REFLECTIONS

LYNETTE HEYWOOD

FISHER KING PUBLISHING

Published by
Fisher King Publications
The Old Barn
York Road
Thirsk
YO7 3AD
England

fisherkingpublishing.co.uk

For Dad and Gary... our souls will
never disconnect but my heart misses
you both incredibly

I stared at the brown package in my hand. It had been posted through the front door and was addressed to me.

I looked around the big house. The high white walls of the hall, the family pictures that smiled at you as you went up the stairs. The family pictures that represented everything except for the true meaning of the word family. So false and contrived, it was enough to make you sick.

She wasn't in. She was never in. I was glad of that. I would enjoy the peace whilst it lasted.

I threw my car keys into the vase that stood on a wooden plinth in the hallway and opened the mysterious package.

It contained a videotape. The word "enjoy" was written across it. I was confused and intrigued. I kicked off my shoes, ran to the kitchen and took a bottle of white wine from the fridge., A single wine glass was drying on the draining board; I grabbed it and ran upstairs to my room.

Along with a TV and video player I had everything you could want, but sometimes everything isn't enough. Material things can be meaningless.

I loaded the tape into the video player, and pressed play. I didn't know what to expect, but I certainly wasn't anticipating what appeared on the screen.

Someone had sent me a video of my boyfriend, Jamie. There he was in his full manly glory – cock out, prancing around like an amateur porn star. And the worst part was that he wasn't alone.

I sat down on the bed and felt the bile rising in my throat as I continued to watch the filth that had invaded the room.

I just couldn't work it out, I'd been seeing him for eighteen months or so and he had been lovely. He'd been the first person I'd let make love to me. I was eighteen and had been saving myself for someone special.

Well, there was clearly nothing special about him, he was a prick.

The tears were rolling down my face as I stared at the TV and took in the reality of it all, I shook my head in disbelief. How could he do this to me?

I felt distraught and appalled that he had been unfaithful in the most degrading way. And to make it worse, he had let someone film him doing it. Who else had seen this?

I grabbed the remote control and switched off the set. I ripped the curtains from my windows. I wanted to wreck everything that was around me.

I took some deep breaths and stared through the bedroom window at the big tree right outside. In summer the leaves would wave at me happily, and in winter, its bare branches would thrash hard against the window. Throughout the seasons it would comfort me.

I stared at the leaves and wondered how many would grow and fall from the same branch.

Was it like that for us? Were we just leaves that fell off our branches whilst the rest of the tree grew and carried on thriving? I watched the wind pick up slightly. As the leaves parted, I could see the soft cloudy sky with a tinge of orange sun glistening in the background. There was always *something* between the parted leaves.

Yes, the world was beautiful, but unfortunately, it was marred by some of the people in it. All my life, I had been treated with disregard by those who I was supposed to trust.

I'd trusted Jamie but seeing that video of him made me think that everybody must be the same. I felt the barriers slamming against my chest, colliding with my heart as they did. I made the decision that they would never come down again.

I paced the bedroom in anger, I felt the anxiety take over and I could barely breathe. I felt sick.

It was OK, I told myself. It was going to be OK. I wasn't dead, although growing up there were plenty of times I wished I had been. But I'd got through all that. I'd made it this far, and I hadn't broken. I was not going to crack over a stupid boy; he would get his – I would make sure of it.

I opened the bottle of wine; I needed a drink. I sat on the edge of the bed and poured a full glass, devouring it quickly, thinking about the situation.

The phone rang.

I nearly jumped out of my skin at the sound of it. I decided not to answer as I knew it would be Jamie. He knew I'd be alone. He'd be phoning to come over as he did nearly every night. We would laugh, eat junk food, get drunk and have sex.

He could fuck off. If I ever saw him again, I would kill him.

I poured a second glass of wine and put the TV

on, but I just couldn't bring myself to watch it, so switched it off.

The third glass of wine barely touched the sides. I threw the empty glass onto the carpeted floor and lay back on the bed, feeling drunker than I normally would after just three glasses of wine.

I closed my eyes, feeling dizzy from the combination of booze and shock. I needed to see who he was with. Who was the girl? I hadn't paid attention to her, only to him, and now I wanted to know who it was.

I pressed play again and forced myself to watch the seven-minute-long tape to the end.

The realisation of what this meant gripped my chest tightly, the pain was almost unbearable.

I was done with him – he was over and out of my life. It was her I was more interested in now. That bitch.

I never imagined she would go that far. She had no morals – I knew that. But in my wildest dreams, I didn't think she would stoop this low. I stared at her sucking his cock; she was giving it her all. I dived off the bed and ran into the bathroom, where I threw up the entire contents of my stomach.

I slumped to the bathroom floor, wiping the sick away from my mouth with my sleeve. The cold tiles felt soothing against my hot skin.

I couldn't imagine ever getting those images out of my head; this wasn't some stupid teenage girl caught up in a moment.

I knew she was a whore; she had always been a whore. She fucked anybody who looked her in the eye. And now there she was fucking my boyfriend.

It was time it all stopped. I would make her life hell as she had made mine. She would pay every single day for the rest of her life, as she'd made me pay, pay for nothing.

In this situation, most young girls would want to talk to their best friend – their mum. I was envious of friends who had that kind of relationship with their mums. I had no such luck but had craved it all my life.

She had been cruel, using her vile mouth to bring me down and make me feel terrible about myself. Her slaps left me feeling embarrassed and vulnerable. Then there was the other stuff. I had loved her and always wanted to please her. I'd forever tried to make her love me even after a tragic accident. An accident that I was responsible for – it was my fault – she had screamed at me often enough.

I was worn out with it; she had always put one thing before me. It was the thing that kept her thriving, that kept her alive. She was an addict, a glutton whose only goal in life was to get fucked. She was addicted to sex, and there she was naked, shameless, and on film fucking my boyfriend.

No, my mum wasn't my friend, but she was no longer my worst enemy. I was hers.

I needed to go back. To where? I did not know,
But it wasn't here, for I no longer belonged.
For here was arduous,
Here was sombre and tedious.
There was somewhere I hadn't been for a long
time.
There was someone I had forgotten along the way.
But when I remembered her, my heartbeat felt
sublime.
The girl there was solitary and kind.
The girl here was lost in mind.
And I was desperate, desperate to find her for a
minute,
Let her know that I forgave her, as I lost her
within,
In such a place where it would stay definite.
The thought of getting her back made my soul
shine with glee.
It made my heart expel the brightest light,
I needed to get her back, for she was the real me.

I stared at the reflection in the window, our noses almost touching the glass. The late sun setting peacefully made her face look warm in the orange glow. I was looking outside, but I was always looking at her, looking back at me.

I was staring at the shoulder length mousey brown hair that wouldn't look so frizzy if it had been brushed. With huge brown eyes, I was staring at a slight woman with a natural curve to her figure. I was staring at luscious thick lips that were a natural pale pink. But I wasn't sure who I was staring at.

I was forgetting who I was. It seemed like an eternity since I'd felt OK. My priorities were now non-existent, and I'd stopped thinking about me – I no longer mattered.

Flashbacks danced in my mind. The place comforted and disturbed me, but sometimes we go to the bad memories to get a sense that we're alive. You've not lived if you've not hurt.

I was there again, remembering.

I shook my head as if doing so would clear the thoughts; for a moment, I'd forgotten about those times – those horrendous times that had defined who I was today. But there was a part of it that I had missed and a part that I craved. Those were the parts I felt I needed to go back to. But I never would.

Our last encounter hadn't been pleasant. Again, I shook my head. I didn't want to go there. I rarely allowed it to enter my head. But there were times the internal conflict was that bad that I could have pulled off my own head.

I couldn't think beyond that... I could never go that far back.

Maybe it was time to revisit some of me, if only for a short while.

Yeah, a short visit wouldn't do anyone any harm.

I thought about my next move as my head went into turmoil, and my heart pounded fast in my chest.

She was out there somewhere and I would find her.

Three weeks later, I sat cross-legged on the floor of my flat, reading the Manchester Evening News. Flicking through it, reading every line, looking for bargains, reading the obituaries. Then something caught my eye, under miscellaneous.

"Submissive woman wanted for sex. Will pay two hundred pounds."

There was a phone number to contact "John". It was a 071 number, so I knew John must be in London.

After reading it over and over, I decided to do it. It would be the release I needed. It would remind me of who I was.

Surely this was better than having an affair, not that that would go amiss right now, but yes this was easier. It was just sex, a transaction – no emotion required.

Staring at the paper, I thought about my recent life.

I was lonely more than anything. But I also felt frumpy and unattractive. I'd gotten my shape back after the birth of my daughter Jody, but *he*, my partner, had not come near me for months.

I used the term partner loosely as we were far from being partners in anything. I knew there was no one else involved. He just wasn't "up for it" anymore.

And I had to see if I still had "it" – I needed to know. And London could give me the answer. But London was a long way to go, given that I lived in Manchester.

It was strange how I came to live on this

Manchester council estate. If I'm honest, I would have probably avoided it in the past. I never would have thought that I would have fitted in and I probably didn't. I was different to the people that lived here, and they knew it, even if they didn't say it.

I didn't have a choice. I'd had to go into a homeless shelter at one point, and I was lucky to be housed here. The flats were like gold dust apparently.

I was surrounded by streets where every house looked the same except for the ones that had their kitchens at the front. Burglary was on the up and robberies seemed to be a daily occurrence. Car windows often got smashed for access to the stereos inside.

Pit Bulls and Staffordshire Bull terriers walked the streets freely. There were times that it would take me hours just to walk to the shops because of the detour needed to avoid the vicious-looking mutts that gave the impression they wanted to devour me in one. "It's alright," their owners would reassure me, "Oscar doesn't bite, daft as a brush he is."

But a daft brush with sharp teeth was the last thing I needed. I was taking no chances. I'd been bitten once, God how I'd been bitten, and I didn't intend to let it happen again.

But I had to admit the majority of people around here were nice, all kind with warm souls.

I remember when I first arrived. We'd been offered what they called a cottage flat, the name certainly didn't fit the description. It was an upstairs flat with two bedrooms, quite a large lounge, and an adequately sized kitchen. The flat below was probably exactly the same layout. It was next to two houses, each with two floors. Our gardens were all connected with nothing but a couple of privets separating them.

It feels like years ago now that I'd been greeted by Irene, my new neighbour.

'Hiya love, you moving into number 26?'

No, I'm just unpacking a small van for the fun of it. 'Hiya, yeah, I'm Julie.'

'You pregnant love?'

No, I've just eaten a lot of pies. 'Yeah, due any day.'

I smiled at her, hoping that would end the conversation.

'That yer hubby?' She pointed at *him*. He was unpacking the van.

Never, ever. 'No, my partner.'

I looked at him. Two nights of passion and here I was moving in with him and having his baby. It couldn't get any worse. I felt like I was in some sort of crazy dream.

'Right love, do you want a cuppa?' asked Irene.

I wasn't used to this sort of behaviour; Irene's openness and friendliness was something I would never forget.

Ten minutes later, she sat in our new living room with two brews, one for me and one for him, while she weighed up the place.

She talked about her two kids, David and Bernie, who were both around the same age as us. By our third brew, I felt like I'd known them all my life.

'Young lad lived in here before you,' she told

us. 'Think he got put down,' she added almost whispering.

'They don't put humans down,' I laughed, nearly choking on my brew.

She laughed with me, 'No, you daft cow! He's in prison.' She turned to him, 'You pulled her off a spaceship or something?' she cackled at her own humour.

He said nothing.

It was then that I realised I would have to learn a different language if I was to survive in my new abode.

Jody was nearly two years old and I loved her, but I felt detached from everything.

He was a perpetual nightmare. I found him pathetic with no sense of anything – I didn't even refer to him by his name.

He was a nice enough lad, and he loved our daughter in his own way. But even at twenty-four, he acted more like a kid than Jody did. I just couldn't gel with him, and I'd stopped trying.

A sudden noise from the flat below made me jump and brought me back to the here and now.

I read the ad for what felt like the hundredth time. Fuck it I was going. He could look after the baby.

He knew I had an old friend who lived just outside London. I could say I was visiting her, and that I needed some space. It was allowed.

He probably wouldn't even notice I was gone. If I disappeared off the face of the earth, it'd make no difference to his existence.

That was it, I'd made my mind up, I was going

to London to have submissive sex with John. I felt a thrill in my stomach as I thought about it.

I needed to go to the phone box at the end of our road to sort it out whilst it was on my mind and I had the courage. Jody and her dad were both in the bedroom having a nap so I wouldn't be missed.

On my way, I called into the corner shop. I needed change for the phone. The slot took 10p, but I bet a call to London was going to cost a bomb.

The corner shop was on one side of a semi-circle of retail outlets. There was a hairdresser above it called Kolash. It was the only hairdressers in the area, so everybody on the estate went there to have their hair done by Sharon and the girls.

The other shops included the chippy, a hardware shop and a new Indian takeaway, which was becoming a real hit, mainly because they offered delivery. If you couldn't be bothered getting off your arse to cook or walk to the shops, it was ideal.

'Hiya Assam,' I said as I entered the shop. Assam was behind the counter, but it was his father that owned the shop.

'Aw hiya love, how have you been?' He was always bubbly and was popular in the community. 'Twenny Benny's?' he said, reaching behind him. He knew me well.

He handed me twenty Benson and Hedges. At nearly £3.50 a packet it was becoming an expensive habit, but cigarettes and the odd bottle of wine on a Friday night were my only treats.

'Hey, I've got sommat in the back you'll like – you've got a kid, haven't you?' he asked.

'Yes.' I nodded my head. '

'Girl or Boy?' He was rubbing his chin as though he was trying to remember.

'Girl, Az. Jody.' I reminded him.

'Yeah, yeah, that's right. Come with me.' He took me through a little doorway in the shop. It didn't have a proper door, just a red, white and blue plastic strip curtain, which I enjoyed walking through.

'Got some little shell suits here?' He kicked a box that lay amongst many other boxes of shell suits in polythene packaging.

He grabbed one for me. 'This'll fit her?' He held up a shell suit that would have fit a nine-year-old.

'Az that would fit me,' I smiled.

'I'll see if I have a smaller one, they're only two quid, and they're designer.'

I rolled my eyes and felt that familiar feeling of frustration. I hadn't come in to buy a shell suit, I'd come in for cigs and change.

'They're all blue Az, I'll give it a miss. Thanks though.'

'OK. If I get owt else, I'll let you know.'

'OK, thank you.'

I paid for my cigs, got my change and left the shop. I crossed the road to the phone box.

I looked around before I opened the door. My hands were shaking. I stared at the telephone number that I'd carefully written down on the back of an old receipt. I started to sweat, and it wasn't long before my hot breath was causing the windows to steam up. I wrote on them to distract myself. The stench of piss was starting to grip my throat.

I picked up the receiver and waited for the dial tone before dialling the number, looking out of the phone box window in every direction just in case I saw somebody I knew.

I didn't know how I would speak, or even what I was going to say.

I put the receiver back down and slumped my body against the plastic windows that had replaced the glass ones many years ago. I was worried that if someone walked by, they would hear me.

But the thought of going to London, having sex with a stranger and getting paid for it, made me excited and I got back in the zone. Again, I picked up the receiver, waited for the pips to bleep and put in my money.

A man answered.

'Hello?' His accent was slightly southern.

'Hello. Can I speak to John, please?'

I sounded husky, trying to use my sexiest voice.

'Speaking,' he responded.

'I'm calling about your ad in the Manchester Evening News.'

I hoped the information would suffice and he would know exactly why I was phoning.

'Really? Are you based in Manchester?'

I tried to work out his tone and decided that he was probably a murderer.

'Er yeah,' I murmured. My sexiest voice and any confidence I'd felt had fallen onto the shitty floor in the phone box, along with the piss and an empty cider bottle.

'How old are you?'

'I'm 26.'

'I will send you your train tickets, what's your address?'

I went all hot. I couldn't give him my address. Jesus.

'Erm,' my hesitation was evident.

'Like that is it?' he laughed. 'Not told your husband?'

'I don't have a husband,' I was offended.

'Do you know the name of your local post office,' he asked.

'Erm. There's a little one on Southmoor Road,' as if he knew where Southmoor Road was, 'but I don't know what it's called.'

'OK, call me at the same time tomorrow, and I'll have more details for you. Oh, and what's your name?'

I hesitated, 'Charlotte – Charley,' I lied.

I don't know what made me pick Charley, but I liked it.

'OK Charley, we'll speak tomorrow.'

Before I could say 'OK' he'd put the phone down. It wasn't a very sexy phone call; I'd half imagined rubbing myself up in a phone box. But I was relieved it was over.

I stared at the receiver in shock at what had just happened, but my thoughts were interrupted by a loud banging on the phone box door.

I couldn't believe it. It was bloody Scott from next door. I went hot from head to toe. What if he'd heard me? How would I explain myself? I opened the door.

'You look hot. Everything OK? Who yer phoning?'

'No one,' I lied.

'So, you just stood in the phone box for the sake

of it then?' He laughed sarcastically and looked right at my breasts. 'You done? I wanna use the phone.'

I stepped out of the phone box, carefully folding up the piece of paper that had John's number on and tucking it into my back pocket.

'Who's Jane?' asked Scott, looking at the name I'd written on the steamy window.

I winced at the sound of her name, but I looked straight at him and shrugged.

I lit a cigarette for the short stroll home. Feeling calmer as I inhaled the smoke, I headed back, knowing I wouldn't sleep tonight. I had to do it all over again tomorrow, and the thought filled me with trepidation and dread but sheer excitement too.

I had a boring night, which involved Jody screaming her head off and him just sitting there ignoring her. He was bloody good at turning deaf whenever she cried, and I was sure the more she wailed, the more he switched off.

I wondered if other mothers felt like this as they crooned and smiled at their toddlers. They spoke about how much joy they brought them, the cake baking, the model making. Me, I hated the whole set up.

I finally got her settled. I stared at her, fast asleep in an old cot we'd bought out of the 'The Loot', a local rag where you could buy just about anything. It had cost us twenty quid.

I smiled at her little blonde curls and her jet-black eyelashes as they rested on her little red cheeks.

She was only two years old, and as much as I hated my situation, I was aware that it wasn't her fault. She was so innocent in all of this, needing *her* mummy to love her. But I needed *me* to love me first. I was tired and I was lost.

'Wanna joint?' he asked as I came back into our living room.

'No,' I snapped.

I didn't want to share anything with him. I wanted to tell him to fuck off. I wanted to ask him why he'd even asked me. He knew I hadn't smoked that shit for years now, even though I secretly missed it.

But I couldn't be arsed saying anything else. I was beyond arguing with him. When you're arguing, at least you are communicating, and I didn't even want that from him.

I felt trapped with a man that I didn't like. He was totally uneducated, and he made the whole atmosphere even more depressing than it already was. I looked around our small flat. It was full of clothes strewn everywhere. The carpets hadn't been hoovered in days. The carpet on the stairs that led up to our living room was hanging off, and one day, I swear to God, one of us was going to trip and fall down. Not Jody though, as we had a big piece of wood across the top of the stairs to safeguard her.

I sighed. What a life. What was I doing here? And what was I doing to my child?

I had no way out, nowhere to go and he didn't even realise that we'd got to this level. He had no idea, he was hardly with it at the best of times, but his lack of awareness was enhanced by the amount of weed he smoked.

That night I lay thinking about my adventure, fantasising about 'John'. I imagined him to be dark with blue eyes.

When I finally fell asleep, I dreamt I was in a stunning hotel. It had all the mod cons, and John was pouring wine while I lay in a silk nightgown watching him, admiring his strong muscular body. His chest was really hairy.

I stroked my legs, feeling the warmth between them, something I'd not felt in a long time. But before I knew it, even my dream was shattered when my oh-so-wonderful partner decided to get into bed, pulling all the covers off me as he did.

I lay there shivering and waiting for the right time to drag them back off him. I wanted to be on the phone, making plans for a day out of here.

I didn't have long to wait and was soon walking up the road to the phone box. I was fantasising about what John would say to hook me in. I needed hooking right in.

I wasn't bothered who saw me this time, and there was no hesitation. I picked up the receiver, put my money in and dialled John's number.

'Hello, can I speak to John, please?'

'You're keen.' His condescending tone fucked me off, but I was supposed to be submissive. I rolled my eyes at the thought of it.

'Oh, you told me to phone you at the same time,' I murmured. I was pretending to be disappointed in his response.

'I've posted the tickets. They'll be at the post office, with a PO Box number on them. Your train will leave Piccadilly at seven-fifteen on Friday morning and will take you straight to Euston.'

I felt a tinge of disappointment. Today was only

Tuesday.

He continued with his instructions. 'Get a black cab outside Euston station, the address is with the tickets.'

'OK,' I whispered.

'You sound cute'. He was dead serious.

'Thanks,' I tried to sound shy.

'Phone me again when you get the tickets.'

'I will.' I responded. I had a lump in my throat and was genuinely lost for words.

But maybe he liked that because he said, 'Can't wait to teach you a few things. You sound very naive.'

I went all hot as the wave came over me. I knew immediately what he wanted.

'I can't wait to learn a few things.'

'How old are you?'

'Still 26.' I replied. 'Although I look much younger.'

I did, to be fair. I was slight, like a girl, but my body was definitely a woman's. I had curvy hips, a slim waist and big breasts. My long mousey hair was messy in a natural way.

'I like the sound of you already.'

'I can't' wait to see you,' I whispered, genuinely enjoying the moment.

'Oh, you won't see me,' he laughed, it was menacing.

'What do you mean?' I asked nervously.

'Don't worry Charley, you'll be fine.'

I was going to tell him the truth and tell him my real name but quickly thought better of it. I decided I liked being Charley – maybe Charley would bring me back to life.

'OK Charley, I'll speak to you when you've got the tickets. I'll have to save this hard-on for you, until Friday.'

I got a thrill between my legs and couldn't control my gasp. I had what I needed, I had the control, the ball was in my court, he had a hard-on for me.

'See you Friday.' I whispered, trying to keep the excitement from my voice, but he'd gone.

I did a hop, skip and a jump, well Charley did. Julie never did any such thing. But I'd decided that Charley would change Julie. And though I knew what I was doing was wrong, Charley was going to help me put the mess right, which would only help Jody.

I felt better already.

Chapter 2

I'd given it a day or so before I put Jody in her buggy and headed to the post office. I didn't have far to go.

There was an opening at the rear of our flat that led onto a field set back from the road. I could see this view from my flat window, lots of trees and nice green grass. Trains infrequently ran by the side of it, and a small railway bridge took you to the post office just over the other side. It wasn't far from where Jody's grandparents lived, but we wouldn't be visiting them today.

Jody was happy that we were getting out of the flat and was being cooperative in getting ready. The weather was typical of a July day in Manchester – patchy white clouds over a bright blue sky. When the sun shone through, it was hot.

I decided I would collect my milk tokens and family allowance while I was at the post office. I grabbed my yellow book out of the kitchen drawer that was full of useless shit – single gloves, sticky tape, spare fuses, old keys, odd pegs.

He was still in bed as usual. It didn't matter what time of day it was, if he didn't have anywhere to be, he'd be in that bed. I was surprised the fucker didn't have bed sores.

I left Jody behind the wooden plank at the top of the stairs while I carried the buggy down, then I went back for her. As I started to carry her down, ever so carefully so as not to trip on the risen carpet, I started to shake. The carpet beneath me felt slippery and unsafe.

One of these days, I would end up in a pile at the bottom, having fallen and broken my neck. The thought stopped me dead in my tracks, and I ran back upstairs.

'Grab Jane a minute,' I shouted.

He came out of the bedroom dishevelled and half asleep.

'What you on about?'

'Grab Jane for me,' I repeated.

I heard it the second time and corrected myself.

'Grab Jody.'

'Don't even know your own kid's name now?' he grinned as he grabbed his daughter.

Like a madwoman, I began to frantically rip the carpet off the stairs.

'What the fuck you doing?' he asked.

'One of us is going to have an accident.'

I was crying now, great big tears of fear. Pulling the carpet off the grippers.

It came off with ease, it was that old and shoddy. I sweated and panted hard as I tore it up.

Jody and her useless dad both stared at me in disbelief.

'One day I'll break my neck trying to avoid this mess,' I was not to be argued with, and he knew I was right.

I opened the front door and threw the carpet into the garden. Ran back up the stairs, grabbed my daughter, strapped her in the buggy and stormed off to the post office, still in tears.

Fancy having a carpet like that and letting it get in that state – it was an accident waiting to happen. An accident I never wanted to see again in my life.

I'd calmed down by the time I'd got to the post office. The small building had grills on the window and graffiti sprayed all over the brick walls on the outside.

It was packed, and I could see a line of mums with buggies waiting to collect their family allowance.

I wondered if the envelope had arrived as I waited in anticipation in the queue.

The middle-aged lady behind the counter recognised me.

'Hiya Julie love, how's our Jody today?'

'She's good, thanks,' I smiled as I looked down at her beaming up at the lady from her buggy.

'Charley, who lives underneath me, has asked me to pick up an envelope. Do you think it would be ok if I grabbed it for her?'

'Charley? I don't know a Charley on your road.'

I took a chance and gave her a big wink.

'Oh, OK. Yeah, if you sign for it love.' She winked back.

'Yeah, course,' I smiled, relieved. 'Oh, I need to cash my family allowance too'.

Twenty minutes later, I had Jody tucked under one arm and was almost running up the stairs. The buggy would have to wait outside the flat. I was too excited to open the damn envelope.

Lazy arse had gone back to bed; he was awake, he was just a layabout.

I took Jody in and dumped her on his tummy.

'Your daughter wants you,' I muttered, and walked into the bathroom.I sat on the toilet and hurriedly opened the envelope. It felt like it was my birthday!

"Charley" was written neatly across the envelope, followed by a number and the name of the post office.

Two train tickets were inside, along with a 20-pound note and a letter written in blue pen.

Dear Charlotte

I enclose the tickets to London Euston as promised. When you get out of the station, there will be a row of black cabs, jump in one and ask them to take you to:

New Cottage Tavern

Finchley Road

It's not far, but I've enclosed £20 for the inconvenience.

I'm looking forward to getting you to do things that will make you feel hot between your legs. I've been hard since you last phoned me.

Call me once you've received this.

John

I was shaking and had to get my composure before I did anything else.

There was a bang on the toilet door.

'You gonna be long? I need a shit!'

I shuddered and quickly pocketed my tickets, folded the letter and money as neatly as I could and flushed the chain.

I watched as the dark water swilled around the manky bowl and suddenly, I felt ashamed of my dirty toilet.

I opened the door. 'Watch Jody. I'm going to get some bleach.'

I needed to get myself out of this rotten life and if I needed to start by cleaning the fucking toilet, then so be it.

I walked to the shop, passing the phone box because I knew I'd feel better about calling John once I'd got a bottle of bleach to start cleaning up my life.

The hardware shop was open. Outside there were stainless steel mop buckets, washing baskets and bins of various shapes and sizes. There was a pile of mats for sale next to the open door.

Inside it was dark. The old shop keeper, Lenny, had ginger hair, a hump on his back and long bony fingers. He looked like he belonged in some sci-fi film, not selling mop buckets and other degrees of shit. He gave me the creeps.

'Y'Alright Lenny?' said a familiar voice.

I turned around; it was Az from the corner shop.

'Hello Assam.' Lenny was a very polite man, and I suddenly felt bad for judging him for his looks.

I could hear them chatting away as I headed over to the bottles of bleach, which were conveniently located next to the cheap toilet brushes. I grabbed one of each item.

'We sell bleach,' Az said with a wink as I walked towards the till.

'Oh, right.' I tried to smile.

'Ignore him love,' said Lenny. 'Two pounds for those.'

He popped them in a brown paper bag for me.

As I paid, I looked out of the window at the

phone box across the way and felt a familiar hot thrill between my legs.

'See you Az. Thanks Lenny.' I said as I skipped out of the shop.

'She's bloody weird that one,' Az muttered as I left, but I didn't care.

While Julie was buying bleach to clean a filthy toilet, Charley was making plans to go to The New Cottage Tavern in London, to meet with John for a submissive shag.

Chapter 3

I raced to board the long blue and yellow train. I had just found a seat when the guard announced that we were leaving the station and the train pulled away.

It was Friday and Manchester Piccadilly Train station had been packed. I'd left the house at 6am after a day spent bullshitting him. I didn't care. I knew he'd look after Jody, and that's all that mattered. Anyway his mother would be there; she was like a fly around shit with baby Jody. But at least I could be sure my daughter would be safe.

I felt a pang of guilt – I was leaving my little girl so I could have sex with a stranger. What kind of mother was I?

I sat back in my seat and tried to relax. As we left the station, I spotted the old Refuge building with its green tower. It had once been the tallest building in Manchester but was starting to diminish in the new up and coming city.

It already felt like a long day, and it was only 07:15. I'd gotten the 102 bus from the bottom of our road, which had taken me directly into the city centre. I'd sat upstairs so I could have a cigarette. The bus was empty; it appeared people didn't get the bus to work anymore.

I remembered the dark and cold winter mornings when men stood at bus stops in their donkey jackets and big steel toe capped shoes. They'd have a cigarette in their mouth, whilst holding a flask of tea in one hand and the morning newspaper in the other.

That seemed like a million years ago.

I was lucky enough to have started off in more luxury than that. I had begun my working days with a nice car and didn't really have to do the bus. How life had changed. I suppose it didn't matter what your start in life was, what mattered was how you let the impact affect the here and now.

I closed my eyes for a moment whilst I tried to get my head together. I took some deep breaths and tried to get any thoughts of home out of my head.

Time to refocus on what I was doing right now. I was going to have sex, I was just going to do as I was told, I didn't have to initiate anything. The feelings of excitement flooded over my body.

I opened my eyes to check that I'd put my bag on the overhead rack. It was there, and I relaxed again. I'd borrowed the bag off my mate Sandra, and she'd lent me some half-decent clothes. I didn't have many friends, but Sandra lived next door with Scott and seemed nice enough.

We'd often meet in our back gardens when we were putting our bin bags out or bringing the washing in, and she'd sometimes say; "I'm making a cuppa do you want one?"

She had a small family, two little boys with about nine months and half a day between them. How she did it, I would never know. Scott was a painter and decorator; a good-looking bloke who always appeared to be having a conversation with my tits instead of my face. If I was honest, I could tell that it all felt too much for him – being a dad, a provider. He seemed bogged down by it all, but it was clear he loved his kids, and he did what he could for his family.

The train was warm. I was glad I'd worn a T-shirt over my green and yellow leggings. The fact it was a "Smith's" T-shirt and didn't match my leggings didn't matter, nor did it matter that I had my old, ripped, fit for the bin converse on. I planned to get changed in the toilets at Euston so that I was fresh for my date.

I looked around at the other passengers. I believed that everybody was fighting some sort of war with their soul. Appearances meant nothing.

The couple opposite me were middle-aged; they were dressed very hippy-like. Her long blue hair was frizzy and unkempt.

The train guard broke my reverie.

'Tickets please.'

I handed mine to him, I'd had them firmly in my hand so as not to lose them.

'You're in the wrong carriage. Come with me. Bring your bag.'

My stomach lurched. Where was he taking me?

He marched through the carriages; I was getting nervous now. What was going on?

'In here madam.'

He pointed towards the first-class carriage. Wow! I was gobsmacked.

An all you can eat and drink buffet was being served.

'Thank you,' I said.

I placed my bag on the much bigger rack and sat down in the much larger seat that was far more comfortable. The tables had cute little lamps on them and ashtrays for people who smoked.

I looked around, there was only a couple of other

people in the whole of the carriage.

A businessman caught my attention, he looked middle-aged but very smart, I didn't see it very often. I was impressed with his dark blue suit, light blue shirt and tie. His expensive coat had its own seat next to him. He certainly looked sophisticated.

He must have felt me looking at him as he peered over his newspaper and caught my eye.

I helped myself to a glass of red wine and curled up on my huge seat. Outside the world was drifting by. We went through beautiful countryside, and I could see the old buildings as we approached Macclesfield station.

Before I knew it, I was on my third glass of wine, and getting cosier and cosier. The noise of the engines made me feel sleepy, and as the rhythm of the train swayed me gently from side to side, it was becoming difficult for me to keep my eyes open.

I fell into a deep sleep.

Chapter 4

I was nervous as I got out of the black cab. I was finally face to face with the New Cottage.

It wasn't what I'd imagined because, for some reason, I thought it was going to be an actual cottage. I realised now that the idea of a little thatched cottage in the middle of London was daft.

In reality, the New Cottage was a normal-looking pub that had a cottage feel about it. It was lovely actually. Outside, it had pretty little benches and baskets of flowers hanging from the beams that held up the beautiful wooden balcony for the guests. There were little Swiss shutters on the windows, giving it a romantic feel.

I slowly approached the front door, hoping this wasn't too complicated and that John would know it was me.

I wore a short leather skirt, a white vest top and high-heeled black boots. I'd put my long hair up in a butterfly clip and wore large, hooped gold earrings. I felt sexy and knew I looked it.

I was barely through the door when I heard; Charley?'

I looked up and saw a man in his late thirties, he was tall and blonde and extremely good looking.

'John?'

'No, but come with me?'

He walked off towards the back of the pub, and

I had no choice but to follow him. He went behind the bar and asked me what I wanted to drink.

'Half a lager,' I replied.

And down it went in one fell swoop as if I'd not had a drink for weeks.

The jukebox was belting out Elton John's 'Sacrifice', and I quickly looked around the place. It was full of daytime drinkers, enjoying the sun and getting ready for the weekend.

The man beckoned me towards him, which meant I had to go behind the bar.

'Up there,' he said and pointed towards some stairs which obviously took you to the living quarters of the pub. 'You'll find a sleep mask on the door handle – put it on, then knock on the door. I will give you your money when you come back down.'

A sleep mask? I got a flashback of John saying to me on the phone, 'you won't be seeing me.'

As I walked up the stairs, sweat started to trickle down my face; I think it was caused by my nerves as well as the intense heat that hit me.

I saw the door, and the man was right, there was a black leather sleep mask hooked on the door handle.

I was getting a tingling feeling between my legs, but I was also apprehensive.

I thought about what I was doing and what I was getting myself into, it could be dangerous. But the fact that I'd just walked through a pub where lots of people had seen me was reassuring. Surely If I was going to get murdered, they'd have been more discreet about it.

I gulped as I reached for the sleep mask and put it over my face, it was tight, and I couldn't see a thing. I was in complete darkness. I took a deep breath and knocked on the door.

I could feel my whole body shaking as the door opened. There were no words, just a hand gently taking mine and leading me very slowly along what I assumed to be a hallway. I could smell a stale yeasty smell, which was probably connected to the pub. I imagined the walls to be yellow from cigarette smoke. I could feel the beams as I reached out to steady myself.

I was in darkness and trying to imagine what the person holding my hand looked like. His hand felt strong but gentle. I sensed there was more than one person, and for a minute, I panicked and almost swiped the mask from my face.

There was a female in the room, I could taste her perfume; it smelt familiar, reminding me of a long time ago, and it made me feel a bit dizzy.

I was pushed gently to sit down. I was dying to scream, 'Say something, someone. Who is there?' but I knew I had to play the game.

The surface I sat on was soft, obviously a bed. I touched the sheets, nothing special, just nylon.

I was pushed gently to lie down. I was shaking now and didn't want it to appear obvious, so I tried to concentrate.

I was horny though.

She started undressing me, starting with my boots.

She groaned as she rubbed her soft hands up and down my legs.

She pulled off my skirt, followed by my top.

His strong hands undid my bra.

He stroked my breasts. His masculine hands felt slightly rough as they caressed my nipples, I sighed and went with the beautiful feeling It was giving me.

She was taking my knickers off slowly with her mouth, her tongue occasionally licking my pussy through my knickers. Her perfume was putting me off, but I tried to ignore it.

I was starting to get wet.

She was licking me, biting me gently, my clitoris went hard as her tongue darted quickly in and out, it felt warm, and the top of my legs tingled as her saliva dripped into me.

She stopped, and I heard them both moaning pleasurably, he was obviously fucking her now. I went to touch my wet pussy, but one of them gently moved my hand away.

Then he stuck his cock in me. I hadn't expected it and it felt so hot, so fucking hard and so big. I gasped as though in pain, but the pleasure soon took over as he went in and out of me, gently, slowly; he felt so good.

She straddled my face, wanting me to lick her. I stuck my tongue out as she rode it, slipping up and down on my face.

He groaned loudly, obviously turned on by what he could see. I couldn't see a fucking thing.

I couldn't help it, it was all too much, and my body needed this release; I couldn't hold onto it any longer. I came fast and I came hard. And oh my god it was strong.

He also came fast and hard, spraying himself all over my stomach. As he did, I felt her hot pussy swell up on my face. She screamed dramatically.

The next thing I knew, I was being taken out of the back door of the New Cottage. I'd not been allowed to take my mask off. I wanted my money, so I headed back to the front of the pub, looking for the blonde guy. It was then that I saw her. I got the heavy smell of perfume and the realisation dawned on me...

I jolted awake. My leggings were damp, and I was aware that I might have been gasping during my dream orgasm. The businessman looked over his newspaper, stared into my eyes and then smiled at me. I felt my face flush red.

The train pulled up in Euston. I needed to get ready in the toilets and jump in a cab.

I wasn't as nervous now because I knew exactly where I was going and what would happen. She would never be there though, that was just a dream. She would never be there again.

Chapter 5

I approached The New Cottage, and it didn't look much different from how it had in my dream. A picturesque pub in a beautiful London setting. The hubbub of the road surrounding it was astounding to see; there were people everywhere.

I stood outside for a minute and wondered what I'd be greeted with. People were already sitting drinking in the sunshine that lit up the pub walls. Water glistened, feeding the magnificent plants that grew all around the lovely establishment.

As I entered, I noticed the stunning structure and felt the warmth of a city pub that had the feel of a country inn. It was a really good combination and difficult to capture, but this place had it.

This time I was met by nobody. Not that there was a last time, but the dream had felt so real. I headed straight for the bar, which was already attracting a crowd.

I looked at all the men on their own wondering which one was John and whether he'd seen me come in. Was he even here? I didn't really have any instructions, just this address. His name probably wasn't even John, just as mine wasn't Charley. I felt like everybody's eyes were on me. I was really conscious that I was here on my own, and I felt vulnerable.

I waited at the bar until a sour-faced barmaid asked me what I was 'avin'. I decided another red wine wouldn't go amiss, ignoring the fact that this would be my fourth.

She slammed a large glass on the bar. I wasn't sure if she was rude or just southern – people certainly had a different way about them down here. My friend from London once visited Manchester and couldn't come to terms with the fact that everyone was smiling at her. I had to explain people were just friendlier up north.

After my next couple of gulps, I was starting to feel more confident. I wore a white gypsy top and flowing skirt, my brown sandals made me look a bit hippy. My frizzy, mousy brown hair was loose, and I certainly wasn't sexy, but I'm sure the red lipstick put a mar on that thought. He wanted submissive, so my look was intentional.

The jukebox was playing 'So Far Away' by Dire Straits, and I immediately thought of Jody. I could have left there and then, grabbed my bag, and hailed a black cab back to Euston. I pictured her little face in my mind but told myself that she'd be ok and that I would spoil her rotten when I got back.

Thankfully, my thoughts were interrupted.

'Hi, are you Charley?'

I nearly fainted on the spot, but instead looked to the man stood on my right and replied.

'Yes, I'm Charley.'

'I'm John,' he smiled.

I was shocked by his appearance. He must have been about thirty for a start. His stunning blue eyes shone brightly as he smiled. His natural white teeth would be perfect if they weren't slightly crooked at the front. His messy light brown hair with natural blonde streaks hadn't seen a pair of scissors for months. He certainly wasn't what I imagined.

'Er hiya', I stretched my hand out to shake his but pulled it back quickly. What the fuck was I doing?

He smiled, not perturbed in the slightest.

'Can I have a bottle of your finest red please?' He asked the sour-faced barmaid.

I gulped down the glass that I had in front of me. It did me no good whatsoever, my vision was becoming blurred. I needed to get my head together.

'Let's take a seat,' he said and pointed to a booth in the corner.

I picked up my bag and realised how big and awkward it was given why I was here. We walked towards the booth. We were lucky to get it because the pub was getting more packed as the lunchtime crowd had started to drift in.

The music on the jukebox seemed louder, which I welcomed. Music had always kept me company, and I needed it right now. It would take away the fear of any uncomfortable silences.

Right now, it was blasting out Bruce Springsteen, and part of me wanted to get up and dance; I loved the man.

'I love Bruce,' I decided to tell John.

'Yeah, he's good.'

I grinned at his accent.

It was definitely a southern accent, but it was beautifully entwined with an Eastern European twang, and looking at him, I thought he was probably Polish or Ukrainian. I wasn't sure and, given the state I was in, he could have even been German.

He sounded different from the phone call, which seemed to have happened weeks ago now.

'Where you from?' I asked him as he poured me my fifth glass of red wine; it wasn't even one o'clock yet.

'Do you ever stop for breath?' he asked, sipping his wine.

My heart skipped a beat, and my stomach did a somersault. His tone suggested criticism and I couldn't cope with it. I wasn't sure if he was serious or not, and my nerves got the better of me as I threw the wine back. I was trying to work out what I was doing wrong.

I snatched the bottle from the table and refilled my glass, spilling some of it as I did. And as I spilt the wine, I spilt my words, forgetting that he'd just offended me.

'On the train, I had a dream that I came here and got fucked whilst blindfolded. There were two people there, and I'm sure one of them was my mum.'

I heard myself say it, but almost didn't realise that I'd said it out loud.

He heard it and looked me deadpan in the eye.

'That's some crazy shit.'

The wine had gone to my head, and I'd already forgotten what I'd said.

I'd gone numb, and the tables around me were becoming dreamlike and surreal. I had to get my head together. I was losing it.

'What?' I needed him to repeat himself.

'Are you on drugs?' he asked me.

I laughed.

'No, I'm fucking not.' I was aggressive, but he was fucking me off now.

He just stared at me. His blue eyes were so intense but so bright at the same time; he was gorgeous.

I stared back at him but couldn't keep his gaze. I felt uncomfortable. It was clear he didn't think I was good enough, and I was making a fool of myself. The word "submissive" came into my head. My god, what was I doing? He didn't want any sort of personality. He just wanted sex.

'Do you still want sex?' I slurred, still knocking back the red. Again, I couldn't believe what had just come out of my mouth and shouldn't have been surprised at the response.

'No, I don't think you're what I'm looking for Charley. I'm sorry.'

He looked like he just wanted the time he'd wasted back. He was so inconvenienced it was untrue.

I felt devastated, embarrassed and offended all at once, and it didn't combine well with being pissed out of my head.

'Well fuck you.'

I flew up out of my chair and threw the remnants of my glass all over him.

He didn't flinch.

I grabbed my bag and stormed out, barging passed the crowd as I did so, upsetting a couple of people on the way by knocking their drinks out of their hands. I was like a bull in a china shop, leaving a trail of destruction behind me. I'm surprised I got out of there alive.

The bright daylight was a shock to my system; I thought it would be dark. It felt late. I felt dizzy as I looked left and then right. I had no clue what to do or where to go.

I staggered up the road with no plan of action. I just wanted to sit down somewhere and get my head together. Then I'd go back, and I'd show John what he was missing.

It wasn't long before I came to another pub. I went in. Julie was telling me to go home, but Charley was saying fuck it. Julie didn't stand a chance. Charley was ordering a brandy and coke before she even crept into my thoughts.

This pub was a traditional London pub, but really rowdy. The tiles inside made it look like an old-fashioned toilet. Bob Dylan was droning on about Maggie's farm, and the clientele were older and more working-class – the very people I was trying to get away from.

I stood at the bar and it wasn't long before I was joining in with the rowdiness. We swayed along to Lou Reed's 'Perfect Day', then jumped about to "The Clash." The floor was soaked in spilt beer and there were cigarette butts everywhere.

I wanted John. I needed to tell him that I wasn't a knob, and I wanted my 200 quid.

I still had his number, so I checked my purse for change and went to find the phone in the pub. It was on the wall at the side of the bar.

He answered, or someone did, but I couldn't hear a word as it was too noisy. I had my fingers in my ear trying my hardest to hear what was being said. I shouted, 'I'm sorry' down the receiver and hung up in frustration, I swaggered back to my brandy and coke.

I woke up and felt the comfort of a bed, but I had no idea where I could be. I was almost afraid to open my eyes, although I somehow knew that I was safe. I knew that I'd made it through whatever challenge had been sent to me and that at least I was alive.

I tried to remember the day before – the train, the dream, New Cottage and John. I could hardly remember any of it. I vaguely remembered an old pub and making a call. That was it, that was the last thing I remembered.

Now I was here, wherever the fuck that was. The walls around me felt familiar, all of them white and all of them tall; it was an old house for sure.

My head hurt, and my eyes ached. I had to forget everything for a moment and try and go back to sleep. I knew the rest of the world was also sleeping and that no one could get me right now. I needed to gain some sort of strength. I was broken and not worthy of anything. The pain across my head, along with my anxiety, pounded away at my soul.

I was going to lie here for as long as I possibly could, no one was bothering me, and no one held me at gunpoint. I was in a bed; I must have been safe. I closed my eyes but couldn't get that old pub out of my head. I know what I wanted and needed and that was stillness so that my nervous system would be better prepared for what was about to be thrown at me.

Of course, I couldn't go back to sleep. The relief was flooding through my body as I lay there and thanked god that I was alive.

Wherever I'd been between the old pub and now

was giving me a nightmarish feeling. Fear of what could have happened was making me feel sick to the core. It felt dark, and I felt fearful.

Although I didn't know exactly what, something had gone on. How did I end up here? My thoughts were all over the place. I tried my damnedest to recall what had happened after I'd gone back for my brandy and coke. Nothing was registering, but a fear enveloped my body.

The quiet knock on the door sent me reeling. I felt the bile rise to my throat, I had to swallow the acidic taste and shuddered as I did so. I had no idea who could be behind the door.

I couldn't say anything. I wasn't even sure now if I'd even heard a fucking knock on the door.

But I must have because they knocked again. This time a little louder.

This time they didn't wait for a response, and as the handle turned on the white oak door. I swear I stopped breathing.

A man stood in the doorway, he looked familiar, and he felt familiar, but it wasn't quite registering where I'd seen him before. Until he smiled at me and I realised that it was the businessman from the train.

'Hi, he said in a northern accent. 'How are you feeling?'

'Blackout. I've had a 'Blackout,' I whispered.

Chapter 6

And just like that, I was on the Euston to Manchester train on my way home. I'd never had so much excitement in my life, and nothing had really happened, or if it had, I didn't remember it. But it was definitely an adventure.

Thanks to Phil, the businessman off the train, I was safely on my way back.

He told me that he had bumped into me during a brawl in the old pub. It seemed like a bit of an odd coincidence, but who was I to judge. The man might possibly have saved my life. This morning, I could just have easily been found by some bloody road sweeper, lying dead in a gutter.

Phil said that I was out of it, so he'd followed me. He said he'd felt a sense of responsibility towards me and he had to make sure I was safe. He said he took me home and put me to bed in his spare room. He seemed genuine enough, and since he'd let me go and caused me no harm, I had no reason to question his intentions.

I'd ended up shamefully telling him the tale of how I'd come to London for submissive sex, and that the punter didn't like me, so I hadn't even been paid my £200.

I didn't remember what happened after I had screamed sorry down the phone to John. Hard as I tried, I just couldn't recall anything else; I remember walking back to the bar, and that's it.

I wasn't sure if I was just paranoid, but somebody could have spiked me. Put something in my drink when I'd gone to use the phone. I surely hadn't drunk enough to blackout but I was thankful that Phil hadn't been a dirty bastard or, worse still, a murderer, as this could have been a very different story.

I felt rough as I sat back in the huge first-class seat that this time I'd allocated myself correctly.

I wondered if I should try the "hair of the dog" tactic and get myself a red wine, but the thought made me gag.

I decided to close my eyes and sleep the rest of the way so I could regain some of my strength.

I went back to the bar and spotted my brandy and coke. The noise level was high – the revellers were drunken and happy but rowdy, all stomping around the sodden floor, singing along to The Proclaimers.

I downed my drink and felt a slam to my head. I needed to get out, I felt hot and sick, as though I was going to faint. I headed towards the door, and that's when I spotted him.

John's bright blue eyes caught me in a gaze that I couldn't get out of.

He started walking towards me, and I shouted 'Sorry', but I heard it in slow motion. I shook my head as though it would increase the speed of my speech, but I couldn't speak anymore. Everywhere around me was coloured as though I had rainbow-tinted glasses on. I couldn't see straight.

I think he went to grab me, but someone stopped him. The other man looked like he was

pushing him away from me. I went towards them.
I desperately wanted to speak to John and explain
why I did what I did. I lost my footing and fell flat
on my arse. They picked me up, both of them. I was
mortified. I looked around for my bag and decided
that I had to get out of there and out of London.

I wanted to go home back to Manchester. I
was aware of the state I was in. I needed to get to
safety. Maybe I was safe being amongst so many
people, but safe or not, I was struggling to keep a
focus.

Leaving a trail of destruction behind me once
again, I vacated the pub. My long flowing skirt
stuck to my legs as it was soaking, my white gypsy
top was covered in red wine and smelly ale. It was
early evening now, but again I was shocked as it
felt much, much later.

I saw the bus stop and headed towards it; my
gait was clumsy. It took me all my might and
strength to get a couple of hundred yards up the
road. I didn't even know which way Euston was.

I jumped on the first bus that came and asked
the bus driver if he went near Euston Train Station.
If he answered me, I don't remember. I looked in
my bag and wondered if he would take milk tokens
for the fare, then saw I had a couple of quid in my
purse left over from my family allowance.

I found a seat on the bus, and asked everybody
around me if the bus stopped near Euston? No
fucker answered me or wanted to make any eye

contact with me.

I looked towards the back of the bus and noticed a man standing there. He was unusual looking with jet black hair; he had the look of a Native American. I think he smiled; it was hard to focus.

I put my head back and closed my eyes for a minute. Just for a minute. Suddenly, the bus driver was making a racket about me leaving the bus.

I opened my eyes and looked around. There was only the Native American left on the bus with me. Fuck me, I thought, panicking. I could see we were in a huge bus depot.

'How do I get to Euston from here?' I slurred to the bus driver.

He pointed to the subway through the bus depot.

'Walk under there, and across the common, then follow the main road to the station.'

The Native American was shaking his head, he wanted my attention, he was shaking his head fiercely.

'No?' I asked him, trying to get more information from him.

He pointed to a bus which was parked up in front of us and nodded his head.

I said loud and clear and pointed to the bus.

'Does that bus go to Euston train station?'

He nodded his head; he was relieved that I'd got it.

I staggered off the bus I was on and headed over to the one in front of me. The Native American

followed me and made sure I got on the bus,
watching me intensely.

'Do you go to Euston train station?'

'Yes love,' the bus driver said and took my fare.
I sat down on the only free seat, next to a man
whose head was down as though he was asleep. I
didn't care; I felt desperate and lost now.

'Does it definitely go to Euston?' I asked him
even though I thought he was asleep.

'A fellow Manc?' he asked in a soothing voice.

I felt relief.

'Yes, yes.' I said.

'I'll let you know when we're at Euston, don't
worry?'

I stood up, remembering the Native American.
I wanted to wave to him and let him know I was
thankful. But I couldn't see him, my eyes darted
around the desolate bus station and he was
nowhere to be seen. As the bus drove off, I strained
my eyes, looking for him, in one last hope.

I felt sure that he'd been sent to guide me...

I was tapped on the shoulder by the guard wanting
to clip my tickets. I jumped in shock but reached for
my purse to get them for him and was gobsmacked
to see a wad of twenty-pound notes.

I gave the guard the tickets, and as soon as he
walked up the train, I got the money out and counted
it. £200 and I had no idea where it had come from.

Chapter 7

A few days after getting home and recovering, and not least, reflecting on what could have happened to me in London, I was still feeling grateful to be in one piece. The more I thought about it, the more I was sure I'd been drugged.

If my dream on the way back from London was anything to go by, I might not have got home at all. Walking through a subway and across a huge common, while pissed and drugged out of my head, would not have ended well.

The dream felt real to me, and it was all I had to go on to put the dishevelled pieces together of an extraordinarily complex jigsaw. But I'd never know for sure. The whole bus journey did feel familiar, as did The Native American, who I'm sure was sent to guide me. I got Goosebumps when I thought about him and almost felt afraid in a really odd way. I still wasn't sure how Phil fitted into it all.

I shook my head in disbelief and took stock of my shit life. I made the decision that there would be changes, and it would be immediate. It was as though I'd been given a second chance. The whole thing was surreal. Going to London for sex with someone I didn't know had been so risky. The fact I was safe and sound was a sign. I had to do better, do more with what I had.

I'd arranged for a new carpet to be fitted in the hall. I'd been to the post office and paid my £30 BT bill and was told the line would be re-connected in twenty-four hours. I needed my phone if nothing else.

I told "him" that he had a week to find somewhere else to live. I decided that he was the main drain on my life, there was absolutely nothing there. I had no feelings for him whatsoever. There probably never had been any feelings from my side, and so it really wasn't his fault.

If he was honest, he probably felt the same way about me. I'd not been a fun girlfriend, I'd been difficult, low all the time, and depressing. The weed had probably helped him through it.

I wasn't in a good way when I met him.

I had just gone through the most difficult relationship. The end had felt more like a bereavement because it really was the end. It had left me with so much internal conflict – love was supposed to be unconditional, but it never had been.

So, when I met him, I felt like I had no one else in the world, and I suppose it was sex and nothing else really. That had soon worn off when I became pregnant. In the world I'd just left, I wouldn't have given him the time of day, never mind a daughter. It was the circumstances that had thrown us together and what a mess that was. But we had Jody now, and I knew him and his family did love her.

I tried to explain to him the best I could why I wanted him to leave and made it clear that there would never be a problem with him and his mum seeing little Jody. It was going to break my heart to hand her over to them, even if it was part-time. But I also wasn't daft. I would need to be free at times. I wasn't going to play the game of "yer not seeing yer kid." It wouldn't come to any good, especially for me, and if I was ok, Jody would be too.

The cheeky sod agreed to go; he didn't bat an eyelid. I was relieved and offended at the same time. Relieved because I couldn't have coped with a fuss or a fight but offended because it just affirmed that it wasn't right. Not even a "why?" No pleading and begging from him. It was like he'd been waiting for permission to leave.

And I was gobsmacked when I'd returned from playgroup with Jody and he'd actually gone. There was no sign of him or any of his shit. I felt lighter already until I realised he'd taken the fucking telly.

I shed a tear for Jody and looked at her little face. I felt so guilty that she didn't have any choice about what was going on in her little world. Her life had just changed paths, and she would no longer live with her daddy. I remember that feeling so much, but I hadn't had a choice either.

My daddy went, but he never came back. I was five years old, and I missed him so much. He had always made the bad times better, but I realised and even understood why he had gone. In the end I didn't blame him; if I could have left, I would have. I just wish he'd stayed in touch somehow, but she wouldn't have had that. I know he loved me. I'll never forget the tears in his eyes the day he left. I remember him kissing me and telling me to be a good girl. I remember feeling scared and confused and looking at her. She was putting on her lipstick. She couldn't have cared less.

I kissed Jody's soft red cheeks, with tears rolling down my face and told her it was going to be ok. She didn't understand a word but said "mama" three times, the lump in my throat wouldn't go, as I continued to think about my dad for the first time in a very long time. Was he alive? Did he think about me, about us? Then I cried for her.

I looked into the empty space in the corner; it was only a telly. I'd filled plenty of empty corners, and I could get one off the clubman. Sandra had one off her clubman that had a box built into the back of it that you had to put money in. And if there was no money in it, there was no telly. I could do that.

I took a deep breath and told myself that this was for the best and that Jody would always have her dad and his family. The atmosphere here wouldn't have been doing her any good anyway, and if mummy was happy, Jody would be happy. But mummy was far from happy.

I cleaned the toilet for hours on end that evening. A sense of loneliness enveloped my body, but I had a clean toilet, a new carpet on my stairs, and access to the outside world, or at least I would in twenty-four hours. And I had my little girl.

I put Jody to bed. Thankfully, she was tired, and her eyelashes touched her cheeks no sooner than her head touched the pillow. I watched her for a while and envied her peace and her innocence.

I wasn't tired and welcomed the alone time. I opened the large window in the living room, sat on the windowsill and lit a cig, blowing the smoke playfully at the reflection in the glass.

I looked at the big open space outside my dingy flat, lost on a huge council estate – the fields and the trees not far away. I could hear dogs barking in the distance and people in their gardens finishing off their summer night, boozing, laughing and chattering. It was more than comforting and probably only a few doors down.

I looked towards the field and could see someone walking their dog. I could just make out a small Staffordshire bull terrier, wrestling with the branches. He was oscillating wildly as he gripped a branch fiercely whilst his owner walked the perimeter of the field, enjoying the interaction with fresh air. They were becoming silhouettes, shadows of the summer night.

I took another drag of my cigarette and leant on the wall with my feet up to my chest, blowing the smoke out of the open window.

The night sky still had shadows of the sun, and it wasn't quite dark. Her reflection was always watching.

I thought about London again. I thought about John and cringed at how the whole thing had turned out. I should have kept a level head, but I hadn't, and there was nothing I could do about it. It wasn't a date, but for some reason, I liked him and could have actually gone on a proper date with him; I even thought it could have worked between us. But then again, he must have been a bit dodgy to be advertising for sex, so he wasn't someone I'd want to get serious with. He was fit though. I hugged my legs close to me.

Then I thought about the £200. It must have been Phil who put it in my purse whilst I'd been dead to the world. I shivered at the thought of me being asleep in front of a stranger – my god.

I jumped; I thought I heard a knock at the door. I was a bit apprehensive about answering the door at this time of the night. I wouldn't be able to see who it was. The front door was at the side of the house, and you had to walk down through some very tall bushes to get to it. It was dark, and there was no light.

I ran into the kitchen and climbed up on the sink to open the window at the side of the house. I leant over as far as I could.

'Hello,' I half-whispered.

'It's me, Scott, from next door.'

I shouted down to him, 'One minute', and ran down the stairs to open the door.

'Aw sorry to bother you mate. I saw the living room lamp on and wondered if your fella has a bit of weed he could sort me out with.'

'Er come in.' Not sure why I was asking him to come in as my "fella" no longer lived here, and there was no weed left in the house that I knew of.

He went up the stairs and climbed over the board. He knew the drill he'd been in before.

'Sit down, if you like?' I was polite, 'I'll have a look for you.' I thought there might be some in the kitchen drawer and I was right. I wanted to laugh; he might have taken the telly, but he'd forgotten his weed, who'd have thought. I split it into a couple of little bags that he'd also left behind.

I went into the living room and threw Scott a bag, he was pleased and asked, 'how much?'

'A tenner,' I said quickly. I hadn't even thought about money, but I certainly wasn't going to turn it down.

'Where is he?' he asked, rummaging in his pocket whilst looking around the small flat, as though someone was going to come through the door.

He's gone,' I replied.

'What do you mean?'

'He's gone, left, done one, fucked off.' I couldn't make it any clearer.

'Hey?' He was genuinely confused.

'Hey?' I was genuinely confused at his confusion.

We both started laughing. 'We've split up, he's moved out.'

'Oh my god mate, are you ok?'

'I will be,' I smiled.

'Hey, shall I make us a nice joint?' he smiled.

God, I really did welcome the company, and one wouldn't do me any harm.

'Go on then, fuck it.' It might actually relax me a little bit.

He skinned up as I wondered if it was ok for him to be here with me. What about Sandra?

The flat actually looked cosy although I'm sure the lamp's ambience was helping it look a bit less like a shit hole.

'Do you wanna brew?' I thought it polite to ask.

'No ta. Do you have a beer?'

'Not really. You're lucky I had weed. I've got nowt in the fridge but got weed for the neighbour.'

And we both laughed again.

Why did I want him to like me? What was wrong with me? I had such a need for men to like me, for them to want me.

It was like I was coming back to life after a long

time of just existing. I didn't want to have sex with him. I wanted him to want sex with me.

He lit his big fat joint and passed it to me.

The smoke filled my lungs, and as I inhaled, I felt the sensation from the weed take over my body. Every inch of me started to feel relaxed and at ease, my eyes felt heavy but nice.

'That's a big one.' I said, obviously referring to the joint.

He laughed as he took a drag and almost choked laughing a cloud of smoke clogging his throat, he started coughing whilst trying to suppress his laughter.

It started me off, and before we knew it, we were literally rolling about on the floor laughing our heads off and I couldn't even remember what had started it.

I kept trying to tell him that I was laughing at his choking, but every time I thought of his face puffing up like a squirrel storing his nuts, I'd start laughing again. The tears were rolling down my face. He finally stopped laughing and was trying to get his composure and said, 'you only said "that's a big one".' And we were off again. I couldn't breathe through laughing, and then I laughed even more as I thought about me getting his kit off in my mind while he nearly choked.

We finished the rest of the joint in silence, both stoned and deep in our own thoughts. I was now seriously trying not to laugh as it really wasn't funny anymore.

We'd somehow ended up sat on the floor with our backs leaning on the settee.

We were close, and he was touching me accidentally on purpose. I had a v neck vest top on, black with black leggings and bare feet. I was nothing special, but I knew I was attractive to an onlooker, just not to myself.

I liked the spark; I liked the feeling it gave me. I thought of Sandra, but I was too stoned to care. I wanted to roll into his arms, but I'd do no such thing.

'So, what happened with him?' he asked.

'Nothing happened, ever. Well, maybe once.' I grinned referring to Jody.

'I know the feeling,' he smiled, 'she's always too tired and makes no effort. It's draining.'

'Well, it was more than just that, to be honest, but that was a massive part of it. He made me feel unattractive,' I looked into his eyes, knowing my sad-looking brown ones would hook him in.

I was right. He rubbed my leg slowly, tickling the skin beneath my soft leggings. The feeling sent an electric shock through my body, and he leant forward to kiss my lips. I kissed him back hard and boom, she was back.

I ripped his clothes off like a wanton whore who had been starved of sex.

'I'm so fuckin' horny,' I drooled.

He had obviously not had sex for months either as his reaction was as fierce as mine.

He actually ripped my vest top in two and dragged my leggings off, followed by my pants. I grabbed at his jeans, trying to get the buttons undone, all five of them – fucking Levi 501's were a pain in the arse.

He jumped up and sat on the settee.

I went to straddle him, but he turned me around so that I had my back to him.

I was going to come before he even entered me, I was that excited.

He started to push me down onto it, guiding me, holding my arse.

His hands felt strong and firm.

I was aching between my legs.

He was moaning softly.

I lowered myself slowly savouring every second of the entering of his cock.

It was warm, it was so hard, and it felt gorgeous as it hit my spot.

I was panting trying to keep hold of my orgasm.

I was wet, and I could smell my sexiness.

I rocked up and down, using my hands to push myself.

Within minutes, he grabbed my arse and pulled me down with some force, hard on his cock.

I could feel my whole body go into a beautiful spasm.

We both groaned in pure delight and ecstasy, knowing that the other one was coming hard.

I stood up and turned around.

'My god,' he muttered, 'you're fuckin' beautiful.

I smiled and said, 'it's getting late.'

And with that, he left.

I went to bed that night feeling elated and on top of the world. I kept hearing his words "my God, you're fuckin' beautiful".

Not only was I on my own and free to think and

feel what I wanted. I'd just had what I'd needed for months and my god it was worth the wait. I felt wonderful. Then I decided I needed a bath, the need to wash it away was as strong as the need for it in the first place.

I got up and ran myself a bath, making a coffee to wake me up a bit. I sat in the bath until it went cold, wanting to make sure his smell had gone from me.

When I got back in bed, I lay there and wriggled about trying to get comfortable. I couldn't quite get used to the fact that I had all the room in the bed. Eventually, I relaxed and thought about where I'd come from. It hadn't been the best journey so far, and my experiences had left me feeling low at times. Some days, it was even hard to move. I thought about the state of the flat and decided that I would get it straight little by little; it already felt a bit straighter now that he had gone.

I had to carry on, I knew that much, and I would. I was forgetting my past, or I was until I had the dream on the way to London. She was in it; I shook my head. She wasn't allowed in; I'd just got rid of one drain and there was no room for any more.

I decided that I would be alone forever. I would have to have sex though. I started to get the feeling between my legs, and I welcomed it. I fell asleep, and as I did, I put my hands between my legs and rocked myself gently into a beautiful orgasm that made me dream of John.

Chapter 8

The next few days, I worked hard on the flat while Jody played or followed me about or cried or wanted feeding, but slowly I felt I was getting there.

It was Friday, and her father would be picking her up tonight and taking care of her until Sunday.

I was looking forward to being "me" for a couple of days. Not that I planned to do anything. But the idea of doing nothing unless it was for myself felt good.

I went into the back garden to empty the carrier bag that I'd been using for a bin. I stopped dead when I saw Sandra busy emptying her rubbish.

Too late, she'd seen me. She didn't look very happy, or maybe I was totally paranoid.

'Morning,' she said.

'Morning,' I responded. 'Are you OK?'

'Scott has fucked off,' she murmured, almost embarrassed.

'When?' I was trying to look her in the eye but could feel the heat rising in my cheeks.

'Oh, it was a few weeks ago now, but It's just kicked off again. He was supposed to be having the boys so I could go out with the girls tonight and of course, he's suddenly decided that he's going out and can't change his plans. They're going to my mum and dads' now, but it's not the point.'

'He's gone as well,' I said, nodding toward my flat. I did a little laugh in an attempt to comfort her and let her know she wasn't alone in her circumstances.

'Jesus, are you joking?' she asked.

'Nope! Deadly serious and I'm better off for it. Jody is going to his mothers with him for the weekend, and I'm looking forward to the peace if I'm honest.'

'Come out with us,' she said excitedly.

I could usually tell if someone was just offering an invitation to be polite, but I could see by her face that she genuinely wanted me to go out with her.

'We're walking round to The Royal Oak at 8pm. Be ready, and you can come with us. It'll be a change for you. And there's a disco on.'

'OK,' I said, surprising myself. 'See you later,' and I ran back upstairs feeling excited.

'Deffo?' She shouted as I ran off.

'Deffo,' I promised.

Oh my god, I was going out with the girls. What to wear? I made a mental list of every outfit I owned and decided I didn't have one thing that I could wear to the pub. I couldn't use the clothes I'd worn in London as they were Sandra's.

I went into a cupboard in the bedroom and pulled out a suitcase that was buried at the back. I'd sworn I'd never open it again, but it was full of old clothes from my previous life and I needed something to wear tonight. I'd not been out for years, and I wanted to look good.

I settled on a tight, short black skirt and a frilly, black, off-the-shoulder top. The frills were multi-coloured but predominately yellow, so I grabbed a huge yellow belt to break it up. I had yellow shoes to match. I would look better than anyone in that pub and the best out of all the girls going out tonight. I had no doubt.

I looked in the mirror at my long frizzy hair. It looked limp and I decided some products wouldn't go amiss. A visit to a hairdresser wouldn't go amiss either, but I had more chance of bumping into Madonna at the end of our road than having my hair done by a hairdresser.

There was a knock on the door. It would be Jody's dad coming to collect her; she was all ready to go. I ran down to let him in and spotted a brown envelope on the floor. I scooped it up; it had my name written on the front of it. I quickly opened it and found a wad of ten-pound notes folded neatly. I looked for a note or some clue, but there was none.

The banging on the door got louder.

'OK, 'OK,' I shouted, staying calm as I didn't want to upset Jody before she went.

I opened the door to be greeted with, 'What the fuck are y'doing?'

His face irritated me.

'Wait there.'

I shut the door in his face. He could wait outside for that comment. I couldn't be bothered with his bollocks.

I went and got Jody, who was gabbing happily waiting for her daddy. Her bag was all ready, changes of clothes, but no nappies. If he wanted nappies, he'd have to buy them, like I did.

I got the buggy and made sure she got off safely, with as little interaction with him as possible.

'Bring her back Sunday at seven.'

'I'll bring her back when I want.' He was adamant

in his tone, which was actually quite refreshing. I didn't know he had it in him.

I closed the door and looked again in the envelope, counting the tenner's; there was twenty altogether – two hundred quid. How bizarre I thought.

A trip to the hairdressers was possible after all. I grabbed my bag, left the flat and walked to the shops. I was going to Kolash for the first time; I needed a complete overhaul of the mess on my head.

The little banner above the door was white with a pencil-drawn image of a woman's head with a hairdryer either side of it.

As I was about to open the salon door, I heard someone shout my name and recognised the accent immediately.

'Hiya Az,' I said even before I turned around.

'You getting yer haircut, Julie?' he asked sweetly.

'No, I was wondering if they sold cigs in there,' I said sarcastically.

'Ah Julie, what's wrong with my cigs?'

I rolled my eyes and opened the door to the salon.

'You should smile more y'know Julie, you're a pretty woman.' I half smiled as I bounded up the stairs nervously.

I was immediately met by the tension that was often experienced when walking into a hairdresser's and quickly regretted being so rude to Az, who meant no harm.

The owner, Sharon, had the tightest blonde perm I'd ever seen. The top of her head was tight curls, but then they were right down her back too. She had a lovely warm smile and asked what I wanted in a very professional manner.

She was polite, but when she spoke, the other girls looked across at me. I felt them looking me up and down and checking me out.

One was drying an older lady's hair.

'I remember, Brenda, when my mum used to put elastic bands in my hair instead of bobbles.'

'Jesus Christ,' Brenda cackled, 'rip yer bleeding hair out them. I used to put knicker elastic in our Bev's hair, she'd go mad if she knew.'

They both laughed.

The other girl had squashed a purple cap onto some poor buggers' head and was going for it with a crochet hook, as the poor woman winced in her chair, holding on to the cap for dear life and making small talk.

'We got married in the con club us love, and had a communal buffet, everybody brought butties. Those were the days.' The girl with the crochet hook grunted clearly uninterested.

I told Sharon I wanted some streaks and a cut and blow.

'Can you wait for ten minutes?' Sharon asked me. 'You're lucky; I've just had a cancellation.'

I could wait all bloody day really, so I didn't mind.

'Yeah, no problem.'

'Do you want a tea or coffee?'

'Yeah, I'll have a coffee, please,' I said and looked around for a magazine to read. They were all hairstyle ones but never mind, it was something to look at.

She called over to a lad who was doing someone's hair, and I gathered they didn't get on as the atmosphere between them was tense.

'Go on then, Robby,' she said to him, 'brew up for the client.'

Her tone was firm, though there was something unnecessary about the way she'd asked him, but I liked her style.

Robby picked up on it but didn't take it out on me and he kindly brought me a coffee.

'There you go love, get that down your neck.'

I smiled; he was nice.

The radio started playing Wet Wet Wet's "Angel Eyes", and the mood lightened.

'We went to see these last week, didn't we T?' Sharon shouted across the room to the girl who was blow-drying Brenda's hair.

'You shoulda seen her Brenda,' "T" said to her client, 'You'd have thought Marti was singing to her.'

'HE WAS,' screamed Sharon.

Everyone laughed, and the whole salon burst into song in time to the radio.

I relaxed a bit as the tension was lifted, and I thought about John's stunningly beautiful blue eyes.

Robby joined in and pointed at me as he was singing the lyrics "Angel Eyes" I felt my face turn as red as a beetroot. He then said, 'your eyes are stunning though.'

For a split second, I thought he was flirting because he wanted me. But I shook my head and instantly removed the thought. There was a time and a place.

A couple of hours later, and after a good laugh, I

left the salon with a beautiful shoulder length curly bob and blonde highlights that made my brown eyes look slightly hazel and my black eyebrows and eyelashes more prominent in a good way.

Sharon had asked me if I'd wanted a perm to lift it, but it had a natural curl already if teased right. I refused her upsell but was impressed by the way she'd put it.

I walked back to the flat. I'd picked up a bottle of wine from the shop to drink whilst getting ready, a bit of Dutch courage was much needed for tonight.

I stared at myself for ages in the mirror. I couldn't believe the difference a good hair cut made. I thought about a time when my hair was always pristine, then shook my head.

I was here now, and I was doing OK... ish.

I thought about the two hundred quid that had come through the door and wondered if it had a link to London. There was no one else in the world that would post me that amount of money.

But I never gave my address and as I thought about it, I went all hot. Jesus what if I had given it to someone, whilst drugged out of my head. My God, I must have. I started to feel anxious and was pacing around the flat when it dawned on me that I still had his phone number in my purse. I would phone him and ask who had posted me the money, then I felt crazy. I couldn't just phone him out of the blue and ask about two hundred quid. Surely it was a coincidence, it being the same amount as the money in the envelope from London.

Oh my god, I was really starting to feel stressed. I took the envelope out of my bag and looked in it in case there was a letter hidden in the deepest darkest corner. I'd already looked several times so knew for a fact that there wasn't.

It dawned on me that the envelope had the name "Julie" written on its front. That meant only one thing – it had no connection to London. I had been known as Charley.

I poured myself a glass of wine and ran a bath; it was 6pm, and I wanted to be ready in good time.

The wine definitely relaxed me as I lay in the bath, wondering what the night ahead would bring. Fleetwood Mac was playing full blast from the radio.

After the bath, I scrabbled about for some usable makeup. My findings consisted of an old tray of eye shadow, so worn down that there was more tray than powder, a mascara and a very worn-down lipstick. It was so used that I'd need a cotton bud to dig it out and apply it to my lips.

At two minutes to eight there was a loud knock at the door, my stomach did a somersault. I knew it would be Sandra and her mates – mates I'd not even met before. But I had this. I took a deep breath and opened the front door.

I knew I looked nice with my new hairdo and black and yellow outfit.

'Alright?' They all seemed to yell at once.

Sandra introduced me to Clare and Angie, who seemed nice if not a bit rough around the edges, but everyone around here was like that. I had no problem with any of them.

'You look top,' Sandra crooned, looking me up and down. 'Can't actually believe how nice you look.'

'Cheers. I must look a twat most of the time then,' I joked with her.

I was used to the banter and tried to give it back, but I was always conscious that one wrong word and I would offend someone.

'I believe yer old fella's left ya?' Clare asked.

'Well, I kicked him out in all honesty,' I responded with a smile on my face.

'Why? Who yer shaggin'?' Angie said, laughing at her own crassness.

A flashback of me sat on Scott's cock shot through my head.

I laughed. 'Nobody... yet!' I said, with a wink.

'Ay this might be yer lucky night, there's some fit bits in the Royal Oak.'

'Let's go then,' I laughed, and we all stomped to the pub together laughing and joking and slagging off men.

'They all fuck off in the end,' Angie harped on.

I thought about my dad and thought she was perhaps right.

The pub was rocking. The DJ was in the corner, surrounded by his coloured lights; it made the pub feel darker than it was, which I preferred.

I liked his choice in music as he played all the biggest hits from the eighties. No wonder it was rocking.

We stood at the bar and all of a sudden men surrounded us like flies' round shit.

'Who you with love?'

'Yer wanna drink love?'

'Your fella must be a right dick to let you out on

yer own.'

'Yeah, I will have a drink,' I said to the second guy who looked alright. 'I'll have half a lager please.'

The cheek of me, but I didn't care. I was going to get all I could tonight.

'Half a lager,' he laughed. 'Half a lager? Are you sure?'

I nodded.

'Half a lager it is then.'

I threw back the drink and it felt nice on top of the wine. I felt a bit giddy and swayed to the music as Womack & Womack's "Footsteps on the dance floor" took over the disco, and the atmosphere ramped up.

'What's yer name?' Mr-half-a-lager shouted at me.

'Charley, my name is Charley,' I shouted back.

The girls laughed and went along with me, thank God.

The halves of lager were coming thick and fast, and I was getting more than a bit giddy. Angie and Clare were dancing with each other but in a ridiculous fashion, exaggerating their moves looking like a right pair of lunatics and half of the pub were laughing at them. They were hilarious.

'Do yer wanna grab a bit of fresh air?' Mr-half-a-lager asked me.

'OK,' I nodded.

We headed outside, where we could still feel the atmosphere and hear the loud music. I felt happy in the midst of it all.

He walked me over to a small alley that led to the

estate. He grabbed me and kissed me, and I found myself kissing him back, but I wanted more.

I reached down to his pants and rubbed him, feeling him go hard at my touch.

Suddenly I heard one of the girls shouting me. 'Charley?' It was Angie. 'Where are you?'

I ran from behind the alley, laughed and said, 'I'm here.'

'Come on, we're going into Manchester.'

Her enthusiasm was higher than mine. I didn't want to go anywhere; I was enjoying it here.

Mr-half-a-lager was gutted. As I got in the taxi, he ran out of the pub with a beer mat and a pen and asked me for my phone number. I laughed as I wrote it down for him.

We asked the taxi driver if he had any good tapes and Sandra, who was sat in the front, had no qualms in going through his glove compartment looking for something decent to put on. I'm not sure I agreed with "Music for the jilted generation" by The Prodigy, but it certainly set the scene for a "Full Throttle" ride into Manchester.

The taxi driver turned the volume up. The girls were screaming "yieow yieow" then "efffffa," then laughing loudly, even the taxi driver was joining in and we were off.

We headed down Princess Parkway, passing Maine Road, the Manchester City football ground. It reminded me of another reason for getting rid of 'him'. It was like football was crucial to life, and his passion towards "City" and nothing else used to irritate me.

It wasn't long before we could see the lights of

Manchester. I used to work here once upon a time, and it used to excite me. Tonight, I felt a bit anxious, but I was doing well and going with it.

I sat back as the girls danced about in their seats as Mr Flint blurted out lyrics of Voodoo. The taxi driver was certainly enjoying it and sang along loudly. The atmosphere was loud but fun.

'Do you want a sip of my lager?' Sandra asked him. He actually took a swig, and we all screamed with laughter.

The streets were full of revellers. We approached via Oxford Road, the part of Manchester where mainly students congregated.

We approached a little green doorway on Princess Street and the taxi man charged us £8 for the luxury.

'Aw come in with us,' Clare begged our driver.

'Yeah, come on,' the others joined in.

'My wife would fuckin' kill me if I went home tonight with hardly any money because I went to the Cypress with four gorgeous women instead. Sorry girls. Thanks for the offer; go and enjoy yerselves and give us a ring when you need a lift back.

We all laughed, told him we loved him a hundred times and jumped out of his taxi.

We piled into the club and as I looked above the door, I could see Cypress Tavern written in green writing.

The music was blaring and the clubbers were jumping up and down on a soaked floor full of cigarette dimps. I thought of the old pub in London. It was a similar atmosphere and a similar genre of music. This was the northern version and given most of the music had been generated in the North the atmosphere was definitely more that of loyalty and love.

Joy Division were tearing love apart loudly. Men jumped up and down to Ian Curtis's haunting tones as though they connected with him. Maybe they did.

Angie shoved a brandy in my face.

'That was quick, how did you get that?' I asked.

'What?' She screamed.

I just shook my head, I couldn't be bothered saying it again, for her to say "what" again.

We went into a back room; it didn't feel as loud in there. There was a tiny bar, and people were skinning up everywhere.

There were some local lads in, who the girls all seemed to know. We sat with them and they seemed a good crack, passing around their joints and sharing their beer. I found that living on a council estate, everyone knew each other and couldn't seem to do enough for each other. It really was a different world to where I came from.

I was lagging now and finding it hard to keep up until The Smiths came on. "This Charming Man," ripped through my soul and I found myself standing on the table, dancing like Morrisey and loving life.

Suddenly I saw the Native American from the bus in London. The shock made me lose my balance, and I fell flat on my fucking face.

One of the lads picked me up off the floor, and we were laughing, me out of embarrassment and him out of pure amusement.

The Native American was nowhere to be seen.

'I'm gonna go,' I said.

'I'll take yer,' he shouted, his beer breath made me gag and the volume of his voice made my ears pop.

I left but not before I scouted every inch of the club to see if I could see my guardian angel. I couldn't. He'd gone. Maybe I was having some kind of breakdown and imagining him. Maybe I was just pissed and needed my bed.

It wasn't long before I was outside, walking up Princess Street in Manchester and before we knew it, we were approaching Moss Side.

'My car is here,' he said.

'Hurry up,' I shivered. 'I'm fucking freezing.'

He fumbled about for something in his pocket, it looked like a coat hanger, but it could have been something attached to his keys, he reminded me of a jailer.

'Quick; get in,' he said.

I got in the passenger seat, and he sped off at what felt like a hundred miles an hour. I felt sick but lay my head back and tried to take some deep breaths.

The car was skidding everywhere, and I started to realise that he couldn't drive.

'What are you doing? You idiot. Your driving is shit,' I slurred.

'Not my fuckin' car, is it? So, I'm not arsed.'

'What do you mean?' But I knew what he meant; I knew he'd stolen it.

'Let me out,' I shouted. My god here I was again in another situation that could end up disastrous, and even in my drunken state, I felt scared.

'Don't be fuckin daft. We'll be home in a minute.'

He stopped at some traffic lights. I saw my chance and dived out of the car right opposite the huge Southern Cemetery. He sped off at full speed, and it was then I saw the blue lights. He's fucked, I thought.

I flagged down a taxi and was lucky that it stopped. I thanked him as I jumped in the front seat, trying to say my address as clear as I could.

'I just wanna go home.' I muttered and pressed my head against the window. We passed the big hospital on the parkway as we drifted at a normal speed. We passed The Mersey Lights a pub notorious for trouble. It was emptying out, its revellers reluctant to leave. The bouncers on the doors had their work cut out tonight. Cars were beeping their frustration as partygoers kept staggering into the road.

'Lock yer door,' instructed the taxi driver, making sure none of them would get in. As we waited in slow-moving traffic, the red glow of the traffic lights glared in my face. Annie Lennox was playing on the radio.

No more I love you's
The language is leaving me
No more I love you's
Changes are shifting
Outside the words

Her powerful voice pierced through my heart and the need for her to know that she couldn't reciprocate the feelings brought a tear to my eye. I also would never again be able to say, "I love you." It was as simple as that.

The taxi dropped me off on the corner of my road, and I walked as best as I could towards my flat. I couldn't wait to get in and crash out on my bed.

A man was walking towards me, he was a bit older than me and had light blue jeans on and a checked shirt. He was of a big build, and when he approached me, I became nervous.

'Have you got the time love?' he asked.

'Not on me, but I've got a clock in my bedroom,' I winked.

The next thing I know, we were stripping off in my bedroom, all inhibitions gone. No name asking, just pure filthy, fast and furious sex.

I felt the heat of his body and the quickness of his breathing, I remember the feeling of him inside of me and me rocking backwards and forwards so that my pleasure was fierce on his hardness. Jesus, he must have thought he'd won the pools.

He was certainly grateful, as he lay there afterwards, trying to catch his breath.

I wanted to fall into unconsciousness but at the same time was trying my best to stay awake until he left.

'Er I'll be off,' he said. 'You're fit, you know, but you need to be careful. I could have been a nutter.'

I shut the door after him and stumbled back up the stairs. I grabbed my bag so I could get a cig and noticed the piece of paper inside it. It was John's telephone number.

I stared at it and could just make out the number

if I shut one eye.

Fuck it, I was going to phone him.

I didn't hesitate.

After a few rings, I heard, 'Hello'. It was him. I pictured his sparkly blue eyes and his messy light brown hair.

'Hello,' I said, trying my hardest to beat my drunken slur. 'It's Charley.'

There was silence on the other end of the phone as I gripped it hard to my ear to listen.

Finally, a response. 'Charley, what do you want?'

'I can't get your angel eyes out of my head.' I slurred. 'A man has just asked me for the time, and I said I had a clock in my bedroom; and can you guess what happened next?'

'I'll tell you what, Charley, phone me back when you're sober, and maybe you can explain what the hell you're on about.'

The phone went dead.

I phoned back.

It was engaged.

I pressed redial.

It was engaged.

I put the piece of paper in my bag and noticed that the brown envelope had gone. I rummaged through my bag in desperation, looking again and again in the same places. But it had gone. I couldn't fuckin' believe it. The man without the time must have had it; there was no other way it could have gone.

I needed a bath. But I wasn't up for it.

I threw my bag across the living room floor, feeling sorry for myself. I got on the settee and fell asleep, wondering why John wouldn't speak to me.

Chapter 9

I dreamt I was in a beautiful church listening to the bells chiming loudly, making a beautiful tune. I became aware of a phone ringing from an office somewhere in the church. The candles were lit around me, and the church's warmth made me feel safe, but the shrill was increasing. The ringing bells disappeared, and all I could hear was the shrill of the phone. Somebody needed to answer that phone.

I woke up and quickly realised that it was my phone that was demanding to be answered.

I dived up fast off the settee and felt the sharp pain in my head from the hangover that had decided to break into my skull as I slept.

I picked up the receiver, my mouth was dry and sticky. 'Hello.'

'Oh, hello,' came the southern crossed European twang. I knew immediately it was John and my stomach lurched as I tried to recall the conversation that I'd had with him last night. I decided that me and alcohol were a bad mix. I did an internal groan as I recalled the 'I've got a clock in my bedroom' scenario.

'What do you want?' I knew my tone was rude, but I didn't care. I felt awful.

'I have only met you once and spoken to you a couple of times, but I can feel that you're troubled.' He seemed sincere.

'I'm sorry; I need to go.'

I put the phone down. Not because I didn't want to speak to him but because I really did need to go.

I ran as fast as I could to the toilet, thankful for once it was just in the next room.

The sweat was pouring from me. I sat there, thinking that I hadn't even had that much to drink, but I suppose I did have a load of lager. And there was the wine I had before I left. Then the brandies in the Cypress on top. Bleurgh! The thought made me queasy. I leant my sweaty head on the toilet wall; it felt cool on my hot face. My eyes were gravelly, and I needed to get back in bed.

The phone started to ring again. Jesus; in all the years I'd had a phone, it had barely rung, and now it had rung twice in ten minutes. I had to ignore it. I couldn't move.

Twenty minutes later, I was in my bed, welcoming sleep, and as I lay there, I remembered that the brown envelope had gone out of my bag. Ah well, at least I'd got a nice new hairdo out of it, and that had to count for something.

I tossed and turned. I was desperate for sleep but the pain was too severe; I couldn't get passed it, so I decided on a cup of coffee instead.

I got up and walked into the kitchen. The rain was pounding on the window. I shivered. I didn't have any curtains up in the kitchen. Being on the top floor I didn't really care, but in that instant, I felt cold. The day was black, it was so dark that I had to turn the light on.

I shivered as I watched the trees on the field blowing in a summer gale. I wasn't moving today, that was for sure.

I made my coffee and checked in the drawer to see if there were any paracetamol left. I usually kept a bottle in the kitchen drawer, just in case. There were two left, so I put them in my mouth and welcomed the hot coffee as it helped them go down.

I threw the empty bottle back into the drawer with the empty Piriton packet that I took to help me sleep.

I went back into the living room to call "his" mother, to check on Jody. I was sure she would be OK, but the call would make me feel better.

I could hear them all in the background when she answered. Jody had a big cousin on that side of the family called Jess. She was obviously there. I could hear laughter and lots of chattering from them and immediately felt better. I smiled and after some polite conversation, said that I'd see her tomorrow.

'Actually Julie,' his mother began, 'I'm off work now for two weeks. We're going to have a week at home, then we're going to the caravan for a week. Me and Pete were thinking that, if you didn't mind, Jody could stay with us and then come to the caravan. The fresh air would do her good. I mean it would give you a break. I know it's been hard for you.'

'You don't care how hard it's been for me. I'm not stupid.' I was harsh. 'But yes, its ok Ann. She sounds happy, and that's what's important. What about clothes though – do you want me to drop some over?' I asked, concerned that she'd taken so little with her.

'We'll pick up some new ones for her, spoil her a little bit if you don't mind?'

'OK, OK. Well, enjoy your holiday then and give her a cuddle every night for me?' The lump in my throat was hard to swallow.

She was shocked by my response and couldn't get off the phone quick enough. They were only over the bridge, not too far away, and I know Jody thrived at her grandparents' house. They were good people even if their son was a bum.

As soon as I put the receiver down, it rang again. I thought Ann had forgotten something.

'Hello' I answered.

But it wasn't Ann. It was John.

'It's me again.'

It being him shocked me, and again I was lost for words.

'Hiya' I said once I'd gathered myself together. 'I'm sorry about before,' I said, remembering how rude I must have sounded.

'You rang me last night and told me that you'd had sex with a man who asked you for the time?'

'So?' I said, 'that's nothing to do with you.'

'OK, but you phoned me about it, not the other way round. You do need to watch what you are doing,' he went on. 'You were in a state when you were here. You're lucky you were looked after. You were begging for sex.'

I wasn't sure what to think. This was coming from a man who was advertising for a submissive shag, and now here he was with adapted morals. It seemed odd to me. And what did he mean I was begging for sex? I was too embarrassed to ask.

'Who do you live with?' He asked me.

'I live with my daughter,' I responded, unsure why I would tell him the truth.

'Why did you phone me last night?'

'Probably to beg for sex.' I was sarcastic in my response. 'I don't even remember calling you.'

'It doesn't matter,' he said. 'I was simply curious.'

'I lost my envelope,' I said out of the blue.

'What are you talking about?'

'Never mind.' I wondered about the first envelope in London that had come from nowhere. Was there a connection?

'Go on,' he urged.

'It's nothing; I got £200 posted through my door in an envelope and ended up losing it.'

'Not surprising given the state you were in,' he said. I didn't like his tone. 'Do you want to come back to London?'

'Not right now. I'm too hungover.'

'Do you drink a lot?' he asked.

'No, I don't actually. I'm just pissed every time I speak or see you.'

'I've seen you once.'

'Why didn't you want to sleep with me?' I was interested to know.

'It was never going to be me. I didn't put the advert in the newspaper, I was just there to meet you. You looked too lost and vulnerable. I mean, you were so drunk and drugged up, and you have issues.'

'I didn't take any drugs, I was spiked! And what issues? You can't tell if someone has issues from half an hour of meeting them. And what do you mean, it wasn't going to be you?'

'It doesn't matter. It all worked out for the best.' He wasn't going to divulge. 'You do have issues though. There is definitely something going on around the need for sex.'

I laughed.

'I've laid down every night for twenty-six years, trying to find myself and who I am. I've tossed and turned at my regrets and the internal conflicts that torture my soul. My head spins in absolute turmoil and chaos. You've met me once and think you've got me summed up in one – fuckin' hilarious. I wish I'd have met you sooner. You could have saved me a lot of sleepless nights.'

I slammed the phone down. Who did he think he was? He could take his assumptions and stick them up his arse.

There was definitely something going on around the need for sex though. He was right about that, even though I'd never admit it to him.

The rest of the day didn't get any better. I'd been out for one night, and my phone was ringing like Busby's hotline.

Mr-half-a-lager phoned me, turns out his name was Steve. He was declaring undying love for me after one short meeting and wanted to know if I would meet him at the Royal Oak for a drink. He seemed nice enough, but it wasn't what I wanted.

I didn't want to go out with anyone. I didn't want another fella. I'd had enough and wanted to simply enjoy myself and remain single for now, perhaps forever. I didn't need to be tied to a man, to have to explain myself anymore. No, I didn't want that. Besides, I needed to learn to love myself before I let anyone in, and I wasn't capable of that. The past never left me and made me feel void of any feelings.

I refused Steve's date politely, giving him some excuse about having no babysitter, even though I was free to do what I wanted for the next two weeks. I took his phone number and said if I could get a sitter, I would call him and let him know.

He was happy at that and waffled on for a further five minutes before asking if he could phone me again. I said he could if he wanted to. I was hoping he'd somehow forget. I knew he wouldn't. Why did I get myself into these situations? All I wanted was peace.

I'd just gotten rid of Steve when there was a knock on the door. It was Scott asking if I fancied a spliff with him. You couldn't make it up.

I had to blow him out too. I explained I'd been out with Sandra and really needed to get some sleep due to a hangover. He laughed and said, 'maybe another time.'

'Maybe,' I replied and shut the door, thinking that was the last thing I needed.

I went back up the stairs, grateful for my new carpet as it kept my feet warm. I made another cup of coffee, thank God for coffee. I sat on the windowsill watching the rain. This was my new favourite spot. I could have sat there for the rest of my life – nobody bothered me, and when I looked at my reflection, I saw "her".

I was attuned to the nature that was my back garden. I loved watching the little birds flying from branch to branch, looking for food. The rain was beautiful, and it touched everything.

I watched below, as Sandra took her soaking

wet washing off the line, with one of her children clinging to her ankles. I hadn't seen her since I'd left the club and it dawned on me that she must have wondered where I'd gone. Then I wondered why she'd not knocked on to check. I started to get paranoid that Scott had told her about the other night. My stomach was in knots for a minute, and it took me a while to calm myself down.

I looked again, and now Irene, my neighbour from the other side had joined her. Bless Irene she was helping her get the washing off the line.

I sighed loudly. So much had gone on over the last few days. I didn't feel good about myself really.

I had a near-miss in London, slept with my neighbour's partner, not forgetting the total stranger I'd let in last night. I'd been in a stolen car and lost the remainder of my 200 quid.

I tried to relax and took a long drag of my cigarette. I had a flashback of "The Native American". He had been there, in the Cypress Tavern.

What was going on? Or was it me? Was I going mad? He must have been there, or I wouldn't have fallen off the table.

Who was he? My dream must have been my subconscious, somehow reminding me of what had happened on that bus. Because I'd only seen him in my dream. Yet he was real in the Cypress Tavern.

The whole thing was weird. Then I thought about "her". Was she having me spied on?

I decided to put on my biggest, baggiest jumper and knock-on next door to test the waters with Sandra. I wouldn't settle until I knew whether she knew about me and Scott.

She seemed off with me when she opened the door.

'Oh, alright?'

I was taken aback but appeared confident.

'Yeah, I'm OK. What time did you get home?' I asked her.

Her face softened. 'Do you wanna brew?' she asked me.

The kids were noisy but cute. I missed my Jody but appreciated the space, although I wasn't doing anything productive with my time.

She'd painted her kitchen green, and her white cupboards were standard. The drawings and paintings that were splattered all over the cupboards did the job of cheering it up. The toilet was at the back of the kitchen, albeit in a separate little room. I still couldn't get my head around that in this day and age she still had to come down in the middle of the night for a wee.

She had a little wooden table with some nice wicker chairs, two blue and two natural and a big orange vase on the table with fake yellow and orange roses. Her kitchen window had gingham curtains, and they made it look homely.

'I got in about 2am, and I'm flipping knackered. But we had a good night. What happened to you though?' she said as she was putting the kettle on. You could just about hear the little radio in the background.

I told her about my fall and that it had sent me into meltdown and that one of the guys from the estate offered to take me home in a stolen car.

'Oh my god,' she laughed. 'That'll be Spenner; he's a bloody nutter.'

'Well, I must have looked like a nutter when I did a Starsky and Hutch right out of the car, rolled onto the pavement like a ninja and lay there until he'd driven off.'

She laughed again.

I was glad she was laughing. It meant she didn't know about me and Scott.

'I heard some news last night, and it really did my head in,' she blurted out.

I gulped and waited for the accusations to come firing at me.

'What's happened?' I asked whilst the top of my legs went clammy and started to shake.

'Scott's been sleeping with someone else. I feel sick.'

I didn't know what to say and was about to burst into tears and start apologising.

She stopped me just in time, by saying, 'It was Angie who was out with us last night. She's supposed to be my mate.'

She was the one who then burst into tears.

'How could she do that to me?'

As if I had the answers.

She was sobbing now.

I felt helpless and like a fraud.

'Has it been going on for long?'

Not that it mattered.

'Dunno, don't wanna know. She was legless last night and seemed to take great joy in telling me. I knew he was fed up, but of all the fuckin' people, he had to sleep with her.'

'What you going to do?' I stood up to comfort her, but she point-blank refused.

I felt awkward.

'What can I do? I need to move on. And he was only asking me the other day if we could try again. I even thought about it, but there's no way now. That's the straw that broke the camel's back, that is.'

I wanted to tell her to fuck him off, and that she'd be better on her own and that men were bastards.

But I said nothing. Anything I said at this point could have been referred to at a later date as me putting a spanner in the works for my own benefit, so I kept quiet.

One of the kids started to cry, and she instantly went into mummy mode, which made me smile, but also gave me a sad feeling.

That's what mummies do, they drop everything for their baby.

Mine never did that. She only abused me. I wasn't a great mum, but I'd never abuse my baby girl. I'll never know why she did it to me. Maybe it was something I did, she clearly never liked me.

I had to stop thinking about her, it never did me any good.

The last ten minutes hadn't done me any good either. I needed to get out and leave Sandra to her problems. I had enough of my own.

'I'm going to get off.' I said, noticing that my accent was attuning to theirs and that I really was losing myself.

I berated myself all day for making such a mess of things and was feeling quite low by the early evening. I ran a bath and decided that I would walk to The Royal Oak, to see if I could find Steve or any other bloke I could get my fix from. It was the only thing that ever made me feel better, but I knew it was a short-term solution; it was barely worth it given the mortification it would bring in the aftermath.

Despite knowing it was a terrible idea, I started to feel excited as I thought out my plan of action.

I would get dressed up and put some lipstick on, and when I saw Steve, I would lick my lips and had no doubt that we would be back at the flat in minutes.

The thought was giving me that feeling. I got in the bath, and the hot water on my naked flesh only made the feeling stronger.

I opened my legs and rubbed myself and said John's name out loud. The thrill of his name on my lips, shot between my legs and my nipples hardened in the cold air. I squeezed one of them hard, and literally screamed as the beautiful flow throbbed hard between my legs.

I didn't need to go out. I was happy right here.

Chapter 10

After my bath and my change of mind about going to the pub, I decided to give the flat a once over. After all, this was the idea in the aftermath of London, to get myself sorted and make this place a nicer home for me and Jody.

I heard a commotion outside, just as I went to get my yellow duster and tin of Mr Sheen out of the kitchen cupboard.

It was Irene, and her children, David and Bernie. I could hear David's ever so camp laugh, which without fail, always made me smile. It almost made me laugh out loud as it contagiously rang in my ears. He had the loudest laugh in the world, I was sure.

I leant over the kitchen sink so that I could give them all a wave.

Irene was a small woman with short jet-black hair. She always wore a black straight skirt, with a t-shirt in summer, and in the winter, she'd replace that for a polo neck jumper. She was what they called the salt of the earth, simple and honest, and good in every way. She spoke with her eyes, and her mouth wasn't far behind. She had a couple of cleaning jobs on the go, one at the bank in the shopping centre and another at the school. She'd seen their dad off years ago.

David was plump with short black hair; if he grew it, it would be curly, but he wore it really short. He worked down the road in the old Dresser Rand building, so was often at his mum's. He'd often knock-on and come in for a brew with me or a smoke with "him". Or I'd bob in for a brew at theirs when he was about.

We didn't spend loads of time together, only because me being me, I refused every invitation to join him on a night out, even though I wanted to go. But I really liked David, he was so funny, warm, and if I didn't have the steel barriers around my heart, I might have let him in a bit more. He never gave up on me or got fed of the grump that I often was.

Bernie was the double of their mum, again she was short, but not as plump, with longer black hair and was really pretty but could have taken more care of herself. She dressed a lot older than her age, mirroring her mum's straight skirts but jazzing them up a bit with striped tops and trainers. She was another soul who I warmed to, albeit she never had much to say. How could she get a word in with him around? Bernie had a different job every week; according to Irene, she never lasted in them. Her mother would say she needed to stand up for herself and stop letting people walk all over her.

Irene spotted me, looking down on them and waved madly, fag in mouth, beckoning me to go down to see them. I grimaced at the thought of it. I had always loved their company whenever they bobbed round but could I really be arsed going down and joining them just to say hello to everyone.

'Julie, Julie,' she screamed through her own laughter. I could hear her loud and clear, and I hadn't even opened the window yet. 'Come down. Come see what these two buggers are up to.'

Reluctantly I went downstairs and across the path into her garden.

'Do yer wanna brew?' She asked before I had chance to say hello. 'Make her a brew David, while I finish my cig.' She pointed towards the back door that led into the kitchen.

'She can make her own fuckin' brew, she's got two perfectly good working hands there, haven't yer love? Kettle's in the kitchen.'

His smile beamed right across his face. I loved his sparkly eyes. He was a soul – a little loud and very noisy, but definitely a soul.

'Y'alright, Julie love? Yer know me don't you kid? I call a spade a spade, say it as it is. Right, now get that kettle on. I'll have two sugars in my tea, ta girl.'

Everyone laughed at his cheek, including me, and it felt nice to be amongst something that felt like fresh air.

Ten minutes later, we were all sat in Irene's living room with a can of lager each. The tea idea went to pot after Irene declared that she had no milk.

'Plenty of lager,' she laughed. 'But no bloody milk. I'll go to winey after and grab some,' she said, referring to the local off-license.

'Yeah, and don't forget, you'll need more lager for when we've supped this lot,' David said, wiping his mouth on his sleeve.

'You've got one each, that'll do.' Irene smiled and held up her can as if to say cheers.

'One each? I'm here for the night mum. Are you our Bernie? Better get to that chippy, never mind the winey.' He cackled again.

'Eh, mum? Remember when you used to batter our Bernie?' David suddenly spurted out of nowhere and at the same time burst out laughing. It was obviously a family joke and not a confrontation or he wouldn't have laughed after it. I hoped.

'She used to fuckin' leather her, you know Julie.'

'Aw don't our David. I feel awful when you say it like that.'

'You did though mum,' Bernie joined in. 'You and dad would come in from the pub, and he'd batter our David and then you'd batter me.

She too was laughing at the story. The only humour I could find in it was the way they were all sat calmly laughing their heads off about them being battered as kids.

David noticed the look on my face and tried to reassure me. 'Don't worry. Didn't do us any fucking harm love, look at me. I'm a tough puff for it. No one would mess with me I'd knock any fucker out.'

Tough puff made me burst out laughing. I loved him for it.

'Yeah, but I didn't mean to leather our Bernie, you know,' poor Irene said, having thought about it. 'It was because he was Bernie's dad and not yours. So, I thought if I leather his kid, he might know what it feels like and leave my kid alone.'

David spat his drink out everywhere, hitting Bernie on the back of the head with his spray. She fell on the floor laughing so hard her face looked stuck, and tears rolled down her eyes.

'Aw see that's why I love me mam,' he shrilled. 'She did it for me and to get back at him, not to hurt you, Bern.'

'True fuckin love that.'

My stomach was actually hurting now and I

couldn't get my breath.

I had images of Irene going for it, hitting poor Bernie to rescue her son, even though Bernie was her daughter. Absolutely unbelievable and quite sad really.

It was the way they were all telling it that was funny.

'Did your dad hit you a lot?' I asked him, trying to be serious.

'Hit me a lot?' he yelled. 'He threw me down the stairs once because I'd been swinging on a swing down the brook and fell off and caught my pants on a stick and ripped them, nearly breaking my fuckin' neck and all. I went down them stairs so fast on my stomach girl let me tell yer. My bastard head went straight through the leccy cupboard door, or it would have done if it hadn't had been hanging off its hinges. My face was squashed right onto the fuckin' leccy meter. When the fucking leccy man came to read the meter, I knew it off by heart.'

He then did a great big sigh followed by a great big roar of a laugh.

Again, I sucked in the biggest laugh and actually thought it could be my last breath it was so painful. I was howling now, and David's laughter was making me howl even louder because it was so loud.

Irene screamed with laughter but then quickly started choking on the cigarette she'd just taken a drag of. Holding on tightly to her can of lager so as not to spill any, she was laughing and choking and almost barking at the same time. It was hilarious but bloody scary to watch. I thought she was going to die.

Bernie was laughing even louder and still on the floor, going nowhere fast, her hair all sticky from the lager spray David had given her.

The tears were streaming down my face, and again I couldn't get my breath. I was certainly not laughing at his dad throwing him down the stairs. It was his animation and exaggeration in his storytelling that cracked me up and made my heart laugh like it had never laughed before.

He was bloody hilarious, and Jesus what a man to be able to get through all that abuse and laugh about it; his sexuality didn't even come into it.

I could tell he didn't always laugh though and that he was a troubled soul like me. We definitely had a connection I could feel it. He knew too, as he winked at me with a big cheesy grin.

'Right, what do yer want from the chippy?' Irene asked us all. I wasn't comfortable taking food off them and stood up, ready to make my excuse and leave.

'Errrr, where do you think you're going?' David asked me. 'Yer going nowhere lady, you're having chippy with us. Mam's paying. She got her giro today girl, have what yer want.'

'Giro?' I asked. 'I thought you worked Irene?'

'I do but I don't tell them bastards, do I love?'

I wasn't sure what bastards she meant and decided I didn't need to know.

'I'm having chips and gravy with a sausage barmcake.' Bernie announced. 'Have the same as me.'

'Er yeah OK, I'll have that then.'

I wasn't really feeling that hungry but having

thought about it, I'd not eaten all day so probably could do with some dinner.

Irene wrote down everyone's chippy order on the back of a ripped cigarette packet, grabbed her shopping bag off the back of the door and set off to the shops on her own.

'Don't forget the lager mam.' Bernie shouted after her. Then added, 'Wait for me. I'll come with yer or you'll forget sommat.'

She grabbed her coat and ran out.

'Don't forget the milk,' David screamed after her.

We got the knives and forks ready. 'No need for plates babe, we'll eat it outta the paper.'

'You put kettle on, we'll have to have a cuppa tea with our chippy, it's the law.'

There were so many different laws around here, I was still getting used to them and actually enjoyed being a part of them when I allowed myself to be. The times like this for me were few and far between but were probably the most settled I'd ever been in my life. Just a shame they weren't my family.

The girls were back with a crate of lager, milk and a chippy tea. Not that either of them had been a girl for a long time; they were well passed that milestone. Well, Irene was at least. They were gabbing happily. I felt a pang of jealousy for a minute, although Irene would treat anybody like one of her own. She was just that sort of woman and I genuinely did feel welcome.

'Hey, we put that lottery thing on, it started tonight, and we could be millionaires if we win.'

I was intrigued, I'd heard it was coming but wasn't quite sure what it was.

'What do you have to do?'

'Yer just give Az a pound,' Irene started.

'Yeah, but it's not just Az's shop, there are other shops and they have to have a lottery machine mam. You're making it out as if you can just give Az a pound.' Bernie continued.

'No, I fuckin' wasn't,' defending herself, Irene went on, 'I was just using Az as an example, he got a machine today.'

'Pah,' said Bernie. 'I don't even know what you're on about now. I'm confused.'

'Yeah, well it doesn't take much,' her mother chastised.

'You are never gonna fuckin' win that thing,' David interrupted sucking the leaking gravy through the chippy paper. 'You've got more chance of being hit by lightning, especially with those fucking shoes on love.' He pointed to Bernie's silver trainers or whatever they were.

She slapped him affectionately across the head and took her place at Irene's kitchen table.

We all had our brews with our chippy, followed by more lager, laughter and funny stories about their childhood. The love was so strong and Irene clearly loved her kids, even though she'd leathered one or probably both of them over the years.

I didn't have any funny stories to tell them back, but it didn't matter; it was nice to just listen and giggle and to try and guess what happened next.

David and I took our lagers to the back door so that we could have a cig.

'Need to give this shit up me,' he complained as he took the longest, hardest drag of a cig that I'd ever seen. Everything he did was dramatic but hilarious at the same time.

Bernie and Irene seemed to have been raising their voices in the kitchen behind us.

I heard Irene suddenly shout, 'No, you threw yours in the bin.'

'I did not!' Bernie responded, pushing her mum out of the way so she could get to the bin first.

'Yours is the one in the bin.'

'How can it be, mines in my hand.' Irene was shaking her lottery ticket in Bernie's face.

'And I've won a bloody tenner.' She was still waving the ticket in the air.

Bernie, quick as a flash, grabbed it out of her hand.

'Give it back now.' Irene was fuming.

Bernie was double-checking the numbers quick.

'This hasn't won a tenner; it must be the one in the bin.'

Like a shot, they both ran to the bin.

Bernie was screaming, 'you fuckin said it was mine. MOVE!' She elbowed her mum out of the way.'

Bernie got to the bin first and reached for the ticket, but Irene grabbed the back of her hair pulling her to the floor as she did so.

David quickly pulled his cig out of his mouth and threw it to the floor and ran into the kitchen, screaming at the top of his voice.

'Right stop it now! You look like a pair of fucking animals fighting over a piece of meat. Gerrup now!'

He dragged them both up off the floor and panted as he said, 'Don't tell me this is over a fuckin' tenner?'

He grabbed the ticket out of Bernie's hand and ripped it up into tiny pieces.

'Now it's nobody's ticket. Right come on our Bernie, I've had enough now, order us a taxi and we'll get going.'

'Aw I'm sorry our Bernie,' Irene was clearly upset by what had just happened.

I just stood there in awe of the whole thing. Half amused, half afraid that it was really going to kick off, but David had sorted it out. Thank God.

It was now time to make my exit.

'Right, you lot, I said affectionately. 'I'm definitely off. Thanks for my tea and a really funny night.'

'See ya girl,' David shrilled.

'Yeah, see ya Julie.' Bernie looked ashamed. 'Sorry about before ... it was just ....'

'It was just you proving you'd kill me mam for a tenner,' David interrupted.

'Ha-ha.'

'See ya Julie. Call for a brew in the morning love.'

'I will Irene.'

And I ran across the garden through the gate, opened my front door and ran up my stairs to the safety of my windowsill.

As I lit my cig and curled my knees up to my chest, I stared at my reflection and smiled at her. I was thankful that I still knew how to laugh.

The dark sky was clear and the stars were shining

brightly. I knew I needed to have this nice feeling more often, but the bad feelings weren't by choice; they were just there.

I needed to go to bed, my hangover was still buzzing somewhere in the back of my head with the added effect of the lager and chippy I was feeling tired.

As I jumped off the windowsill, I heard my letterbox bang hard.

I ran out of the living room and looked down the stairs and could see a brown envelope. I quickly ran to the bedroom window and looked up and down the street but could see no one. I even opened the window but could only see Sandra going into her house.

'Did you see anybody coming up my path just then?' I shouted down to her.

'Ay?' She sounded bewildered.

I repeated the question and she just shook her head and looked up and down the road herself.

'There's no one been round here.' She shrugged her shoulders and went back into her house.

I ran downstairs to retrieve the envelope; inside was two hundred pounds all in twenty-pound notes folded neatly.

Total rewind of happy feelings. My head was now in turmoil again.

Who was posting this money?

It had to be something to do with John. I'd told him on the phone that I'd had lost my last envelope.

I was going to ring him and have it out with him.

I made myself a coffee, got myself comfortable and dialled his number. Given that the last time I'd spoken with him, I'd slammed the phone down, I had some front.

'Hello' he actually sounded sleepy, but it wasn't that late.

'Hello, is that John?' I knew it was, so wasn't sure why I was asking.

'Hello, yes it's John.'

'It's me, Charley.'

'You speak like you expect me to be sat here waiting for you to call me.'

Why did he make me feel rude and inadequate?

'Well yes, I can see why you thought that.' I couldn't be arsed with his games. 'I phoned you because I've had another envelope drop through my door with another two hundred pounds inside it. Do you know anything about it at all? I know the first envelope was put in my bag when I was in London and it's too much of a coincidence for some random Manc to be posting envelopes through my front door.'

'I don't know your address Charley. How could it be me?'

'Well, it can't be you, because they've just hand-delivered it.'

'So why are you phoning asking me about it?'

My god, he was really difficult, almost emotionless in his stance. I changed the topic slightly.

'What did you mean the other day when you said that it wasn't you who had put the ad in the paper? Who did put the ad in the paper, and why did you meet me?'

'I was sent to see what you were like, that's all.'

'Sent to see if I matched the criteria?' I was guessing since he was being so vague.

'Yeah, sort of?' He grunted. 'You ok anyway, Charley? Have you been being careful?'

I thought about the night I'd had, I thought about the moment when I shouted his name in the bath; if only he knew.

'I don't have to explain anything I do to you. I'm a big girl and can look after myself.'

'Well, you can't, can you?' He was referring to London.

'I'm OK, aren't' I? I'm safe now.'

I don't know whether I was paranoid, but I'm sure I heard him hesitate again.

'I don't know,' he said. 'Are any of us safe?'

Yeah, definitely a weirdo this one

'OK so you don't know anything about the two-hundred-pound cash payments that I keep receiving.'

'No.'

'OK, I'm going then. Thank you.'

'OK.'

'OK, bye.'

'Bye.'

My early night had gone right out of the window. I lay there for hours, tossing and turning about the money, trying to work out if the envelopes were being posted at the same times.

Then there was the conversation with John. I definitely felt some distant connection with him, even though he never said much. There was definitely an element of care coming from him. I almost laughed out loud. He was hard work and maybe that's what I liked – the challenge.

I turned over again, my body becoming hot.

Then I thought about Irene's lot. What a funny, beautiful, mixed-up family. I started to feel calmer as I thought of those two women fighting over a lottery ticket. I giggled and closed my eyes.

I said, 'thank you' out loud and dropped off into a deep and peaceful sleep.

My dream led me to the living room of the flat, where Jody was walking about. She was older, probably about four. She was asking me if she could go to the toilet. I was busy trying to fix the television that had been broken. Jamie, my first boyfriend, had broken it and I wasn't sure why.

She asked me again 'Mummy, can you take me for a wee, please?'

I started going out of the living room door, so I could take her for a wee.

And I remembered that I'd not put the wood up against the top of the stairs.

I saw it in my dream before it happened.

I heard the scream.

I ran to the top of the stairs as fast as I could.

It was too late.

She was there lying face down behind the front door.

She was surrounded by brown envelopes.

I shot up quickly and was panting, trying to catch my breath. I was sweating in fear and could hardly breathe.

It wasn't Jody in my dream at all.

It was Jane.

Chapter 11

I couldn't move with the pain. I sat on the windowsill all day and thought about Jane; I couldn't look at her reflection today.

The dream had been traumatic for me and had probably been triggered by all the talk about child abuse with Irene's lot.

As much as I had laughed, and I did laugh, the stories had resonated with me, and that's probably why I'd found a connection with David.

God knows what people go through in their lives; it's no wonder the world is fucked. Most of us have feelings hidden in the depth of our soul. Some of us live in peace with them, refusing to re-connect. But some of us live with constant conflict and fighting that goes on in our own minds. And while you continue to be angry with the world and at other people, you constantly hit yourself across the head with an angry stick.

I thought about Jamie, my first boyfriend, and the film of him with my mother flashed in my mind. He'd got off scot-free that one, come to think about it. I shook my head; I didn't want to think about it.

I had been working so hard not to let these thoughts surface, for they brought me so much conflict and turmoil that I would find it difficult to focus.

I thought about the accident and how she'd blamed me for it all my life. The thought sickened me because I was there and knew exactly what happened. As a child, I believed that I was to blame.

But as I'd grown into an adult and relived the scene a million times a day, I knew it wasn't my fault; it was hers.

She had been being mean again. It was my turn on this particular day.

Jane had suffered her turn the day before.

Every day without fail, one of us, especially me for some reason, would endure the cruellest abuse.

If it wasn't our faces being rubbed in food, it was red hot baths. If it wasn't blowing cigarette smoke in our faces, it was the gripping of the back of the head.

Then there were the insults. They didn't leave you, and at such an early age, they became your beliefs.

So, you believe you are ugly. You believe you are stupid. You believe you couldn't do anything, especially when everything you did got criticised. She would say "you should have done this" or "you should have done that", proving that she never thought I was good enough.

I tried to get rid of the image of her laying at the bottom of the stairs with Jane. But Jane's limp, lifeless body never left my mind.

I thought about the years afterwards, about the layabouts she would bring home and her lack of dignity as they fucked her within earshot of me.

The only good thing from that was, once she'd had sex, she was lovely, and all was well for a few days. It got to a point where even I'd look forward to her next fuck.

My mother – what a mess.

To look at her, you wouldn't believe it. She was

perfect, a stunning woman with jet black hair and the darkest eyes you ever saw. She was always stunningly dressed. She religiously had a blow-dry on her hair every Friday, and Saturday was nails day.

She had money, hence the expensive lifestyle. I suspected she'd fleeced my father as I'd never known her to work a day in her life.

Yet she drove an expensive car, and our family home was very affluent. To the outside world, we looked like a very lucky family.

I thought about my father, who left not long after the accident. I really don't think he could take anymore, and this had devastated me. I'd lost them both; they'd left me alone with her.

As I got older, I realised that it was all her and not him. He probably didn't have a choice, and she wouldn't have allowed him to see me. I wasn't allowed to mention him; she used to make me recite, "daddy is dead".

If I ever showed any emotion or asked after him, she would grab my face hard and almost spit in my face saying, "repeat after me, daddy is dead. Do not ask again.".

So I didn't.

Instead, I'd thought about him every day and had done for the last twenty years. I tried hard to see his face when I closed my eyes, but all I had was a blurry image, tall with black hair. His eyes changed with my growing imagination, but I'll never forget the tears that rolled from them the day he had to leave me.

Then there was Jane. I couldn't help it, I started

crying. The dream had reminded me of her little face and her dreadful fate. I cried like I hadn't cried in a long time. I cried for my dad, I cried for Jane, I cried for the mother I never had, and I cried for me.

I walked over to the phone; I needed to check on my little girl. I needed to make sure that she was ok, it had only been two days, but it had felt like I'd not seen her for ages.

Ann answered.

'Hello 2747.' She always recited the last four digits of her telephone number when she answered the phone ending on a sort of high on the 47.

I rolled my eyes.

'Hello Ann, its Julie. How's Jody?'

I could tell she was a little bit nervous; she probably thought I'd phoned to say I wanted her to come home. But I'd agreed for her to stay for the fortnight, so wouldn't go back on my word.

'She's fine,' she hesitated. 'She's really having a ball. Our Jessica is here and won't go home, so we've got them both, and then next week, we're off to the caravan. Do you want to speak to her?' A pause, and then, 'Jody, come and say hello to mummy.'

I imagined her shouting from the hall and pictured Jody in my head, toddling over to her. I heard her babbling through the phone and could tell she was drooling; it made me smile.

'Oh, my bloody ear is soaking,' Ann laughed when she came back on the line.

I laughed too.

'Thank you,' I said, and I was genuinely grateful for her having Jody. It was really helpful, and she loved her and was looking after her.

It was warm, so I made myself a coffee, grabbed my cigs and lighter and went and stood at the front doorstep for a bit of fresh air. I appreciated the warm morning. I was pleased that the sun was so bright and took a deep breath so that I could taste the air.

I had to walk along a path with tall bushes on either side, along with overgrown grass and wildflower to get to my gate. It was nice, and it was private. Nobody else had to walk along it unless they were coming to knock on my front door.

I had a little entrance on one side of the path that led me into Irene's garden, but that was one I made by constantly splitting the bushes; it became a permanent opening. I lit my cig and instinctively walked towards the gate, admiring the density of the green leaves; they were lush as the sun shone upon them and smelt so fresh.

I got to the gate, or at least to the two concrete posts that marked where it should have been. I made a mental note to phone the council and ask them to fit one for Jody's safety. It wasn't a main road outside the house, but it was busy enough.

I heard talking, so walked forward slightly; I had a smile on my face as I guessed it was from Irene's house. But I was shocked to see her and Sandra deep in conversation and unaware of my presence. I was just about to say hello when they both stopped dead in their tracks.

Irene grabbed her chest and said, 'Jesus, you frightened the living daylights out of me then. Bloody sneaking about.' Her tone was different.

I looked at Sandra; her arms were folded, and her nostrils flared.

'Yeah, yer fuckin' good at sneaking about, so I've heard,' she said.

I felt the heat rise up my neck and up to my face. I actually thought my head was going to blow off.

I didn't know what to say.

I looked at Irene, but she put her head down. I almost felt betrayed by her, yet I knew I had no right.

'I took you out with my friends; you saw how upset I was about Angie. You even tried to put your fucking arms around me, and the whole time, you were shagging him too.'

I still couldn't think of anything to say. I just stared at them both.

I decided to deny it. 'Look, I don't know what you're talking about.'

'You fuckin' liar! He told me.'

'Well, I'm sure he's to be trusted.' I pulled a face that suggested she would be off her head to believe a word he said.

She seemed to buy it or was at least contemplating it.

'No, I know him. I know when he's telling the truth. I've known him ten years.'

'Did he tell you the truth about Angie?' I retorted.

Why the fuck had he told her, he had nothing to gain, surely.

I turned around to walk off, but a sudden pain in my head shocked me as she yanked hard at my hair.

The fear gripped me, and I was back in a place that I couldn't allow myself to be. I'd had enough of that all my life. The red mist was in my vision, and my boiling blood was like a pressure cooker in my head.

I turned around swiftly, grabbing her throat, and spoke through gritted teeth. 'Never ever do that again.' She looked scared, and I immediately punched her in her face.

She dramatically fell to the floor.

I nearly laughed. Then felt sick when I realised what I'd done.

I'd caught her lip, and it was bleeding. She wiped her mouth, looking at the blood on her hand.

'Phone the police Irene. She's a fucking animal.'

'Don't Irene, for fuck sake. She did attack me first.' I almost begged.

'Leave me out of it, the pair of you. And you get up off the floor, Sandra, you look a right dick lying there.'

I actually offered my hand for her to get up and thought she was going to take it until she dragged me down on top of her and started to pummel me in the back.

Irene was screaming at the pair of us now.

Jesus, I'd only come out for a cig.

The crowds were starting to gather; it must have looked like something from Billy Smarts because I certainly felt like Coco the Clown. I was mortified.

'Look at her showing her arse at her age,' one woman shouted to her mate.

'Ought to be ashamed of themselves; they're bloody mothers,' another joined in.

I pushed Sandra to the floor with both of my

hands hard and grabbed her throat. I tightened my grip looking straight into her eyes. I didn't care. The red was everywhere. 'You will never win. Don't fucking do it.'

Then all of a sudden, a strange sense of calm came over me, and I pulled myself up, leaving her there lying on the floor, shouting and screaming with a busted lip, trying her hardest to get up. She looked like a dying fly, with her fucking legs everywhere.

I ran into the flat and shot up those stairs like a rat up a drainpipe before I did any more damage. I had felt it again when I had my hands around her throat, I wasn't going to stop.

I was shaking like a leaf and threw myself on my bed. I was crying out of anger, fear and a bit of resentment.

How dare she fucking attack me like that. It was Scott she should be angry with; he clearly didn't know how to keep it in his pants.

But I was more bothered about Irene than Sandra. She was like the mum I didn't have, and I really didn't want her to be disappointed in me.

I cried until I couldn't cry any more. I was all cried out. Sunday was supposed to be the day of rest, and I'd never felt so much unrest in my life.

Fuck it, I washed my face with lots of cold water, got dressed and put some makeup on. I put my hair up with a banana clip that I'd found. It looked nice as the bottom part of my hair fell beautifully on the back of my neck. I shoved some earrings in, grabbed my high heels. Where I was going, I had no idea. I just needed to get out of there.

There was a sudden banging on the front door.

'Babe, y'up there?'

I nearly cried with happiness to hear that voice. David.

He carried on banging hard, and whereby it would normally bug the life out of me, I'd never been happier to hear it.

'Woah. Woah. Julie'. He sang through my letterbox, making me laugh.

'I'm coming, one minute.'

I ran down the stairs and opened the front door to find him and Bernie standing there.

'Ay me mum told me what happened with scrapper Sandra, she said you knocked her right out. Go on girl. Knew you had it in yer, me.'

He was beaming, waiting for me to add to the gossip that he'd already got from his mum.

'Oh, she seems to be under some illusion that I've slept with her fella.'

'Got a big dick him,' David gasped and then started howling.

'He has,' I winked, and we all started howling.

'How do you know, anyway?' I asked him.

'She told me.' He grinned and pointed at Bernie.

I nearly fell off the doorstep, I laughed that hard.

'Jesus,' I laughed. 'Stop it, Sandra will hear us.'

'Fuck her,' David bitched, 'don't you think she's all innocent in this love, she's not behind the door, let me tell you. She was shagging his uncle for years, babe. She and Scott got back together, but it was never right since. That's hard to forgive and forget, so that's probably why he shagged about, probably getting his own back, and I don't blame him, dirty bitch.'

'Are you joking? So why did she attack me?' I actually felt better knowing this, even though, in actual fact, we were all in the wrong.

'Coz she's a nutter, that's why Julie,' Bernie finished off for him. 'Anyway, we've ordered us a taxi, we're going to Canal Street, you coming?'

Canal Street was where the gay community socialised. The atmosphere was supposed to be amazing, and if it was a street full of David's, I knew why.

'I've got about thirty quid to last me all week,' I said. Then I remembered the envelope full of cash; it was tucked under my pillow.

'Ah, it never kills ya having no money, you'll get by. Az at the corner shop does tick; he'll never see you go without just tell him yer know our Bern. And you'll get yer family allowance Tuesday surely?'

'Yeah, I know Az', I smiled.

'Come on, you deserve a night out after that piece of shit twatted you. And you look like a fucking drag queen with that muck on your face, so you'll fit in.' He was referring to my makeup. 'Looks like you're going for an interview at Foo Foo Lammas!' He always followed his one-liners with an outrageous scream that you just had to laugh at.

'Come on,' said Bernie, 'we'll have a right laugh, and besides, you'll keep me sane, and I won't have to put up with him all night on me own.'

'What do yer mean?' David was offended. 'If it wasn't for me, girl, you'd be stuck in that flat night after night.'

'Yeah, and so would you love.'

'And so would I.' I was feeling left out. We all laughed again. I felt pleased I made them laugh.

The beeping of the taxi made us all jump.

'You tell it to wait; I'll get my stuff.'

As I left the flat and got into the taxi, I saw Sandra peeping out of her curtains.

I felt sorry for her really. I was only glad these two had my back.

She stuck her two fingers up and stared right at me. Jesus, I wasn't sure she was going to be easy.

And on the other side, I saw Irene waving at us all excitedly from her front door.

'Have a good night, love,' she shouted, 'and make sure them two look after you.'

Chapter 12

The Village was buzzing, alive with all sorts of beautiful and flamboyant characters, men dressed as women and vice versa.

There were people in stunning costumes and people who were ordinary in their approach.

Such a wonderful mix; it took my breath away.

There was a row of beautiful bars, all with flags hanging from them and tables next to the canal – such a peaceful looking setting marred by the revellers who so brought it to life.

We started off in the New Union where we grabbed a pint and listened to the banter. There were people everywhere, and the jukebox was playing loudly, creating a lively atmosphere as the evening sun came in through the open door.

David was eyeing up the talent.

'I'm fucking starving me, can't wait for a kebab after, or shall we get one now?' he asked.

'No,' Bernie said, 'even if you get one now, you'll still want one after.' She was downing her pint.

'Right, we'll have one more, then go and party at Mantos,' David said, downing his pint as fast as Bernie. 'Can I have three more?' he asked the barman.

'Can we go to New York, New York for one too,' said Bernie. She obviously had her own plans. 'I wanna see if that Paul is in there; he's fit.'

David howled, 'He's fucking gay, you daft cow.'

'Well, he's easy on the eye; I can look, can't I?

And besides, I might turn him.'

'You won't fucking turn him, for Christ sake, Bernie. Are you thick? And you won't be fucking touching him either lady. I might though.'

'You wouldn't? He's mine,' Bernie was genuinely gutted.

'He's not fucking yours. He's fucking gay, you daft cow. Anyway, you fancy Az, don't you? You can't have them all.'

I was laughing again; it was like going out with a comedy duo.

We finished our third pint and headed up the road. I was in a haze, the sun was setting and I was tipsy; I felt amazing, and the day of unrest was disappearing.

The noise and chattering that I could hear around me was making me feel emotional. People were laughing loudly and bantering with each other. Everyone was so friendly.

A woman came towards us, her make up thick and dramatic, her hair thick and blonde – it was obviously a wig. Her fishnet tights made her legs look long and slick, if not a bit muscular. When she spoke, I realised it was a man in drag.

I smiled at her and admired her for having the balls to come out and be who she wanted to be.

'You playing rugby tomorrow, our Della?' David asked her.

'No, not after tonight's shenanigans, and I've not even started yet,' Della replied with a deep voice.

We all chatted by the canal for a while just outside New York, New York, until Bernie raced across the forecourt after spotting a table.

'Ere come and sit down; I've robbed us a table.'
She was incredibly pleased with herself.

We all sat around the table, and I watched the
world go by. I was amazed by the lesbians. For some
reason, I'd imagined they'd all be in Doc Martins
with shaved heads and tattoos. Some of them were,
but there were also lots of other beautiful young
women who didn't fit my idea of how a lesbian
would look.

One of them looked over to me and smiled. I felt
a flutter between my legs. I'd never had a flutter for
a woman before. Then I thought about my dream on
the train. Hmmm she was pretty.

I smiled back shyly and sucked on the bottle of
Budweiser as seductively as I could.

'I'll get us a drink. What you having Della?' I
asked to be polite.

'Gerrus a pint love.' I smiled at her.

The bar was buzzing, the DJ in the corner played
a bit of Kylie.

I needed a wee, and the toilets were over the other
side of the bar. I made my way through everyone
dancing and singing.

When I got in the toilets, I shouldn't have been,
but I was surprised to see men in there too. I suppose
it didn't matter; in here, they were all one in some
respect.

She was in there too – the pretty lesbian.

'Hi,' she smiled. She really was pretty; her hair
was blonde down her back with a kink in the end.
She was younger than me, I was sure, but I didn't
really have a clue.

She wore a pair of denim shorts and a short black

top; she had a big black heart tattooed on the top of her arm, it was distinctive, and it was sexy.

'Hi,' I smiled, suddenly becoming conscious of myself and of the beer I'd consumed.

She nodded toward a cubicle, and for a moment, I was confused.

'Wanna go in?' she asked, licking her lips.

I got the message.

'Yep sure.'

She followed me in, locked the door and started kissing me straightaway.

Her kiss was hard and passionate; her lips felt soft, and her tongue warm on mine.

She was rubbing my whole body up and down with her soft hands and biting my neck gently.

She grabbed my breasts hard, and I succumbed; right there and then, I would have done anything for this girl.

She pulled my top off and cupped my breasts free from my bra. She started to suck hard on my nipples. I was groaning as she took turns on each nipple, she pulled hard with her mouth and caressed them with her tongue at the same time as sucking on them. I'd never felt such a pleasurable feeling; I wanted it to last forever.

'That's beautiful,' I told her.

She pushed me so that I was sat on the back of the toilet cistern; my breasts were throbbing hard, so I rubbed them as she twisted and pulled my nipples.

She pulled my knickers off and spread my legs, touching me ever so gently with her fingers. Then she put her face between my legs and licked me up and down, her tongue exploring every inch of me;

it felt like velvet. I grabbed her blonde hair as she expertly stroked me at the same time.

I gasped in pure delight as I came in her mouth; she sucked me as I did so, and all I could feel was her warm lips. I was panting and lost for breath when she had finished.

She let herself out of the toilet, leaving me there with my tits hanging out and a throbbing between my legs that wasn't going away. I felt absolutely amazing.

I did what I originally came in to do – a wee. I went to the bar to order the beer, looking around for the pretty blonde, but she was nowhere to be seen.

I went outside carrying beers for all. They were still laughing and joking. Bernie had spotted Paul and was crooning over him – daft cow. I smiled to myself.

'Hey, I just had sex in a toilet… with a girl,' I blurted out as I sat down.

'Oh my god, they both screamed.'

'Bet you've never had your fanny licked liked that before girl?' David said, wagging his finger in my face.

'No, never.'

The night got better, and the shenanigans carried on into the twilight before we headed back to my flat with kebab all over our faces. But what a night.

They had to top and tail on the settee, and I found an old blanket for them to share. I did have a tiny spare room, but it was full of shit.

I was elated. I had friends staying at my house, and for the first time, I got in bed with no regrets. Well, the thought of the fight swept through my mind, but

I quickly swept it right back out. I thought about the pretty blonde girl with the hot mouth. She'd blown my mind, and I thought about the scene again as I started to drift into sleep.

'Night John Boy,' David screamed from the living room.

I giggled and shouted back, 'Night, Mary-Ellen.'

'That's about right,' Bernie roared, 'suits you does that name our David, you've always been a right Mary-Ellen.'

I crashed out with a big smile on my face.

I felt like I'd been asleep for ages when something disturbed me. I heard a noise outside. I lay there for a minute listening. Through my slightly open window, I could hear it was Sandra. I had no idea of the time, but it was getting light, so it must have been at least 4am. The birds were whistling, but I could hear the voices outside becoming raised.

I got up and looked through the side of the closed curtains. I could see a black car parked right outside my gate.

Sandra seemed to be having a debate and was leaning into the passenger side window.

I couldn't see who she was talking to, but she looked angry, and her arms were flying in the air, yet she wasn't shouting.

She stepped back as the car door opened. I nearly died. It was the Native American. He had a suit on and looked very official for this time of the morning. He looked up at the window and stared right at me. I almost fainted on the spot.

I jumped back in shock and sat down on my bed. I felt sick. Who was he?

I stood up and looked back through the gap in the curtain and could see he was pushing her into the back of the car. I'm sure he was hitting her, but I just couldn't quite make it out.

The car sped off, and I knew immediately something was wrong. Sandra didn't look comfortable at all.

What the hell was going on?

Chapter 13

I hadn't gone back to sleep. I'd gone in the kitchen so as not to disturb those two. They were snoring so loudly that it was beginning to get on my nerves. I felt anxious enough, and I just wanted them to wake up, so I could speak to someone.

I was convinced that this was something to do with me. There was too much going on, but it all sounded ridiculous when I tried to make sense of it.

I climbed over the sink and sat on the kitchen windowsill, lit a cig and drank the coffee I'd managed to make with very little milk.

I looked out at the early morning sun. It was climbing behind the trees, stretching and yawning, flickering orange light between the green leaves.

I looked down into Sandra's garden, and it dawned on me. The kids! Where were the kids?

Maybe they were with Scott. I hoped they were somewhere safe. Oh my god, I half wish I hadn't been woken up by it all.

'Is that you Julie love? Stick the kettle on.'

I was relieved to hear David's voice and waited for him to come into the kitchen.

'What you doing up there? You'll break yer friggin' neck if you fall, you daft cow.'

'I usually sit on the living room one, but I didn't want to disturb you two.'

'You couldn't disturb our Bernie babe. She gets Rigor Mortis when she sleeps.'

For once, I didn't' laugh at him but said, 'David, something really odd is going on.'

'What's up Julie? Is it because you're a lesbian?' I couldn't believe him.

'I'm not a lesbian David. I think Sandra's been kidnapped.' I was deadly serious.

'What? Why? How? I mean... what do you mean? Have you gone stark raving mad?' He laughed. 'People don't just get kidnapped, don't be so bloody dramatic.'

'Well, I saw her getting pushed into the back of a black car. It looked as though it was against her will. The man had a suit on and looked very official. Who is dressed like that at 4am in the morning? They were having some sort of disagreement. It was just odd. And as he was pushing her into the back of the car, I am sure he was forcing her.' I didn't say it was the Native American (who probably wasn't even a Native American). For some reason, I felt protective towards him.

I went on to explain, 'I've got stuff going on that's weird, but that's another story and a long one. But I'm sure the person who pushed her into the back of the car is erm...'

I couldn't explain it without sounding like a lunatic. What did I say? That I was totally paranoid, that I thought the man had come for me, and that there was a similarity between me and Sandra. That I was being followed by a Native American who was in my dream. And that I kept getting two hundred quid shoved through my letterbox.

Having just put it like that in my head, I decided I was totally paranoid. This was nothing to do with me. But the whole thing was bloody mad.

'Erm? Erm, what?' David asked. 'You're not

making any sense; get that coffee down yer neck, give yer head a shake, wake up proper and try again.'

'Have you run out of milk?' He was mooching about in the fridge. 'I can't fuckin' believe you; I'll bob down and ask me mum for some.'

He ran off down the stairs, and I finished off my cig.

I didn't need to give my head a shake; I was convinced that what I saw wasn't right.

Ten minutes later, Bernie walked into the kitchen, scratching her head and holding her back as though she was in agony.

'Y'alright Ju?' She asked, oblivious to anything that was going on.

'Morning Bern,' I smiled. 'David's just ran to your mums for some milk, but I'll put the kettle on.'

I decided to try again.

'Bern, I think Sandra has been kidnapped. I saw a bit of a commotion last night, and she was being pushed into the back of a car.'

'Are you joking Ju? Was it Scott has he finally cracked?'

'No, I don't think so.'

Before I could carry on, David came pounding up the stairs, out of breath and with a bottle of red-top in his hand.

'The fucking police are at Sandra's. You were right; summat's definitely gone down.'

Oh my god, I couldn't believe it. I grabbed my face with both hands.

'What do I do?' I asked them as they were legging it to the bedroom window to get a good view.

'Shall I go down and see the Police and tell them

what I saw.'

'No, shall you fuck. You stay where you are, and stay out of it, our Julie. It's nowt to do with you.'

That was the way round here; say nothing and keep quiet – the "no grassing" code. I wasn't sure, but I'd go with it for now.

The phone rang as they were in the bedroom.

It was John.

'Julie'

He thought I was called Charley.

'Hello.'

'You need to listen to me. No fucking about, this is serious.'

I was shaking.

'You need to be out of the house as soon as you can. I have someone picking you up in two hours.'

I didn't know what to say. I was scared and confused.

'What do you mean, I have to get out? Get out of my flat? How? Why?'

'A car will be with you in two hours, it's a black Jaguar. The guy picking you up will explain everything.'

My head was spinning.

'What guy?' I felt sick. 'What do you know John? What's going on?'

'It's a long story, and we don't have time. Please Julie, trust me? My name's not John, it's Pavel.'

'Fucking Pavel?' I was gobsmacked.

'Yeah, Charley, fucking Pavel.'

'OK, fine,' I resigned. Now wasn't the time.

'Look, I will explain, but not now. Take my number with you. I will be in touch.'

'I'm not sure.'

And I wasn't; why would I be? I didn't know this man. I'd only found out his real name three seconds ago.

'Julie, Sandra has got you in trouble. You need to get out; we're coming for you.'

God, I knew that had been connected to me. But why?

'What does anybody want with me? I don't have anything, and I haven't done anything.'

I had though, I had done something. It was a long time ago, but I had done something.

'I will explain later, it's complicated, and you've got less than two hours now. The clock is ticking. Do not tell a soul, do not phone the police. We are looking after you.'

'Why?' I had no idea what was going on; I was getting into a state.

David and Bernie were still in the bedroom watching the shenanigans that were going on outside.

How would I get rid of them now? As I thought it, they barged into the living room.

'The kids were left in the house.' Bernie was crying. 'They've just got hold of Scott to come and get them; nobody has a clue where Sandra is. It's awful. I don't like it; it's like flipping EastEnders round here at the moment.'

'Turn it in mard arse, and let's go and see what our mams got to say,' said David and they left.

'Sorry,' I spoke back into the phone. 'My friends are just leaving. I'm not sure how I'll get out without them seeing me though, they live right next door.'

'You'll have to be careful then, won't you?' His tone was changing.

So did mine.

'Sorry Pavel. I can't just go on a whim. You could be fucking anybody. How do I know you're not trying to kill me, have me raped?'

His words stopped me dead in my tracks.

'Because I'm your brother Julie. Just get in the car when it comes, and I'll call you later.'

He put the phone down.

I looked at the window and saw "her" staring at me in total utter shock. I had to have a cig and then I had to get my head together and start to think straight.

My brother, how could he be my brother? Was he my dad's, or was he hers? I was trying to remember his features; he was fair, they were both dark. But I was fair. It didn't make any sense. Nothing was making any sense.

Then I thought about Jody.

What about Jody?

How long would I have to go for?

How far was I going?

Where was I going?

What was going on?

The panic took over my whole body, and I got that sudden visit from an old foe. It was as though I had tripped over and quickly had to save myself from falling. I actually gasped as the shock rippled through my body. My palms became really hot and sweaty. My whole body started to tremble, and I couldn't get my breath. My breathing became fast and heavy, and pins and needles tingled down my arms to my hands.

I gripped my chest and climbed off the windowsill before my weakness had me fall off. I staggered over to the settee, where I sat down and put my head between my legs and tried to gain control of my breathing. I was blowing rapidly. I closed my eyes and tried to relax, but I couldn't get the situation out of my head. It was here, and it was happening. I couldn't do it. I wouldn't even be able to get off this settee.

I'd had enough. I wasn't getting past it this time. I couldn't do it again. I couldn't put myself through these feelings. I'm sure I'd be better off dead. I thought of her, and I thought about Jane. I thought about the pain I'd felt all my life.

I thought about what was happening now, and I thought I was going to die. The feeling was getting worse. I was trembling from head to toe whilst drenched in my own sweat.

I tried to breathe; I tried to get in the moment. I couldn't.

I got up and staggered into the kitchen, gasping for breath, unable to feel my arms.

I saw her in the reflection of the kitchen window. It was Jane. I tried to smile, but she looked so sad and desperate. She would always look how I felt because Jane was my twin sister, the other half of me.

The thought of getting her back made my soul
shine with glee
It made my heart expel the brightest light
I needed to get her back, for she is the real me.

Chapter 14 - David

David and Bernie were at their mum's house. They'd temporarily moved in under the false pretence that they were looking after their mum when in actual fact, they were just downright nosey.

The atmosphere was buzzing as they thrived off the drama of the past couple of days. They'd spent their time trying to guess what had really happened to Sandra the other morning.

Irene's house was cosy, with a brown leather three-piece suite that was too big for the long but narrow living room, and the matching armchair was squashed right next to it.

She had pink and blue floral wallpaper with a plain border and pictures of David and Bernie as children in big gold frames.

The curtains were brown and matched the three-piece, and the crisp white nets made the room bright. The big blue furry rug took up most of the living room floor but made it look homely.

'Brew up mum. I fancy another brew, do you Bernie?' She was eating a packet of digestives that she'd found in the cupboard. 'Tell you what girl, if you don't stop feeding your face, we're going to have to rub butter around the front door frame so we can squeeze you out.'

'Shurrup, David. I'm stressed out. It could have been me that got kidnapped.'

David howled with laughter. 'Why would anyone want to kidnap you? You daft cow.'

'Sometimes it's about being in the wrong place

at the wrong time.'

He shook his head as he handed his mum his cup for another brew.

Irene grabbed the cup and walked into the kitchen.

'Tell you what?' she said. 'There's more to this than meets the eye. I'm not having it. First of all, Sandra gets forced into a car, leaves her kids, then comes back later that afternoon. And from what I've heard from the neighbours, she was on a fucking date with some bloke. Now we've not seen or heard from Julie for two days. No, I'm not having it, me.'

'I'm not having it either mum,' Bernie agreed. 'There's more to this than meets the eye.'

'I just fucking said that our Bernie. There is more to this than meets the eye.'

'Jesus Christ, what's with all this eye meeting?' David was getting impatient.

'It's fucking simple,' he said. 'I'm telling ya, they've taken Sandra instead of Julie, and then realised their mistake, paid Sandra off so that she keeps her gob shut, and then they've come back for Julie.'

'She might have just gone away for a couple of days; she did seem pretty freaked out the other day,' said Bernie, trying to keep it on a lighter note.

'No Bernie, I'm not having it. Hey, do you think it was sommat to do with that fight they had? Gutted I missed that, you know mum. Did Julie knock her out?'

'David, she twatted her right in the face, a proper sharp jab.'

David and Bernie laughed. Bernie said, 'Have

you heard our Rocky there?'

'No,' Irene went on, 'Julie snapped, you know, Sandra grabbed her hair, and Julie just lost it, I was worried. She had that look in her eyes.'

'Don't be so fucking dramatic mum, for god sakes.'

They were all having a good laugh when there was a loud knock on the door.

'You get it David,' said Irene.

He stood up bold as brass and went to answer the front door.

'Hiya, Sandra, come in love.'

'Make Sandra a brew mum,' he ordered. He raised his eyebrows at Bernie as he nodded his head towards Sandra and mouthed, 'what the fuck?'

Bernie just shook her head, confused.

'Do you want a cuppa love?' Irene asked Sandra raising her eyebrows to David as if to let him know that she was as shocked as he was.

'Yes, please Irene.'

'What happened, Sandra love?' Bernie just came straight out with it. 'Julie said she saw you being bundled into a car.'

'Well, she didn't quite say that did she?' David said, bringing her back down to earth with a stare of death right in her eyes.

'But what did happen, San?'

'What do you mean?' Sandra looked genuinely confused.

'Well, the police were at yours early doors Monday morning saying that the boys were alone.'

David was clever and left it at that.

'Ah, it's all a big mix up.'

Irene came in with the brews.

'What sort of mix up love?' she asked. 'The police don't just come out for nothing.'

'Er, I'd been on a date, and Scott saw his arse and brought the kids back and left them.' She was trying to be confident, but it wasn't working.

'Well, Scott didn't know anything about it when the police fetched him to get the boys,' Irene continued probing. 'So, you went on a date at 5am? Got in a car and thought the kids were with Scott? Doesn't add up to me.'

'Have you seen Julie?' Sandra changed the subject.

'No, we've not seen her since Monday morning; we stayed at hers and were woken up by the police.'

Her face went pale, and it was obvious she was panicking.

'Has any of this got anything to do with you two fighting?' David asked her.

'Jesus, I only came round coz I'm feeling shit about the whole thing. Scott is kicking off now and wants the kid's full time. I don't need a fuckin' interrogation. I've been interrogated enough.'

She started crying, and they backed off, trying to console her instead.

'Sorry love,' Irene was hugging her, 'you know what it's like around here, people want to know the ins and outs of a cat's arse. You have your brew.'

She looked at David shaking her head.

'Not having it,' she mouthed.

'So, what's he banging on about now?' Bernie asked, trying to change the subject or at least redirect it.

'He wants the boys, doesn't he? I wouldn't mind; he's living at his mums, but I know he couldn't hack it full time.'

'You should just agree until he gets fuckin' fed up. They all do in the end.'

She just shook her head; it was clear she was agitated.

'How are you lot anyway?' Her behaviour was odd, and they were all too honest to let it go.

'What the fuck is going on Sandra, you can trust us; seriously, is everything ok?'

She put her head between her hands and started crying.

'Aw love, let it out. It must be a stressful time for you, but there's more to it than meets the eye.'

Bernie went to laugh but thought better of it when she felt Irene's glare upon her.

Sandra was not letting go of anything and was adamant that it was nothing more than a date that had turned sour and that she was genuinely worried about losing her two sons to their father.

'I'm going to get off,' said Sandra, meaning she wanted to go home.

Nobody persuaded her to do otherwise, and the minute she was gone, it erupted.

'Not having it,' Irene said for the fourth time in twenty minutes.

'She's full of shit,' David agreed.

'I was dying to laugh when mum said there's more to this than meets the eye,' said Bernie.

And the three of them roared with laughter.

'Hey Bernie, don't you have Scott's phone number?' her mum asked her.

'Yeah, I think it's in my bag, why?'

'Phone him and get him round here. He'll tell us what's going on.'

'Are you both daft? I can't just phone him and ask him to come round,' Bernie whined.

'Give us the phone number, I'll fucking phone him,' David held his hand out impatiently, waiting for her to give him the phone number.

She gave in, and ten minutes later, there was a knock on the door.

'Fucking hell, he was quick Bern, bet he thinks he's in with a chance,' David was laughing.

'He fucking might be love.' Bernie flicked her long black hair as she went to answer the door.

He came into the living room confident but friendly too.

He was tall and stocky, a good-looking lad with dark brown hair that was always cut immaculately.

'Alright,' he greeted them all.

'Alright, Scott.' They all replied at once.

'Do you want a brew?' Irene sounded like a broken record.

'I'll have a beer if you've got one.'

'Fucking hell, you don't want much,' said David. 'I'll have one too mum.' His laughter lightened the atmosphere.

'What's going on with Sandra, Scott?' Irene got straight to the point while Bernie went to get some cold beers out of the fridge.

'Fuck knows what's going on. I got woken up by the police at 6am Monday morning, saying someone had reported her to the police because they'd heard the kids crying nonstop. Whoever reported it told them where I lived, and thank God they did, or they could have put them in a home. I can't get my head around it all.'

He looked genuinely upset.

'She's never done anything like that before. I think she's losing the fucking plot. It sounds like she'd been out all night and left the kids on their own – knocks me sick.'

'Do you know she attacked Julie the day before this all happened?' Irene asked him.

'No way, what happened?'

'She said you told her that you slept with Julie.'

'Well, that's a lie, I did no such thing. I mean I did sleep with Julie, but I never told Sandra.'

'Well, who did then?'

'Dunno Irene,' he replied. 'Where's Julie? Is she next door? I should go and say sorry.'

'No, she's not there,' David explained, 'she must have got off Monday; she'd had enough; maybe she's gone to stay with family.'

David explained that Julie had seen Sandra being forced into the back of a car around 4am Monday morning. That it didn't look like she was just getting in from being out and that it didn't look like a date.

Bernie joined in and said, 'The fact is that deep down, we all know that Sandra wouldn't leave the lads for two minutes, and you shouldn't be giving her such a hard time, Scott. She went pale when Julie was mentioned. It's obvious that there's more to this than meets the eye.

Everyone started laughing, leaving Scott looking baffled.

'Sorry mate, it's just that mum's said, "there's

more to this than meets the eye", a million times tonight. But she's right to be fair. There really is. It doesn't add up. We need to find Julie because I've got a feeling they've come for Julie in the first place and took Sandra by mistake or something like that. Then they've sent Sandra home, paid her to keep her gob shut. Or they might have threatened her with her life – you just don't know. But they've come back and took Julie; no one has seen her for two days now.'

'You sure she's not in her flat?' Scott asked.

'Well, we've knocked on more than once now,' David said. 'No answer.'

'Hey, I've got a spare key that I keep here for her, in case she gets locked out,' Irene suddenly remembered, 'I keep it in the kitchen drawer.'

Seconds later, they were leaving Irene's like they were all on a secret mission, telling each other to shush and bumping clumsily into each other. They cut through the path in the bushes and were soon stood at Julie's front door.

Bernie was cowering behind Scott. Irene was looking up and down the path in case they were seen.

Scott was the alpha, and he took the key off Irene and put it in the lock, but he couldn't do it.

David took over, 'ere give it me,' he said, grabbing the key from Scott's hand.

'Hey it's already open,' David exclaimed. 'No wonder you couldn't do it.'

David led the way up the stairs with Scott right behind him. Bernie's nose was practically up Scott's arse. And Irene took one more look out of the front door before shutting it behind her.

David gasped as he opened the living room door. Scott walked into the back of him, causing a pile-up behind him.

Irene tripped on the top stair and said, 'What the fuck is it, David?'

She soon saw for herself.

The living room was covered in it.

The four of them were silent.

Even David was lost for words.

Chapter 15

Bernie turned and ran down the stairs like a madwoman, slamming the front door as she left.

The rest of them stood squashed together in the doorway of Julie's living room.

The place had been wrecked, and there was blood-red paint splashed all over the walls; someone had scrawled "Murderer" in the paint. It looked gruesome, to say the least. The settee had been ripped to shreds with a knife, and the telly had been flung across the floor.

They looked at each other in dismay as they took in the scene in front of them.

'It looks like something from a horror film!' Scott was uneasy.

Instinctively they all marched into the bedroom, which looked untouched.

Just a ruffled unmade bed with a plain yellow quilt thrown across it and one green pillow. Jody's cot was on the other side of the room.

'It feels weird,' David whispered. 'Ghost-like.'

And as he said it, the little musical toy in the cot started playing twinkle twinkle little star. David jumped out of his skin, causing Scott and Irene to jump out of theirs, screaming as they did so.

David grabbed both of them as though they had the answers. 'What's going on?' He was shaking.

They all ran out of the bedroom and into the kitchen, which looked untidy but nothing untoward.

The knock on the front door started them off again, and Irene, gripping her chest, said, 'That's it

I'm going. Come on you two.'

Bernie was stood outside waiting for them, too scared to enter.

'What did you knock for? You daft cow,' said David, waving his hands everywhere.

'What's happened?' She asked him.

He didn't answer her but ushered everybody towards Irene's.

'Quick, just get back to ours.'

Scott was speechless and followed them like a lost sheep,

Once back in Irene's, they were all at once trying to tell Bernie what they'd seen.

'I thought it was blood at first, did you Scott?' Irene asked him but was telling Bernie at the same time.

They told her how someone had ripped the settee to shreds with a knife, and then they explained about the music in Jody's cot turning on.

Bernie was listening avidly and was in total shock as she took it all in.

'So, where's Julie?' she asked, 'Shouldn't we phone the police?'

Irene had already lifted up the receiver to do so, and she dialled 999.

Within the hour, the police were at the door. The neighbour's curtains were twitching again. They'd not seen this much entertainment in years – first the catfight, then the police at Sandra's, two potential kidnappings and now this.

Irene let the police in and put the kettle on for everybody.

'Tea love?' She asked the policeman and his

young colleague.

'Not for me, ta.' The older policeman was stern.

His young colleague wasn't and said, 'I'll have a tea, two sugars, please love.'

'What's going on?' The policeman asked, getting his notebook out.

Irene, David and Scott all started to relay the scenario back to the policeman, who was trying to write it all down as he tried to take in every word until he raised his voice and said, 'Stop! One at a time; I can't understand a word any of you are saying.'

'You,' he pointed at David.

He told the policeman the whole story from beginning to end, leaving out the fight, as that really didn't seem relevant, until Irene stepped in and told them all about it anyway.

The policeman explained that he would take a look next door and urged his colleague to finish his brew. Then they left.

Irene saw them out and shut the door.

'Fuckin narcy bastard.' David clearly didn't like the policeman. 'Any need for him. They'll not do anything; you know they never do. But the young one looks like Will Smith, his dark brown eyes and little bit of a tash was enough to get the heartbeat going. Aw, I wonder where poor Julie is?'

Scott said he felt sick about it all and that he was going to get off. He asked them to let him know if they heard anything back from the police.

As he went to leave, the police knocked back on, came into the house and asked everybody to sit down.

They all looked at each other as if to say, "what now?"

They'd found an empty bottle of paracetamol on the kitchen floor and some other tablet packets and had come to ask questions around it.

'Do you know Julie well?'

They didn't really; they'd only been neighbours for a couple of years.

'What's her surname?' Do any of you know?'

They looked at each other confused, until Irene remembered.

'It's Robinson. Julie Robinson. I remember because she asked me to pick up her family allowance for her once when she had a cold. I'd forgotten all about it as I have a cleaning job and had to go to work that day. So I took her book and asked...'

'It's ok love, we don't need to know the ins and outs, just her surname, and you say it's Robinson?'

'Er yeah,' Irene was put out at being cut off and started rubbing her fringe, sticking it to her forehead out of embarrassment.

'So?' David was curious. 'What you thinking officer? That Julie took an overdose, then sprayed her own walls with "murderer" and hid her own body after she'd slashed her own settee?'

'No sir, we don't think that; we are just looking at the facts that we have. We have radioed through to the station, and they're contacting the local hospitals as we speak? Other than that, we have to do some further investigations.'

The policemen asked them all a few more questions, then said they would contact them if they needed any further information.

They took addresses and phone numbers, shut their books and said they'd be leaving now.

As they walked out, "Will Smith" looked David up and down slowly and then followed his boss out of the front door shutting it hard behind him.

'Did you see what he just did then?' David asked anybody who would listen. 'He couldn't take his gorgeous eyes off me. We need to phone the police every day just so I can have a look at his truncheon. What do you say ladies?'

'An empty bottle? What do they mean?' said Bernie, away with the fairies as usual.

Everyone ignored her.

Scott shook his head and said again that he needed to get off. Bernie looked disappointed, anything for a cheap thrill.

'Let's have a beer,' David suggested, not ready to turn it in yet.

'Go on then,' Scott said as he was feeling about in his pocket.

'I'm thinking,' David looked serious. 'Julie did say to me the other day that she had "weird stuff" going on. I wonder what she meant by that?'

Scott pulled a piece of paper out of his pocket. 'Hey, I forgot; I found this as I was going up Julie's stairs.'

It was a receipt but on the other side was a phone number beginning with 071.

They all stood around the piece of paper as though it also had the answers written on it.

'Phone it.' Irene said.

'Sod that.' Scott was having none of it.

'You phone it Bernie,' he handed her the piece of paper.

'I'm not phoning it.' She was almost trembling.

He handed the paper to David and told him that he had to do it.

David contemplated the task ahead and was stuck for once as to what to say. He had no idea who would answer the phone, but it was weird that it had been found on the stairs in the flat.

'What shall I say?'

'Just ask them if they know Julie and where she is. It's a London number. Sandra said she'd been to London and was really weird about it. She lent her some clothes, but Julie wouldn't say why she was going or who she was going to see.'

David snatched the piece of paper off him.

Irene wasn't happy about a call to London and said it would cost a fortune. They said they'd all club together if it was too expensive, and she relented somewhat, sipping her beer from the can as she sat down to watch the show.

David picked up the phone. His hand was shaking. Scott read the number out to him so he could dial it with ease.

'It's ringing.' He turned his back to them as though it would make it easier for him to hear.

'Hello.' he said, his voice deeper than normal. 'I'm just wondering if you know anyone called Julie?'

There was obviously a reply because David carried on.

'I'm from Manchester. I'm her mate; she lives next door to my mum.'

Scott, Irene and Bernie all looked at each other in wonder.

'No, No.' He was shaking his head. 'Er, just wondering if you had any idea where she's gone; she's not been seen for a couple of days...Yes, we've called the police... Not much really, they seem to think she's taken an overdose – they found evidence they said.'

He turned around and shrugged his shoulders at the others. 'We found it in her flat.'

He was obviously being asked where he'd got this number from.

'Oh right, ok then. Cheers, bye.'

And he put the phone down.

'What did they say?'

Irene was chomping at the bit.

'Nowt,' David replied. 'He just said that he didn't know her.'

'What do you mean he said nowt, he obviously said something, because you were talking back to him David?'

David was deep in thought, trying to work out the conversation that he'd just had.

'He was foreign him, I'm sure he was. He asked loads of questions, let me waffle on and then said he didn't know her.'

'What was his answer when you asked if he knew Julie?'

'He didn't answer me. He just asked me where I was from and how I knew Julie.'

Thinking aloud, David asked, 'So if he didn't know her, why would he want to know how I knew her?'

He slurped down his beer; this was driving him mad. Someone had taken Julie; they'd dropped their phone number on the floor of her flat, or had they? Could Julie have dropped the number? Who did she know that lived in London? Scott had said she'd been to London a couple of weeks ago. So who had she gone to see?

There was more to this girl than they knew. And they didn't really know her. For her to have disappeared, and for that to happen in the flat. She had obviously had some sort of "no good" in her life.

The more he thought about it, the more he decided that Julie must have done something for this to happen. Her words were ringing in his ears. She seemed to be so sure that Sandra had been kidnapped the other morning.

'I'm going to bed,' he announced. 'But tomorrow, I'm going to be asking some questions. I'm going over to her ex's and finding out what he knows. We don't even know where she's from, but she's definitely not from round here. She doesn't talk like us, so why is she here? What has she done?'

Then he started laughing. 'Hark at me! I sound like inspector fucking Morse.'

'Inspector fucking gadget more like,' his mother said, quick to get in on the act.

David got into bed. His old room was almost untouched, albeit Irene had walloped the wood-chip wallpaper a couple of times, with a touch of magnolia.

The curtains were dark blue to go with the dark blue carpet with black dashed in; it was worn in parts. The bed was made and the flowery quilt cover didn't match anything. The old dark wooden wardrobe stood in the corner, the handles making it look like a great big face.

There was a portable telly on the bedside draws that matched the wardrobe. David contemplated turning it on, but you could never get a clear picture anyway, and he knew he would spend all night messing with the little round metal aerial that was neither use nor ornament. He decided against it.

He lay there thinking about Julie, and he remembered her saying she'd had sex in the toilets in New York, New York. At the time, it had gone over his head. It was a very promiscuous place, and it wasn't unusual, but all of a sudden, it seemed wrong.

He thought about the fight she'd had with Sandra and the way his mum had described it. Julie had really lost it, apparently. He thought about the state of the flat; no one would do that for nothing. And then the trip to London and the foreigner who had sounded so sexy, but also very guarded.

He dived up out of bed and picked up his jeans; he needed to check if he still had the phone number as he wasn't sure what he'd done with it.

He was going to make it his business to find out what was going on, so he was going to phone him again and be a bit more direct. He was going to make him tell him what was going on. He was sure that he knew – he was too cagey.

As he lay there, he could hear giggling outside his door and realised that Bernie had dragged Scott up to her room. 'Dirty cow,' he said out loud.

He turned over and pulled the covers over his head; the last thing he wanted was her groaning like a bitch in heat.

He then heard his mother and laughed to himself.

'You can't be doing that in here, you two. Come on Scott, you'll have to go home. You're not on Bernie; it's not a bloody hotel.'

He didn't want to hear any more; they all did his head in. He needed to get a good night sleep so he could get out on the job tomorrow.

First thing, he was going over to her ex's house. See what that slimy fucker had to say.

Chapter 16

David rose early. He was a natural early riser, and it was never long after his eyes had opened that he needed his fix – a cup of tea.

He pulled the covers back and got out of bed, slipping on an old silk dressing gown from back in the day.

As he reached the top of the stairs, he could smell the familiar smell of a fry up. He let the smell waft up his nose and took in the delicious smell of the bacon his mum was cooking.

He looked at his big belly and thought about the diet he was constantly on and off. 'Ah fuck it,' he thought. 'I'm not fat; I'm just big-boned.'

He nearly ran down the stairs; he was that excited.

'Morning,' he greeted his mum and was surprised to see his sister sitting there. Although, if there was food to be had, she was never too far away.

'What happened last night then? After Scott got kicked out love?' He laughed.

'Shurrup.' She couldn't be bothered with him; it was too early for a full-on David.

'There's a cuppa here, love.' Irene basked in her role of being the doting mum.

He gulped his brew. 'Aw, I love my tea in the morning me.' As if no one knew that about him.

They all sat down for fried eggs, with a crispy edge, crispy bacon, sausage, beans and the biggest pile of buttered toast you've ever seen.

'That looks lovely mum, thanks,' said Bernie still smarting from getting caught out with Scott.

They ate in silence.

'Gorgeous that love.' David said once he'd demolished his fry-up and four cups of tea. He stood up.

'Right, I'm going to get ready, and I'm going over the bridge to find out some more about Julie. The police won't keep us informed – we're not family. So I'm going to find out for myself. Glad I booked a week off work now, are you Bernie?'

'You know I've lost my job David,' she said, glaring. 'You're such a bitch.'

His laughter could still be heard even when he was safely in his bedroom.

He came down, ready to face the day ahead.

'You walking over with us or what?' he asked his sister.

'Erm, you should have asked me before, I'm not dressed, and I can't come like this.'

'Go get dressed then, and I'll have another brew. I'm dead bloody thirsty. Must have been those couple of cans last night.'

Half an hour later, they were walking through the estate. The weather was still warm, and people were everywhere. The kids were off school, so plenty was going on in gardens; some had paddling pools in them from the night before, half-deflated and half empty and all the little shops were busy.

They walked past their old primary school and reminisced about their days spent there.

'Aw, it only seems a minute ago, doesn't it?' Bernie said and stuck her head through the dark blue painted railings.

'Hated it me Bern. I remember a right old bag,

Miss Wood. She used to wear a two-piece blue suit, and she would slap your arse at any opportunity. She was wicked.

It's child abuse that.'

'Yeah, but was that because you'd put drawing pins on her chair, our David? I'd have slapped your arse too. Bullying that,' she mocked.

They both laughed. As they passed the school, they came to the railway bridge they had to walk over to get to where they were going.

The grass verges were full of kids playing football and riding around on their bikes. It was lovely to hear them up and about so early and having fun.

'Remember when our mam used to give us a bottle of water and a couple of jam butties between us, then kick us out for the day?' Bernie was reminiscing.

'Yeah,' David smiled, 'and she'd say don't come home until it's dark, and then if we were late, we'd get leathered.'

'These kids don't know they're born.' Bernie sounded older than her years.

It wasn't long before they reached their destination. Julie's ex's family lived at the end of the green.

David walked up the path while Bernie waited at the gate. She was definitely the quieter, more reserved out of the two and didn't like confrontation at the best of times.

He banged on the door and waited to see who answered. It was "his" mother, Ann.

She was a slim woman with very neat short hair, it was streaked, with highlights of blonde running through it, her eyes were deep brown, and she wore black leggings with a blue and white striped T-shirt. She wore a couple of nice gold chains around her neck and lots of gold bracelets. It made her look a different class, but she wasn't. Her and her husband had obviously worked hard and done well for themselves. Her house was bought, it had nice wooden framed windows, and her front door was oak, her garden was pristine.

Her face was soft as she said, 'Hiya love.'

She knew who he was, but they'd never really spoken. She knew he lived next door to Julie or his mother did. She was a bit put out as she looked behind towards where Bernie was stood at the gate.

David was full-on as usual.

'Er hiya. Is your son in? The one who's got the kid to Julie.'

'You mean Andrew? No, he's not. What do you want him for?' She immediately went on the defensive.

'Well, we've not seen Julie for days, and we're a bit worried about her.' David explained.

'Well, what's that have to do with our Andy? They're not together anymore. She kicked him out a couple of weeks ago. Anyway, I just spoke with Julie this morning.'

'Did she say where she was?' David was thrown by this information.

'No. I assumed she was in her flat. What's going on here?'

David explained the goings-on, starting with the fight with Sandra, but leaving out the reasons behind it. Ann was nodding her head as though she could imagine Julie losing it.

He told her about the suspected mix up between Sandra and Julie and how Sandra had been kidnapped in the middle of the night, only to be brought back in the morning. And then the state of Julie's flat and how the word "murderer" was painted all over the living room wall. Ann was gobsmacked as she listened.

He explained that they'd phoned the police who had suspected she'd taken an overdose, and whilst it hadn't made sense, something was definitely amiss.

And finally, taking a deep breath, he told her about the telephone number they'd found on her stairs and about the foreigner he'd spoken to in London claiming not to know anything about her, yet still wanting details about the two policemen who were investigating.

'She went to London a couple of weeks ago,' said Ann, in an attempt to add to the story.

'Yeah, so I heard.'

David sighed. He wanted to hear something he didn't already know and felt frustrated.

'So did she not mention anything at all when you spoke to her this morning?' He asked in the hope of some clue.

Ann said she hardly knew Julie, but for some reason, she always felt nervous around her. She said she was always nice to her as the thought of losing contact with Jody would kill her and Pete (her husband) and that she was happy that she had Jody for a couple of weeks. She showed concern that Julie could have taken an overdose and wondered if she had called her from a hospital.

'I have no idea love; your guess is as good as mine,' said David. 'Where is she from?' He wasn't giving up. 'Because she's not from round here, is she?'

'Well,' said Ann, ready to gossip, 'She is very secretive about her past – our Andy doesn't even really know that much about her. She's from Lymm, in Cheshire, originally and was brought up in a very big house apparently, on The Avenue. Really posh! But her mother kicked her out, and she was in a homeless shelter when our Andy met her; he was the cleaner there. But she's never let on what went on and why her mother kicked her out. There was some huge fight, but there has to be more to it than that. We all fight with our kids, don't we love?'

'Oh yeah, definitely!' he pointed at Bernie, who was biting her nails at the gate, waiting patiently, 'Just last week, my mum and sister were kicking shit out of each other over a lottery ticket.'

She laughed, and David thought she seemed nice enough, genuine with a heart of gold, he could see that.

A young man was making his way up the path and grunted something to Bernie, who had stepped back to let him pass her.

'Alright mum?' Andy greeted his mother.

He was a tall, wiry lad with a similar hair cut to his mother; he had her deep brown eyes, which also looked soft.

'Alright mate?' He said, without even looking at David.

David bent his head and nearly stuck his face in Andy's face, making him look at him. 'Julie seems to have gone missing, and nobody knows where she is.'

Andy shrugged.

Ann repeated David's story to Andy, and David was happy to add in bits to make it sound more mysterious than it was. He didn't mention anything about her sleeping with Scott, which was unusual for David; he'd normally enjoy stirring the pot.

'Yeah, I can imagine her kicking off,' Andy said. He had been listening intently. 'She had a right temper on her at times. She used to snap at our Jody loads. It used to do my head in, but there was no telling her. She knew best. Glad to be out of it, to be honest.'

He went to walk in the house but stopped as though he'd had another thought.

'God knows who would have done that to her gaff. Although I have no clue as to what she used to get up to – she definitely had some sort of mad past.'

'Your mum said she's from The Avenue, up in Lymm? How come she ended up here? What went on there then?' David really was taking on the role of Inspector Morse now, and Bernie was getting fed up, wondering what the point was.

'Dunno really, she just said her mum was a nutter and had leathered her all her life. Then she apparently overstepped the mark somehow, and Julie said enough was enough, whatever that meant. She rarely spoke to me about anything, never mind her past. Bit of a weirdo if you ask me.'

He shrugged, then continued.

'She'd been in the homeless gaff, where I used to work for about six months when I met her. We hit it off; she was a right goer at first.'

'Andrew!' His mother reminded him that she was stood there.

'Sorry mum, but she was. Then as soon as she got pregnant, that was it; she hardly spoke, never mind anything else. She was always depressed and lay on her arse all day in her own world; she didn't give a shit about our Jody.'

David listened and took it all in.

'What about her dad? Did she have an old fella?'

'Left her when she was a kid. Again, she didn't speak about him much. She didn't get angry about him, though. She told me that she wasn't allowed to mention him as a kid. From what I can make out, he got sick of the mother's bullying and temper. She does sound like a right psycho, to be fair. No wonder Julie's off her head.'

'Andrew!' Ann gently slapped him over the head.

'Wonder if she's at her mum's,' David said.

'Nah. No way. They hated each other man. She hasn't seen her for years, not once during the time I've known her anyway. Called her "the enemy" or "the psycho" – no way she'd be there.'

'The enemy?' David asked. 'Really? The enemy?'

'Yeah, straight up. She hated her man and would go in a right mood if she was ever mentioned. I'm sure once she even called her a murderer.'

And the three of them gasped as though it was some missing piece from the jigsaw.

'What?' Bernie shouted up the path.

'What you on about?' David shouted back.

'You all gasped. I want to know why.'

'You should have listened then, you daft cow.'

She braved it and walked up the path. They all seem friendly enough towards each other, and she did know Andy, sort of.

'Hiya,' she said to Ann, 'I'm Bernie, David's sister.'

'I'm Ann, love.' She smiled at Bernie.

Andy went into the house, but the rest of them stood at the door, gabbing.

'Why don't you come in, and we'll phone Platt Lane Police Station and see if they have an update on Julie? Then I think I'll drive up to her mother's.'

David jumped at the idea. 'I'll come with yer if you want a bit of company.'

'Yeah, sure love.'

They all piled into the house. The long hallway led into the kitchen, and there was a door to the right that led into the living room. You could see into the living room because the doors were made of wooden frames but had Perspex panels. This was considered quite posh.

Ann opened the door, and her living room was very welcoming. There was a light brown stipple over the fireplace, which had a brass fireguard surrounding it.

The settee was a deep beige with pale brown stripes running through it. She had vertical blinds up at the window and nice flowery curtains. There were vases of flowers on the coffee table, making the air crisp with their strong scent.

'Do you both want a cuppa?' Ann asked Bernie and David.

'Tea two sugars for both of us, thanks love.'

Poor Bernie, she could never get a word in.

Ann turned to her son, who was lounging on the settee. 'Andy, make the brews please, and I'll phone Platt Lane.' He did as he was told.

Two little girls came into the room; Jody and her big cousin Jessica. Jody's blonde curls were tidily put into a little scrunchie on the top of her head, and she looked cute in her little pink summer dress and pink sandals. Jess had two plaits that went down her back and had a yellow summer dress with yellow sandals. She was probably about four but was enjoying mothering little Jody.

Bernie admired the two little girls. 'They're bloody adorable.'

David pulled a face as though they had rabies. He didn't like kids. Little brats who were always whining at one thing or another.

Ann went to use the phone; it was in the hallway on a table that had a cushion on it quite old fashioned, but it was probably her mother's before her.

Andy came into the living room with the brews and acknowledged his daughter and his niece.

'You alright girls? Are you playing nice? Give us a kiss Jody.'

'And me,' piped up Jessica and ran to him and gave him a big kiss. Jody wasn't bothered but gave her daddy a kiss anyway.

Ann came in and said that she'd phoned Platt Lane, who had said that the case was closed. They'd spoken with Julie today, who had said she was fine and that she would sort the flat out once she returned and that she was staying with a friend for a few days.

As she went to sit down the phone rang again, she ran into the hall to answer it.

'Julie?' She almost screamed. 'Where are you? I've got David and Bernie here worried sick. They say the flat has been vandalised and the police have been involved.' She didn't let on that she'd just got off the phone from the police.

David ran to Ann's side, she passed him the phone.

'Baaaaabe, where the fuck are ya? We've been worried sick about you girl? Is there sommat going on or what?'

'Right, right.' He responded, nodding his head. 'Ah, how come you didn't tell us?' He was questioning her.

'Alright babe, well, you take care and hurry up back, we're missing ya?'

He put the phone down.

'She's full of shit that one,' he said, waving his hand in the air. 'I can tell when someone's lying a mile off. And she was lying through her back teeth then. She couldn't even look me in the eye.'

Ann started laughing. 'She couldn't see you.'

'No Ann.' David was deadly serious. 'I mean it. If she could have seen me, she wouldn't have been able to look me in the eye. I'm telling ya.'

'Where did she say she was?' Ann asked, arms crossed.

'She said her mum wasn't well and that she was staying with her for a few days to look after her.'

'But the police said that she said she was staying with a friend?'

'Yeah, full of shit.'

They were walking back into the living room, and Andy had heard the commotion.

'There is no way on this earth that she is looking after her mum. I'm with David on this,' he nodded his head towards David. 'She's lying.'

'I'm a bit worried now,' Ann said, her arms folded. 'I think we should drive to her mother's and check her story out.'

'You're dying to get to that mother's you, aren't you Ann love, have a nosey about. Yer best get yer best frock on, so we don't get shown up.'

Ann took his humour well and laughed.

'Why are we even getting involved?' Andy asked.

'Because she's Jody's mum love, and I don't want her to be in any sort of trouble or in a situation she can't get out of. She wasn't telling the truth on the phone just then, so something is not right.'

'Why are we getting involved?' Bernie asked David.

'Because we are. She's alright, our Julie, and I don't want her to be in any trouble.'

'You just called her a liar,' Bernie reminded him.

'Yeah, she's a liar, and yeah, she's probably a wrong un, but I do love her for some reason. And like Ann said, she might need our help. She is troubled, like me. I can feel her pain Bern.'

Bernie didn't know whether to laugh or cry and instead rolled her eyes.

'I'll come with you Ann. I could do with a drive out, not moved with all this going on; it's been dead stressful.'

Bernie thought if the wind changed right now,

she would forever have her eyes stuck to the back of her head. She couldn't believe what a bloody drama queen he was.

'I'm going back over the bridge David.' She waved bye to the girls and headed off.

'See you, love, nice to meet you.' Ann was distracted and wanted to get a wriggle on.

'Ok,' Ann said. 'Get the girls ready Andy, and let's go to her mother's.'

'I'm not coming. I've got somewhere to be in half an hour.'

'Well,' Ann ordered. 'Help me get the girls ready.'

Within seconds, there was excitement; it was as though they were off to the beach for the day. The girls were jumping up and down. Andy was grabbing little bottles of juice for them. Ann made sure she had spare knickers for the kids and a packet of baby wipes.

'Feed the dog Andy, and we'll get off.'

'Jesus,' David said, 'we're only going up the road.'

'I have to be prepared,' explained Ann. 'Better to have it and not need it than not have it and need it.'

'You two are off your heads,' Andy laughed.

They were away, with David sat in the front passenger seat and Ann driving. The little girls sat in boosters in the back.

They drove in silence towards Manchester Airport to get on the motorway that would take them to Lymm.

Ann slammed a tape into the car stereo.

'How've you managed to keep that safe?' David asked, referring to the car stereo.

'I can pull it out,' she smiled.

'Then why was it still in the car? You can't take any chances round here. Every bleeder wants a car stereo.'

She laughed as Astral Weeks crooned out of the speakers and Van's one in a million voice filled the car. Van had the range to be a delicate croon one minute then the roughest growl the next. The album lyrics reached beyond language.

David looked out of the window as they drove through the estate where he grew up. He passed all his old haunts.

The Red Rose on the corner, still going strong. As they drove further up, they passed what he remembered his mum used to call a "home for naughty kids". She'd threaten them both with it every so often when she'd had enough. Had enough of the next drunken bum. He loved his mum and knew that she'd done her best for him and Bernie. But he still shuddered at the fear he used to feel about going in the home for "naughty kids". It had always intrigued him.

He reminisced as he passed The Newalls, a pub where he'd spent many a night in his late teens. He smiled as he thought about the DJ in the backroom and Friday's soul night, where he'd play the same songs week on week. He almost laughed out loud as he remembered DeBarge's "Rhythm of The Night". He had visions of himself stood watching the girls dance, not wanting to take any of them home but to be able to throw his handbag on the floor too, metaphorically speaking, and dance around it, arms swaying, hips gyrating and head nodding to the music. It wasn't the done thing back then.

It had been really difficult for him being gay and growing up on a huge council estate in the '70s and '80s. There were so many "lads" around, and he'd found it hard fitting in. He was always accepted, he got along with everyone and was easily liked with his loud and charismatic ways, yet he could be as rough as the rest of them. He had known he was gay from being a young lad when he fancied Mr Pickering, the PE teacher. He'd been about eleven at the time, and all his mates were talking about girls and lady teachers with big tits. But he couldn't stop looking at Mr Pickering's muscly legs. He remembered how uncomfortable he'd felt.

He had laid in bed that night and cried because he didn't want to like boys; he wanted to be "normal" like everyone else. Girls were great, fun and bitchy; he loved their company. But early on in his life, when he thought this was only happening to him, he knew he would never want to even kiss a girl, never mind anything else.

He fought for years and tried to be "normal", but once he admitted it to himself and told himself that's who he was and that it wasn't wrong, he felt better about it. He grew gracefully into a man and wasn't afraid of his masculinity or femininity; he loved the fact he had both.

He'd been worried about telling his stepdad. He knew his mum wouldn't care less. He'd had the fight and the torment for years in his head, and the most difficult thing in the world had been the internal fight. The external fight would be simple in comparison, so fuck his father; he'd have to lump it.

He lumped David instead, right across the fucking head. Calling him all sorts of vile names. He then left his mother, which David blamed himself for, for years. Especially as his stepdad's last words before he left were that her son knocked him sick to the core. But he knew in his heart that his views were wrong and that his mum was definitely better off without him. She had found happiness in so many other things than a vile drunk that beat her kids.

They flew up the M56, David in deep thought.

Jessica broke the reverie and shouted from the back.

'Nana, I need a wee.'

'How long can you hold it for?' Nana asked.

'Not very long.' Jessica was frowning and really thinking about it.

'Ok, there's a pub off this roundabout; we'll call in there and have a wee.' Ann started to indicate left so she could pull in.

When they entered the pub, it was quite busy considering it had just opened for the day. A couple of groups of lads were obviously starting out with breakfast for a stag do. They were a little bit rowdy, and were ordering eggs and bacon, challenging each other to have a pint with it.

David felt the stares. Then one of the lads started wolf-whistling him and asking him where his handbag was. He then heard one of them say, 'fucking puff.'

He walked right over to them, hand on hip. 'What a bunch of hard men you are, I'm fuckin shaking' in my shoes here. There's about 10 of you lot versus me, a nana and two little girls. You're the fuckin' puffs.'

He spun on his heel, and as he did, the locals and a couple of bar staff clapped. He went bright red and said, 'Come on Ann, let's have our wee's and get out of here before I twat the lot of them.'

Ann laughed and headed off to the ladies with Jessica and Jody.

David had his wee and went and waited for them in the car.

Soon they were back on the road. In fact, they were only minutes away from their destination.

Ann turned right, and they were on The Avenue. She leant over to David and asked, 'Right what now? Do we just knock on all the doors and ask for Julie?'

She was looking at David rather than the road.

'You just keep looking straight ahead girl, or we'll be up someone's arse in a minute.'

She looked over him, trying to see out of the passenger window.

'Ann!' He yelled as she got a bit close to a man on a bike.

She slammed on the breaks to avoid hitting him. She couldn't have anticipated the smash to her rear as another car slammed into the back of them.

Her car shunted forward, giving her and David an almighty jolt. David thought he was going to hit the dashboard. He reached out with both arms as if to save himself.

'ARRRRGGGHHHH!' he screamed.

'SHIT!' Ann screamed.

Thankfully, the girls were in their boosters and had only been jolted slightly.

'I can't breathe,' David was grabbing his chest.

Ann was more concerned about her granddaughters, who were more upset at the adult's reaction than the crash.

'It's ok, it's ok,' she crooned, trying to reach over to the little girls.

'Bloody hell Ann, you could have killed me.' David was wiping his brow.

The huge bang on the window brought them all back down to earth.

The knocking belonged to a big woman – big in height and big in weight. Her hair was immaculate, and the sunglasses on her head were Gucci. Her large earrings were real diamonds. She wore a lightweight, slightly see-through white T-shirt that showed off her huge breasts.

She continued to bang on the window, but it wasn't the banging that was frightening them; it was the scars on her face. She'd obviously been burnt, and her face was disfigured.

'What's that?' David was almost ready to dive in the back with the girls so they could protect him.

'Good God, David, don't be rude!' said Ann, and she wound down her window very cautiously, with a most hesitant look on her face.

David jumped out of the car.

'Sorry,' he announced. 'She nearly hit a biker and had to brake, but you shouldn't have been driving so close to us. You must have been right up our arse.'

She smiled with only one side of her mouth. But it was her eyes that caught his attention; they looked through the very core of him and sent a chill up his spine. He didn't like her one bit, and it was nothing to do with her face.

'You're absolutely right,' she said. 'I've just come over to check if everybody is ok and the driver looked like she was in a funny position, so I was concerned she was hurt.'

By now, Ann had got out of the car.

'Look, I'm so sorry,' the woman said, turning her attention to Ann. 'As your son,' she pointed to David, 'just said, I was driving to close. If you come back to my house, I will pay you cash for the damage, best that way. Then we can let the boys in blue do what they're paid to do and not waste time on a scratch like this.'

It was a bit more of a scratch. Ann's red mini metro's bumper was badly dented.

The woman pointed towards her big Range Rover.

'I think my car is ok, so don't you be worried about that.' There was definitely a touch of sarcasm to her tone. 'Do you want to check if yours still drives?'

Ann jumped into the car and started the engine, and there didn't seem to be an issue.

'Follow me, I only live up the road, and I'll pay you cash for the inconvenience.'

David jumped in the car, muttering. 'God, she's weird, don't you think? She reminded me of Cruella De Vil.'

'She was an oddball, wasn't she?' Ann agreed. 'I'm worried. We should phone the police. Pete will go mad.'

'Well, let's get to the house, and we'll tell her that we want to do it the official way.' David was nodding his head. 'Yeah, it's not right this.'

They pulled up outside a large house. The creepy woman used a remote control to open the huge wooden gates that hid her beautiful house from the world.

'I don't believe it.' Ann gasped.

'What's up now Ann?'

'It's her house!' Ann was excited.

'I know it's her house; she's pulled up outside it.' David was exasperated and thought that maybe Ann had banged her head.

'No, I mean it's her; she's Julie's mum.'

'Shit, you're joking,' David said.

Before they could say another word, the gates were closing behind them. They silently drove behind her until she stopped on gravel right outside her front door.

'What shall we do? He asked Ann.

But before she could answer, the woman was bounding over to the car. Such a big woman, she must have been six foot tall.

They got out of the car, and David helped Jessica out, whilst Ann picked up Jody. Her thoughts were on overdrive. What if this woman really was a psycho, and she was putting the girls at risk?

'You know what,' she said, 'We'll just get off, and I'll sort the bump out myself.'

She was nervous and looked at David for back up.

'No, I insist,' the woman said before David could respond. 'I want to give you payment for the damage. Don't worry, you'll be duly compensated. Besides, we're in now,' she grinned. 'Please come in; I'll be no more than a couple of minutes. I have the cash in my house.'

David wondered what had happened to her face. She had clearly been an attractive woman. Her weight and height would have had no bearing on her looks once upon a time. You could see that.

They followed her through the front door of the house. The hallway was huge, with tall white walls and high ceilings with beautiful chandeliers.

There was a grand staircase; it was wrought iron and beautifully stained oak wood.

On the walls leading upstairs, there were two expensive canvas photographs. The first one was of two little girls – twins, in fact. And the other was of a man with the twins and this woman. They looked like a happy family, and you could see just how stunning she was as a young woman.

'Just let me get you some cash from upstairs.'

She left them in the hallway and headed up the staircase.

'That must be Julie on that picture.' David was trying to take a closer look.

'There's two of them,' Ann gasped. 'She must have a twin?'

'Oh my god.' David also gasped.

They jumped as the front door opened and were confused when the postman walked in bold as brass but stopped dead in his tracks when he saw them.

'Er, where's Susan?' He asked.

'She's upstairs,' David explained, guessing that "Susan" was the woman they'd followed in.

'Ok, I'll wait here; she knows I'm coming.'

David and Ann just looked at each other and shrugged.

Ten minutes must have passed, and Susan still hadn't come down the stairs. Ann whispered to David. 'What do you think she's doing?'

'How do I know what she's fuckin' doing,' he whispered back. 'Why don't you go up and ask her?'

'Do you always have to be so sarcastic?' Ann asked through gritted teeth. She was losing her patience now. Jody had fallen asleep in her arms and was getting heavy to carry. Jessica held on to her other arm; she felt like a bloody packhorse and really wanted to get out of this house.

'She knows I'm coming.' The postman said again.

'Riiiiighhhht,' David responded, not wanted to engage in any conversation. Although he did have a sneaky look up and down – nowt like a man in uniform, he grinned internally.

Another ten minutes passed before Susan meandered down the stairs in a very sleazy fashion. She'd changed her clothes and was now wearing a black, off-the-shoulder dress. It was low cut, and her huge breasts were almost touching her chin.

'Rob,' she exclaimed. 'I forgot you were coming darling.'

He smiled like a puppy wanting his treat, and by the looks of things, he was about to get one.

Susan looked at Ann and David, and her eyes lay firm on Jody, who was stirring.

She squinted her eyes as she weighed her up.

'Is Julie here?' David asked outright.

'What?' She was deadpan. She looked back at the canvases and then spat as she spoke the words. 'Julie is dead.'

David looked at Ann and then at Jody.

'Get out.' She hissed and threw a brown envelope at David's feet. 'Get out now.'

Jody started to cry. Susan zoomed right into her little face, and the realisation dawned on her.

'Who is this child's mother?' Again, she was spitting as she spoke. 'Who are you, and what do you want?'

Postman Rob tried to make his exit.

'WHERE ARE YOU GOING?' She screamed her shrill was terrifying, and they all jumped.

Rob stopped dead in his tracks and stayed put.

'Come on David, grab Jess, and let's get out of here.'

'What is that child's mother's name?'

She walked over to Ann, reaching her in seconds.

'This is my granddaughter. I can feel it. This is Jane's daughter.'

Ann was worried. She had no idea what was going on, or who Jane was, but just knew she had to get her granddaughters out of this house quickly.

David picked up the brown envelope and scooped Jess in his arms.

'Look, there has been some misunderstanding, and we need to get these girls home,' he said.

'Why are you here?' Susan demanded. 'You were driving 20 yards from my house; you were coming here.'

David thought quickly.

'We were looking for our friend Julie. She's

gone missing, and her flat has been vandalised. She called us this morning and told us that she was here, so she's obviously sent us on a wild goose chase and believe me, we won't be chasing anymore; she's clearly a psycho.'

'If she's gone missing, you should leave my granddaughter here with me.'

Ann jumped in, 'That's not going to happen. I'm her grandmother; she stays with me.'

'Right, this is getting a bit too much for me,' Rob intervened. 'Susan, I'm going. I've got to be back at work in ten minutes.'

She walked over to him, almost as though she'd forgotten Ann, David and the girls were there. She grabbed his shirt collars and started to kiss his face as though she was starving hungry.

'Quick,' Ann hissed, 'get out.'

They left through the front door as Susan and the postman were fiercely stripping each other's clothes off.

They ran to the car and could see that Rob had left the gate open when he drove his van in.

They dived in the car and didn't even fasten the girls in. They would do that once they got off her property.

Ann tried to do a U-turn on the huge drive, but Rob's van was in the way as she had parked too close to the Acer that was planted next to the front door. She couldn't manage to get past it.

'Fucking hellfire.' David cursed. 'What the hell are we gonna do?'

Ann put her foot down hard and smashed into the front of the van knocking it out of the way; she took half of the Acer with her, but she got through.

'Go on girl,' David yelled in excitement. 'Get us outta here.'

As he looked back, he thought he saw a young woman looking out of one of the bedroom windows. He squinted his eyes, and as he did so, Jody blurted 'mama' out of nowhere.

He looked again, straining his eyes, but there was nobody there. He was losing the plot.

Ann drove like the clappers up the drive and through the gates. She didn't stop until she was at the end of The Avenue.She stopped to fasten the girls in properly, then headed to the motorway, getting them back to safety as quickly as she could.

Chapter 17 - Julie

I woke up from a dreamy sleep. It felt like I'd been in and out of sleep for days and had continued to feel exhausted. Right now, I felt like it was lifting, and I was coming out of it. That last panic attack had really taken it out of me. They often did, but this one had been extreme.

I know I'd been offered food and even been given some. But I was sickly, everything had felt hazy, and as of yet, I didn't recall any conversation with anyone.

I sat up and stretched. I looked around the bedroom; it was a fair size and pristine without a thing out of place. The walls were a deep pink with beautiful wooden dado rails. The floor had been sanded to its natural state and the furniture matched. A beautiful long solid pine dressing table housed a telly – I bet that one didn't have a coin box fitted to the back of it. The beautiful huge pine chair with a deep pink and light green cushion on the seat just finished it off. The matching pink and green curtains were gently being blown in the breeze from the open window.

I got out of the solid pine bed and went towards the open window to see if I could gauge where I was in the world.

I couldn't see anything apart from beautiful countryside. The view was limited due to the house's angle, so if there were any more houses around me, I couldn't see them. There was a tiny stream at the bottom of the garden, and I watched as the sunlight played with its ripples as it bobbed up and down, glistening brightly, causing little rainbows as it did so.

I tried to recall what had happened.

I'd had the call from Pavel and had gone into some sort of mental breakdown. I had debated taking the paracetamol that I thought I'd had in the kitchen draw.

The fear of the unknown was just too much, and then thoughts of Jane were triggered, and they had taken over every cell in my body. Jane's death, the guilt, the sudden departure of my father, and her, with her horrible burnt face. That and not knowing when I would see Jody again sent me over the edge that I'd been teetering on for so long.

I remember wanting to end it there and then.

As my thoughts were going back to the flat, they also brought back the feeling in the pit of my stomach.

I remember getting the bottle of tablets, and there wasn't any left. I'd thrown it across the kitchen floor, and then there was a knock on the door. The knock.

Pavel had said two hours; it had been two minutes, or had it? It was all a blur.

The knock jolted me into action. I grabbed a carrier bag out of the kitchen drawer and ran around the flat like a madwoman, looking for pyjamas of all things. I remembered my envelope and threw it in the carrier bag. I grabbed some overnight clothes and knickers and some leggings and a top and threw them into the carrier bag with the envelope. I thought about my toothbrush, so I ran into the bathroom and grabbed it off the windowsill along with a roll-on deodorant. They also went into the carrier bag.

I ran back into the bedroom and grabbed my suitcase from the cupboard. I finally grabbed Pavel's number, which was always next to the phone, and my box of cigs.

I ran down the stairs, opened the front door and couldn't believe who was standing there. I stopped in shock and asked. 'Who the hell are you?'

It was the Native American from my dream and from the Cypress Tavern. The kidnapper. I knew that much, but who the hell was he?

'Just get in the car; we have no time. I will explain later,' he said, his voice low and gravelly.

I had to trust him as I wasn't sure what the alternative was. So, I quickly ran up the path making sure that nobody was about, looking over towards Irene's and then at Sandra's but the coast seemed clear.

He quickly opened the backseat door for me, and I was met with the smell of beautiful luxurious leather.

I looked out of the windows and realised they were blacked out. It made me panic somewhat.

'Where are you taking me?' I asked.

'To safety.' His eyes stared at me softly through the mirror. I trusted him and lay my head back on the comfy seats and closed my eyes. I felt absolutely exhausted.

The rest was a blur. I don't recall leaving the car.

And now here I was.

I thought about Pavel and wondered if he'd phoned me. I wondered where I'd put his number and started to look for the jeans and T-shirt that I'd shoved on the other day. I'd somehow managed to fold them up on the beautiful pine dressing table next to the telly.

I couldn't find it; it wasn't in the jeans pocket where I distinctly remember putting it. My carrier bag was hung on the beautiful pine chair whilst my suitcase was placed neatly under the dressing table. I wasn't sure what possessed me to bring the suitcase. I had some clothes in it from back then. I certainly didn't need them here. It had occurred to me though, that there was a load of paperwork in the zip compartment.

The night I left my mother's, she was asking for the case back. I was in no mood and completely defied her. That woman, my mother, came into my head every fucking day. It was time I put her to rest. I shook my head vigorously as though that would cleanse her from my head. I grabbed the carrier bag and sat on the bed while I emptied it.

The number wasn't in there. I was starting to get agitated as I sat there on the bed, trying for the life of me to remember where I'd put it. There was a knock on the bedroom door. I opened it and was surprised to see a young woman stood there. She was younger than me and noticeably confident in her demeanour.

'Hiya. I'm Fiona. I was just checking that you were ok. I was told you weren't very well, and I wondered if we needed to call a doctor.'

She stroked the front of her hair and looked at me. I could tell she didn't really care if I was ok and that she was doing as she was asked.

'Erm, I think I feel better now, thank you? Where are we?' I asked.

'We're in my dad's house in Mobberly.'

I kept her at the bedroom door as though it was my front door and wouldn't open it fully as though I didn't want her to see in.

'Do you know what is happening, and do you have a number for Pavel please? In fact, can I use a phone? I need to check on my daughter.'

'Pavel isn't contactable at the moment, and don't ask me why because I don't know.' She put her hand up in the air and was very dismissive.

'What do you mean, not available?' My heart was starting to race.

'I have no idea what's going on with them all at the moment, but I'm sure my dad will explain when he gets back later. He's just asked me to check on you and make sure you have something to eat.'

'Can I use the phone, please?' I asked her again.

'Yeah, if you want.'

God, this woman had no emotions in her face whatsoever. She was deadpan when she spoke. But I was intrigued by her face. She was really unusual in her looks, and the small scar on her chin made her look even more attractive than she was. But she was starting to irritate me, and I wasn't sure why. She was just so unfriendly, although I didn't know why I expected her to be anything else.

'The phone is down the hall if you want to use it now?' She was pointing down the hallway outside my room.

She was taller than me, probably about five foot ten. She was extremely slim with a very flat chest. She was wearing a retro t-shirt that looked like it was from the 70s with slim flared jeans. She looked like a student and probably was. Her short black hair was styled messy on purpose, and it fell gently across her face. Her dark brown eyes were deep-set, her cheeks were hollow but in an attractive way, and they made her cheekbones look more prominent.

I could see the resemblance to her father.

She took me down a long hall. The decor must have been similar all through the house as again the floors were sanded, and Indian runners broke up the ambience. The paint on the walls was a musky green, and there were plants skilfully placed in pots along the floor. There was a pine table, and on it was a white dial phone.

'I'll stand here; you must not tell a soul where you are?' Obviously, she was following instructions.

'Why? Where the fuck am I?' I spat. She was really irritating me now. How stupid. I had no clue where I was to tell anybody.

I picked up the phone and actually felt comforted by Ann's usual "2747" greeting. I wanted to be there, I wanted to feel safe, and I wanted to see Jody.

'Hi, Ann,' I looked at chiselled cheeks and threw her a look of disdain. She wasn't perturbed as she leant on the wall, arms crossed, picking the bits off her T-shirt.

I checked on Jody and even had a little chat with her in Jody style. I smiled through my tears.

When Ann came back on, I asked when they were going to the caravan and if there was a number there that I could contact them on.

Ann asked me to call back, as she did have one but would have to phone her sister for it.

I agreed and put the phone down, feeling sad and scared.

'Hey,' Fiona grabbed my arm gently. 'It'll be ok you know.'

I was taken aback by her empathy; maybe she was human after all.

'I'm sure it will, something tells me it will, but we don't have a clue between us what is going on. We don't even know why I'm here, or do you?' I asked in the hope that she would shed some light on what was going on.

'No, I don't. It's typical of this lot. I'm always left in the dark. I didn't even know about you until this morning when dad drafted me in. I have enough to do, and now I'm stuck here.'

She laughed. 'God, I don't mean to sound rude. I know it's not your fault. I do know it's something to do with my uncle and that he's in some sort of trouble. They need to grow up the lot of them. Settle down and be normal.'

'Is your uncle Pavel?' I asked.

'No, I don't know what is going on with Pavel either.' She laughed again, holding her hands out palms up. 'He just tries to keep in with the oldies. I just know that dad got a call and had to go to London on urgent business.'

'What business?' I asked.

'Honestly, Julie,' I was surprised she used my name, 'I have no idea.'

For God sakes, what was I involved in? These people could be child traffickers, be part of a paedophile ring. How was I part of this madness? The trip to London had been down to an advert in the paper. How on earth had I met my brother if that was the truth? It was too much of a coincidence. I find an advert in the local paper for submissive sex, and it turns out I nearly did it with my brother.

He must have known immediately who I was; otherwise, the story could have been quite different. How on earth did he know? I was wracking my brains. It was absurd.

I needed to eat. I told Fiona I was starving and asked if there was any chance of food. She smiled broadly, and it lit up her whole face.

'Tell you what, you go back to your room, and I'll grab you some food. Be warned though, I'm a shit cook, so you'll have to make do with whatever I concoct for you.'

I went back to the room and grabbed my cigs; there was one left. Fucking story of my life. I went and sat on the windowsill. "She" was there staring back at me; she looked annoyed. I felt annoyed, she looked scared, and I felt scared.

I relaxed as I inhaled in the smoke, taking deep breaths as I did so.

This was fucking ridiculous. I'd been here two days now and was none the wiser. Again though, I thought about what the alternative could be and was thankful that I was safe. Well, at least for now anyway.

I knew Jody would be ok with Ann and Pete, and she would have a ball with Jessica in the caravan. She deserved a little holiday, bless her little heart. Again, my eyes filled up with tears.

I knew she was better off without me. I was always miserable around her. Always feeling shit. She would be having so much fun and cuddles right now. I felt a surge of anger flow over my body. It was all my mother's fault, she was a fucking animal, and she'd damaged me so much that I was struggling to love my own daughter.

The tap on the door got me out of it. I ran to it and opened it for Fiona, who had a big tray in her hands.

'Here, let me take that off you,' I offered.

'Don't worry, I'll leave it here, next to the TV.' She placed it carefully on the pine dressing table. 'It's probably awful, but at least it's edible,' she said and went to leave the room.

'Hey, can I use the phone again shortly?' I asked. 'I have to call back for a phone number of the caravan park where my daughter's grandparents are taking her later this week.'

'Do what you want; you're not in prison, don't forget.'

'Do you have a pen and a piece of paper?' I asked.

'Give me a minute.' She bent down and corrected her flares, making sure they were correctly placed over her converse. 'I'll grab you one from my room. You eat your food.'

I sat down. She'd brought me some toast and boiled eggs and a cup of tea. There was also some sort of Danish which looked gorgeous. I was starving and wolfed the lot in almost one hit, drinking the tea down fast.

She was back with the pen and paper for me and

walked me to the phone so that I could phone Ann again.

As soon as she picked up the phone, she screamed. 'Julie. Where are you?'

I listened and felt sick as she explained that my flat had been broken into and wrecked. But I had to stay cool. One, because Fiona was listening to every word, and two, because I couldn't let on where I was. I was quickly thinking of something to say.

I heard a kerfuffle on the line, and then I heard David's voice.

'Baaaaaaaabe.' He yelled.

He also wanted to know where I was, but now I had my story.

'I've had to come and look after my mum,' I lied. 'My uncle got in touch and told me she had some awful flu and that she was bedridden, and she is, she's not well at all.'

He didn't believe me. I could tell he absolutely knew I was lying.

'Yes,' I continued. 'I'll be home in a couple of days. Don't worry about the flat. I'll get it all sorted when I'm back. Miss you too.'

That wasn't a lie because I would give anything to see him and Bernie right now.

As I put the phone down, it rang straight away, startling me and Fiona.

She rushed to pick it up. The conversation was sparse, but I was interested.

'Ok,' she was nodding.

'That's not good.' She was looking at me as though I could hear the person on the other end.

'She's ok, and yes, I'll ask her, but I gather all is

ok there.'

'Ok, you take care and keep in touch, so we know what's going on.'

'Yes, I know that; yes, you've told me that before.'

She hung up.

I watched as she walked up the hall, leaving me stood next to the phone. I was about to ask her what was going on, but she had her head down. Was she crying? It was difficult to tell.

'Is something wrong?' I asked her.

'They've all been arrested.' She was wiping her tears, thinking I'd not seen them.

'Who?' I asked.

'Dad, Pavel and my uncle.'

'Oh my god. What for?' I asked.

'He just said it had been a huge mistake. I do worry though. I know there has been some bad blood between some old boys in London. It's all gone a bit tits up, and they're warring between themselves. I don't know the story, but this happens all the time, and next week they'll all be on the same side, doing someone in for favours. My dad is a good man, but he does know some hefty men. But his solicitor is fabulous; she'll have them out by this afternoon.'

'Where's your mum?' I asked, not sure where the question came from.

'Mum died giving birth to me.'

'Oh my god.' I was genuinely saddened for her.

'Yeah, it doesn't make me feel particularly good at times. She pressed the corner of her eyes to prevent the tears and then laughed because she felt stupid. 'God, I'm sorry,' she said. 'I don't know what's up with me today.'

'God, don't worry, I could cry on fucking demand right now. I feel shit too.'

'I grew up feeling like it was my fault, like I was responsible.' She shrugged. 'I know it was a medical mess up, but it doesn't stop the guilt.'

I knew how she felt about the guilt thing. As soon as I thought about Jane, I got the twang in my belly, like a snake had just decided to do a somersault in my gut.

'You know we're going to have to stay in the house,' she said. 'If they're protecting you, it's for a reason, so we should make sure that we stay safe. You will have to stay here until dad gets back. He said he wouldn't be days. He also asked if Jody was safe?'

'Yes, Jody's safe,' I said, not wanting to tell her where she was. 'So, do you think I'm in some sort of danger?' I asked. 'I must be,' I answered my own question.

She shook her head. 'Fuck knows.' She laughed. 'As I said, I only got drafted in this morning. He told me nothing other than I needed to look after someone. That's my dad for you though. He also said I was to show you the safe room. Come with me. I think he's worried that whoever he is warring with might come for us. He said any sign of trouble, this is where we had to go.'

As I followed her down the long hallway, I wondered if this was about my mother and what had happened years ago. I wondered if she had decided to get me back after all. She always said she would. I suddenly felt sick.

Although I wasn't sure what the connection between her and London could be. Unless Pavel was her son, but if he was working for her, why would he protect me? Was he protecting me?

Nothing about that woman would surprise me. She had her fingers in many pies, and she was capable of anything. I shuddered, and my guard went up. So far, I was safe, and Jody would be at the caravan in a couple of days for a full week. God, I hope things were a bit clearer then.

Fiona walked into my bedroom and shut the bedroom door behind her. I realised I was still in my pyjamas and suddenly had a flashback of the girl in the toilets on Canal Street. I got the feeling but pushed it away. This wasn't the time or the place.

She beckoned me over to a door on the same wall as the dressing table and what I assumed was some sort of closet or a small built-in wardrobe.

She opened the door wide, and I was right; it was just a cupboard full of shelves.

'Watch me carefully,' she said.

I did, and she unhooked a latch on the side of the shelves, and it was almost as if another door opened, and I nearly died when it did. She pulled the shelves towards her on a hinge, and there behind it was a set of stairs, leading to what, I had no idea.

'What's up there, fucking Narnia?' I almost felt excited.

'Go on up. I'll show you how to lock yourself in once you're in. Although if anything does happen, I'll be right behind you.'

I sat on the stairs and saw how she carefully shut the door into the bedroom, lock it with the key that was originally on the outside, and then pull the shelf back into place. Once shut, she used another key to lock that as well.

'What's up here?' I asked.

'Go up,' she said, and I did; she wasn't far behind me.

At the top of the stairs, there was a loft space with no windows. She showed me where the light switch was. There were two sofas and a coffee table, but not much more – such a cute room.

'So, if we hear anything untoward, we run up here to safety. If nothing else, dad is prepared.'

'Ok.' I agreed, then added, 'Do you know what, it might just be safer if I were to go and stay at one of my mates, this is making me feel uncomfortable?'

'You're not in prison; you're not being held hostage. You can do what you want for me, but I trust my dad, and if he says you should be here, then you should be here. You could leave and be followed, and besides, he's locked the gates, and they're about 12 foot high. At least give it until tomorrow. He'll be back, you'll see. They can't hold them for more than 24 hours, and if I know my dad's solicitor, he'll be home before that. Please be patient. The London lot are not to be messed with.'

I felt like slapping her across the head. Instead, I went and sat on one of the sofas and put my head between my legs and took some deep breaths. I needed to keep my wits about me, and I needed to stay calm.

'I'm going to get a shower and get some clothes on, I told her. Can we get down from here? I'm starting to feel claustrophobic.'

'Yeah ok,' she replied.

I was beginning to feel trapped in this huge house, with a room to escape into if we were attacked in the middle of the night.

I barged passed her and let myself out through the shelf and through the cupboard door back into the bedroom.

I grabbed a towel off the side and proceeded to the en-suite bathroom.

Again, I couldn't breathe. Fuck off, not now, I told myself. I really didn't need any of this. I wasn't sure my nerves could take anymore.

The shower had a huge head, and when I turned it on, the power of the water was overwhelming. I stepped into the heat as the water sprayed my face. I already felt better.

I stood directly underneath, closed my eyes, and allowed the feeling of relief to wash through every inch of my body.

As the water pounded the top of my head, I felt like it was washing my mind, clearing it of any bad thoughts. I felt the heat wash through my head as it caught my breath.

I tilted my head so the same heat could hit my face making me feel exhilarated.

I turned around, and it hit my shoulders.

Wash away the weight from them, so I can enjoy life's experiences.

I leant back slightly as I let the fast and furious water hit my chest. With my eyes closed, I breathed in deeply.

Wash away the heavy feeling so that I can feel lighter.

I let the water hit my breasts, and as it did, I rubbed my nipples softly.

Wash away all the negativity so that I can feel free.

I closed my eyes and relished the beautiful sensation on my nipples.

I leant back as the water embraced my stomach. I took another deep breath.

Wash away all my fears and the snake that lies within so that I can live easier.

The water felt like tiny stones as it hit my thighs. I could feel hot drops between my legs.

Wash away the pain so my strong legs can carry me easily through this difficult life.

My feet tingled with joy as the water kissed them both.

Wash away the burden so that I can stand tall.

I turned around and leant forward so that the heat of the spray lashed all over my back.

Wash away the guilt so that I feel supported.

I opened my legs and didn't even have to touch myself as the water hit me, giving me so much pleasure until the top of my legs tingled with joy.

I sat on the floor and lay back, holding myself up with my elbows. I was sweating in the steam, and the fierce water came for me, hitting me hard between my legs.

I gasped, and my breathing became shallow as it happened. I came with such a force that I've never felt before.

Wash away the regret so that I can start again.

Chapter 18

The shower had made me feel amazing. I definitely believed that water responded to my emotions. I felt a lot of positive feelings. I had a realisation that I was the only one who thought my negative thoughts, and that's all they were, thoughts. Surely, I could change them around, albeit maybe now wasn't the right time to become all positive and inspirational. I had to get out of this mess first.

I lay on the bed, and tiredness took over me. One thing I'd learnt from depression or whatever it was that was wrong with me was that I was always exhausted. I was always sluggish.

I must have dropped off for a good few hours before I was awoken by the presence of someone else in the bedroom.

I sat up quickly and rubbed my eyes.

'It's me, Fiona. They're in the grounds,' she whispered.

I got out of bed quickly, whispering back, 'who?'

'I don't know,' she said, still whispering. 'But I've just heard the dogs barking like mad from the next house up, and the big light just lit up our drive, and two cars were parking up.'

'How did they get in?' I asked. As I did, we heard an almighty bang; it sounded like a car backfiring or a gunshot.

We both made a dash for the safe room.

We could hear them coming up the big stairs at the bottom of the long hallway. It sounded like there was a lot of them.

Fiona's hands were trembling as she tried to unlock the cupboard door that led to the safe room. The key flew out of her hand into the air and onto the floor. I swear I was going to piss myself. My legs had turned to jelly.

'Stay calm, take deep breaths, come on,' I whispered. 'You've got this.'

She managed to pick the key up and unlock the door, but as she took the key out to lock it from the inside, she dropped it again.

We both bent down to pick it up and smacked heads hard. I felt dizzy, and I'm sure she did.

We grabbed each other instinctively and helped each other in a moment of despair and blurred vision.

We quickly pulled the big shelves towards us, and Fiona shut the cupboard door, locking us in safely.

As she was shutting the shelf door back to its original state, we heard the bedroom door open and then silence.

She locked the shelf door ever so quietly, and we stood there for a minute in sheer dread with sweat dripping off our faces as we heard people in my bedroom.

I grabbed her hand, and we crept up the stairs. This time we didn't turn the light on. I guess we were both too afraid in case they saw the light coming from the room somehow.

We both went towards one of the sofas and climbed on it together. We held each other tight, both shaking and breathing heavily, teeth chattering in total fear.

We didn't speak for what seemed like hours. The only audible noise was that of our breathing.

We had no way up there to assess anything that was going on. We had no idea if they were still in the house, or maybe they had decided there was no one home and, with a bit of luck, took off.

'Do you think they've gone?' Fiona whispered. It was as though she had just read my mind.

'I've no idea,' I whispered back, 'but I'm not about to go down to check,' I smiled. Not that she could see me in the darkened room.

'How's your head?' I asked her.

'I'll have a big lump in the morning,' she said.

'Me too.' I said, rubbing my forehead. I winced as I felt the small lump that was forming.

'What happened?' I asked her.

'I was in the kitchen having a cup of tea and reading my book when I saw the gates open and the outdoor lights come on. I'm not sure how they managed to open them though, only a few people have access. I saw two cars and panicked when I didn't recognise them. And that's when I ran up to you. You know the rest.'

I didn't know what to say. I just sat there feeling very afraid, rubbing her hand in mine for comfort and wondering what the hell would happen next. You couldn't write this shit. I knew that for sure.

Fiona released her hand from mine and sat up straight. She seemed to be coming round somewhat. She had stopped shaking.

'We can put the light on, you know, and we can talk without whispering. This is a safe room with a purpose. The room is blacked out and soundproof. Dad doesn't do things by half. Also, there is a little fridge over there with drinks in and a toilet behind that door. Sorry, I felt so dizzy then I couldn't think straight.'

She got up and switched the light on, and even though I believed her, I almost thought it was going to trigger some sort of reaction. It was better for the light. But we had no way of knowing what was going on in the house. They could have set the thing on fire by now, and we could just be sat here waiting for the flames to reach us.

I shuddered at the thought and started to pace around the room, the room was small, but there was enough room to pace.

'Is there no way of knowing if they've gone?' I asked her. 'Is there no secret window anywhere?'

'No,' she responded. 'I'm just hoping and praying that dad is on his way home. Can I ask you, are you my dad's bit on the side?'

Her question came as a surprise.

'Jesus, no,' I cried, 'absolutely not.'

Then I started laughing. 'I only met him the other day. This is something to do with a trip I took to London, a trip I wish I'd never taken.'

She laughed too and looked relieved. She must have had her fair share of her dad's women.

'Sorry,' she said. 'I never know with him. He's a right gigolo, or at least he thinks he is.'

We didn't say much more on the subject, and she walked over to the fridge and grabbed us both a soft drink which I welcomed.

We sat cross-legged on the floor, opposite each other. It was as though we were about to engage in deep conversation or meditate.

'What do you do?' I asked her. 'You look like a student?'

She told me that she was studying for a degree at Manchester University. She explained that she was studying psychology and was in her third year. She said that she wanted to be a counsellor and had studied neurolinguistic programming and Cognitive Behaviour Therapy. She was looking at helping vulnerable children and youths, and it sounded like an interesting career.

I sat and listened. I couldn't help but think she'd bumped right into a psychological mess with me. I was a psychiatrist's wet dream.

'I have so many issues, Fiona,' I blurted out.

And suddenly, as though they had been sat there waiting for an opportunity, the tears flowed as I started crying. I felt ashamed as it wasn't what I was expecting to happen. I didn't even know this girl, and here I was, a blubbering mess.

'Let it all out,' she said, going into professional mode.

So I did.

After I had finished, she looked at me and asked me if I felt better. It was as though the tears had washed my mind and my eyes, and I could see things clearer.

Chapter 19

'Have you ever told anyone your story?' she asked me.

'God no, never ever.' And I hadn't. I'd never sat there and let it all out. The only person who knew my story was me. And I was sick of hearing it, along with "could have" and "should have" and "why didn't I do this" and "why didn't I do that". It had slowly become a volcano in my head, ready to explode its hot lava everywhere.

'Tell me,' she said calmly, 'start at the beginning and tell me all of it. Don't miss anything out. If it gets too much, we'll take a break. All I will do is listen.'

I took a deep breath.

I was four years old, playing in the garden with my beautiful twin, Jane.

The sun was shining. We had so many wonderful toys. Part of the garden had been made into a mini playground; it was wonderful. Little swings and slides, all on soft bark in case one of us fell.

There was also a little water play feature and a sandpit with amazing shapes to play with.

This is one of my earliest memories.

I remember hearing shouting coming from the kitchen. They were arguing again – my mummy and daddy. She was shouting loudly, and daddy seemed to be trying to calm her down. Then I could hear pots and pans being thrown, and she was swearing, calling him names. I remember feeling so scared and sick in my stomach. I looked at Jane, who carried on playing. She never seemed as alert as me, but thinking back, she might have been blocking it out.

Daddy rushed out of the house and into the back garden where we were playing. He had blood all over his face and shirt. Mummy was laughing loudly. She said he was stupid. She told him to go and to come back when he wasn't so stupid. He left the garden. I'd never known where he went. But the image of my hero with blood all over his face and shirt never left my head.

Then it was our turn. She was fierce, and she looked angry. I remember she told us both to get in the house and that playtime was over.

Jane put her toys down immediately and walked in. I didn't want to go in the house, mainly because I felt safer out here. I was frightened of what was to come.

So I carried on playing as though I hadn't heard her.

She bounded over to me and slapped my bare legs. Hard. Not once but several times. I felt the slaps sting my little legs, and the tears stung my eyes, but I refused to cry. Even at an early age, I didn't want her to have the satisfaction that she'd hurt me. It wasn't the slaps to the legs that hurt; it was the horrible angry look that was on her face that I could never get out of my head. She frightened me. She was a huge woman.

The abuse went on for us both. Our dad was hardly around. If he was, she seemed calmer with us but worse with him. She was always lashing out at one of us. The best thing he could do was stay away.

Then one day, Jane and I had been playing in our room. We had a beautiful bedroom, all pink and girly, and there was two of everything. Everything we wore matched, from our little dresses to the ribbons in our hair, even though Jane's were always neat and mine always came untied and loose.

To look at us both, we probably looked like we were from the perfect home. It just shows you that abuse has no prejudice; it will strike all classes, so long as there is an evil perpetrator.

I remember we both jumped as we heard her high heel shoes thudding on the stairs; she was on her way up. We were babies and yet, gave knowing looks to one another early on. We were one; I felt what she felt and vice versa. She might have hit us in turns, but we both felt it twice over.

She called us both out of the room. Jane had wet herself, probably out of fear. I remember quickly grabbing a pair of knickers for my sister before "she" came into the room.

But I wasn't fast enough.

She called Jane a dirty girl and said that she

would smell of wee all day now. She quickly changed her and, of course, had to change me because we had to match. When she finished, she pushed us both out of the bedroom. We must have had somewhere to go, but where, I'll never know.

I had kept the clean knickers tightly in my little hands so that she wouldn't see them. Jane was complaining that she'd hurt her foot. I knew she hadn't; it was her way of getting sympathy. Even though it didn't always have the desired effect.

Mother picked her up and carried her on her hip, about to go downstairs.

But then she spotted the knickers and asked me what I was doing with them. Before I could answer, she called me ridiculous and asked me to put them back where I'd found them.

I dropped them.

With Jane still in her arms, she went to slap me hard across the head, just as I bent down to pick up the knickers I'd dropped.

This caused her to lose her balance.

I had to pause my story to regain my composure for the next part. The tears were coming, and Fiona reached out for my hand as she could see I was getting upset.

The noise they made when they both fell down the stairs has never left me. It was horrendous. The crying and wailing, the thudding of their bodies and the clanking as they hit each step of the stairs was horrifying. I just stood at the top of the stairs and watched in absolute terror.

Fiona told me to stop. She said firmly that we needed to break.

I lay back on the floor and took some deep breaths. This was the first time I had ever said it out loud. It had been in my head for twenty-one years, but I'd never said it out loud.

Fiona got me a bottle of water out of the little fridge.

I was dying for a cig.

'Bet you could do with one of these?' Fiona pulled a twenty packet out of her pocket and handed them to me with a lighter. I nearly kissed her.

I lit the cigarette and longed for a window so I could see Jane. I longed to look at her and let her know that I had spoken about her. I inhaled that familiar taste and breathed the smoke into the small space. It spiralled slowly as the light shone on it, making me blow some more. I thought about what I'd just spoken about. Fiona remained quiet as though she was allowing me to absorb in my own thoughts.

After I'd finished and thoroughly enjoyed the cig, Fiona asked, 'You ready to go again?'

I nodded my head and continued my story.

After the fall, it became chaotic in the house. Mum had screamed Jane's death out loud for weeks, howling, crying, all with a broken arm. But it was totally self-absorbed. My dad and I were in as much pain, if not more. That's if you can measure the pain of grief. It didn't matter. Jane was her "baby" all of a sudden. She was hers, her daughter, she gave birth to her, she was her youngest child being the second twin. She couldn't believe how upset we were. As though we had no right.

It made it worse that she told everybody I'd pushed them both. I had to see a doctor, some sort of shrink, and she reminded me constantly that I'd pushed them. Until I got to a point where I believed it. The knicker story reformed in my head, and I saw myself actually pushing them.

For me, the pain felt unbearable. I couldn't get the image out of my head, and when I asked my dad when I would see Jane again, he said, 'never, sweetheart, never.'

I would lie in bed, night after night, trying to comprehend the word never and asking myself how long was never? If he had said five hundred years, it would have meant I had hope, but never?

Every day she blamed me, she hit me, and called me a murderer. Every day I believed her. I went into a shell and wanted to curl up and die and go with Jane, but it never happened.

Then dad left, he was told to go. I know now he would have had no chance against her. I remember him crying and saying he had to leave.

I was beginning to feel tired by my story.

'Are you ok?' Fiona asked me gently.

'Yes, I'm ok. It's hard; it's never been said out

loud, even though I never stop thinking about it all.'

I cried every night for my dad. The pain matched that of losing Jane because, at the time, I didn't understand why he had left me without taking him with me. He knew she was a monster, and so for a long time, it left me wounded.

But as an adult, I know how powerful she is, and I know he must have been grieving for Jane. The poor man was driven from his own home and lost his twins in the blink of an eye.

At five years old, I was alone with her, and life was worse than ever. The years passed and I became used to her. There were times I even felt sorry for her. There is obviously something very wrong with her.

Then there were the number of men she would have come to visit her for sex. The house was huge, and there was no need for me to see such behaviour, but she was never discreet, and at times, I think she was putting on a sexual show for me.

I used to feel very scared as a child, uncomfortable, but the weird thing was after each visit, and for a few days afterwards, she would become the mum I dreamed of.

She would let the man go, then come to me with a kiss and say, 'I need the bath, sweetheart. I need to wash the monsters away, and then we'll watch an old film on the telly.'

And she'd get snacks and fizzy pop, and we'd watch the huge telly. We'd actually snuggle up on the huge sofa we had, and I used to take in her strong perfume. For a moment, I would forget the horror and enjoy the pleasant feelings and her warmth.

That's the reason you return to your abuser. Because for a moment, you do believe that they love you. I believed at that moment that I was her world, and I would instantly fall right back in love with her. It was always short-lived, and then she'd start again. I'd want to tell her, 'Mum, it's me, you loved me yesterday.'

The tables turned when I was eighteen.

My education hadn't been so bad. I'd worked as hard as I could at school, but I couldn't settle into the regime and timetables. I got into trouble a couple of times for being disruptive. I soon learnt to keep my head down or feel her wrath. I learnt very quickly that school was my escape. While I was at school, I didn't have to deal with her, so I worked hard and left with high marks in my exams.

After school, I got a job working in Manchester for a Chinese computer company. I was the receptionist in a very affluent office in Spring Gardens. Businessmen would come in to see our specialists. I'd make them coffee and offer them biscuits and escort them to their relevant meeting. I would answer the switchboard all day long, transferring clients to their respective counterpart.

I'd met Jamie there. Jamie Morano, he was dishy, very Spanish looking. He seemed to be the only bit of normality in my life. He became my first boyfriend, and I fell for him hook line and sinker. I was so in love with him.

Most nights, my mother would be out on one of her jaunts, and he'd come round, and we'd laugh, have crazy sex, and eat junk food in what seemed like blissful happiness for me. I was hooked and head over heels in love. He'd met her a couple of times, and she was pleasant enough, other than her passive-aggressive remarks about me, which made me wince. I wanted Jamie to see me as perfect and not look at me through her eyes.

I came home from work one evening. Someone had posted a brown package through the door, addressed to me. I remember thinking nothing of it at the time. I had no idea what it could be.

It was a videotape. I was intrigued, but for the life of me, I wasn't ready for what I was about to see. I remember watching it with bile in my throat as I witnessed my mother and Jamie having porn like sex.

Once again, she'd got me. I must have been the only thing in her world that she was set to destroy, and I'll never know why. I felt betrayed, sickened because I had stupidly thought Jamie had been as in love with me as I was him. I never saw Jamie again, and hopefully, for his sake, I never will. Never has anything destroyed me as much as he did.

I approached her about the video. I asked her what the hell she thought she was doing. I'd never confronted her with anything in my life. But to me, this was the final nail in my very well nailed down coffin.

I was cooking dinner at the time because she would never do such a thing. We were having pasta. I was using the big pan with two handles. She laughed. Her laugh got louder and louder.

The water in the pan was boiling, and I was about to put the pasta in. Instead, I picked up the pan and threw the lot all over her stupid fucking face.

She soon stopped laughing.

Fiona was aghast. She asked if I was ok and if I needed another break. I shook my head. I was nearly finished, so I might as well carry on.

After the drama of the ambulance coming and her being rushed off to hospital, I wasn't sure what to do with myself. I had nowhere to go; I knew no different. So I waited for her to return.

I couldn't believe the mess that was her face when she returned. At the time, I thought she deserved it, but now I've had time to think, I know that nobody deserves that.

She negotiated my punishment with me. I had two choices.

The first choice was that she phoned the police and reported it as a crime and would ensure that

*I spent the rest of my adult years in prison. I
believed her.*

*The second was that I would sleep with her
men. She could no longer entertain them, so I
would have to take over.*

*It was the first time I realised they had been
paying her for the deed. She must have been
expensive to sustain the lifestyle that she did.*

*I agreed to the latter and quickly started to have
many visits, and I'm ashamed to say that it made
me feel very powerful. The men were desperate
for sex, some in sexless marriages, others lonely
weirdos whose only sexual encounters had been
with themselves. Their desperation in their need
for sex made me feel alive. It was the only time in
my life that I felt good.*

*I had confidence that I'd never experienced
before in my life. The adoration for my body
and the excitement my body gave them made me
finally feel worthy for a moment. But as soon as
the moment was over, I was left feeling ashamed,
sickened and guilty. It was like a drug for me,
an instant high with a massive come down. I've
constantly wanted to go back to that place of
feeling that but fought against it. Until the time I
went to London.*

*She made me do this for a year before
physically kicking me out. This came out of the
blue for me. I wasn't expecting it. She told me
I had an hour to pack my bag and that I would*

be taken to a shelter for the homeless in a place called Chorlton.

She even attacked me for taking my suitcase. She had said it was Jane's and not mine, but I was no longer listening. She wasn't getting the case off me out of principle. I was fucking sick to the back teeth of her.

As I left the house of horror in Lymm, she shouted, 'I will get you back for the murder of my little girl. I will have you, for the mess you've made of my face. So keep looking over your shoulder; you're going to need eyes in the back of your head.'

The shelter was a dive. I had nothing but my suitcase with items of clothing which I'd quickly packed. She gave me no money, just wiped me out of her life.

I cried, and I cried, and I just wanted to go back to sitting on the huge sofa with my mum eating snacks and watching films. Despite everything she'd put me through, I still wanted my mother's love.

I looked at Fiona.

'And then I suppose the rest is recent. I met Andy when he worked at the homeless place where I was staying. We had a few nights of wild sex that actually wasn't wild at all, and I became pregnant with Jody. As much as I love her, I just don't know how to be a mum. I've never been taught. I asked him to leave after my trip to London, and then I slept with my friend's fella. I'm ashamed, but at the time, I craved that power. I slept with a man who was just walking past my house, and then I had sex in a toilet with a girl I'd never spoken to. Sex is the only thing that keeps me alive. Then I berate myself and say it's because I'm the same as my fuckin' mother. I even have to have the bath afterwards.'

I sat up quickly. We were both silent, not because of my story, but because we both heard something. Someone was trying the door down the stairs. They were really pulling at the handle.

We stared at each other in silence, a thousand words telepathically spoken. I was searching her eyes frantically as she was mine. The sweat was pouring from my head, but I couldn't move my hand to wipe my brow. I was frozen.

They got it open; the door actually opened.

Our eyes were screaming at each other, still no words, yet this was the deepest conversation I'd ever had. I had felt fear before, but this was something else.

Then they all rushed in, and our eyes told each other it was over.

Chapter 20 - David

The whole situation had sent David to his bed for a couple of hours. They'd gone on a whim to find Julie and ended up having a car crash that nearly killed him. Well, maybe that was a slight exaggeration, but he was definitely suffering from some sort of injury; his neck was killing him.

They'd then been subjected to the Yeti that was Susan Robinson, Julie's mother. And he'd been convinced for a minute that the fucking postman was going to kidnap him, Ann and the kids.

And to top it all, Jody had shit in her nappy, so the car stunk all the way home. He gagged until the tears were streaming down his face. He was a state.

Ann had dropped him off at his mum's, where Bernie and Irene were waiting for all the gossip.

'Did you find Julie?' Irene interrogated him as soon as he'd walk through the front door.

'Fucking 'ell, let me get my bastard foot through the door,' he groaned. 'It was horrendous,' he exaggerated, 'absolutely horrendous. Do us a brew mum, I've not had one for hours.'

He told them the whole sordid story while they sat there, mouths agape.

'Jesus Christ, she sounds like a weird woman,' Irene said. 'You're not to go there again David. She sounds like a nutter. I wonder why she said Julie was dead?'

'God knows.'

'Hey David, Az has given me a job at the shop; he said I could do four hours a day. It's a start, isn't it?' Bernie piped up, totally oblivious to David's nerves being shot to hell.

He couldn't believe his sister sometimes. He was sure she had a screw loose. How could she talk about herself at a time like this? Selfish cow.

He had gone to bed because he couldn't be arsed with any of them. He needed a nap and to absorb what had just happened to him.

He lay there for a while thinking about Julie and what a weird set up she had been brought up in. Going by the pictures he'd seen, Julie had a twin. She must have gone through that loss and never said anything. She certainly had a lot going on, did Julie. No wonder she was a bit cuckoo, he thought. He wondered how she'd gone from that huge house to a cottage flat in one of the biggest council estates in Europe. He thought she'd either had to escape the madness that was her mother, or she'd been kicked out.

Either way, she was best out of it. That he was sure of.

He tried to recall what the Yeti had said. She was insistent that Julie was dead. It was strange for a mother to say that, although he guessed she had nothing maternal about her. Did she mean Julie's twin?

Then there was the postman, what a strange scenario that was. Was Susan Robinson with all her airs and graces some sort of brass? Was she getting paid for sex, or was she paying them? The postman was familiar to her but not boyfriend familiar and the way she went into some sort of trance when she thought he was leaving was terrifying.

He remembered the state of the tree and the postman's van after Ann had driven straight into them, but he reassured himself that she'd had no choice. God knows what would have happened to them if she hadn't have got out the way she did.

Then he remembered the brown envelope and shot up quickly to grab his jacket. He'd put the envelope in one of the pockets.

He got back in bed and opened it. He couldn't believe his eyes. It was full of money, all in twenty-pound notes. He counted it out on his bed and couldn't believe it was a thousand pound, a grand. 'A bag of sand,' he said out loud.

His mind went into overdrive. He could buy a new three-piece suite for the flat, a new wardrobe, even book himself a cheeky holiday; he was bloody loaded.

Then he brought himself back down to earth and realised it was actually Ann's money for the damage to her car. He went to put it back and told himself he would drop it off for her later.

Fuck it, he thought. The damage didn't add up to a thousand pound; he betted her car was only worth £500.

So he took a handful of the money and ran downstairs.

'Right girls, where do you want to go? And I mean anywhere, anywhere you both want. I've got three hundred quid in my hand, and we're going to have a ball. Come on ladies, today is your lucky day.'

Irene and Bernie were gobsmacked.

'Oh my god, where did you get that from,' Irene

asked.

'Ask no questions, and I'll tell you no lies.' David was wafting the notes in the air. 'Come on think'. What shall we do?'

'Blackpool,' Bernie yelled.

'No babe, somewhere classy, not fucking Blackpool.' He grinned. 'Get your glad rags on, he ordered, and I mean your best. I'm going to take you to that dead posh restaurant, the one with the famous chef. I think he owns it; he's called John Thomson.'

The girls ran upstairs excitedly while David showered and changed into the only decent clothes he could find. His jeans were clean, he found some shoes and an old shirt he had left there. Fucking hell, he thought – his chest was almost bursting out of it. But it would have to do.

The girls came down, all dressed up to the nines.

Irene had her special white coat on. She saved it for best. It was long and woollen and probably a bit warm for an evening in July. She'd had it for twenty years and only worn it twice before. Shows how many times she had to dress up in her best, bless her.

Bernie had tied up her long black hair. She had a little pretty blue bow with white dots tied in the front of it. She wore a blue top, off the shoulders, with white dots on it that matched her bow, and a pair of white pants. Her white trainers matched them nicely.

They all complimented each other for twenty minutes whilst they waited for the taxi that David had ordered.

They giggled in excitement all the way to the restaurant.

David was explaining to his mum and sister where the money had come from.

'The Yeti threw an envelope at me for the damage caused to Ann's car, but there was a bag of sand in it.'

'A bag of sand?' asked Bernie, 'what good is that to anyone?'

'A grand' David started laughing. 'You know sometimes Bern, I think I got the brains, and you got the looks. Well, I'm not even sure you got that our kid. Although you look belting tonight girl.'

Bernie blushed, and they all started laughing.

'Ah, you never say anything nice to me our David, thank you.'

Irene smiled. The atmosphere was lovely.

They arrived at the posh restaurant car park. David paid and tipped the taxi driver and told him what time to come back for them. They walked up the steps to the door that would lead them in.

They all hesitated for a minute, feeling a bit intimidated by such a beautiful place.

'Come on, let's do it; we're as good as anyone else.' David pulled the door open, and they found themselves stood in the most quaint and classy place they'd ever been in.

They couldn't believe just how posh it was. The white walls were adorned with candles in luxurious candle holders, and the huge windows were shaded by expensive wooden blinds that let the sunlight in so naturally. There were little tables everywhere covered in rich fabric tablecloths and fancy napkins with gorgeous cutlery laid out properly. The black wooden beams finished it off a treat, and it was just so inviting. Irene got a tear in her eye.

'Aw, David, I love it here.'

He smiled at his mum. 'It's nice, isn't it?'

The maître d' came over to them. He was French and welcomed them in a most beautiful fashion.

'Bonjour, Madam, Monsieur et Mademoiselle.'

Bernie started giggling; David nudged her and threw her a look.

'Hiya mate. Can we have a table for three please?'

'Er, of course. Do you have a reservation, sir?'

'Aw, no. It's my mum's birthday, and we just decided to come here. Someone recommended it; we were told the food was delicious.'

Bernie giggled again.

The French maître d' smiled at her. 'What is so funny, mademoiselle?' he winked at her, and Bernie was smitten.

'I'm sorry, I'm just a bit giddy.' She straightened her face quickly.

He said he had a table, and as he walked them to it, a stunning looking middle-aged chef came from the kitchen; his eyes were like the ocean.

He walked straight over to Irene. 'Your coat madam?'

Irene looked down at her coat. 'Yeah, what about it?'

'Can I take it for you?' He smiled and went to help her with her coat.

She went as red as a beetroot. 'Ah, thank you very much.'

David couldn't breathe. 'That was him, mum!

That was John Thomson. He's dead famous, and he just took your coat for you.'

'I think I've got a tenner in that pocket. Do you think it'll be ok, our David?'

He burst out laughing. 'Jesus mum, he makes a tenner a second. He's not gonna go in your pocket, you daft cow.'

The maître d' held out the stunning black leather chairs for them one at a time, then he handed them each a menu. He quickly brought over a bottle of white wine, showed them the label and said, 'I recommend this crisp French wine for you.'

He poured Bernie a small glass to taste. She knocked it back and carried on looking at the menu.

'Was the wine ok madam?'

'Aw yeah, thanks, it was lovely.'

She turned her attention back to the menu.

David was embarrassed. 'I'm sorry,' he said to the waiter. 'We will have the wine please.'

After the waiter left, David said, 'Right, it's dead posh in here. Let's not act like we've never been to a nice restaurant before, for God sake. They must think we're off the estate.'

'We haven't been to a nice bloody restaurant before David, and we are off the bloody estate. Got a couple of hundred quid, have you? You're not bloody Rockefeller. We are who we are. Get a grip.' Irene was livid at his newfound snobbery. 'And don't forget you bloody nicked that money, Lord Fauntleroy.'

Before David could snap back, the waiter was back with some bread and oils for them. They tucked in whilst browsing the menus.

'Not sure what any of this stuff is. What you having David?' asked Bernie, confused as ever.

'I'll have the steak,' he said. 'Can't go wrong with steak, mash and vegetables. I'm starving.'

'Think I'll go for the scallops,' Irene added.

'I'll have scallops then,' Bernie played it safe. She decided that if Irene liked them, she probably would too.

The waiter took their order and filled their wine glasses up. They gulped it down quickly and asked for a second bottle.

They were buttering their bread and dipping it in oils, telling each other to save enough room for their meal, which came quicker than they expected.

John Thomson brought Irene's and told her to enjoy. He also brought her a glass of champagne and wished her a happy birthday. She was all a dither but thanked him whilst flicking her short black hair and wishing she'd had time to get her roots done. Two other waiters brought Bernie's and David's food and gave them both a glass of champagne to toast their mother's make-believe birthday.

'Aw, I love it here David.' Irene said it again. 'It almost feels like it really is my birthday!'

David looked at his plate. 'Where's the food?' he whispered.

'What's up?' Bernie asked him.

'I'm starving, and I've licked more mash potato off the back of the masher than they've put on my plate. It's tiny.'

Bernie started laughing, really belly laughing.

'Give over,' Irene said to Bernie. 'You look bleeding stupid sat there laughing on your own. Get it eaten our David, don't be so ungrateful.'

She cut up her scallop, put a piece in her mouth and immediately spat it out.

'Mum!' David whispered loudly. 'You can't do that.'

'Jesus,' she said, 'I thought they were going to be like the scallops from our chippy – spuds with batter on. They're fish; I hate fish.'

'Just eat the veg then mum, give them our Bernie. In fact, give them here, I'll have them.'

She lifted her plate up and scraped them onto his plate.

'Can I have a bit of your steak then?' she asked.

'Aw, you're joking,' he said and proceeded to cut it in half. 'Eeeew!' he said. 'There's blood everywhere. That's hanging.'

He threw half a piece of steak onto Irene's plate. The other diners were starting to look over at them now.

He ate the scallops, steak and the mash, as little as there was.

'I need a pudding now, do you two?'

They both nodded.

He was looking around for the waiter, and he came walking over to them.

'Do you have a dessert menu please?' He asked in his posh voice.

'Why do you keep putting that voice on?' Bernie asked him, laughing again. 'You sound a right knob.'

'You look a right knob,' he retorted.

He burst out laughing at the look on her face. His big, loud laugh made the people on the next table jump. They gave him such a dirty look.

'Seen enough?' He asked, giving them the David stare of death. 'You'd think they'd never heard laughter before,' he said loudly.

They ordered their puddings, and again they were disappointed by the sizes.

'Can we have the bill?' David asked.

The waiter brought them the bill. David nearly fainted at the total, but he was pleased that he had enough to pay it.

As they were leaving, John was waiting with Irene's coat and, as he helped her with it, he asked if she'd enjoyed her scallops. She told him they were lovely and thanked him profusely for getting her coat. He gave her a great big kiss on each cheek.

'Ooh, I think I'll come again,' she giggled.

'I don't think you fuckin' will,' David muttered under his breath, and they went outside to wait for their taxi.

'Where shall we go now, David?' Bernie asked him.

'Chippy our kid, fucking chippy. And the winey.' They all screamed with laughter.

'What an experience though, hey girls? A famous chef taking mum's coat and a real Matey D.

Again, they all screamed.

They stood and waited for their taxi and admired the luscious trees that surrounded it. You could just about see the tiny post office set back through them.

'How the other half live, hey mum,' he smiled.

'Yeah, but I bet they don't have great kids like I do,' she winked. 'Here's the taxi. Come on, let's get to that chippy.'

Chapter 21

David's head was banging when he woke up. His mouth felt like the bottom of a birdcage, and his lips were stuck together. He needed water but didn't have the strength to lift his head off the pillow. He lay there for a minute thinking of the laugh he'd had with them two last night. He smiled at the thought of the restaurant and vowed he would go again, if only to listen to that maître d' talk for half an hour.

The reverie was soon broken by a loud, frantic banging on the front door. He heard his mum and Bernie racing to answer it. He sat up and tried to listen to what was going on but couldn't make head nor tail of the matter. He sighed and pulled his dressing gown on, rubbing his head as he did so. The throbbing must have been visible from the outside, it was banging that hard.

He went downstairs and was greeted by a hysterical Ann. She was in a right state.

Irene was trying to calm her down whilst Bernie took solace in the kitchen, offering everybody brews. It was the least she could do, and the only way she could cope with all the drama.

'David,' Ann cried. 'That horrible bastard had me arrested last night. She told them I had been drinking and that I'd damaged her property and the post van. I was sat in Hall Lane Police station on the estate for hours. They've let me out but said I will have to go to court. She has made up so many lies about me, you wouldn't believe it.'

'What?'

Bernie brought them all a cup of tea. Ann explained that she had been packing and getting ready for the caravan when she heard a knock on the door. She thought it was Pete or Andy as they were both out. She thought one of them had forgotten their key. She said she ran downstairs and nearly fainted when there were two police officers there to arrest her.

The cup of tea was literally shaking in her hand, and she was spilling drops of it on Irene's settee. Irene tried to ignore it.

'As they were telling me that they'd have to take me to the Police Station for questioning, there was another knock on the door. They let me answer it, and I swear I nearly dropped dead. It was her, Susan Robinson. She barged right past me, and there was a lady behind her, who I later found out was from Social Services.'

'Jesus, Ann. I can't believe this.' David was genuinely gobsmacked.

'All they were going on about was the huge plant pot with the big tree in it being a family heirloom. And that I should have reported the damage that I did to the van. Then they confirmed that they had seen evidence of me driving recklessly and speeding off, as her house has cameras everywhere. And that's not the worst of it,' she broke down sobbing.

Bernie couldn't take anymore and explained that she had to get a shower as she was due at work in an hour. David shot her such a look. What was up with that girl? She was so fucking self-absorbed. He was going to have a word with her later.

'What else happened?' David asked. He was

feeling a bit nervous now. He had also been there with Ann. The situation had been harrowing, and he would tell any fucker who tried to arrest him. He wouldn't be taking any shit.

'She's got Jody.' Ann could hardly say the words.

'Who? Her? The Yeti? What do you mean she's got little Jody?'

He was stood up now and pacing up and down his mum's living room, genuinely concerned about the little girl being with that woman. He kept bumping into his mum, who had also started pacing.

'The police and the lady from the Social Services told me I had to hand her over to her other nana. It's been the worst moment of my life so far. Her little face, she didn't even know who that woman was and was putting her arms out to me. Oh my god, I can't believe this is happening. I need to get her back.'

She resumed her sobbing.

'I told the police that we didn't know where Julie was. She laughed and said Julie's dead. The policeman must have thought I was mad. I told them that she was a monster and that Jody had never met her before. But the bitch insisted that she was her nana.'

'They believed her, and of course they bloody would. A rich, affluent woman versus a council estate neurotic female. I had no chance. So she took her. The police took Jess too, but she's back with her mum now. The whole thing is a mess. Where the hell is Julie? We need her back now.'

The woman was in a state, and no amounts of cups of tea could calm her down.

David thought quickly on his feet.

'Where's that phone number for that London guy?' He asked his mum, who started to look high and low for it.

'He knows where Julie is; I know he does. This has just got serious. That baby could be in danger. The woman is a fucking nutter; it stands out a mile off. I'm going to tell him, and I bet we see Julie very soon.'

Irene eventually found the number, and David didn't hesitate. He picked up the phone and dialled the number, but it just rang out.

He gave in and put the phone down. 'Don't worry Ann, we will get that baby back'.

Ann sat and wailed her heart out. Irene sat next to her and put her arms around her.

'Come on, it's going to be ok; we'll get little Jody back for you.'

'What if we phone the police and ask to speak to the sergeant at Platt Lane, explain what's gone on. He might just listen to you; it's worth a try. You've got to do something,' David suggested.

Bernie came back into the room, overhearing the last part of the conversation.

'To be fair, when Andy gets home, he will be able to phone the police and get Jody back. He's her bloody dad,' she said.

'Fucking hell, that's the most sensible thing you've said all your life, our Bern,' and they all set off laughing, even Ann.

But she was right. In all the panic, they'd forgotten that Andy would have more rights than a nana. One would think so, anyway.

'Thank you, all of you. I feel a bit better now, or at least I will do once Andy gets home.'

As they were finishing off their brews, there was a knock on the door.

It was the police.

David was shaking now and wondered what they were going to say.

Irene let them in and went to put the kettle on. That kettle was on overtime of late.

'Are you David Bates?' the officer asked, all surly and cocksure of himself.

'Yeah.'

'We've had a complaint. Were you at Susan Robinson's house in Lymm yesterday with Ann Davidson?'

'Yeah,' David responded. 'The lunatic drove into the back of us, asked us back to her house and went bat shit crazy on us, and now you lot have given her this woman's granddaughter. You might want to go back and question your mates at the station. They've put that kid in danger.'

The police officer ignored him.

'Mrs Robinson claims that you have stolen money from her property. She'd like it back, and she might consider dropping any charges.'

David thought about the envelope that was tucked safely under the wardrobe upstairs.

He shook his head, bewildered by the questions.

'Do you have a warrant to search my house? Because if you do, I'll give you the address, and you can go and look all you like.'

'If you just hand the stolen money back to us, we can forget the whole thing.'

'And say I don't have the stolen money to hand over, say there was no stolen money, and Mrs Robinson is just making this all up? Or maybe question the postman who was happily trying to get his oats whilst on duty. Maybe he took this fucking money.'

He wasn't coming up for air.

'This is bollocks. It's just an easy way out for you guys. I know, let's go and pick on the council estate lot. Let's take their kids and accuse them of stealing money. Well, I'll tell you, I've never stolen anything in my life, and you can tell Mrs Robinson that I wouldn't give her the steam off my piss, nor would I touch her fucking money, and she can shove her accusations right up her fat arse.'

'Er, so you've not got the money?'

'What fuckin money? She hit us up the back of our arse because she was driving too fast. She asked us to go back to her house so she could pay us in cash because she is dodgy and didn't want the police involved. We got there, and she must have forgotten she had a client there, left us hanging about for half an hour while she got changed. Went cuckoo at us for being at the house and started screaming for us to leave. And she said her daughter Julie is dead, but she is in fact very much alive, just missing, and you lot have done fuck all about finding her.'

David was fuming.

'We panicked because she started getting angry and shouting. Her postman friend said he was leaving, and she nigh on started having sex with him, so we made our exit. Check that on her fucking camera.'

The officers knew they were on the road to nowhere with this one and said they would leave it for now and be back if they had any more questions.

'Fire away. If you've got any questions, ask me now? And please get that baby back from that monster and drop any charges to this lady here. It's absolutely ridiculous and unfair.'

'We will look into your requests,' one of them said, and they left with nothing.

David ran upstairs and got the envelope from under the wardrobe.

He took it downstairs and handed it over to Ann.

'What's this?' she asked.

'It's the fucking money they came for. She threw this at me when she was losing the plot. I didn't steal it; she threw it at me. It's yours for the damage to the car. When all this is over, you take Jody and Jess on a proper holiday; you deserve it for what she is putting you through.'

Bernie said she had to go to work as she was starting her job at the shop today for Az.

'I'll walk you down our Bern,' David said. 'I need some cigs. Ann, you wait here, I won't be long, and we'll try the London number again. Then if all else fails, we'll get a posse together to get Jody from that woman, don't you worry.'

'Yes, finish off your cup of tea, love,' said Irene. 'We'll wait until your Andy is back home, and then we'll sort this out. If I have to, I'll go and grab Jody out of her hands, the bastard. It's going to be ok Ann; you've got us on your side.'

Chapter 22

David and Bernie were walking happily to the shops. It was a nice morning, and they could hear the birds whistling as they walked past the tiny, wooded area near the railway bridge.

They laughed about the night before. They'd ended up dancing in the kitchen after their chippy supper, supping cans of lager from the winey.

'My fuckin head's banging,' David told her. 'Hey, it's good of Az to give you a chance. You'd better get it right this time lady. Just keep your head down, and if the floor needs sweeping, fucking sweep it Bernie.'

'I will David,' she smiled. 'I'm excited about this. Besides, Az is dead cute. I think he likes me.'

'Babe, don't be dipping your nib in the office ink,' he laughed. So did she, even though she had no idea what he was on about.

As they were approaching the block of shops, David's attention was turned by someone he knew coming out of the hardware shop. He ran over to him, leaving Bernie to cross the road that separated the two blocks. Just as he went to shout the guy's name, he heard an almighty bang, followed by a harrowing scream.

He turned around, with the feeling of dread in his stomach, and as he did, he saw a big black car speed off. He didn't even think to take the registration number. Then he saw Bernie lying on the floor, blood everywhere where she'd banged her head on the kerb.

'BERNNNIIIEEEE!' he wailed.

Someone had driven straight into her, sending her flying. They must have hit her hard because she was lying on the other side of the road, left for dead. He ran over to see how she was, as did a few other people, including Az.

'What the fuck,' he shouted loudly, 'phone an ambulance quick!'

The girls were all coming down from the hairdressers, and Sharon was shouting, 'get her a blanket; there's one upstairs in the salon. Quick!'

She sat down next to Bernie and tried to stop the blood running from her head. She stroked her head. 'Come on Bernie. Come on girl.'

It was that typical estate camaraderie. Everyone knew each other, and by God, if one of them was hurt, they all were there at once.

David ran to the phone box to phone his mother. He could see Sharon was with her and knew she was a good girl. His mother was there before he'd got back from the phone box, with a much-shaken Ann whose day couldn't possibly get any worse.

The ambulance was quick, thank God. Bernie was unconscious but breathing. Sharon had covered her up to keep her warm, and her girls were making David, Irene and Ann cups of sweet tea; it was the northern medicine for everything.

The paramedics were as fast as lightning. One made a hole in Bernie's back and attempted to blow up her lungs which must have collapsed. He was doing it with a pump whilst telling everyone to give them some space.

It was a sickening sight to see. The beautiful girl had never done anyone any harm and wouldn't hurt a soul, and yet, there she was, fighting for her breath.

David was pacing. He didn't know what to do with himself.

'I seriously can't believe this has happened,' he said to Az. 'Look at her, for fuck sake, who would fucking do that to her?'

He gave Az a fiver and said, 'can you get us some cigs mate?'

Irene was sobbing sat on the kerb next to her girl, stroking her head and talking to her. The paramedics were asking her not to move her in any way and not to upset her.

'Can you hear me our Bernie, its yer mam? Come on love, wake up. I need you Bern.' She looked up to the paramedic. 'Can we just take her home please? I just want to take her home. I'll look after her.'

'We're just going to get her comfortable, make sure her lungs are fully inflated and get her to the hospital,' he smiled.

They put Bernie in a neck brace and cleverly slid her onto a stretcher. She groaned somewhat, and Irene nearly dived on her.

'Step back love, I know it's hard, but we need to be really careful because she's got a head injury, and she might have a spine injury. So let us do our job and get her as comfortable as we can.'

David went over to where Ann was. She was in as much shock as he was. 'I'm sure it was her Ann – Susan; it was a big black car, but I'm sure it was her.'

'The police are here now. Let's tell them exactly what you saw love.'

'I didn't see fuck all, only heard the thud and our Bern scream.'

He started to cry.

'Come on love, you be brave for your mum'.

She put her arms around him, and they both stood hugging each other and crying. The ambulance men lifted Bernie into the ambulance, their blue lights were flashing, and they were getting ready to go.

The police were questioning everybody who was stood about, but they'd only just come out to help and hadn't seen anything.

Irene asked David to go in the ambulance with his sister, and she would get in the car with Ann and follow them to the hospital.

David climbed into the back of the ambulance and looked at his sister with a mask on her face to help her breathe. Her face looked squashed in the neck brace. There was blood all over, and they were trying to stop it from running in her eyes. They managed to put a patch on it to keep it at bay.

'Is she going to be ok?'

'I don't know mate. She's taken quite a knock,' he said. 'Her face is yellow, and both lungs were collapsed. I suspect she's broken her ribs when she fell onto the kerb, and they've cut her organs. So, let's see what they say when we get to the hospital.'

'Is she going to die?'

'I don't know mate,' he said again. 'Let's see what the doctors say. We'll do everything we can for her.'

David stared at his sister as they made the short

journey to the hospital. He wanted someone to tell him she'd be fine, that it was just a scratch.

'Come on our kid. Don't you fucking leave me. You really are the other half of me. I can't do this without you. Mum will break without you. I can't manage that without you girl. I can't cope. I need you Bern. Please, please don't leave me. I'll let you have the double room when we go back to the flat.'

He grabbed her hand and started stroking it. 'I don't think I've ever told you our Bern, but I love you so much, you know. We've been through everything together, and I've never thanked you for being my little sister. But thank you. I couldn't get anyone better. So please don't leave me yet. Let's get you right and get you back home. We will stay at mums until your right.'

The tears were falling down his face. He had no idea what the outcome was going to be. She couldn't die, she couldn't, he thought. But people did die every fucking day; why would they be any different. She really could die.

She was met at the hospital by a lot of white coats, and David was taken to the relative's room. Ann and Irene were not far behind him.

They were told she would need a CT scan to assess the internal damage. And that the cut would need looking at on her head, as she had lost a lot of blood.

They sat down in the relative room and drank cup of tea after cup of tea. There wasn't much conversation. David leant on the wall, and for the first time in his life, he prayed to God.

'I know we've never met big man, and I've

never even spoken to you before. But please leave her here with us. She's a good soul and doesn't have a harmful bone in her body. Go and get that fucking Susan Robinson or some pervert, but not her big man, not her.'

He cried silently and hoped and prayed until the young doctor came into the room.

'Hi guys, I'm looking for Bernadette Bates's mum. Is that you?' she asked Irene.

The cup in Irene's hand was shaking so much that Ann took it off her.

'I'm Doctor Parkinson, and I work on the trauma ward. I've been looking after your daughter.'

David was nervous.

'Bernadette has gained some sort of consciousness, and she's asking for you and for David. I take it that's you?' she smiled at David.

'She's had a CT scan, and she has a lot of damage to her internal organs. She has several broken ribs, and one of them has lacerated her liver. She is stable, but she is being transferred to our Intensive Care Unit. That means she will have the very best care and attention. That's what she needs right now. If you want to come with me, I'll take you to her so you can let her know you're here. Oh, we've stitched her face; she's had 16 stitches, so she will have a little scar.'

'Is she going to make it?' David asked the young doctor, and as he did, Irene put her face in her hands as though she didn't want to hear the answer.

'It's too early to tell,' she was careful how she answered him. 'All I can say is her kidneys are doing well, and that's a good sign, but we need to assess the liver damage. Come on, let's go and see her. We have given her a lot of pain relief; she's on a morphine pump, so she won't' be fully with it.'

They followed the young doctor to the Intensive Care Unit. The atmosphere was awful. The patients in there were really poorly, and all you could hear were the monitors that were keeping them all alive.

The young doctor took Irene and David to where Bernie's bed was. Ann waited just outside as there was only two allowed in at a time.

She looked so poorly with tubes coming out of every vein; God bless her. Her face had been cleaned up, but there was a lot of dried blood stuck in her hair. Her stitches were covered up, so you couldn't see them.

'Babe, you didn't have to do all this,' David whispered to her. 'You'll do owt for attention, you girl.'

Bernie smiled at her big brother. She grabbed his hand and winced in pain as she did so. Then she saw her mum on the other side of the bed and smiled with tears rolling down her face.

'Sorry mum,' her little voice was croaky, and she was slurring.

'Don't you be bleeding sorry love,' Irene was choking on her sobs. 'You've got nothing to be sorry for. But the bastard who did this will have something to be sorry for when I get my hands on them.'

'I'm going to be late for work now,' Bernie sobbed.

They laughed gently and said that she had nothing to worry about. Az had seen the whole thing, and he would keep her job open for her, but she just had to get better and get home where she belonged.

The nurse looking after Bernie said they needed to let her get some rest now, and they should go home and get some rest too. It had been a long day for them all, and they must be knackered.

The police were waiting for them outside with Ann.

David gave a statement and told them about the big black car and that he had a suspicion that it had belonged to Susan Robinson, but he couldn't be sure and that it was only a hunch.

They said they would look into it.

Chapter 23

The next few days were spent back and forth at the hospital, and as Bernie lay helpless and in pain in the Intensive Care Unit, David and Irene were by her side. Bernie was out of it due to the morphine drip that she needed to relieve the pain of the broken ribs and torn liver.

'Look at you,' David smiled gently at his sister, 'out of your bloody head, and you've not had to spend a bloody penny.'

She was responsive and certainly knew they were there; she would smile weakly and squeeze their hands.

Doctor Parkinson had been giving them daily updates. Today she seemed different.

'I need to talk to you both,' she said.

David and Irene looked at each other, and the fear on their faces said it all.

They all stepped out of earshot of Bernie.

'She's doing really well. We've scanned her again, and the tear in her liver seems to be healing on its own. But we need to make sure that the blood doesn't clot around it. It hasn't so far, and we're giving her warfarin to thin the blood. Her lungs are weak, so we're giving her a course of steroids to clear any infection and strengthen them. The pain she will be feeling will mainly be from the broken ribs, and as you know, there's not much we can do with broken ribs. They will hopefully heal naturally, but that will take some time. We're going to keep her with us for a couple of days and build up her strength. Then we will move her to a normal ward.'

'So, she's going to be ok?' David screamed and then realised where he was and quickly apologised for his loudness.

'Unless Bernie has a setback or that liver starts to bleed again, then yes, she's going to be ok, in a lot of pain but ok.'

David grabbed his mum and squeezed her so tight that she nearly had to be put on a ventilator, never mind Bernie.

He walked over to the bed. The tears were flowing again; he'd never cried so much in his bloody life.

'Right lady, you're getting leathered when you get out of here.' His usual banter returning but he was a lot gentler. 'Walking in front of a car, you daft cow.'

Bernie opened her eyes.

'Shut your bloody gob our David, you do my head in.'

He laughed and so did Irene. Their girl was going to be ok.

Later, back at the house, he and his mum were gabbing about the goings-on of the last few days. They had been put through the mill, and they were really feeling it. They were both emotionally drained, and fear had exhausted them.

'I wonder how Ann's getting on,' Irene said.

'God, I know,' he said. 'I wonder if she got their Andy to get little Jody back.'

'Give her a ring love and find out; she will want to know how our Bernie is anyway. Aw David, I'm so relieved she's getting better. I thought for a minute…'

'I know mum, so did I. That was awful. Shall we walk round to The Royal Oak and have a cheeky drink to celebrate? I'll ring Ann in the morning. There's nothing we can do, that they can't do, is there really?'

His celebratory drink suggestion was welcomed. 'I'll grab my coat; give us a minute.' Irene got up and started grabbing her jacket.

They walked in the dusky summer evening. David started to feel a bit paranoid, and as they walked, he was looking out for big black cars.

Every two minutes, he would jump nervously.

'I've got post-traumatic stress me mum. I'm a nervous wreck.'

'We've got to get over this,' she reassured her son.

When they got into the pub, all the girls from Kolash were sat in the corner, and they spotted them straight away. Sharon ran over to them and gave them a big hug.

How is she doing?' she asked and started to get teary-eyed and emotional. 'Aw, I've never seen anything like that. Is she ok?'

'She's broken several ribs, and when they broke, they've caught her liver, nearly cutting it in half, and as you know at the scene, her lungs collapsed. But guess what? Our girl is gonna be ok.'

The pub went into absolute uproar. People were cheering and screaming and grabbing David and Irene. Sharon was crying her eyes out. 'I really thought it would be bad news,' she sobbed.

For the rest of the night, they were treated like

royalty. They didn't put their hands in their pocket once.

Az joined them and asked politely if he could see Bernie in the next couple of days. He got upset and expressed his disbelief of the situation and said that he would never forget Bernie just lying there for the rest of his days.

Irene gave him a big hug and happily told him and the crowd that Bernie's first words were to tell her brother to shut his gob and that he was doing her head in. Everybody laughed with joy.

'Thank you all,' Irene was serious. 'You probably all helped to save her life; we'll never know.'

'Well, as soon as she's ready, get her to come to the shop, and we'll do your hair for you both. Come and have a pamper day on us; you both deserve a treat.' Sharon was wiping the black mascara that was running down her face.

'Errrrr? What about my hair?' David laughed. 'I deserve a treat too. It might have been me in that Intensive Care Unit today, and I wouldn't have made it. I'm fatter than her; I'd have had a fucking heart attack and carped it.'

Everyone screamed with laughter again.

'You can go to Fred's, the barbers on the other block,' laughed Sharon. 'Be careful you don't lose an ear though. He's lethal with those clippers.'

The banter was non-stop all evening.

Suddenly David spotted Sandra at the bar. She was with a bloke, and it wasn't Scott. He nudged his mum. 'Look at her,' he pointed to where she was stood.

'Oh aye,' who's that she's with?' Irene squinted

and was just as intrigued. They both watched them as they went and sat in a corner on their own. 'Bit cosy, aren't they?'

David couldn't stop looking. 'Where do I know him from?' he asked himself. 'He looks dead familiar.'

'Who is he mum?'

'I can't even see bloody Sandra me love. Never mind him.'

'God, I know his face, but I can't think where from. It'll come to me.'

And they carried on drinking.

But David being David couldn't let it go. He nearly screamed out loud as it dawned on him.

'It's him! The postman from the Yeti's house. Oh my god. It is. What's his name? Rob, it's Rob, the postman.'

He was about to run over but changed his mind. He decided to watch them instead.

In fact, he couldn't take his eyes off them.

They got up to leave. David shouted over to Az. 'You brought the car mate?'

Az nodded. 'Yeah mate, don't drink, do I? It's against my religion.'

'Come on,' David grabbed his jacket.

They both got out of their seats. Az could feel his pal's urgency. The way these people stuck together was beyond loyalty; it was a deep understanding of one another's needs. There wasn't always a need to explain, and at that moment, it was proven.

'Won't be a minute guys,' David let the crowd know he was bobbing out. He didn't let them know that they were going to do a follow.

'S'up?' Az asked David.

'So much has gone on mate. I even suspect our Bernie's accident was no accident, more like attempted murder. I think that Sandra from next door to my mum has got sommat to do with it. She was just in here with a bit of an odd choice. I want to know where they're going and what they're up to.'

'Right then, let's get off.' Az excited by the prospect, 'And if anyone has hurt your Bernie, I will have them sorted. I'm deadly serious man. Love that girl me.'

'You can love her all you want, but you'll never make a Muslim out of her mate. She likes her booze and bacon too much.'

Az laughed. 'We'll see.'

They saw Sandra and postman Rob getting into a car in The Royal Oak car park. It was a dark blue Ford Montego. She was all giggly, flicking her hair flirtatiously as he was opening the door for her. They sped off and did a left from the pub and another left at the traffic lights. Az was sharp in following them discreetly.

They looked like they were heading to the hospital, which was ok as you could get to Altrincham if you cut through the hospital. It wasn't ok though, when they turned into the hospital car park.

'What the fuck?' David said to Az. 'I'm paranoid now that they're going to see Bernie. Come on, let's get to the ICU quick.'

They parked up and ran through the Accident and Emergency department, following signs for the ICU.

When they got outside the ward, they had to buzz to get in. The nurse, or whoever it was that answered, told them it was a bit late and that Bernie already had a visitor.

David was having none of it.

'Who has she got visiting her? She doesn't know anybody but us. Can you let me in please? I'm worried that it's somebody it shouldn't be.'

The nurse reluctantly buzzed them both in.

'Wash your hands mate,' David told Az, 'and put a plastic apron on.'

As they approached her bed, David stopped dead in his tracks, unable to move.

She had a visitor alright. It was the fucking Yeti. What the hell was going on? He knew for sure now that she'd run his sister over.

'Watch her like a fucking hawk,' he told Az.

He ran back out of the room and into the waiting room, where he picked up the phone and dialled 999.

He went back to the ward where Az was watching like a hawk as instructed. He was stood near the sink and not near the bed but he had a good view.

'She's been talking to her,' he whispered.

'Has she now.'

David walked right up to her.

'What are you doing by my sister's bed?'

He was fierce with his hand on his hip.

'I've come to see my relative, she's also on this ward.'

'Well, my sister's not related to you, so you best move on. You don't fuckin' scare me.' He stared at her.

Bernie was uncomfortable and started getting restless. David was aware that she was getting upset.

'The police are on their way. I know you had something to do with this,' he said, pointing at his sister.

She laughed an evil cackle that must have been her theme tune because she was so good at it.

She proceeded to walk out of the ICU very quickly.

'What did she say to you babe?' he asked Bernie.

'She said she didn't mean it; she meant to hit you.'

David wasn't surprised but felt the sickness creeping into the pit of his stomach. His baby sister was lying here with several broken ribs, her liver cut in half, and two collapsed lungs, and it should have been him.

He gave her a kiss on her head and said, 'I've brought someone to see you babe.'

He beckoned for Az to come over. Az was emotional and became very shy.

'You still look beautiful Bernie. Hurry up and get better. I can't wait for you to get out of here.'

She grinned sheepishly. 'You look fit; I can't wait to get your kit off.'

They both started laughing, and David said, 'she's off her tits; ignore her.'

'Don't ignore me,' she pouted.

'Right, we're going to go girl,' her brother said. 'You take care, and if anyone comes who you don't recognise babe, tell the nurse immediately that you want them to leave. Do you hear me our Bern? I'm being serious.'

She nodded and closed her eyes. She was knackered.

David and Az sat in the waiting room and waited for the police to turn up. After half an hour, they called it a day, but David said he wasn't going to let it drop.

'She did it, Az. She's just told Bernie.'

'Are you sure mate? Bernie is drugged up to her eyeballs.'

'You're right, but I believe her. We've had a bit of a nightmare with that woman. She can't be trusted.'

'Come on, we might make last orders.' Az grabbed him gently.

As they were walking out, they bumped right into Rob the postman and Sandra.

'What the hell is going on here?' David jumped on them.

Sandra was totally lost for words. David told her that the police were on their way and that Bernie was under protection and that she'd better get the fuck out.

'I've got your number snakey fucking Sandra. Stay away from my family. You've had something to do with this right from the start. Where the hell is Julie, I know you know?'

She said nothing but spun on her heels, linked the postman's arm and steamed off down the hospital corridors. David had never seen her move so quickly. There was definitely some sort of mystery going on. He was dying to find Julie. He made his mind up to try the London number again as soon as he got in.

'Come on mate, let's go and get that last pint. I

bet my mum is out of her bleeding head.'

The pub landlord shouted last orders, and as was the rule, they all doubled up.

Singing and dancing and generally happy, everybody exited the pub.

Az was the local taxi and charged people for lifts, but he dropped Irene and David off home first, for free. Then went back to make his butty for the night.

As soon as they got in the house, David rang the London number.

'Hello,' came the foreign accent.

'Hello. It's David. Julie's mate.' David was excited and felt like he'd had some sort of breakthrough. 'All I'm going to say is this is getting serious. Susan Robinson has Jody. Julie needs to come home now and get her daughter. Social Services are involved.'

The silence on the other end of the line was enough. David could hear the cogs turning loudly, even through the handset of the phone.

'Ok, thank you,' came the reply.

David put the phone down, knowing it would get sorted.

He picked up the phone and rang Ann.

'2747', she was grumpy.

'It's David, Ann. Sorry it's so late. Two things. Bernie is going to be ok, and I've made contact with the guy in London. They know about little Jody, so I'm sure we will now see movement.'

'Oh, thank god on both accounts,' she said. 'I just want my little baby back.'

He wanted to tell her about Susan being at the hospital but didn't want to worry his mum, who was in earshot. He would sort that out tomorrow.

After the phone call to Ann, he made another call.

'Alright Az? You free tomorrow? I have something I need to do. Will you pick me up at nine o'clock please?'

He put the phone down and picked it back up.

'Alright Scott? I need you mate. Can you be at mine for nine o'clock tomorrow morning? Yeah mate, she's going to be ok; it's our Bernie Scott; it'd take more than a four be four to wipe her out mate.' He laughed and put the phone down with a quick, 'see you at nine.'

'Where you going?' Irene asked him.

'I'm going to get Jody. I'm not scared of that woman. I know she is extremely dangerous, but I'm going to get that baby for Julie and Ann even if it kills me.'

I sat frozen to the spot as I heard them coming up the stairs. I had no idea who *they* were or what they wanted with us. Did they have guns? Were they some sort of crazy gangsters? My heart was in my mouth. I had my back to the stairs and couldn't for the life of me turn my head round to look. I felt safer not looking. Instead, I looked straight at Fiona, who was in the same predicament. She hadn't diverted her eyes from mine.

'Fiona?' came a voice from behind me.

A look of relief took over Fiona's face. I felt the same relief because I just knew it was ok; it was someone she knew.

'Dad,' she shouted and scrambled up off the floor. She grabbed my hand to take me with her. I got up, spun around and saw her dad, the Native American (who obviously wasn't a Native American at all), with two other men. They just stood there and said nothing. They didn't look like they were to be messed with though.

She ran over to him sobbing, explaining that someone had been in the house earlier and that we'd been in the safe room for hours.

'They've gone now, and they won't be back. It's a good job I came home when I did. Are you girls ok?'

I just nodded my head. I was so relieved that it was him and no one wanting to kill us. I've never been so frightened in my life. Well, I had, but that was scary.

We all left the safe room and went through my bedroom, down the long hall and down the stairs. Somewhere I'd not even been yet.

I thought about Jody and needed to check in at some point. Although I was confident that she was safe and sound with Ann.

The kitchen we ended up in was huge, with a great big island in the middle that had a marble top and stunning huge brass taps. The floors were stone and cold on my feet.

I wondered what would happen next, but after what had just gone on, I was still dumbfounded and in some sort of shock, so I was happy to go with the flow right now.

The two men who were accompanying Fiona's dad had retired to the lounge. Fiona was still visibly shaken, and her dad was trying to reassure her, even joking about the situation to make her feel better. She smiled sullenly and got some wine from the fridge. It was early evening and a warm night, but I was shivering.

I told them that I needed to go and put my jumper on and some socks as I felt cold. They both smiled warmly; their smiles were exactly the same.

I was comfortable. In fact, I had bonded massively with Fiona and was really grateful for the conversation that we'd had. It had certainly lifted something from inside me.

I ran upstairs, looking through the huge windows as I did. I saw Jane in my reflection as I always did and smiled with tears in my eyes. God, I missed her.

I went into the bedroom and grabbed the carrier bag that was hanging off the chair. There was a jumper in it and some socks, along with the rest of the shite I'd grabbed.

I looked under the great big pine unit for my case, and it wasn't there. I didn't understand. I know I had put it there. I searched the bedroom, but it had definitely gone, and I wondered if Fiona had moved it.

As I approached the kitchen, I could smell food, and my stomach growled with hunger. We hadn't eaten for ages.

We all sat down and ate. It was all quite official, and I wondered when someone would tell me what was going on.

And as if he read my mind, Fiona's dad spoke.

'By the way, Julie, my name is Ron, and I have a lot to tell you, but let's eat up first. You girls must be starving.'

'Hi Ron,' I replied. 'This has been a crazy time for me, so I'm extremely interested to understand everything that's gone on.'

I asked Fiona if she'd moved my case. I was starting to relax a little now.

'No,' she answered. 'I put it under the pine dresser for you.' She looked perturbed.

'It's gone.'

Ron got up quickly and went to the other room to speak to the two men.

When he came back, he asked me if I knew what was in the case.

'Just some clothes.'

'Ok.' He shook his head, confused.

We carried on eating the lovely dinner that he'd ordered and had brought in. I was starving and must have looked like a pig shovelling down the food and not coming up for air. Then with a glass of wine, we retired to the big, beautiful lounge.

'Sit down,' Ron said. 'I'm going to tell you everything. Well, everything I know anyway. This will help you understand why you're here and why we needed to protect you.'

I sat down, staring at him intently as he started his story.

'My brother owns The New Cottage in London. The gentleman who ran it for him was running some other seedy businesses on the side. One of them was luring in women for sex. His name is John. He is no longer allowed to run this type of business as he no longer works for us. My brother put a firm stop to it.'

I felt a bit embarrassed and looked at Fiona, who shook her head as if to say, it didn't matter.

'Of course, we now know that you answered the advert to meet John, and it's fine, let's forget that. It doesn't matter. What does matter is that by pure coincidence, or maybe not, we were alerted that you were on your way. We put John straight and told him who you were, so of course, he wasn't interested, or more like he was afraid as he didn't want to be messing with you or, should I say, us.'

I was confused but continued to just listen.

'We sent Pavel to meet you. He's not the brightest spark and was meant to just put you off, give you the money and send you back home. Of course, there was an altercation between the two of you because the daft bastard can't string two sentences together and got the whole thing wrong. You got very drunk and were found wandering the streets of London out of your head.

'We've since found out that another gang were following you and had your drink laced with a drug called Rohypnol. which is a date rape drug. Luckily, we got to you in time, and you got home safely. We needed to talk to you, but we couldn't get near you. For there is a person who is very much involved in your life, who watches your every move. Even worse than that, she arranges for you to be drugged. She is our arch-enemy, Susan Robinson. We all have this in common.'

I flinched at the name. 'My mum.'

'Yes, your mum. Your mum has been watching you like a hawk Julie, and she is in deep with some very bad people and involved with drugs on a large scale. She is a sociopath and a dangerous woman. She has the big boys eating out of her hand because she can get them good drugs in huge quantities and does the best deals.

'She has convinced them that me and my brother are after her blood, and they've become very protective. It meant that we had to stay in London meeting with people we don't want to be involved in and trying to convince them that their Queen Bee is a perpetual liar and sociopath. We couldn't get to Manchester, and then the monster planted a shit load of cocaine on us, and we all got arrested, including poor Pavel, who is still none the wiser. You have something that she needs, and I'm not sure what it is, but God, she needs it because she's not let up about it. I'm now convinced it was in your suitcase.'

There was nothing in my suitcase, only my

clothes. I shook my head in disbelief.

'Anyway, I tracked you down because we wanted to give you money regularly until we could catch up with you in person. I didn't approach you as I knew that your every move was being monitored. So I approached your neighbour Sandra who I thought could be trusted. You seemed to be friends. I gave her a stash of envelopes with five hundred pounds in and asked her to post one through your door once a week. Then you phoned Pavel and told him you kept getting sent two hundred pounds. I realised she must have been stealing from us.

'I grabbed her one evening and gave her the fright of her life. I hadn't realised until then what Susan had promised her and her boys in exchange for destroying your life. She was frightened and told me that in the next day or so they were planning to come to your flat for you. She wasn't sure what they were going to do, but she knew something, and it was enough. We got you in the nick of time.'

I sat there in shock at the thought of Sandra involved in all this. To try and destroy my life? That wasn't exactly a bed of roses. My god.

I couldn't even find any words to respond to him. I bet he thought I was a bit thick. I just sat with my mouth wide open and hadn't taken one sip of my wine.

'I have been following you to make sure you've been safe. I'm sorry if I frightened you, I'm not a professional, and you saw me a couple of times.' He laughed out of embarrassment.

'I suspect that Susan knows you are here, and that's why she sent people round earlier. Of course, she knows we were all arrested in London because she arranged that too.'

He was obviously conscious of my silence, but I was trying to absorb the whole thing.

'We do need to get out of here and drive to London for a couple of days. Our solicitors have given the police a lot of detail, and Susan will be under surveillance now. She can't continue to go around destroying people's lives. It's nearly over, but in the meantime, you need to make a decision. Do you want us to get Jody so that she can come, or is she ok where she is?'

I was missing my daughter now incredibly. After the conversation with Fiona, I'd grown so much, and after hearing all this, I felt a massive need for her for the first time. But I needed to think of her, she was at home with her loving family, and it wouldn't be good for her to be dragged across the country to be with a load of strangers.

'No, I want her to stay where she is. She is loved and safe,' I whispered.

'You're coming with us too,' he said to Fiona. 'It's not safe here, not until she's been arrested.'

'Yes, that's fine. I wouldn't want to stay here, but are you missing something out here dad. Because I've just put two and two together, and I'm waiting for you to say it, but you haven't.'

'I don't understand,' he rubbed his chin as though he was in deep thought.

'Why do you both have Susan Robinson as an arch-enemy? What have you all got in common with Julie? She has no idea!'

I was feeling exhausted at this point but had

wondered myself how it was all connected.

He stood up.

'Julie, my brother is Steve Robinson. He's your dad. And you're going to meet him very soon.'

I dropped the wine on the floor and looked at them both. I saw it. I knew it. I felt it.

'And Pavel is his son?' I asked. My hands were trembling, and my mouth had dried up.

'Yes, your dopey brother is Pavel,' he grinned affectionately. 'Your dad was married briefly before Susan. They had Pavel, who stayed in Europe with his mother until about ten years ago, and he's lived with your dad ever since. Now he will meet his daughter again, and Pavel will meet you again, under quite different circumstances to last time. Your dad has so much to explain Julie, but he has loved you every single day since you parted.'

He went on.

'My brother is a man of strength, but that woman has bullied him for most of his life. It's an obsession, and she clearly loves him; she just has a funny way of showing it.'

I was crying now and felt a huge bellow of relief flowing through my body. I felt that I'd come home. I was here with my actual family. They both hugged me, and I could smell the familiarity in them both.

Before I knew it, we were packing up and heading for the big black luxurious car and then to London.

I phoned Ann before I left. This time I didn't have Fiona breathing down my neck because, of course, I was free, and I was using my uncle's phone. It was fine.

Pete answered. I asked if Jody was ok. 'Yep,' he replied, 'not sure where they all are now, but they were ok when I left this morning.'

I smiled and felt reassured.

Fiona and I got into the back of the car and she snuggled up to me. 'Hey, you're actually my big cousin,' she grinned from ear to ear.

I smiled back and felt the warmth in my stomach. I knew I had a connection with her, or I wouldn't have opened up like that. The jigsaw was coming together, and now I was going to see my dad again. I couldn't wait.

Chapter 25

It was late in the evening when we arrived in London. It wasn't easy to drive in the city as the traffic was never-ending. I listened to the horns beeping aggressively at one another, and truck drivers scream profanities to each other.

They seemed to drive a lot faster than we did in the North, and it took my breath away as Ron weaved through the traffic with ease. Each and every time felt like a near miss.

I looked out of the windows and enjoyed seeing the people in their summer clothes, enjoying drinks sat outside. Restaurants were full to the brim, and people were carrying large bags of shopping. Late night shopping in London looked like a thrill.

The city was alive. The atmosphere was buzzing as we passed the big red and blue signs that indicated the underground. As the crowds were coming out of the stations, just as many were piling in. It was amazing to think that there were probably as many people underneath us as there were on ground level with us.

I started to feel nervous, as I knew we would be soon approaching The New Cottage, and half of me wished that we were still on the motorway with two hours to go. I didn't think I was ready. What was I going to say to him? What would he say to me? And then there was Pavel. I sat back and thought about all the conversations we'd had.

He had really frustrated me, like a big brother should I suppose. Then I cringed at all the sex talk. Jesus, he must have thought that I was some sort of lunatic. Then I forgave myself because I had been really affected by my mother, and actually, it was no wonder after all that woman put me through. After seeing my twin sister die and then be blamed for it. All those years of wishing I'd saved her. Then to be subjected to the men that wanted sex against my will. It felt wrong to enjoy it, but even that was probably the impact of the abuse. So I forgave myself again.

I sat in the back of that car and forgave myself for lots of other things, including throwing boiling water on her face. It was one of the hardest things to think about. For as much as I despised the woman, it was a dreadful thing to do. Her reaction never left my mind. I shook my head to clear it.

It was wrong, and I should have walked away from her cackle, but I didn't. I believe our paths are chosen, and it was meant to be. Nothing could have prevented it, and there was definitely no way of going back. I promised that I would be kinder to myself. Because no matter who comes into your life, the only relationship that lasts forever is the one you have with yourself, and I was going nowhere, so I needed to love me.

We were approaching a car park. I hadn't been concentrating and didn't recognise where we were. I assumed we were at the back of The New Cottage. I felt sick.

As Ron was parking up the car, I really did think I would be sick.

'I'm going to faint,' I told Fiona. I went hot and dizzy, and everything around me became surreal like.

She felt my head. 'Gosh, you're hot. You are anxious. It's natural. Close your eyes and take some deep breaths,' she said. 'We are in no rush. Can you hear me, Julie?'

I heard Ron ask if I was ok, and there was silence as they waited for me to get my composure.

I took a few more deep breaths, opened my eyes. 'Let's do this.'

Ron helped me get out of the back of the car. He was gentle with me. 'Come on darling,' he said. 'I promise it's going to be ok.'

We walked into the pub. It was reminiscent of the last time I was there. I could smell the smell. I looked around, consciously looking for my father, who in my head was a distant memory. I'm sure I would know him when I saw him.

They took me behind the bar and up the stairs that led to the living quarters. I tried to swallow my gulp, but my mouth was dry.

We approached a closed door, and I imagined him sitting on a couch with a suit on and wondered if he still had black hair. His brother certainly did. I wondered if Pavel would be here with him.

Ron handed me a sleep mask. I stopped dead in my tracks and suddenly went extremely hot.

'Just joking.' He smiled, but I didn't smile back. His joke triggered a creeping doubt, and I felt uncomfortable.

He opened the door, and I walked in behind him. He smiled at me and gestured with his arms towards a couch where Susan Robinson sat, surrounded by three or four men in black coats.

The heat enveloped my body, and my legs turned to hot jelly as I fell to the floor in shock.

When I woke up, I was still in the back of the car, soaking wet with fear and trepidation. I was confused and delirious.

Fiona had got a damp cloth and was mopping my brow tentatively, and Ron was looking concerned.

I realised that I had fainted or had some kind of fit. What had just happened was just a dream. It was ok after all. I was ok.

There was a commotion outside the car. I could hear it because the car door was open, giving me fresh air.

I heard the shout.

'Is she ok, Ron? Is she ok?'

I heard him. I felt him. I wanted him so much. I got out of the car weakly, still shaken, but found the strength to run at him.

I collapsed into his arms sobbing whilst he held me hard, squeezing life back into me. The familiar smell; I could have been blindfolded, and I would have known that smell. I might have fainted again if he hadn't let go. But let go he did, and then I saw him. I saw the tears in his eyes. The same tears he'd cried when I was five years old. I saw his beautiful sparkly green eyes and his greying hair, but it was him. After looking at my face for a full five minutes, he pulled me to him again, and I was enveloped once again by that smell. I was crushed by his strength and by the strong arms that were my dad's.

We both sobbed for a moment, just staring at each other. Then it dawned on me and hit me like a freight train. It was him. The businessman off the train. It was Phil, the man who rescued me from the bus the last time I was here. Of course, he was in it with the Native American. Of course, they saved me. They were my family.

I looked over to Fiona and Ron, who were sobbing just as hard as we were. None of us could speak.

I heard more noise in the car park, and there he was – Pavel. My brand-new big brother. I ran over to him, and we hugged.

'Do you still want sex with me?' he jested. I laughed out of embarrassment and briefly thought of the inappropriate thoughts I'd had about him.

'I'm sorry,' I said. 'I didn't even fancy you. You're bloody ugly.'

We all laughed and walked into the pub where a great big glass of red was waiting for me.

'You're just having one lady,' Pavel winked. His beautiful blue eyes twinkled as he joked with me.

I sat snuggled up to my dad. He still had tears in his green eyes.

'I have so much to explain to you, my darling girl.'

'Dad, you really don't. I understand, and you have nothing to explain at all.'

'I want to,' he smiled. 'I left you behind with that monster.'

'Dad, you really don't,' I said it again. 'I know why, and I forgive you. I've never doubted you, honestly. I always knew you wouldn't have had a choice. It was horrendous, but I knew if you could, you would have saved me. So please don't beat yourself up anymore. We have the rest of our lives together now. Let's not focus our energy on the past. Let's move forward together.'

He grabbed me again.

'You're your daddy's girl alright. Cut from the same cloth,' he said. 'Thank God,' he laughed.

'I'll drink to that,' Pavel raised his glass. 'At least you're nothing like her.'

They all laughed, but I missed the joke until Ron whispered, 'He hasn't even met her, so he doesn't even know what he's talking about.'

I loved the banter between them and was happy to be part of it.

As I sat there sipping my red wine, I wondered what was next. Then I decided that if you plan your path step by step, it's not your path. You will be directed, and it will be chosen for you, so the outcome couldn't be controlled. It would just happen. I was going to go with it and believed it was all going to be ok.

We sat, and we talked for hours and hours. Dad and I tried to reminisce the best we could, but it was difficult. Unfortunately, there weren't very many good times, and it hurt because if there was, Jane was with us. We also talked about the future. Pavel and I had a banter, and amidst it all, Fiona and I smiled at each other. I would never forget our unspoken bond and loved her with all my heart. They say blood is thicker than water, and right now, I believed that to be the case.

Pavel locked the pub up for the night. We all trooped upstairs.

'Anyone hungry?' My dad asked. No one was. I

couldn't have eaten anything; I was too excited.

I was shown to my room for the night. Outside the door, my dad held me again as though it was the last time he would ever see me. He said that he would be there in the morning and every single morning to come. As I shut the door behind me, I threw myself onto the luxurious bed and let out all my tears. They were tears of joy and relief, but I sobbed and I sobbed.

I wasn't going to sleep, even though I had exhausted myself. My head was in overdrive, even more than ever before.

I closed my eyes for a second and thought about my little Jody. She had a brand-new family: her granddad, her uncle Pavel. I smiled when I thought about him. His character matched those phone calls. I thought he was being standoffish, but really, he hadn't had a clue bless him, but I already loved him for it.

She would have a great uncle Ron and a big cousin, Fiona. I felt so excited and wanted her here with me now. I just knew that my life was going to be different from now on. I already had a sense of belonging, a sense of being someone.

I heard a phone ringing. It didn't sound far from my room. Maybe the office was nearby, but it sounded loud, like the old bell phones. I didn't think much more of it as I lay there reminiscing and feeling overwhelmed by the evening and the whole thing.

Not long after, there was a knock on my door.

'Come in,' I shouted as I sat up and switched on the little lamp beside my bed.

It was Pavel. He wasn't sure what to do with himself.

'I'm not having sex with you,' I laughed. Knowing, of course, that he hadn't come into my room for sex.

He sat down on the end of my bed.

'What's up, big bro?' I asked him. He smiled, but he looked serious.

'That was David on the phone. She's got Jody, Julie. Susan has got Jody.'

I didn't know how many times I could survive the feeling of dread that was running through my body yet again. But this time, it came with a surge of strength. This was no time to go under. It was time to draw in on my inner power and get her back and get her back now.

'I want to go back to Manchester right now,' I said to my brother.

'They're all drunk,' Pavel reminded me.

'Then get me a taxi. I'm going now to get my daughter. I'm going to break down her door and get my baby girl from that monster.' I had to stop myself from thinking of what she could do to Jody.

'I can't let you go all alone.'

'Then come with me,' I ordered him. 'Let's get a cab to the train station and jump on the next train.'

'You're a nightmare. Can't we just wait until the morning?' He was pleading now.

'Pavel, Jody is with the woman who abused me all my life. She abused a grown man, our father, and she killed my twin sister. I can't wait until morning. Please, we need to go now.'

'Ok then. I'll leave them a note for the morning, so they don't' think we've done a runner.'

We both agreed to go and get dressed and meet on the landing in twenty minutes.

'Be quick, please,' I begged.

Twenty minutes later, we were ready to go. He guided me out through the back door, and we went onto Finchley Road, where we hailed a black cab.

'Euston Station,' Pavel instructed.

I looked through the streets of London again, but this time with a huge knot in my stomach.

'I hope she's ok?' I whispered to Pavel in the back of the taxi.

'She will be sis,' he smiled. 'She will be.'

Chapter 26

It was approaching one o'clock in the morning by the time we arrived at Euston station.

There were no trains to Manchester for another couple of hours. I couldn't believe it; I hadn't anticipated any sort of delay.

We sought out a coffee shop just outside the station, and I ordered a cup of coffee, but Pavel wanted a cup of tea. I smiled inwardly at the irony. I thought only the northerners loved a cup of tea.

The radio was playing loudly in the kitchen, and as Blondie sang, 'oh, your hair is beautiful.' I marvelled at the speed of the waitress as she served us her wares. Apron on and cig in her mouth, she never batted an eyelid. She had no interested in us whatsoever.

We found a seat so we could sip our drinks in peace. I chose to sit near the window so I could watch the hub and the bub of the world outside. It comforted me, and I needed comforting right now.

The area around the station was still really busy, and there seemed to be no slowing it down.

I watched as the late-night stragglers hung about the train station. There were homeless people in cardboard boxes, which they'd made a makeshift shelter from. They were begging for money with little tin cups or a cap turned upside down. I felt sorry for them, we didn't see as many in Manchester, so it fascinated me.

'I can't settle,' I told Pavel.

'I can imagine,' he said.

This was really weird. Here I was sat with "John". John, who I had phoned to meet in London for submissive sex. John, who I called when I was pissed up, who I abused because he didn't want any sex, never mind submissive sex. And now it all added up. I looked at him and still thought he was beautiful, and I still loved his accent.

'Hey, so when I first called and spoke to John from the phone box, was that not you?'

I suddenly remembered the brief dirty talk we'd had and realised that it couldn't have been him.

'Did Ron not tell you the story?' he responded.

'Yes.'

'So, you know it wasn't me.'

'Well…' I wanted to explain myself but couldn't be arsed.

It had all shifted. He was my big brother, and I kept shaking my head at the whole idea of him. He didn't look like my dad, but there was definitely a resemblance to myself and dad. But it was deeper than just looking like us; he was part of us. I felt it.

I sipped my coffee from the little white cup that came with a saucer. It always tasted better from a shop.

'I wonder what happened.' I thought out loud as if Pavel might know. 'I know how protective Ann is over Jody. What did David actually say?' I asked. 'In fact, how did he even get your number?'

'David has phoned me before, looking for you,' Pavel smiled softly.

I was gobsmacked. I thought about it and realised what he'd said on the phone about the flat being vandalised. They must have gone up and found it in a state. Thinking back, I was so delirious after the phone call with Pavel that I don't think I locked the door. They must have found Pavel's phone number, even though I was convinced I'd picked it up.

'Of course, even though I knew he would worry,' Pavel's accent was reverting back to his native tongue, probably because he was knackered, 'I couldn't speak about you. But really, he did worry. And then last night, because I think he knew you were with me – he is very clever. He just said, "this is serious now. Susan Robinson has Jody." He knew I hadn't kidnapped you, and he knew you were with me. He wanted to get you the message Julie.'

I sighed and felt tears in my eyes. That lad was so bloody loyal, and it sounded like he'd been looking for me. He was definitely my good friend. When all this was over, I would be giving him and Bernie the biggest hug. First, I needed to get my baby back.

'Did you leave a note for Dad?' I asked Pavel.

'Oh no, I forgot!' he said. He really was daft, but he was harmless, and he was here with me now, so I was grateful.

'Shit, they will panic when they wake up Pavel.' I was genuinely concerned that they would wake up and think that I'd done a runner.

'I will call dad as soon as the time is reasonable.'

'Where are you from? What's your story?' I asked him, smiling. It dawned on me as he smiled back that our smiles were identical. It really was weird.

'Dad was working in Germany and met my mother. The story is long and boring,' he said. 'You know boy meets girl and all that palaver? My mother was young and moved back to be with her parents to the East of Europe when I was a very tiny baby. So originally, I am German with an Eastern European name. Dad must have returned to England and met your mother and settled into life here. Years later, he returned, looking for my mother, who he had never forgot.' 'No wonder.'

'Yes, but unfortunately, my mother was now happily married to my stepfather with two other children. However, they all agreed that it would be in my best interest to get to know my biological father. It was nice because we met properly for the first time, and he wanted a relationship and to pay towards my upkeep. I was about fifteen when I started to visit him in England for many years until it was time to move here and live with him permanent.'

He paused as though he was thinking carefully of what to say next.

'Apparently, when your mother found out about me, she went ballistic, and our poor father paid for it dearly. He has a scar on his arm where she tried to stab him with a knife.'

'My god.' I was shaking my head, but I wasn't surprised.

'I think after Jane died, our dad couldn't take anymore and had to leave her. She probably had a massive say in it also. He has always had many regrets for leaving you. To a point, it's made him ill.'

I shook my head and couldn't believe how a person could make another person feel so bad. Absolutely awful.

'What do you mean, ill?' I was worried instantly for my dad. I couldn't cope, having just got to know him and then something be dreadfully wrong with him.

He is on medication for his nerves, he explained.

'She's vile,' I spat.

'She is coming from a place of fear.'

'She's a twat.'

'What makes her a twat though?'

I laughed, 'I don't know, nor do I care, and it's not for us to sit and analyse. I just need to get my baby away from her.'

'No wonder you have issues.' He was deadly serious.

I looked at him, and I laughed.

'You're obsessed with my issues. Yes, I've got issues, is it any fuckin' wonder?'

'No,' he deadpanned me. 'Not really.'

I rolled my eyes at him and stared out of the window, sipping my coffee. I saw Jane in the reflection through the coffee shop window and then felt guilty. I hadn't looked for her in a few days, but to be fair, there had been a lot going on. I tried to smile at her, but she looked stressed and tired. I couldn't muster the energy, not even for her.

I thought about my journey without her and suddenly felt sad for her as I often did. I gulped my coffee down and looked again through the window. I looked her straight in the eye through the reflection and, in my mind, asked her to look after Jody until I got there.

I felt really tired now, and my vision was becoming blurry. I chased the little flickers of lights that were in my eyes by blinking them away. They were making me feel a bit dizzy.

Four coffees later, I was as high as a kite but knackered all at the same time. Pavel was bearing up but wasn't far behind me.

'Come on,' he said, 'it must be time to get the train. At least we can sleep for a few hours.'

Twenty minutes later, we were on the London to Glasgow train calling at many other stations, one of them being Manchester Piccadilly.

The train was comfy, and the high seats were relaxing.

Pavel sat near the window, and I sat in the aisle seat. I would be too claustrophobic sat squashed by the window. I like to stretch my legs, but for now, I had them curled up in front of me.

I looked at the seats ahead of me; some were facing us. I couldn't cope with staring at someone for the next three hours, so I went to close my eyes. Then I saw something I could have actually stared at for three hours.

He was dark, he was handsome. He gave me the look, and I was immediately worried that he would think Pavel was my husband.

I had visions of meeting him in the toilets halfway through the journey and...

'I actually know what you're thinking,' Pavel nudged me in the arm.

'Ouch,' I said, rubbing my elbow.

'Jody,' he reminded me.

'Jesus, don't you think I know that,' I hissed.

'You were planning to meet him in the toilet to show him your clock.'

I burst out laughing.

'You were?'

'I was, but it's gone now, thanks to you.'

We had such a strong connection that he could read my mind.

I leant my head on my arm and snuggled up to him. The noise of the train whirring around in my brain, the rhythm of the wheels meeting the track. The occasional sound of movement and the odd cough in the carriage. The dimmed lights made me feel so sleepy.

The guard was coming up the carriage, so I got our tickets ready. He silently clipped them. I closed my eyes and tried to think of good things because even though I knew there was a battle ahead of me, I knew I would win. I would kill to get my girl back.

I pictured her little face when she met her granddad and her uncle. What would happen? Would we leave the flat because things would now drastically change? Then I thought of David and how I wanted him and Bernie in my life and how I don't think I could leave Irene without me as a neighbour. But there I was, trying to control my path again. I had to go with the moment, and it would all fall into place.

I thought of the last couple of days. Telling my story to Fiona while being hidden in a safe room, with potential murderers let loose in the house. Then being rescued by my uncle, driving to London to meet my father and brother and now back again. I was absolutely exhausted beyond belief.

I heard Pavel snore loudly and jump as he did so. We both laughed quietly but not for long. A deep sleep took over us both.

And we snored and slept and didn't move an inch until we arrived... in Glasgow.

David woke up early; he had quite a day ahead of him. He had to do something to help Julie, and that was to get Jody back. He knew that as much as Ann loved her, she didn't have the wherewithal to do anything about it. She was waiting for Julie to come back, but something untoward was going on with Julie, he was sure about that, and he knew it probably had something to do with the mother.

He was expecting Scott and Az to be there at 9 o'clock. Despite their faults, they were loyal to the core. It was the estate law; if one of you was in some sort of trouble, you'd all muck in.

He sat and waited for them, sipping his beloved cup of tea. He'd only had three up to now, so he had a few more to go before he could fully function. He thought about his flat. Although David didn't live with Irene full time, he might as well have done lately. Him and Bernie had grown up in that house, so they enjoyed the homely welcoming feeling. Irene would never be free of them. Nor would she want to be.

He shared his flat with Bernie. It was on the other side of the estate, but they were never there, and because Bernie had come out of work, the social was paying for it anyway. David didn't even have his name down on it. He thought long and hard about that. He decided once things had settled here and Bernie was better, they needed to get back in it before some fucker reported them and they had it taken off them. Council flats were precious commodities, and it was dead man's shoes getting one these days.

His thoughts focused back to today. He knew he could rely on the lads, and he had a plan. He'd been up half the night thinking about it, but he had a plan.

There was a part of him that also wanted to put that bitch in her place. He knew she'd ran over Bernie, and even though Bern was off her tits, she'd said as much. Why would she say that if it wasn't true, and what the fuck had Susan Robinson been doing visiting Bernie? And that snide Sandra was obviously involved in all this somehow? He couldn't get his head around it.

But he had got his head around his plan, and he was excited to execute the fucker.

Irene came downstairs yawning and pulling at her dressing down.

'What time have you been up since, our David?' she asked him, rubbing her eyes.

'Wasn't too early, about half six.' He held out his empty mug. 'Go on then, I'll have another, seeing as you're asking.' The cheek never left him.

'I didn't say a fucking word; you're a cheeky sod.' She grabbed his cup off him.

'I'm going to the hospital after,' she explained. 'They'll be moving our Bernie today. I want to be with her, so I can check what's going on and see where they're moving her to.'

'The milk will be out of date by the time you get that brew done.'

'I'm going. I was only telling you about our Bern.'

'I know about our Bern, mum. I was stood next

to you when the doctor was telling you.' He rolled his eyes and shook his head. 'Off your head you.'

The knock on the door stopped any response from Irene's ever-ready mouth. And sure as anything, Scott and Az were at the door.

'That'll be two more brews then mum.'

Irene didn't have to be told twice and headed into the kitchen. She switched on the little portable telly that Az's brother had managed to get her from the cash and carry. It was a belter and her pride and joy. She loved watching the morning telly and doing her brew. She only had to pay Az's brother a couple of quid a week. She would just cut down on the cigs, she thought, as she bent down and lit the one in her mouth on the cooker.

'Do you want me to do some toast? Have you got time?' she called.

'Yeah, go on mum, ta,' David replied, thinking of his stomach as usual.

He was busy telling the lads what had gone on, even though they already knew about Bernie. He explained that they needed to get Jody back because she really was in the hands of a madwoman.

The plan was for Scott to go in and seduce her. David had done a bit of asking about and knew that Susan Robinson worked on word of mouth and that more or less anybody could turn up. The woman was a sex maniac.

'I'm not shagging her,' Scott shook his head. 'Fuck that.'

'All you need to do is somehow get in, get her to the back of the house, and I'll nip in and run upstairs and get Jody.'

Az laughed. 'Listen James Bond, it's not gonna be that simple, say the kid isn't even upstairs?' David laughed back. 'That's where you come into it. You'll have to fuckin' look for her downstairs while he's giving the Yeti one.'

'The Yeti?' Scott gulped. 'Is she a big girl, this Susan Robinson bitch?'

'You'll see.' David kept his smile inward, he didn't want to tell Scott too much, or his plan would be shot to hell.

They supped their brews and wolfed down toasted Warby's bread with real butter on. You'd never tasted proper toast until you'd tasted Irene's.

'Right,' David stood up and handed his mum his cup and plate. 'Let's get this party on the road. Tough puff and fuckin' Laurel and Hardy.'

They all burst out laughing, and off they went.

'Be careful,' Irene shouted after them.

They got into Az's car.

'Right, just before we get to the house, you're gonna have to swap over, and Az and me will duck down so she can only see you,' David said, giving out orders to his comrades.

It wasn't long before they were approaching Lymm and nearing their destination.

David was panicking and said that maybe they should pull over and swap seats.

'You said outside the house, mate,' Az reminded him.

'Yeah, I need a cig now, don't I? Pull up so I can open the door and have a quick drag of one.'

'I don't believe you,' Az said. 'You're such a pussy. We're nearly there; I thought you was in a hurry to get little Jody man.'

He shook his head as he pulled over, allowing David to have his much-needed cig.

'Right, I'll level with you. She's not an easy woman, so yeah, I could shit in me knickers right now.' He was deadly serious.

'Aright,' Scott said. 'Keep your knickers on, and don't be shitting in them, for fucks sake. And hurry up because if you think you're shitting your knickers, how do you think I feel? I've got to try and turn this bitch on.'

David burst out laughing. 'Honest, she's easy prey, and I'm telling you if you can't get this one into bed Scotty lad, you might as well call it a day. Saying that, I wouldn't say no to you.'

They all laughed in the smoked filled car. They were used to David's humour and were never offended.

Az and Scott swapped places, and Az gave him a rundown of the workings of the car. They set off again with David giving Scott the instructions on how to get to the exact house.

'Right, we're here. Az, make yourself scarce.'

They both lay as low as they could so that if she was looking through the camera, she wouldn't spot them.

'The gate's already open,' Scott said to them both, not daring to move his lips fully in case he was being watched.

He drove straight in and drove slowly towards the front door. 'Fuckin' 'ell man. Am I really fucking doing this?' Scott was getting worked up.

He forced himself out of the car, shutting the

driver's door behind him and steamed in to do the job in hand.

Az and David lay low for what seemed ages.

David peeped up and saw that Scott had gone in. He wanted to give it five more minutes so that Scott had time to work his magic and get her out of that hallway.

'Are we both going in?' Az asked.

'Yeah, you take downstairs and look for Jody, and I'll go upstairs and see if I can find her up there. Just fucking grab her Az and get back to the car. If you have to, drive off and wait for us up the road.

'And what if you get her first?' Az whispered from the floor of the passenger seat.

'I'll have to come in here and wait for you, won't I?'

The next few minutes were vital. The boys had no idea what was going on behind the door. Scott could have been taken upstairs. He could be in a state once he'd seen her face and point-blank refused, then they'd been stuffed.

Given that he'd not come out so far, though, suggested he was up for it.

The boys snuck out of the car and went towards the front door, hoping and praying that it was open. Bingo! David thought as it opened. They got in quick and noticed that there was no one in the hallway.

David ran up the stairs. He almost nodded an acknowledgement at the huge canvas on the wall, as if to let Julie know he was there and that he would get her Jody.

Az searched carefully downstairs. There was

no noise or any evidence that there was a child anywhere downstairs, he thought. There was no evidence of Scott or the Yeti either, so he was a bit worried that David might bump into them upstairs.

He walked through the kitchen very much on edge. There was a room to the left of it. He slowly, carefully walked up to it, his eyes scanning everywhere, looking at every detail. The house was stunning, it was huge, and although Az's family weren't short of a bob or two, this was something else.

He could see a door within the large room, and as he got closer to the door, he could hear his mate panting. Well, he assumed it was his mate, but given what he'd been told, it could have been the fucking Yeti. Either way, someone sounded like they were enjoying themselves.

'Dirty bastard,' he grinned, but it gave him the chance to scan the rest of the downstairs. He quickly left the room and headed towards the back of the house.

There was a conservatory that must have been sixty-foot long in total. It was full of lavish furniture but no sign of any child. The early morning sun shone warmly through the glass. He admired the space around him. He needed to head back towards the front door; he'd pretty much done as he was asked and covered the ground floor.

Meanwhile, David was on the first floor. He was nervous because he'd not heard any commotion downstairs, and he didn't know if that was a good or bad sign.

He approached a huge room that had yet another

doorway to get into it. He walked carefully towards the door, listening for any noise. He heard the sound of a child. She was behind the door. He was sure of it. Jody was behind the door.

He tried to open it, but it wouldn't budge. He kicked it, and the fucker flew off its hinge and spun round and knocked him out. As he blacked out, he thought he saw Julie coming towards him.

There was a commotion from downstairs that made him stir, his head hurt, and for a minute, he thought he was at his mum's.

Then he remembered that he'd been on a mission to get Jody from the Yeti's house. He realised that he was still in the Yeti's house and sat up quickly, rubbing his bruised head. The door that had hit him was now open. Jody was there in the playpen, playing with toys.

The commotion downstairs seemed to be getting louder. He knew he had to get out of there.

He ran to the playpen and grabbed little Jody. He grabbed her dummy and a little blanket he'd seen her holding when they'd been in the car.

'No shitting lady,' he held her at arm's length, as though her nappy was already full and carried her toward the stairs, taking care that he didn't bump into anyone.

The Yeti was screaming now, and he could hear her shouting that she was going to phone the police. From the racial abuse she was spurting, it was clear poor Az had been rumbled. He could tell that they weren't in the hallway near the front door, so he made a dash down the stairs. He didn't look around him. He focused straight ahead with his eye on that front door.

As he opened it, he saw the police coming slowly through the gate. As quick as a flash, holding Jody close to him now, he discreetly got in the back of Az's car and lay there, with Jody silently in his arms. She was bewildered but didn't bat an eyelid as though she was waiting calmly for it all to end.

He watched the police walk up to the house. There were two of them. They went in through the front door, but it wasn't long before their back up arrived.

That was it; they were fucked.

Chapter 28 - Julie

I heard a commotion and woke up wondering why everybody was exiting the train. We had come to a complete standstill as though it was the last stop. I was disorientated.

I looked out the window and could see we'd pulled into a station. I could see the hub and the bub of a lively city. It didn't look familiar, and I was confused.

Then came the announcement from the train staff.

'Welcome to Glasgow Central, where this train terminates. Please take all your belongings as you leave the train.'

I couldn't fucking believe it. We were in bloody Glasgow. My god!

'Pavel, Pavel,' I shook him awake.

He yawned. 'I feel like I've been asleep for hours.'

'That's because we have been asleep for hours,' I groaned. 'We're in bloody Glasgow, for fuck sake Pavel. I can't believe you let us sleep that long. We are absolutely miles away from home.'

I could have cried there and then.

'Me?' he was defensive. 'My arm is still wet, where you were drooling all over me.'

I ignored him.

The guard walked past.

'Excuse me,' I hoped to get his attention. He looked around as I continued. 'We should have got off at Manchester.'

'Manchester is four hours away,' his Scottish accent boomed through the carriage.

'How did ye' miss that lass? You'll have te buy a ticket back. I've not got a machine on me, but you've got time to run te the kiosk.'

I couldn't believe my ears and my luck. But back we had to go, I was starting to panic now.

'What time is the next train back please?'

'It's this one lass. We go back in about ten minutes.'

'You go to the kiosk, Pavel, and get us two tickets. I will wait here so that we don't lose our seats.'

So off he went to get us two tickets.

The train was starting to fill up with the new passengers now, who were going the other way.

I wondered about Jody and how she was faring and hoped to God that Ann had managed to get her back or her bloody father had shown some bollocks and done something about it all.

I wondered how on earth she'd managed to get Jody off them in the first place. But I knew that they weren't messing with an amateur and what Susan Robinson wanted, Susan Robinson got.

It made me feel sick to the pit of my stomach. I knew how worked up Ann would be. Something like this could kill someone. That woman adored that baby and had probably been a bigger part of her life than I had. That I would never ever forget.

Then I tried to think about it rationally and wondered if she would actually hurt her. I don't recall her physically hurting us until we were about four or five. But then my stomach lurched. Of course she would hurt her, if for nothing else but to get back at me, for doing that to her face. I went all hot again. She had no reasoning about her. She was void of any emotion.

There were times when you felt like you needed to turn to God, and right then, at that time on that train, I needed to pray that my baby would be ok. I couldn't stand the thought of that woman damaging her. Like she'd damaged me.

I couldn't wait to be a mum to my baby. I'd never felt this way about it before, but this whole journey had taught me something. I shut my eyes and took some deep breaths to try and free up some space in my head. I had to stay focused. I still had to get back and face the commotion.

I suddenly realised that the train was starting to slowly take off from the station, and I jolted in shock and looked up and down the carriage to see if I could see Pavel. Where the hell was he?

I saw him alright, running up the fucking platform trying to stop the train, which was never going to happen. I nearly laughed, it was that comical, but then I realised the seriousness of it. He would be stuck in Glasgow now until he could get another train. Then he had no idea where I needed to go.

He was waving frantically at me, banging his hands then throwing them in the air in pure frustration.

I stood up at the window. I could have touched him, he was that near. I mouthed through the window to him, 'phone dad, phone dad.' He nodded as the train sped off out of the station, and he could no longer keep up. I saw him throw his arms in the air in sheer exasperation.

About fifteen minutes later, we approached Motherwell, where the guard came over to me and said, 'Tickets please.'

I looked in my purse and my pockets. I had very little cash on me. I didn't know what I was going to do and then I saw it on the seat next to me. Pavel's wallet. So, while he was stuck in Glasgow with no money, I could at least buy a ticket to get home, I hoped. I didn't have to hope for much longer as he had a large wad of notes in it.

I was relieved but didn't know what he was going to do.

For God's sake. I couldn't leave him.

I jumped off at Motherwell, ran across the bridge which led to the other side of the station and waited for the next train to take me back into Glasgow.

It was another ten minutes, so I went to the phone box, dialled 100 and asked her to reverse the charges for The New Cottage in London.

I smelt now, it was warm, and I could smell my sweat. I felt filthy.

I spoke to dad, who was relieved to hear from me. I told him the whole sordid story. He told me not to panic and that he was going to send the Manchester Police to her house to get Jody back.

'Julie, I thought you'd just buggered off and wasn't coming back.' His voice was sombre.

'What? And took my daft brother to boot.' We both laughed.

'See you soon, darling, go and get your daft brother. No doubt he will phone me shortly, and I'll let him know you're on your way back.'

Then I phoned Ann. She was distraught. I calmed her down and told her that the police were going to get Jody and to be on standby to look after her, as I was stuck in Scotland.

'Julie,' her voice was full of angst. 'I love that baby, and I'd never let her come to any harm. She totally manipulated me and the law. I'm so worried about her. I'm so worried you'll never trust me with her again. But you have to know...'

'Ann,' I stopped her in her tracks. 'I promise you, you have been more of a mother to Jody than I have. I will never ever forget that, and you know what, Jody won't either. She adores you. I would never ever stop Jody loving you. I know what this woman is like, Ann. She's my mum.'

She sobbed for a minute and then told me that Bernie had been run over and had been in intensive care. I gasped as she said it. She said David was sure it had been Susan trying to kill him but getting Bernie instead.

I put the phone down with minutes to go for my train. This had to stop once and for all now. The woman had spent her whole life abusing people. She'd killed Jane, she'd almost destroyed dad, I was a total mess, and now she had nearly killed poor Bern. I started to cry. I could only imagine Irene and David trying to deal with that.

What had gone on though? How had all this happened? I somewhat felt responsible because I'd disappeared, but even I hadn't known what was going on.

I jumped on the train to Glasgow and went to get my brother.

Chapter 29 - Manchester

Irene had gone over to the hospital quite early on as Bernie was being moved to another ward. She wanted to be there to understand how far Bernie was from recovering and so that she would know where and why they were moving her.

She arrived at the hospital and headed straight to the ICU ward.

She was met with a shock as she got to Bernie's bed. It was no longer Bernie in there. It was now being occupied by some young lad who'd had an accident on a building site apparently.

He looked shocking as he lay there, and for a moment, Irene remembered the fear of seeing her daughter laying there in a not dissimilar state. She said a little prayer in her head and prayed that he would come through as her daughter had.

She looked around her at all the patients silent and on drips and really did think she was lucky that her Bern was on the mend.

But she was totally confused and looked around for her daughter. She realised that she might have got the wrong bed. In fact, she looked around ICU and wondered if she was in the right ward.

She went to find one of the doctors so that she could ask where her daughter was. She saw Doctor Parkinson as she walked towards the office and approached her.

'Where's our Bernie?' she asked the young doctor, as though she had murdered her.

'We've moved Bernadette to ward F08 in the

main hospital. She is doing so much better and, to be honest, will probably recover better at home. I've asked the consultant over there, who specialises in trauma to the liver, to assess and see what he thinks.'

Irene was elated as she just wanted Bernie home. Even though it had only been a couple of days, it was the scariest couple of days of her life. She was sure Bernie would be better off at home. She could have David's double bed, and she would make her lots of stews and broths to build her back up.

She headed over quickly to ward F08, following the yellow lines on the floor so that she knew where to go.

As she approached the big double doors that would lead her to the ward, she looked around at the greyness surrounding her. Grey floors, grey walls, grey chairs. She sat on a grey chair for a few minutes and watched as porters were pushing patients on beds with drips keeping them alive.

It didn't matter how deadly the patient looked, the porter would whistle, sing and let on to all and sundry. It must have been part of the job spec when they applied.

Teams of doctors and their housemen wandered through the corridors with their clipboards and stethoscopes around their necks. They were obviously on their rounds where they visited their patients, either delivering the good news that they were going home or the not so good that they were going nowhere.

The double doors opened, and a nurse in a blue uniform greeted Irene.

'Hello,' she said.

'Hiya,' Irene returned the greeting but didn't say anything more.

'Have you come to visit someone?' The nurse was patient.

'Oh, sorry.' Irene hadn't realised she was there to help her. 'My daughter Bernie has been brought here from intensive care, and Dr Parkinson from ICU said that she was going to ask the doctor here if he would assess her and send her home.'

Irene was hoping that the nurse wouldn't send her home and tell her to come back at visiting time. She had too much to do later. She'd got a cleaning job in the evening. It was cash in hand, so if she didn't go, she wouldn't get paid. And she needed the money now more than ever as she was going to do David's room up for Bernie, she'd just decided.

'The doctor is with Bernie now if you want to come in.'

Irene was relieved. 'Aw thanks love. You're an angel.'

The doctors were surrounding Bernie's bed, but she was actually sat up and beaming at the attention around her. She smiled when she saw her mum.

'Hiya mum, they said I can go home. I only had the tiniest tear in my liver, and there are no clots, and everything else is ok, 'cept my ribs, but they'll have to mend on their own.'

The doctor smiled at Irene.

'Hi there, pretty much what she just said there.' He smiled and said that he would write a prescription for some pain killers for the ribs. He explained that it was pretty hefty stuff and that she would need monitoring because her ribs would start to become really painful once all the morphine had worn off. He said if there was any deterioration, she should go straight back to A&E.

'Alright love.' Irene was trying to keep up with it all and thought she had it straight in her head. 'How long do you think this will take? I'll have to order us a taxi. There is no other way for us to get home. Do you know where the nearest payphone is?'

'Well,' the doctor responded kindly, 'I'll write the prescription now, and you can go to the hospital pharmacy with this young doctor,' he pointed to one of his housemen, 'And right next door, there is a payphone. The nurses will have Bernadette all ready for you when you get back.'

He shook Bernie's hand, and she said, 'Thank you so much doctor.'

He smiled. 'You're welcome, you take care.'

'Right, you get ready, our Bernie. I'll go and get your drugs and phone us a taxi, and we'll be getting you home. You can have our David's bed tonight. It's comfier.'

Bernie laughed. 'He'll go bloody mad. I can't wait to milk this.'

She told her mum that a woman with a burnt face had been to visit her and told her that she had meant to hit David and not her.

'I don't think this was an accident, mum.'

And as she said it, two police officers appeared at the end of her bed.

'Bernie Bates?' One of them asked.

'We've got a couple of questions about your accident. Are you feeling well enough to answer them?'

'Like you'd be arsed if she wasn't.' Irene wasn't happy that they'd just turned up like this.

Irene was right, and they proceeded to ask Bernie what she remembered about the accident.

Could she remember what type of car it was? Did she see who was driving it? Who was she with? Would David want her to come to any harm? Did she have any enemies?

'Hold on. Hold on.' Irene interrupted them abruptly.

'What do you mean would David want her to come to any harm? No, he fucking would not. How dare you?'

'We have to ask these questions. We were told that David had very quickly got out of the way.'

'He saw his friend over the road,' Bernie said, remembering. 'Our David wouldn't want anything bad to happen to me. He loves me, doesn't he mum?'

'Yeah, he really, really does. But she got a visit off that Susan Robinson, have you been told that? She told our Bern that it was her that hit her and that she meant to hit our David. So what are you going to do about that?'

Irene was fuming now and just wanted to get back home with Bernie.

'Is that right?' The officer asked Bernie.

'Yes, that's right,' she nodded her head.

'Ok thanks, we'll be in touch if we need you again. Can we have the address of where you will be staying, please?'

Bernie gave them her mum's address, and off they went.

'Cheeky fucking bastards. I can't believe what

I'm hearing. They'll do owt for an easy option, blaming our David. I'd blind him, I would.'

Bernie winced as she tried to sit up. 'Come on mum, let's go.'

Irene shouted for the nurse to get Bern ready the best they could under the circumstances, and she went off to get the prescription. The doctor who was originally supposed to be taking her had disappeared into thin air, so she marched off following the signs for the pharmacy, making sure she had 10p so she could phone a taxi.

Chapter 30

David lay in the car with Jody and waited for the police to go into the house. He couldn't hang about. He knew that before long, Jody would get restless. He had to get out of the grounds and back to safety.

He decided the front gate wouldn't be the answer; he would be far too exposed. He grabbed Jody gently. She had fallen asleep now across his chest. He put her dummy in and grabbed her blanket, marvelling at her long eyelashes. He gently moved her hair from her face and set off down the side of the house. He wondered what the hell Scott and Az were doing inside and hoped to God that they could wrangle themselves out of any shit that they were in.

He moved away from the house and walked around the perimeter, hoping there was a side gate or a gap in the bushes or fence. The baby was getting heavy, and he'd only just started.

The back of the house was big, and he didn't want to get near the windows. He could not be seen at this point and thought he should have made a dash for the front gate.

And then he stumbled on a gap between stone pillars. There were two of them, with a wall in the middle that had been built far more recently than the pillars. But at the side of one of them was a small gap. He looked at it and then at his stomach. He went for it.

He held on to Jody tightly and squeezed his way

through the hole, and he was free. He couldn't believe his luck. He seemed to be on a different road than before, and this one had a phone box at the end of it.

Jody was starting to get agitated.

'Don't worry doll,' he whispered. 'I'm going to phone nana to come and get us. We'll be home soon.' He kissed her head. The poor kid must have been through hell, not knowing where she was and who she was with.

She opened her eyes and said, 'mama.'

'Let's get nana first, then we'll get mama, little dolly.'

He sat her on the black seat in the phone box and proceeded to dial the number to Ann's. But he couldn't remember it.

He kept saying, '43627' and got stuck on the last two digits.

He said it again out loud; this time little Jody said as clear as day, '2747.'

He nearly screamed with joy and told her she was a 'clever girl.'

The phone rang, and Ann answered with her usual, '2747', and it dawned on David that little Jody had just mimicked her nana. He was more than impressed.

'It's me Ann. I've got her.'

'Oh my god, David, is she alright? Where are you?'

'We're on the next road at the side of Susan's house. Scott and Az have been rumbled, and the police are there now. They'll probably end up getting arrested, but they'll be ok. And I've got Jody.'

As he was talking away, he could see police cars with their sirens heading towards the house.

'Can you come and get us, Ann?' he asked. 'It's risky, but I'll get caught on foot. They must have it right in for Az and Scott.'

'I've spoken with Julie, David.'

'Oh my god, that's great. I hope she's ok but tell me when you get here. I'm going to try and get to the pub on the roundabout. I don't think it's far.'

He ducked and dived through back gardens and bushes as he had an idea of which direction the pub was. He came out on a main road and could see the pub wasn't too far away.

God, he was shaking now, and Jody was so heavy his back was killing, and his arms felt numb. He needed to shift some of this timber, that was for sure. He was panting like a dog in a bastard heatwave.

He walked towards the pub; it seemed to be getting further and further away, and then he saw Ann's car pulling up. He didn't know where he got his energy from, but he started running. As he did, Jody started laughing, proper belly giggling, which made him laugh. He couldn't believe he had connected with a toddler. She could barely speak, but even she found him funny.

'Right, pack it in now lady,' he was stern with her. 'I'll be on a kidnapping charge at this rate, and you'll not be laughing then when you've got to go back to the Yeti.' He laughed and pulled her close to him. He smelt a familiar smell.

'Jesus Christ. You never cease to amaze me, laughing one minute, shitting the next. Come on, you smelly cow, let's get you to nana, where you belong.'

Ann grabbed Jody from him and held her tightly.

'Right, we've not got time for that Ann. The police will be passing again in a minute. I'll be getting arrested. Let's get back to ours. Yours will be the first place they look.'

What David didn't realise was that the cars that had passed him were Julie's father and the police going to Susan's house to look for Jody.

Ann changed Jody's nappy as quick as a flash in the back seat, gave her a nice warm bottle of milk and strapped her in her car seat.

She flew down that motorway like the wind. Ten minutes later, they were back at Irene's. Irene and Bernie had also just got back.

'Bern!' David screamed. 'How come they've let you out? Are you well enough?'

Irene went and put the kettle on, but not before giving baby Jody a great big squeeze.

'Ann, you must be made up,' she said sincerely. 'We've both got our girls back.'

'Aw, hurry up with that brew mum. I've just been in a police siege and a kidnapping. I'm parched.'

They all laughed, and Bernie squealed in pain as she did so. 'David, don't make me laugh,' she frowned.

Jody was laughing and walking about, happy to be amongst friends and family, but she was knackered as well. She climbed up on to David's knee while he had his brew and fell fast asleep.

'Aw, she thinks I'm a big cushion,' he smiled and stroked her hair and she slept soundly. He picked her up gently and placed her on the settee next to her nana.

'Right,' he said. 'What now? Is Julie on her way back Ann?'

'Julie?' Irene's ears pricked up. 'Have you heard from her? Is she alright? Where's she even been? There have been so many shenanigans because of that girl.'

'None of its Julie's fault,' David defended his friend. 'This is all to do with that Yeti.'

'Well, have you heard from her?' Irene said again, ignoring his defence, probably because she knew he was right.

'Yes, Irene,' Ann interrupted. 'She called me out of the blue today. She knew about Jody as she'd got David's message. I told her about Bernie. She was devastated. She said she was on her way back and that she was stuck in Scotland. That was a few hours ago now, so she should be on her way back. But I suspect she will go to Susan Robinson's for Jody. I have no way of letting her know that we've got her.'

'It will all turn out for the good,' David promised. 'Main thing is we've got the baby.'

Ann put her cup down on Irene's rug while she animated her next sentence. Irene nearly had a heart attack and dived over to the coffee table for a coaster for the cup, sending it flying as she did so.

'Jesus Christ, I can't believe I've done that.' She ran into the kitchen for a cloth while Ann ran behind her, feeling guilty and grabbing a tea towel off the side.

Together, they were on their hands and knees, trying to get the wet patch of tea off the rug. The rain was coming down fast outside as the day had suddenly turned grey. It sounded nice as it hit the window panes. It hadn't rained in a while, and the grass was turning yellow, so a good downpour wouldn't do anyone any harm.

David looked at Bernie. 'Glad to be home, our kid?'

She laughed and then frowned. 'Stop making me laugh our David; it kills.

She looked at him seriously. 'The rain on the window is making me think of us together growing up as kids. The noises are the same, the clattering of rain on the empty tins of paint mum's had outside the window for years. I could sit here now and watch Going for Gold, followed by Neighbours. Remember when we used to do that?'

David was silent for once and a bit shocked. That bump on the head must have made her think a bit deeper. He'd never heard her talk like that. She was normally so black and white.

'Yes, I'm so glad I got to come home, David. Because for a moment, I didn't think I'd ever see it again – our mum's house. Or you or her.'

David had tears in his eyes. He was glad she was home too.

Their thoughts were broken by a loud knock on the door, and everyone froze in their places. Irene and Ann were still both on all fours. Bern was holding her head to one side, listening to the rain and reminiscing.

The door went again.

'Well, you better get it our David. I only live here, but it won't be for me.' Irene's voice was low so that nobody could hear her.

David reluctantly went to the door and was relieved but shocked to see it was Scott and Az.

'Fucking hellfire.'

Scott looked shocked and exhausted. 'That was proper horrendous. Mate, don't be asking me for nowt for a long while.'

'Come in. Come in,' David looked out of the door and up and down the street to make sure the coast was clear. 'Be quiet though, Jody is asleep.'

Az was shaking his head as he walked through the tiny hall into the living room.

'Mate, she thought I was a robber and that we'd both planned it. Him to give her one, which he did, dirty bastard, while I robbed her gaff. She is an absolute nutter. As soon as the police came, she changed her tune.'

Az spotted Bernie in the living room and ran over to her.

'My god, they've let you out. Are you well enough to be out? How do you feel?'

Bernie went bright red and thought about what she must look like, having not had a proper wash for days, and with a pair of PJ's on. She was mortified.

'Hiya Az,' she couldn't look at him, so it looked like she was being standoffish when in actual fact, she wanted the ground to eat her alive. She felt that bad.

David noticed Bernie's decline and knew what she'd be thinking, so he needed to divert Az.

'She's got a bit of post-traumatic stress. Nowt a good night sleep won't sort out,' he whispered. 'Anyway, what happened? Do you mean Susan didn't phone the police for you guys?'

'Well, that's what she said she was going to do, but then the police just turned up. She clearly didn't want them to know she is some sort of drug pushing, high-class prostitute or whatever it is she does. He knows,' he pointed at Scott, who had made himself comfy on one of the settees.

He opened his eyes and noticed Bernie for the first time. 'Jesus mate, you ok?' he smiled. 'My god, you're so lucky mate. Do you know that?'

She nodded her head and smiled softly at Az. 'You ok?' he mouthed. She nodded.

'Right,' David said. 'What has happened? Can someone tell us?'

'The police came looking for baby Jody. There were some non-uniforms too. They stayed outside on the drive and were very pleasant when we managed to get away. But there were swarms of cars,' Scott explained.

Az took over. 'She's said she was looking after Jody and would hand her over to her mother only. It was our chance to get away, but it wasn't that easy. She was making out Scott was her fella and gave him orders to make everyone drinks while they talked through the detail.'

Scott picked up the story again. 'Scary thing is she had no idea that Jody had gone. Who she thought Jody was with upstairs is baffling. You can't leave a kid on its own upstairs for hours. I mean, you'd probably been gone 20 minutes, and she'd been with me for...'

Az interrupted, 'Three minutes?'

David screamed with laughter. 'Fucking hell

mate, you don't do things by half. You were only with her three minutes and she had you taking over the bastard kitchen?'

'Anyway, we managed to make our excuses and leave. The police weren't far behind us. They said they would come back with Julie to collect Jody, and it would be a matter of hours. They were sending a car to meet Julie in Manchester. But that's all we could make out.'

'I hope Julie doesn't panic when she gets there,' Ann said.

'Jesus, do we need to go back?' David panicked.

'No way,' Irene said. 'Ann, phone yours and let Pete know what's going on. She'll phone yours first when she finds out Jody's not there. Get him to phone you here if he hears anything.'

'Good idea,' David said.

Ann did as she was told.

'Right,' Irene continued. 'Let's settle down now and wait. It's all going to be good. What could go wrong now? Does anybody want any dinner? I'm starving me.'

And with that, she toddled off to the kitchen to make everybody food.

Chapter 31 - Julie

I had found Pavel easily enough in Glasgow, and we jumped on to the next train to Manchester. It was an express one but was still going to take us hours, and it would be lunchtime before we arrived back in Manchester. I had to be patient. I was losing the will to live, but thoughts of Jody kept me going.

'I can't believe you came back for me,' Pavel was elated.

'I wasn't going to, but I realised you'd left your wallet and didn't want you to panic. I wouldn't mind, but we could have got the tickets off the guard, so you didn't even need to get off the train in the first place. Never mind, we are where we are.'

We arrived in Manchester, and I was now desperate to get to Lymm. We ran off the train to the taxi rank. There was no way I was getting a bus; it would have taken far too long.

There was a police car waiting near the taxi rank. There was always something going on, but I didn't have time to think about it.

We just jumped in the back of a black cab, I told him the address, and we were off finally.

'You ok?' Pavel asked me in the back of the cab.

'Yeah, I'm ok, getting anxious now. How are you?'

'Proud you've not tried to pull anyone yet?' He grinned.

I rolled my eyes and asked him if he'd been to Manchester before as I saw him looking out of the cab window.

'It's no London, is it?' he said.

'No, it's better.' I defended my city.

We were soon on the M56 heading towards Manchester Airport. I was finding it hard to breathe, so I closed my eyes and took some deep breaths with my head on the back of the taxi seat.

'You know there is a time and a place for a panic attack,' Pavel stated.

'Really, you're not helping. Your ignorance is pissing me off,' I retorted.

'You need to get your child; she needs you. You'll be no good breathless and stumbling about, will you? This is fight, not flight.'

I didn't know whether to laugh or cry, but he had a point in a way.

We approached The Avenue. I heard Pavel's words in my head. I needed to remain focused. I couldn't be having any panic attack now, even though my arms were starting to tingle.

The gate was open. I couldn't see any other cars, police or dads or anybody else's.

'Just park here,' I said to the black cab driver. 'I won't be long. Wait here please. I'm just going to grab my girl, and I'll be back out.'

'Do you want me to come with you?' Pavel asked.

'No, I need to do this alone. It's about time I faced this dragon; it might help with my healing. Thank you anyway.'

'Isn't she dangerous?' Pavel's voice sounded concerned.

'How much more damage can one woman do?'

I jumped out of the cab, walked through the huge

gate, and looked at the house that was once my home. That was once Jane's home. I immediately felt a surge of nostalgia run through my body, but it was shortly followed by a pain in my gut, which made me feel sad.

I looked around the still beautifully kept gardens and the gravel drive. None of it had changed at all. It felt like I'd never left. I spotted the little fountain that had always intrigued me as a child. I used to stare at the water for hours; it was a distraction to the goings-on. At the side of the house, I looked for the tree that I'd grown up with.

As I stood there taking it all in, the heaven's opened, and out of nowhere, darkness took over the sky. The rain pelted down fiercely, hitting me hard in the face. I had an urge to run back to the safety of the cab and Pavel, but I was so near. I couldn't turn back now.

The front door was getting nearer and nearer and bigger and bigger. I could hear my own breath in my ears thudding hard, and with that and the rain, I could barely hear myself think. I felt the bile rise to my throat.

I stood in front of the door, dripping wet and shaking, and not because I was cold.

I lifted my hand up to knock on the door. I winced in fear as I knocked hard.

I waited.

I waited for the moment that I'd never wanted to happen again in my life.

I waited with a dry throat as deep breaths became shallower by the second.

I waited for someone to answer the door, the

matriarch, the woman of this household.

I waited for the monster to appear with eyes of steel and wrath of terror.

I waited for my mother.

I heard footsteps behind the door, and I knew that she knew it was me. She would never answer the door without looking and checking first.

I looked around me, still no police cars, still no dad.

The door slowly opened as it always had done. The smell of her perfume overwhelmed me, and I was taken back to the dream on the train. I had dreamt about her.

And now she was there, standing as though she'd been waiting for me.

She was dressed in black, tits out as usual. The figure-hugging dress gripping tightly at her hips. I felt sickened by her face, it looked awful, and I'd done that. Her eyes were not right; they were devoid of any emotion. She was dead behind her eyes. She had no soul. I looked away.

'Where have you been, you dirty whore? I've had your daughter here because you neglected her.'

She laughed in my face as she had for so many years. The red mist was teetering, but I couldn't lose it now. I needed to get my daughter to safety.

'Where's Jody?' I asked.

'Not fucking here.'

I didn't believe her.

I bravely barged passed her and stood in the familiar hallway. I immediately saw the canvases on the wall and was shocked she would keep them there. What a beautiful family we looked. I stared at them for a moment.

'Yes, perfect, weren't we? Until you killed your sister. Until your father abandoned us. Until you left me for dead and did this to my face.'

She grabbed at her face as though she wanted to pull it off like a mask. She was going to explode. I could feel it. I knew her.

She could never take any accountability for anything. I didn't argue back; that would infuriate her. But I didn't want to stay calm as that would bug her. It didn't matter what I did; she was going to explode.

'Where is Jody?' I asked.

'Not fucking here, you whore.'

She wanted a fight.

I headed through to the kitchen and started checking all the rooms. I shouted Jody's name, and then I knew she was telling the truth because she started to laugh.

Once again, fear took over my body, and the mist was rising like a red-hot spring.

I turned around quickly. She grinned, knowing she had me.

'Where is she? Where is my daughter?'

'Your daughter is not here.' She was calm. 'She was here, and now she's gone. And I don't know who the fuck has her. They tricked me.'

'Who did?' I was starting to think she'd let harm come to her, and one of her men had kidnapped her. I couldn't bear it. 'Please tell me where Jody is?'

She loved that I'd just fed her a great big load of fear. She thrived off another's fear.

'She's not here, darling,' she said softly.

She laughed again. She got closer to me and laughed louder. I stepped back, and she stepped forward.

I was in danger. I knew it, and I'd put myself in danger. I needed to get out of the house. I needed to do it properly and phone the police.

I headed to the door, but she tugged hard at my hair. I instinctively turned around and slapped her hard.

'Fuck off, you horrible, horrible bastard.' The venom was there, and bingo, she had me.

She screamed with laughter. She was genuinely in fits of laughter with tears rolling down her face. I carefully took tiny steps to the side, and I was going to make a dash for it.

Too late, I was going nowhere. She lunged at me and pinned me up against the wall in the hallway. She was a big woman, and I was slight. She was strong, and I felt weak. I had no chance.

She pushed her body hard against mine, staring at me with those eyes. I lashed out and caught her face. Her perfume was making me feel dizzy. She grabbed my throat and attempted to strangle me. Her grip was hard, and I genuinely thought, this is it. This is my ending; my mum is going to kill me.

I tried my hardest to breathe, taking small breaths, but it was getting harder and harder, and I felt the energy being zapped from my core.

I had to hold on. I tried to slip downwards towards the floor, hoping she would lose her grip, but she had gone. She was out of her mind.

The dizziness took over as I started to lose consciousness. And I must have had an out-of-body experience because I saw myself standing behind her. I looked ashen. I looked like a ghost. I watched myself raise a huge stone pan and smack it hard on her head. I heard the crack and a thud. And we both collapsed on the floor.

Chapter 32

Pavel was getting anxious. He thought that Julie should have been back by now. He leant over to the black cab driver and asked him to take him to a phone box.

'You kiddin' me mate? I haven't got all bloody day here.'

'I'm sorry,' Pavel explained. 'This is urgent. My sister could be in danger.'

The taxi driver reluctantly spun the cab, did a left next to the house and drove up the quiet road where the bushes and trees were drenched in the rain that had superseded the summer sunshine.

'Yer in luck mate. There's one right there. Can you bloody believe that our kid?' The taxi driver was genuinely glad there was one nearby. It meant he didn't have to search the whole of Cheshire to find one.

'Wait for me,' Pavel demanded.

He phoned his uncle's house as he suspected that they'd all be there waiting for them, even though they were supposed to be here now.

Someone answered after just one ring.

'It's me, Pavel,' he blurted out. 'Julie is in Susan Robinson's alone, and she's been a while.'

It was Fiona.

'Jesus, Pavel, how long is a while?' Fiona sounded worried sick. 'Dad and Uncle Steve are on their way with a police escort.'

As she said it, he heard them and slammed down the phone.

He dived back in the taxi and said, 'quick back round the house.'

'Bloody hell mate, that was quick, you a rock star or sommat.'

Pavel met with his father and uncle at the gate and shouted. 'Julie is in there.'

The police were all over it now. For some reason, they were no longer defending Susan Robinson but looked more like they wanted her blood.

They all ran into the house while Pavel and his family waited patiently at the gate. Pavel went over to the taxi driver and asked him how much. He paid the man who didn't seem to want to leave now; he wanted to stay around and watch the show.

'What happened?' Steven Robinson asked his son, looking worried sick. 'Did the police not stop you at the train station?'

Pavel looked confused. 'No, we just jumped a black cab' He pointed towards the cab that was slowly driving away from the scene. 'We were expecting you to be here with the police. Julie just ran in and said she wouldn't be long. I asked if she wanted me to go with her, but she refused, saying that she needed to do it.'

'You should have waited until we got here,' Ron said. 'This woman is a lunatic Pav.'

Pavel was devastated; he wasn't feeling good.

They saw movement from the front door, and an officer had left the house and was now walking towards them.

The rain had eased, but the skies were still black. It was a sombre day, and it was about to get worse.

'Erm, Mr Robinson, can you come with me?'

The officer looked towards where Steven Robinson was stood with his son and his brother.

Steven looked at his brother for some moral support. His nerves were all over the show.

'We're all Mr Robinson, and we're all coming in,' Ron said.

'What's wrong?' Steve asked the young police officer. 'I know something's wrong.' His voice was grave.

They walked up the gravelled path and up to the house. The thunder boomed through the skies loudly, making them jump, followed by a huge bolt of lightning that seemed to hit the gravel path, it was that close.

They were greeted by another officer who took them to one side.

'There are two women on the floor, one is dead, and one is not in good shape.'

Steve grabbed the police officer by his shoulders, almost pushing him to the floor. He needed to see if Julie was ok and didn't care about any consequences.

He ran over to the end of the hall where they were. Pavel and Ron were not far behind him.

Susan Robinson looked as dead as she could. She lay there, still and lifeless in a state, her legs were wide open, and one of her breasts had fallen out of her dress. If she wasn't dead, she would have died at the lack of dignity as she lay there.

Julie lay on her back, but Steve couldn't see her face. He ran over to his daughter and could see that she was breathing. He thought she was unconscious as he pulled her head towards him.

'Please don't touch her mate; the ambulance is

on its way.'

'I'm going to make her comfy mate, do not try and stop me.' He wasn't neglecting his daughter for one more second.

'Come on sweetheart. You're ok, you're going to be ok.'

Pavel bent down next to her and stroked her head.

'Come on little sister, I haven't finished tormenting you yet.'

Julie opened her eyes and tried to get up off the floor. Steven tried to push her back down. 'Let me up now. I need to get Jody.'

'Jody is safe with Ann and David,' her dad explained. 'Relax for a minute.'

'I can't relax, dad. I killed her. She was strangling me, and I hit her on the head with the pan. She wasn't letting go of my neck, so I hit her over the head with the pan.'

'How can you have hit her on the head if she was strangling you?' Pavel asked.

'I don't even know. I just remember feeling like I was losing consciousness, and then from nowhere, I had like an out-of-body experience, and I was there in front of me, smacking her hard on the head. Then we both fell on the floor.'

'She sounds very confused,' said a police officer.

The other officers were going about their business, using radios to report back to their relevant stations and trying to establish what had actually gone on.

The paramedics came through the door and went straight over to Julie, who was now making her way to sit down on the huge chair that was in the kitchen.

They got her comfortable, took her temperature

and did her blood pressure. They looked at her neck and in her eyes. They asked her a few questions, like how long she was being strangled. They checked the back of her throat and felt her windpipe.

'Other than a few bruises, she's ok. Just in shock, I think.' The paramedic was speaking to one of the non-uniform officers, who was ready to pounce.

'Julie Robinson. I am arresting you on suspicion of murder. You do not have to say anything, but it may harm your defence if you do not mention when questioned something you later rely on in court. Anything you do say may be given in evidence. You will now be taken to the local station. Do you have a solicitor, Julie?'

'Do not say a word, Julie,' her dad instructed. 'You absolute bastards,' he yelled. 'Do you know this woman has abused this girl all her poor life, and you're going to arrest her for coming for her daughter? Her daughter that you lot just gave away to this woman even though they'd never met.'

Ron was already using the phone and calling his solicitor in London, instructing her to get here with immediate effect, and that money was no object. He told her to get a flight into Manchester and that she would be picked up from the airport.

Julie became hysterical, crying and screaming that she was trying to strangle her. Steven and Pavel tried to calm her down while Ron tried to negotiate with the police for more time.

'We'll get Jody and bring her with us,' Steven said to his daughter.

'No!' Julie said. 'Don't do that. Leave her with Ann. She knows Ann. She needs familiarity right now.'

She paused.

'But can you go to Irene's, next door to my flat and tell them all what has happened please. They must be worried sick, and I feel like I've massively let them all down. Just disappearing and through everything, Bernie's been run over by that fucking animal.'

She looked at her dad, and she started to cry big loud sobs. She was in shock. She was exhausted, and she was near breaking point. 'I can't cope anymore dad. She's got me. I can't cope.'

The officer proceeded to handcuff her and said that they were going to the station.

Julie looked at the heap on the floor and couldn't make head nor tail of it. But she was glad she was dead. She was nothing but a waste of space, an oxygen thief who had no right to anything that this life had to offer.

'Will you take me to Lymm, please mate?' David said to Az. 'I need to know what's going on. There's nowt down here, and Jody's safe and going nowhere. I want to try and meet Julie and stop her from going in that fuckin' madhouse. That woman is dangerous, and she's really got it in for Julie. We should warn her.'

Az was reluctant, given that he'd just nearly been arrested, but he agreed.

Everyone else was dead set against it. Irene and Ann were worried sick.

'You've got what you went for. Why go back now?'

David ignored them all and got into the car. He felt like Starsky and fucking Hutch as Az drove full throttle to Lymm. It was becoming a regular jaunt, and Az didn't even have to think of the way; he knew it alright.

It wasn't long before they arrived in the middle of a scene they couldn't have imagined in their wildest dreams. David climbed out of the car and looked through the open gates into the garden. He couldn't believe his eyes. There were two police cars and two really expensive cars. He knew they weren't there earlier. He wondered if the police had been called because Susan had noticed that Jody had gone. He was beginning to think that this was a bad idea.

He decided to stay outside the gates and wait for Julie to get here. Unless she was already in there and she'd called the police because she was getting nowhere.

On second thoughts, he decided to brave it and walk up the path. He'd be safe from the Yeti with the police about, and he didn't care that he'd took Jody; she was safe with her grandmother. He had not done anything wrong, so they couldn't touch him.

Then he saw Julie.

He was about to run towards her but stopped in his tracks when he noticed she was handcuffed to a police officer.

What the fuck?

'Ere officer,' he called out. 'It was me who came here earlier and took little Jody. Julie had nothing to do with it.'

He was totally barking up the wrong tree, and no one cared what he was saying. There had been a murder, and right now, he wasn't a priority.

He reached Julie. 'You ok kid?'

She nodded and mouthed, 'Thank you,' to him and was put in the back of a police car. He had Goosebumps all over his body, and the hairs on the back of his neck stood on end. He wondered what had gone on. Clearly, something was wrong. He noticed the state of her neck. It was red raw.

Pavel spotted David and guessed who he was. He went over to him, introduced himself and very briefly tried to bring him up to speed with everything. He really needed more than ten minutes amid a murder scene to explain exactly what had gone on the past few days, but David got the gist of it.

He realised that Pavel was the person at the end of the London number and was impressed with what he saw.

He quickly understood that Pavel and Julie's father had taken Julie to protect her from the Yeti. He wished he'd known sooner, then most of this mess wouldn't have happened.

He learnt that Pavel was Julie's brother. He couldn't wait for them to be having chippy at his mums, his family and Julie's family.

He knew that the Yeti was dead. He was shocked and sickened, but soon came round when he remembered what she had done to his sister, not forgetting it should have been him.

And he didn't believe that Julie had killed her, but if she had, it would have been in self-defence.

It took him a while to absorb what Pavel had just told him. The fact he was totally distracted by this stunning man had absolutely nothing to do with it. David was in total shock and felt sick for his Julie. He had such a strong connection with that girl; she was his friend.

If Bernie could hear his thoughts, she would have rolled her eyes, but he was in tune with Julie. They had both suffered, and he totally resonated with her. He thought about the Yeti, and he was secretly pleased that fucking bitch was dead. It could have been his little sister who had died but thank God it wasn't.

Pavel introduced David to Julie's dad and uncle, and David introduced them to his mate Az, who had decided to see what David was up to. David looked at Julie's dad and could see a resemblance but a totally different colouring. He was dark, and she was pale. But you could tell he was her dad.

He looked like a warm and sincere man, but an extremely frightened man at this time, and that was understandable. When David looked at the uncle, he didn't get the same warm feeling; he got a chill running up his back. But they all seemed one team, so he went with it for now and shook the chill away. They caught each other's eye briefly.

'Thank you both for getting Jody,' Steven Robinson said to David and Az. 'If you hadn't have done so, things could have been even worse than they are now.'

He was solemn as he spoke and couldn't muster up any energy to be light-hearted to these lads, even though he felt truly grateful. 'She could have been killed or certainly caught up in whatever went on in there.'

He shook his head in disbelief at the whole situation. He was distraught and worried sick. The atmosphere was tense.

'We need to get to the police station,' he explained to David. 'Julie wants Jody to stay with Ann. Can you make sure that that happens please?'

He took out his wallet and handed David some money. 'That should be enough to fill that car up and get everyone, including little Jody, some dinner this evening. We will be in touch as soon as we know anything.'

He went to walk off with Pavel and Ron and then quickly spun around. 'What's your address David and do you have a telephone number I can contact you on please?'

David gave his details as Steven wrote them in a leather-bound Filofax with a beautiful gold pen.

David was impressed and wondered again how poor Julie had ended up in a tiny cottage flat on a huge council estate, given that her mum and dad were fucking loaded.

'See you soon. Thank you for everything again.'

Pavel shook David's hand and then Az's. Az could see David's blushes and rolled his eyes as they all left the house.

'What is up with you?' Az asked, shaking his head.

'He's fit,' David dabbed the sweat off his forehead with his T-shirt. 'I think I'm in love.'

'He is good looking, I must admit,' Az grinned. 'I think I'm in fuckin' love too.'

David rolled his eyes as a couple more of the police officers left with Julie's family. They got in their separate cars and sped off, leaving Az and David and just two officers.

David couldn't resist going into the house. He couldn't see Susan's body as they had covered her up, but the inconspicuousness of it now made it look worse. It had suddenly become very real. The air was eerie as no one was speaking. They should really get off, but he was intrigued. He'd never been at a murder scene before.

He decided to see if he could get away with walking up the big stairway; he was determined to look around the place. Az followed him.

'What the fuck are you up to now? Yer fuckin' mad, do you know that? Is that because you're gay because us straight men are not into this kind of thing?'

'You straight men are into a lot more than you

know. Believe me lad.'

'What you on about?' Az was frowning at his friend.

'What you fuckin' on about. I don't ask you if you do things just because you're Asian, do I?'

'Yeah, all the fuckin' time.'

They both started giggling because David knew he did and was winding him up, even while there was a dead body not ten feet away. He couldn't help himself.

Az followed him up the stairs. David went into the nursery where he'd found Jody. He showed Az the dodgy door and proceeded to tell him that he'd kicked it and it had knocked him out.

Az started to laugh and wondered how they'd got involved in it all and why they were still there.

'Look at that door.' David pointed towards a door at the end of the room, which looked like it could lead into another room. 'That's weird; I didn't notice it this morning.'

He walked towards it with Az not far behind him. They tried to open it, but it wouldn't open.

They went to walk away, and as they did, there was a slight knock from inside the locked door. David grabbed hold of Az's arm.

'Did you just hear that?'

'What?' Az asked. But no sooner than he did, the knocking started again. It was light but was definitely coming from inside the door.

'Haunted this gaff, man.' Az turned to leave, but David grabbed his T-shirt.

'Fucking Burberry this mate,' Az said as he could feel the T-shirt being tightly dragged around his neck, almost strangling him.

'Fucking Burberry, it's from fuckin Cheetham Hill, yer dick.'

But before Az could say any more, the knocking became louder.

'Right, we're out of here,' David screamed. His scream alerted the two officers who ran up the stairs.

David and Az met them on the landing. 'We were looking for the toilet,' David lied.

'You need to get out of here,' the officer said. He was not happy. 'Quick as you can, do you hear me?'

They didn't need to be told twice; they were off.

Chapter 34 - Julie

I sat in a police cell in Warrington, a small town between Liverpool and Manchester. I still felt sick from the ordeal, and I wasn't with it. I rubbed my neck and throat, conscious of the bruising that felt tender to touch.

I looked around me. The room was sparse even though it was painted white. There were no windows, just a door that kept me from the rest of the world. A bed that looked like a camp bed was pushed against the wall. On top of it, laying on its side, was a mattress. A grey blanket was roughly folded up with a thin pillow on top of it. I shuddered, hoping I didn't need them and that dad and Ron would get me out of here as soon as possible. I wanted to cry, but I didn't.

I pulled the mattress onto the bed just for somewhere to sit and wondered how much worse things could get. Was I going to go to prison? Would I ever live a normal life again? Would dad support me? He didn't need the hassle. I wondered if they'd all gone back to London.

But I remembered that, as I was being escorted from the house, Ron was phoning for his solicitor to fly up from London, so hopefully, she would be here soon, and they would all support me.

I remembered seeing David and got a lump in my throat. He'd got Jody for me, even after my mother had tried to kill his sister. He was an amazing man, and I smiled at the drama of him trying to get Jody back. He would have made a right meal out of it.

I couldn't help it; I started to cry at the idea that I would never see him again. I thought of Irene and Bernie, and I couldn't stop crying when little Jody entered my head.

I'd had enough, really had enough. How much more could I take? I felt like I couldn't carry on. At this rate, I would have to go to court. I would have to be interrogated and tell my story to countless people over and over again. In truth, I didn't even know what had happened. I really had lost consciousness or state of mind anyway. I'd had some sort of blackout. I knew she had been strangling me. But what I did see was me hitting her over the head with a frying pan. I shook my head; it hurt.

I stopped crying and wiped my face on my smelly T-shirt and waited. I didn't know how I felt. I even got lost looking for my own feelings.

I had to ride this out. I had to close my eyes and take deep breaths and think of positive thoughts. There was nothing else left for me to do.

Then I thought about how she'd opened the door to me all brazen and unashamed. It was as though nothing had happened, and no time had passed between us.

I'd never wanted to go back there. I'd never wanted to see her again. There is always hope that you can change how a person feels towards you, especially when that person is your mother. But I knew a long time ago that there was no changing this woman. If we want to change, we have to look deep within, but more than anything, we have to want to change. And in doing so, you had to admit there was damage.

This woman believed she was perfect. That everyone else was damaged. This woman believed she was innocent and blamed others for her own peevish actions. The only way I could free myself from her was to get away and stay away. Luckily enough, she'd kicked me out, so the dilemma of not wanting to leave her was taken out of my hands. I promised myself I would never return physically, although mentally, she never left my mind.

I went back to the scene again in my head. It wasn't me. As much as she was hateful, spiteful and as much as she was strangling me, I don't think I could have done it. Or maybe I could, who knows. I felt like I had taken drugs and was tripping.

As I closed my eyes, I saw myself hitting her over the head with the frying pan, but I had different clothes on than I did now. I opened my eyes. I felt like I was losing the plot, but I was now convinced that someone else had hit her over the head with the frying pan.

It wasn't me. I'd not hit her over the head. I knew it in my soul. It was someone else.

I needed to see what was going on and felt a sudden urge to get out of here. I started to bang on the door. I needed to speak to someone and ask them to get my dad. I needed him to know that it wasn't me. I'd told him in the house that I'd killed her, but I was almost cataleptic. Surely a medical professional would account for this causing a delusional vision, given that I was being choked to death. Surely the impact of that would be the loss of the here and now.

A policeman unlocked the door from the other side. He stood there, arms crossed, back straight, demanding authority and so full of self-importance.

'Is my dad here?' I asked him.

'Grab your stuff, and let's have you.'

I looked back in the cell. 'I don't have any stuff.' I told him.

I followed him down a short corridor where there were a couple of other police cells. He did a quick right and led me into a small office. There was a lady police officer stood in the room. Dad and his solicitor were sat at a table. She had her laptop in front of her and was busy typing away.

I ran to dad, and he stood up quickly and squeezed me hard. I started crying again. The police lady in the room gave me some tissues and a glass of water. And gently asked me to sit down and provided me with a chair to do so.

The solicitor was an older lady but the classiest woman I'd ever seen in my life. She looked like Honor Blackman, the actress. She was stunning and perfectly coiffured. She smiled warmly at me, and as she spoke, I could hear an ever so slight Irish accent. I immediately felt safe and saved. I knew *she* would save me.

She introduced herself as Veronica Statham and explained what she wanted from me. She wanted the whole back story. She explained she had dad's story and Ron's and wanted to hear mine so that she could build up a case of self-defence from a serial abuser.

'I didn't do it dad. It wasn't me. I was being strangled, and I saw somebody hit her over the head with a pan. It looked like me, but how could it have been me? I was having the life choked out of me. It was before I blacked out, so I would have not had a clear vision, surely?'

'Ok sweetheart,' dad reassured me. 'Veronica still needs to know the back story. You've been arrested for murder, and we need to be really clear on what has happened so that we can try and help you not get charged with murder. So, take your time and tell Veronica everything, as far back as you can remember.'

There was a part of me that really didn't want to relive the whole thing again. I'd just done all this with Fiona but under very different circumstances. I didn't feel strong enough to talk about it and be ok and not break down.

Veronica smiled. 'Take your time Julie.'

I thought back to the day of the accident and decided to start there. It was enough; I didn't want to go any further back. I didn't even want to go here. I didn't want to see Jane on that floor again and wondered if it would ever leave me.

I couldn't speak. The lump in my throat was stopping me from breathing. I took a deep breath, inhaled hard and pushed it away. Then I began.

After what seemed like hours later, a couple of toilet breaks and a cup of coffee, I was exhausted and had brought Veronica right up to date. I was also questioned by two police officers, and this would be my statement forever, so I had to keep my head in the game even though there were times I felt again like I was out of body.

It did sound like I had a case for self-defence after years and years of abuse. The talking made me feel better in some respects. But I didn't kill her. I knew how crazy my story sounded, and had I been in a better state of mind, I might have thought more about it, but it was out there now. Every man and his dog had heard me say I'd killed her.

Veronica left the room for what seemed like another hour. She came back with a police officer who said he was Sergeant Elliot.

He was a big man with a dark moustache and greying hair. He had sparkly eyes, and I could tell he wasn't one of these bastards that often let the authority go to their heads. He was older and near retirement, I guess, so he really didn't seem to give a shit. He explained that I would be placed on remand until a court could grant me bail.

I was going to prison. I folded my hands on the table and placed my head on them. I didn't know what to do or say. I just had a feeling of dread all over my body. I couldn't fucking believe this was happening. Maybe I'd wake up, and it would all have been a bad dream. I literally pinched myself and winced, no I was fully awake.

He explained they would take me to HMP Styal. He told me it was actually quite nice and comfortable. I didn't give a shit, I didn't want to go, I'd never felt so out of control in my life, and once again, my only option was to go with it in the hope this would all soon be over.

'What will happen next?' I asked Veronica. She started to tell me the next steps, but I couldn't hear her. I could just see her mouth moving up and down as I thought about my little girl once again. It was like I wasn't meant to see her. I was beginning to feel really anxious about it.

I looked at dad and shook my head. He looked as lost as I did.

'Can I phone my daughter please?' I asked as soon as Veronica had stopped talking. I pleaded with my eyes to Sergeant Elliot, who nodded slightly.

He handed me the telephone as we were all sat in the room. He wasn't stating one phone call only and doing all the spiel, so I felt better, not that I had more than one phone call to make. I just wanted to speak to my girl.

I rang Ann's number and waited for her 2747, but it didn't come because Andy answered. It was strange to hear his voice, and in a way, I wished I was sat in our messy flat with him. He wasn't a bad person. He just got unlucky in a way. He had Jody though, so not so unlucky.

'Andrew? It's me, Julie.' I don't think I'd ever used his full name.

'Jesus, you ok?'

'Long story, and no, I'm not right now. Is Jody there? I'm desperate to speak to her.'

'She's at David's with mum and Irene; they felt safer over there. David has been a hero. Do you know he went to that house, broke in and got Jody?'

I smiled a genuine big smile. I took David's number and explained to Sergeant Elliot, who nodded again, and I thanked him and dialled it eagerly.

I nearly fell on the floor when I heard Irene's quick, rough "hello" as though she'd been disturbed and was put out by it.

'It's Julie.'

The next five minutes went crazy, and for all my exhaustion and the total shock, I couldn't help feeling happy to hear them. The welcome over the phone was stunning. I heard David screaming and Ann shouting. I heard Bernie laughing, probably at David's dramatic face, and then Irene finally saying, 'you alright, love?'

Then I heard a babble and a "mama" at the end of the phone, and I felt elated.

'Baby, baby,' I cooed down the phone. The tears were streaming down my face. 'Jody, its mama.' It was the first time I hadn't felt uncomfortable saying it. She went silent as though she was reacting to my voice. "Mama," she said as clear as day.

I put the phone down as I started to sob. I couldn't take any more. Dad put his arms around me, and Veronica quickly grabbed the box of tissue.

'Come on now,' Julie,' she said. She was stern, but I trusted her voice. 'This will soon be over, and you'll be home in a couple of days, and you will be able to give her the tightest squeeze.'

'Your transport is here, Julie. We need to do some paperwork quickly, and then we need to get you over to HMP Styal. Don't worry, they will look after you there.' My stomach lurched and spun into the tightest knot.

I was going to prison. I remember thinking that I would go when I threw the hot water in her face, but she carted me off instead. I should have been thankful, I suppose. Then I felt the guilt.

She was dead.

My mum was dead.

I saw her lying on the floor and shook my head

to remove the image. Another image that would be etched in my mind forever.

As I went through the door, which would lead me to the van that would take me to prison, I saw her through the window. I saw Jane's reflection, and she also looked sad. Was she sad for mum, or was she sad for me? I tried to smile slightly, but she didn't smile back.

I whispered, 'I'm sorry Jane,' as they led me into the back of the van.

David and Az got back to the house. They couldn't get in quick enough to tell everyone the latest.

They ran into the kitchen, where Ann and Irene were sitting at the table drinking tea. Jody was sitting on a rug on the floor, playing with a wooden spoon and pans. Irene had made some sensory stuff with tin foil and greaseproof paper. She was having a ball. Bernie was lying on the settee in the living room watching shit TV.

'What's happened? Has Julie killed the Yeti?' Irene said, supping on her tea. She laughed at her own humour. 'The Yeti,' she repeated. 'Is she really that bad?' She looked at Ann, who was nodding her head slowly.

'Someone has killed the Yeti,' David yelled.

Bernie hobbled into the kitchen, holding on to her side. She wanted to make sure she hadn't been mistaken in what she had heard and that she didn't miss out on anything else that was about to be said.

'You what?' She leant on the kitchen door to give herself a bit of strength. 'Are yer sure? It was nowt to do with you our David, was it?' She looked worried as she asked her brother.

'Er that's twice he's been accused of murder this week now our Bern. Leave it out love?' Their mother didn't like anyone accusing her kids of anything.

'No, it's nowt to do with me,' he reassured them. 'But what do you mean I've been accused of murder? Who's fucking accusing me of what?'

'No one,' Bernie said. 'ItsMum being dramatic

as usual. When the copper was asking me about my accident, he wondered if you knew anything about it. But he didn't say anything about murder because there was no murder, was there? Because I'm here, aren't I?'

He was none the wiser. It was like having a conversation with dumb and flipping dumber with these two. He could never make head nor tail of what they were harping on about.

'Come and sit over here love,' Irene pulled her out a chair from under the table. 'Make her a fresh brew, our David.'

He was gobsmacked. He'd never made Bernie a brew; they both always made him the brews. He wasn't even sure where the kettle was, but he found it.

Az went over and put his arm around Bernie's waist to help her across the kitchen floor. She looked at all six foot three of him and gave him a sweet smile. 'Aw ta, Az,' she said shyly.

David rolled his eyes and just knew she'd be still hobbling this time next year; she doted on a bit of attention she did.

'Right, so go on now son,' Irene wanted the juices on this one. 'What happened?'

And just as David was about to tell them all the gory details, there was a knock on the front door.

Ann bent down to pick up Jody to put her on her knee.

'Who can that be?' David said, trying to look out of the kitchen window to see if he could see anyone.

'Go and see,' said Irene. 'No doubt, it'll be for you. I only live here.'

He went to the door and gasped when he saw who it was.

'Oh well, well, well. What do you want lady?' His tone was menacing.

'Is she dead?' Sandra looked behind her and was desperate to be asked into the house.

'Is who dead?' He wasn't giving her anything. She could stand on the front doorstep.

'Susan?' she grimaced as she said the name. 'Susan Robinson.'

'What's it got to do with you?' He had both hands on his hips for this one.

'Is Julie ok?' She was shaking now.

'What the actual fuck? You've got some bastard nerve. Don't be coming here asking after someone you've plotted against for months and put in danger. Putting us in danger.'

'David,' she said sincerely.

'That's me name. Don't wear it out.' He leant on the door as though he was bored. 'Come on, spit it out.'

'She's a manipulating vile piece of shit. As if I have had any say in what I've done. She only wanted me to keep an eye on Julie and report back everything. She was planning to kidnap Jody before she landed in her lap, but it all went tits up when her father got to Julie first.'

David thought about it. Could he judge her for getting involved? It would have been difficult to escape the claws of Susan Robinson, once gripped. She must have had something on Sandra, and he needed to know what it was.

'Come in,' he said, his voice a bit softer.

Everyone was shocked when they saw Sandra from next door.

'Er, hiya love,' Irene was standoffish but offered her a brew because it was the "law".

Ann stood up with Jody on her hip.

'I'm going to get off home, Irene. Sounds like there's nothing to worry about now, and I'm going to get this beautiful little lady into her bed.'

The phone rang.

Irene rushed over to answer, and as she said, 'hello,' she waved her hands wildly to try and get everyone's attention.

'It's Julie,' she yelled to everyone.

'Oh my god,' David yelled.

'Give her 'ere,' he grabbed Jody from Ann and ran over to the phone with her.

Ann shouted, 'Hope you're ok Julie?'

And Bernie laughed with excitement at the joy of everyone all of a sudden.

Sandra sat at the kitchen table. They all forgot that she was there for a minute.

After a very quick chat with Julie, the phone went dead.

'Bet she was in a police cell if they think she killed her mum,' Irene blurted out.

David looked at his mother and then at Sandra as if to say, 'not in front of her.'

Az helped Ann pack the car, putting Jody gently in her car seat for her. He told Ann to lock her doors as she was driving home. It was getting late now, and you 'just never know around here,' he said.

Once Ann had left, David turned his attention to Sandra.

'Right, what do you want Sandra?' he asked bluntly. 'Susan Robinson had you by the short and curlies. That's why you had to do as you were told?'

He looked her dead in the eye. 'Yes, she is dead. They don't know yet how it happened. Now, what did she have on you? If you want our trust, it's the only way.' He was sly in his approach.

She looked at Irene, Bernie and Az. 'She knew about my financial situation and knew that I'd claimed as a single parent even when Scott was living with me. She said she would grass me up and that she would phone social services and tell them that I was a fraudster who needed the extra money to feed my drug habit.'

'You've not got a drug habit, Sandra,' Irene said, perturbed by her being worried about something she didn't even do.

'Me and Scott always liked weed though.' She sniffled pathetically.

'So do half of the estate love, and she'll know that. She's had you right over. Guesswork love.'

'Yeah, but she said if a social worker got wind of it, they would take the kids off me. She convinced me that this would happen, and I ended up a wreck because of it. She made me go to the hospital. She wanted me to question Bernie to find out where Julie was. She made me form a relationship with that guy Rob, for what reason I don't know. It sounds dead stupid now I'm saying it out loud. But she really freaked me out, and I really thought sommat was going to happen to my kids.'

David was deep in thought.

'She's picked up on your weaknesses straight

away, took them and made them into mincemeat. She's turned your biggest fear into a close reality in convincing you that your kids would get taken off you. And because you had claimed single parent, like a lot of girls have done, and because you smoke weed, on paper yeah, that's fraud and drugs. When she's describing it like that, it sounds serious and is illegal, hence your fear.'

He was starting to sympathise.

'But in actual fact girl, no one has got the staff nowadays to go looking for a toking mother who claimed a single parent because her partner was in and out more than the Hokey Cokey. It's not like you're throwing back three bottles of vodka a night and leaving them to sit in their own shit while earning three hundred pounds a week on the side, selling yer arse. Anyway, the horrible bitch is dead now, and the more I hear about her, the more I realise that this world is a better place without her.'

He looked her dead in the eye. 'Is there anything else we need to know?'

She took a deep breath.

'It was her who told me Scott had slept with Julie. I was supposed to start a big fight with her and Angie when we all went out, making sure she got injured. But Julie got off early. I had bloody instructions to beat Julie up, but she nearly kicked the fucking daylights out of me. Then I had contact with her uncle and father. They approached me, and I was delivering money from them to Julie. I let them know there was potential danger that night in Manchester. I was scared, but I was also trying my best to do the right thing.'

'It's not even that bad that you've just been a dick,' Bernie said from nowhere. 'But it's caused so much hassle. Look at me. I get why you did it; it's horrible being bullied, but you should never have got involved.'

Sandra shook her head, 'I shouldn't have got involved, but there is one last thing that is really hard for me to admit.'

She couldn't look any of them in the eye. 'I was in the car with Susan that day when she ran you over. She wanted to know who David was, and I showed him to her.'

'Nah fuck that,' Irene jumped up. She was livid, and her teeth were starting to stick out like a dog that was about to bite an intruder. 'You could have lied.'

'She would have found out another way.'

'Nah you didn't have to tell her that. It's not like you just shown her who he was. You were in the fucking car when she hit our Bernie. You must have known what she was going to do. That's not what happens round here. We stick together. Julie's got more nous than you, and she is nigh on a bloody foreigner.'

'She forced me,' Sandra pleaded.

'No, Sandra, love, that's dead fucking wrong, that is. Get out of my house right now. I hope the thud of hitting our Bernie haunts you forever. Now get out. You could have blagged that one. I'm not having it. Get out now.'

Irene pointed fiercely at the front door. She had shown sheer dominance, and for once, David and Bernie were silent. Az sat there quivering in his boots.

'Before I go, there is something else,'

'What?'

'Ah nothing, none of you want to know me now anyway.' She became the victim again. 'But there is someone else at that house that lived with Susan Robinson.'

'I think you're in too deep,' David said. 'And like me mam just said, you need to get out.'

They heard the door slam hard as Sandra the Snake left the house.

Irene was still livid. 'She's not to come in here again. Do you hear me? No one messes with my kids, putting them in danger. Our Bernie could have been dead now.'

She looked at her daughter, who was back on the settee with a big tub of ice cream and a large spoon.

'Where did you get that our Bernie?' Irene looked confused.

'Out the freezer mum,' she said, not lifting her head up for a second.

'Jesus, Bern, it's been there years. I think I bought it one Christmas and we ended up having trifle instead. Do you remember?'

'No wonder you're fat our Bernie,' David laughed.

She shook her head and rolled her eyes and didn't let his bitchiness stop her for once.

Then they all sat in silence for a minute, trying to absorb what had just gone on. It was all mad beyond belief. Sandra had a nerve. She'd committed the cardinal sin in betraying her own; it was unheard of, especially to that degree.

David said to the others. 'Wonder what she meant by someone living in the house with Susan Robinson?'

'Who cares?' Irene said. 'I want nothing more to do with her.'

'But when Julie first went missing and we went to the house, me and Ann, I thought I saw Julie looking out the window. And then there was the knocking in that bedroom. You heard too, didn't you, Az?' He looked at his friend for back up.

David's cogs were going.

As dusk fell on the huge council estate that was home to many, David thought about how their community was a community of honour. It was a community of loyalty, and if you didn't mirror it, you weren't welcome.

He thought about how the other neighbours would react if they knew what Sandra had done, Scott would go off his head and Sharon and the Kolash bunch would scratch her eyes out.

No, he thought, Sandra had shit the bed this time. She'd never be part of anything again. Word would get round that she was in the car that nearly killed Bernie, and she would have to leave eventually. She might have been being blackmailed, but you never betrayed your comrades.

Chapter 36 - The Robinsons

Ron Robinson had a call directly from Sergeant Elliot asking for him and his brother to return to the police station immediately. There had been a vital breakthrough, and they needed help with their enquiries.

Ron knew immediately what it was. It had only been a matter of time.

He knew he should have worked quicker and tried to arrange for an alternative sooner. It hadn't happened, and the law had beat him to it.

He wasn't sure how his brother would take this. Things would certainly change for the worse once he knew. He thought hard and wondered if there was a way out. But he knew that there would be a warrant for their arrest if they went missing. No, he was going to have to face this with his brother, who deserved to know the truth.

Steven Robinson had left his daughter at Styal Prison. He was told he couldn't stay any longer and was asked to leave whilst they did the relevant paperwork with Julie and got her settled in. He couldn't even say goodnight to her or see her to give her any reassurance.

He stood and looked at the building, hoping to get a glimpse of her, but of course, he didn't. The wired fences were high; the red-bricked building was old and could have looked welcoming, but the bars on the windows gave it away. He felt despondent as he got into his car.

He'd arrived home somewhat exhausted by it all

and was ready to pour himself a whisky and try and relax if that was even possible. There was a warm reception waiting for him – his niece and son.

Then his brother told him that they needed to go back to Warrington Police Station. Ron looked panicky and uneasy.

'Can we not go tomorrow?' he said.

Ron explained to him that Sergeant Elliot's tone had too much urgency in it to be ignored. So he and his brother set off back to Warrington.

The sky was now black, and the rain was thrashing down hard on the windscreen of the car as they drove along the M56, passing Manchester Airport, whose bright lights were hidden by the threatening weather. The wipers were on full pelt but weren't making any difference. It was hard to see the road as the reflection of the orange motorway lights were bouncing off the windscreen. The radio of the car blasted out Simon & Garfunkel's "Mrs Robinson" at full volume.

Ron said that he wanted to explain a few things and that he had a feeling he knew what was going on. But the sound of the rain and the radio was making it difficult for him to be heard.

Steven didn't have a clue what was going on, mostly because he couldn't really hear Ron. But he politely acknowledged him as he spoke loudly over the noise of the rain and the radio.

Steven looked at the man who had been like a father to him and was never far away from his side. The man who had blocked Susan Robinson from him, either by payoff or by threats. He had watched him deal with her whilst he recovered from the mental torture and the death of his beautiful little girl. Ron had helped him buy the pub in London, which gave him a huge salary and enabled him to buy a luxurious home in an exclusive part of Hale Barns.

Ron mentioned Susan, and although Steven still couldn't really hear what he was saying, his ears pricked up at the mention of her name. He noticed that Ron sounded different in his tone. He heard him say that it was all her idea, and he didn't want to be part of it.

'Say that again,' Steven demanded, sitting up straight in the car, genuinely just wanting him to repeat himself.

'You heard me!' Ron was aggressive, not realising that Steven hadn't heard anything. Ron thought Steven was sitting up ready for a fight because of what he had just said.

Steven was starting to feel a bit pissed off. 'What the hell is the matter with you?' He asked his brother. 'What the fuck have you been up to now? Ron?'

'She made me promise one thing, and that was to never tell you.'

Steven waited but was getting impatient, and his stomach was in knots.

Ron continued. 'And I'm sorry mate. Some things I had to go with.'

'What the hell have you done?'

Steven grabbed the wheel to get Ron's attention. As he did so, Ron lost his grip. They swerved to avoid a car pulling out of the left-hand lane.

As they swerved, Ron pulled too hard and lost control of the car and smashed straight into the central reservation. He had been doing eighty miles an hour. The car did a full somersault onto its roof, and as it did, another car ploughed right into it, leaving it spinning upside down on the very wet, dark M56.

Coo, Coo, ca-choo Mrs Robinson
Jesus loves you more than you will know
Woo, woo, woo
God bless you please, Mrs Robinson
Heaven holds a place for those who pray
Hey, hey, hey
Hey, hey, hey.

Ron didn't feel the bang. It was the heart attack that killed him outright.

Steven was gasping and fighting against the lack of control he had. He screamed as the car hit the barrier and felt a sense of out-of-body as it did a three-sixty turn. He felt like he was spinning on a fairground ride. He felt the bile rise to his throat, and then he saw his brother. He could see he was out cold and tried to reach over to him. But the gravity kept him held tight in his seat. It was the bang of the other car that took Steven to the dark world of unconsciousness.

'What's that you say, Mrs Robinson
Jolting Joe has left and gone away
Hey, hey, hey.'

Chapter 37 - Julie

I sat on the windowsill, in what was now my bedroom, in what used to be Ron's house, but was now my dad's.

I would never have guessed that all his business and property were in dad's name. Neither would my dad, but it was all his now, and there was a lot.

I lit my cig and curled my knees up to my chest, hugging them as I did so. I looked into the window and grinned at her, then shook my head in total disbelief. It was followed by a sinking feeling in my gut that I couldn't shake off. The last few weeks had been harrowing, shocking and total elation all in one, and I was knackered.

I thought about the accident. It had been fatal for Ron. He'd died in the crash. Dad had been taken to hospital, out cold and in a coma that lasted for over a week. His injuries were all recoverable, and I thanked my lucky stars daily for that.

Fiona had taken the death of her father badly, and that was to be expected. But she wouldn't condone what he had done. She swore that she'd had no idea what her father had been up to. We all believed her. I believed her. I knew her.

I took a drag on my cigarette and inhaled hard, blowing the smoke into the reflection in the window and then wondering why I would want to do that to her. She looked pissed off, and I wasn't surprised. I looked past her through the window. Outside looked warm, but the air was definitely getting cooler. It was blowing in gently through the small window at the top, which was slightly open. It had been a hot day.

I'd come into my room as I often did to still my mind for fifteen minutes. This time was for me to try and gain some perspective on what had gone on. I would do it until I was better. I was determined for this new life to work for me and my baby.

I thought about when I was in prison, sat in a stark cell which I shared with a girl from Blakely who was in for fraud. She was ok, but I wasn't letting her in. My guard was well and firmly up. I didn't have a clue what was going on outside. There had been no sign of dad, or Veronica, or anybody. I was waiting to be charged, and it could have been for murder.

It wasn't until I got the message about the accident that I understood why there had been no contact. I was devastated but relieved I'd not just been left to rot.

I'd been charged with the manslaughter of Susan Robinson. It was black and white to them. I could barely breathe. It was all happening so quickly.

Pavel and David were allowed to visit me, but they were of no help. They were more emotional than I was. In fact, David got asked the leave the visiting room as he was upsetting other prisoners with his bawling. He stammered, 'I'm sorry babe,' as they were carting him out. He was a wreck.

Pavel told me that he was trying to get hold of Veronica without much luck. He told me that he'd been to see dad and that he was still in a coma but doing well. He said it was just a matter of time.

The court day came, and I hadn't eaten properly

for nearly a week. I felt weak in body and even weaker in mind. I was beginning to lose myself and barely had any energy. I had no idea what would happen in court. I just knew I had a different solicitor as there was no sign of Veronica.

I remember standing in the witness stand, which had a screen around it. I had been led up from the cell the court housed. I looked around in total fear. Yet I mustered a smile at my entourage when I spotted them, and I would never forget that moment for as long as I lived. I'd never seen such a turnout, and I couldn't have felt any more loved than I did at that minute.

Irene sat there in her best clobber, a dark blue suit with a slit in the skirt that ruffled around her middle due to the extra weight she'd put on. David, not crying but stood proud in a black jumper and pants. My brother, his blond streaked hair forever growing out of shape, and Fiona, in her brown cords and orange cropped jumper with a shirt underneath. Bernie was probably still recovering, but I was shocked to see Az from the corner shop; shocked and touched. He was suited and booted too.

I saw Ann, her short hair all washed and neatly coiffured, she had a similar suit on to Irene, but it fitted her better, and best of all, she had my baby girl on her knee. My Jody. I gave her a little wave, and she shouted, 'mama' it was heart-wrenching.

They all sat there proud and unashamed of me. It was as if they were on trial the way they'd dressed up for the occasion, and then it dawned on me. They were on trial.

They were here with me, in unity, locking swords

for one of their own, even though I would never be one of their own, they'd certainly adopted me. I felt the tears stinging my eyes. They were on trial with me.

The court was asked to rise as the judge entered. A chill ran through my body, a feeling that was so strong I was starting to feel ill. I looked towards Irene, and she nodded at me fiercely; her eyes spoke a thousand words, words that translated straight to my heart.

'Come on love, you're gonna be alright, you've got this.'

I heard it, and I felt it straight from her heart to mine. I have, I have really got this.

I looked at David, who was grabbing his mouth and kissing into his hand for me. I felt his love and gripped my fists tightly.

They led me to the dock and gave me a copy of the bible to swear on, and I remembered the judge waffling on about my charges.

Suddenly there was a loud bang on the courtroom door as it was barged open.

I remember being in shock when Veronica ran in, dramatically, closely followed by a court official, who she wafted away like he was a fly bothering her.

She was shouting, 'Stop, Stop! We need a re-investigation of this case. This is the person who killed Susan Robinson in a bid to stop her from strangling her twin sister to death.'

I stared at the woman whose hand she was waving in the air. Her mousey brown hair reminded me of mine. I recognised her immediately. How could I not? I'd been looking at her for years. But this time, there was no mirror, no glass window, and no reflection. She was real.

The words twin sister rang loudly in my ears. She stared at me. Her eyes piercing into mine as though she was in disbelief. I went hot and couldn't stand up for much longer. I was going to faint. It was her.

It was Jane.

Chapter 38

The next thing I knew, we were in a confab room. I had fainted, and the court first aiders had to bring me around and help me to a room with two oxblood chesterfield sofas in it. This wasn't a cell, that was for sure.

She was there, almost in front of me, sat on the other sofa. I stared at her. I couldn't believe what I was seeing. It was her; it really was. I went to sit next to her. It was by nature; I'd always be at her side when we were little, so it was an automatic reaction. She wasn't responsive, and I wasn't sure if she was in shock too.

I rubbed her back and bent my head down to look into her face, but she didn't look at me. I wanted to grab her, to feel if she was real. I couldn't believe that she was here and had been alive all this time.

I looked to Veronica for some sort of explanation. She shrugged her shoulders and explained to me briefly that Jane's death had been faked by Ron and Susan Robinson.

I was more gobsmacked that Ron had been involved than I was to see Jane. I couldn't believe that anyone could do this, that anyone could pretend that someone had died in an accident and let us all grieve for her. I thought about the times that my mother had blamed her vicious behaviour on Jane's death. There were even times I'd forgiven her because of Jane's death.

Veronica went on to say that Jane had spent her early life in Sweden with a family who had fostered her, with Susan's permission. I shook my head in total disbelief again. No wonder I was unstable, no wonder we both were.

When Jane turned twenty-one, Susan had got her back and kept her under lock and key, hidden from the world. That was around the time she had kicked me out. I felt sick for Jane, who had obviously endured mental pain and I felt more than betrayed.

Jane sat there listening. Of course, she was in a daze, and of course, she was lost. God knows what had gone on in Sweden, and God knows what had happened upon her return. She will have been put through what I had and worse, no doubt. My mother would have used her body for her own enjoyment. It was awful.

'Jane,' I muttered, hoping to get some sort of reaction from her. She looked up, and tears were streaming down her face. I started to cry with her, and I felt like I was looking through the window. I touched her tears as if I was touching the window.

She pulled away quickly.

'You never saved me,' she hissed in a very mixed accent.

I was gobsmacked, assuming she was talking about the fall. I was desperate to make her feel better. I grabbed her shoulders gently as she sat next to me.

'We were five years old.' I told her softly. 'Mum said that you'd died. I mourned and grieved for you all my life. You were the other half of me that I lost for all that time. And now you're here. I can't believe it.'

I sat back to let her reflect, but she put her head

down sullenly and even stuck her lip out like a spoiled child, refusing to come anywhere near me.

I realised that she might have had some psychological issues. I had to bear with her, and I had to give her time.

'Thank you for saving me,' I continued, trying my hardest to switch her light on, hoping she would come round.

'I hate her,' she spat. As though it had nothing to do with saving me at all and that it was all about just wanting Susan dead.

I didn't know what to say. I was in total shock and didn't know what was going to happen next.

Veronica left the room and returned minutes later.

I forgot all about the situation for a minute as soon as I heard her little voice; my baby girl. Veronica had brought Jody to see me.

She ran right up to me with no hesitation, and I gave her the hardest tightest hug and smelt her hair as I held on to her hard. I had missed this part of me more than I'd ever missed anything.

'Mama,' she smiled up at me. I smiled through my tears and brushed my hands through her huge blonde curls. She wriggled onto my knee and put her head on my chest, stuck her own dummy in her mouth and snuggled into her mama, who was never going to part from her again.

'Ann is waiting for you downstairs, Julie,' Veronica said. 'She's going to take you and Jane home. You are both free to go for now until a full investigation is done on Susan's activity. It's clear to the judge that you two girls have been subjected to her abuse for years. And what she did with Jane is not only immoral; it's totally illegal. We found all the paperwork which backs up Jane's story in a suitcase back at the house. That woman would have a lot to answer for if she had lived.

Jane leant over to touch Jody. I was pleased that she'd taken notice and leant towards her so she could stroke her head or touch her face.

Jody looked up and wailed, 'No mama. No,' she cried and became visibly upset, clinging on to me with all her little might. My stomach turned as it dawned on me that Jody might have met Jane when Susan Robinson took her.

'Have you met Jody before?' I asked my twin sister.

She grinned and replied in her strange accent. 'Yes, you don't think *she* looked after her, do you?'

Her grin sent a chill down my spine. She was a mini version of my mother. I didn't know where she got that grin from, she looked so much like me, but I couldn't make that face if I tried every day for the rest of my life.

Jody settled down when she felt how secure she was. She knew mama was here and that no one would hurt her again. I shuddered at the thought of it.

Veronica said that Jane had been assessed and required counselling and psychological help. She'd been given some medication to try and relax her, and a doctor would be sent to the house to check on her in the morning.

I felt uneasy about it and selfishly wondered for a minute whether Jane had somewhere else to go. But of course, she couldn't go back to that house alone.

I tried to remember that it was Jane, my beautiful twin sister, who I had thought was dead. She would have been through hell and would need to recover.

I was led down the stairs to where Ann was patiently waiting for us. She was as shocked as I was and asked Jane if she was alright. She got a "yes, thank you," at least.

Ann gave me a big hug and told me everyone else had gone back to my uncle's house to wait. She said that she was sorry about what happened to Jody. I reassured her that I had never needed her more than I did over the last few weeks. Without Ann, and probably Andy, I'd be so unsettled about who had my little girl. I told her I appreciated it more than ever. They were her family, and Jody loved them endlessly.

I handed my girl over to her nana whilst she safely put her in her car seat, and we set off to the house. I felt excited, relieved, scared, anxious, sick and confused all at once but felt happy to be going home. And when dad got home, it would be perfect.

The greeting I got was amazing. David's tight hug and Irene's warm squeezes. Bern was there looking a bit worse for wear, but she was there and so pleased to see me, the huge grin on her face said as much. Az was there too, and it dawned on me that he and Bern were a thing now. That made my heart melt. Pav held me tight, and Fiona sobbed, and we became emotional. After all, she'd lost her dad, no matter what he'd done.

I introduced everyone to Jane and told Jane that Pav was our big brother and Fiona our cousin. She smiled, which was nice to see. Fiona fussed over her and took over, sitting down on the sofa with her.

We all sat for hours talking about what had gone on. It really had been a harrowing time. The guys told me their side of their story. How at first David and Ann had taken Jody and Jess to Susan Robinson's house, looking for me. They told me about the car crash they had and how, by coincidence, it had been her, and they ended up running for their lives.

They told me about Snakey Sandra and how Susan had managed to manipulate her into spying on me, and how she was in the car when she'd ran over Bernie. I was absolutely dumbfounded to hear this.

They made me laugh, telling me about Scott going to "the Yeti's" as they called her and doing what he did so that David and Az could get Jody.

I looked at David and watched him flamboyantly telling the tale. I smiled again until they told me about how bad the accident had been with Bernie and how they thought she would die. I was devastated at this bit. I could imagine their whole world would have been shattered if she had have done.

They told me the full gory detail of how *she'd* managed to get Jody off Ann. Ann started to cry.

'Right, stop being so dramatic,' David put her straight. 'She's here now, and she's already shit on me twice.'

We all laughed. He was always just what the doctor ordered, a breath of fresh air, always.

I explained about the first trip to London and how I'd had my life turned upside down through total coincidence.

'You're a dark horse, you, our Julie, going to London for sex,' David laughed.

I explained that unbeknown to me, I'd met my brother Pavel, was followed to safety by my uncle and brought home by my dad. I told them that I'd had no idea until they'd tried to get me before Susan did. I explained the phone call from Pav, and then I told them about being locked in the safe room with Fiona while someone had broken in.

Jane interrupted unexpectedly, 'She wanted your suitcase. It had the papers in it about me being in Sweden.'

She threw me totally. I didn't see any papers in that suitcase, but it made sense as it did go missing, and I'd looked for it just after getting out of the safe room.

I told them about first meeting dad. And then how we'd got the call off David about Jody, so me and Pavel set off to Manchester on the train but fell asleep and didn't wake up until we were at Glasgow so had to come all the way back.

I told them I hadn't realised that David had got Jody and that I'd got into the house but that within minutes, she had me cornered and was strangling me.

I sighed. 'I nearly went, you know; my whole life flashed before my eyes. Then you,' I stared at Jane, 'you saved my life.'

I told them that I thought I'd had an out-of-body experience when I saw who I thought was *me* hitting Susan over the head with a stone frying pan.

'I wanted her dead,' Jane said. Her tone was eerie as she finished off my story. 'I just needed her dead.' The venom spewed from her body, and again, I shuddered.

David squeezed my hand so tight that I nearly yelped. Pavel and I looked at each other.

'I'd do it again if I had to,' she continued. 'I wouldn't stop until I knew she was dead.'

'Well, you clearly did that babe; she's well gone,' David said, trying to ease the tension as she left everyone with their jaws on the floor and shocked to the core.

There wasn't much to say after that, and they all decided to get off. It was getting late, after all. I loved them all and couldn't wait until I saw them again; they made me feel part of something. I didn't want David to leave. He must have read my mind.

'I'm staying here with you girl,' he whispered. 'We'll have to top and tail. I'm not leaving you here with Aileen fuckin' Wournos love.'

I started to laugh, 'Stop it,' I chastised him. 'But yeah, stay here, please.'

Fiona helped me show Jane to her room. We climbed the big stone stairs that led to the massive landing while David and Pav sat downstairs and cracked open cans of beer. I smiled as I could hear them chatting away. Well, David was chatting away as poor Pav couldn't get a word in.

As we got onto the long landing, Jane stopped dead in her tracks, and we nearly backed into her.

'I want to go home. I don't want to stay here.'

I didn't have the head to take the lead. I felt like we were missing an adult, then realised I was an adult and that I would have to deal with the situation. I didn't know where I was getting my strength from; I was on autopilot of some sort. I told her straight that she would have to stay here. At least until dad got home and things got sorted, but right now, whilst there was still an investigation going on, she'd have to stay.

She stared at me with those piercing eyes that looked nothing like the reflections I used to look at so longingly. 'I'll stay, but I won't sleep, so you'd better not.'

And once again, here I was in a situation whereby I was subjected to someone else's flaws, someone else's inability to love, and someone else's cruelty.

I wouldn't have it. I really wouldn't, so she'd better watch her step or she would have to go back to the house.

That night I got in bed, thinking that I'd been harsh on Jane. I also felt the knock-on effect of having such an abusive mother, so I should empathise. I would be the only other person in the world that had half an idea of what she had gone through.

Jody was fast asleep in the little bed that had been put at the other end of the room for her. I was thankful we were together.

I lay there and had to force myself to breathe slower and calmer, or I would have hyperventilated. I couldn't help it as much as I tried. I couldn't get over what Jane had said about me not going to sleep. It really was disturbing me.

I had left David to drink with my brother. I needed to go down and talk to them. I wanted to tell them what she had said and see what their opinion was. Maybe I was hypersensitive, given the fact I was exhausted by the whole thing.

I got out of bed and went down the stairs to the living room, but I couldn't see them. There was a lamp on and some cans on the side, but they weren't there. Maybe they'd gone out for a cig. I wondered if I should go and join them but thought better of it. So I walked right into the lounge and went to sit down on the huge sofa until they came back.

I was not expecting to see what I saw. My mouth, not for the first time that evening, dropped to the floor, and I nearly let out a scream.

Two bare arses were in the air; one belonging to my brother and the other belonging to my best friend.

You couldn't bloody write this shit.

Chapter 39

Over the following three months, there was tremendous change. The court dropped all charges, and Susan Robinson's estate was passed over to me.

At first, I didn't want it, but dad said I was to see it as a type of compensation and that I deserved a fresh start. I had lots of money to play with and lots of good intentions. Of course, I made sure Jane got half, which still left me with more than enough.

I signed the flat over to Andy; he was in his element. I had it all done up for him because, after all, he would have Jody on occasion, and from now on, she would only have the best. The flat had a TV that looked like a huge silver box, but they loved it. He had a state-of-the-art video recorder, and there were no slots for fifty pence's anywhere.

David moved out of his flat, and Az moved in there with Bernie. Against all odds, they were going to give it a go. They were lucky both sides of the families had no issues with colour, race or religion and everybody wished them nothing but luck.

Bernie was recovering well and still loved the attention that the accident brought. So I brought it up often and reminded her how brave and strong she was. Az dropped her off at her mum's every morning so that she could spend the day with Irene while he opened and ran the shop. She must have walked down six times a day to see him, sometimes dragging Irene with her, but Az was always pleased to see them.

Ann and Irene were best buddies. Ann was always

round at Irene's, sharing cups of teas and gossiping about whatever was happening on the huge council estate that had a different story every day.

Irene's home would always be an open house for me. I would never stop going for the warmth and comfort it gave me. I'd never feel it anywhere else.

David and Pavel were very much in love and were another beautiful couple, and I wanted them to last forever. It was my ideal set up, my brother and my best friend. They felt like the family I'd never had. Always fussing and looking after Jody and me. They both knew me well, and that helped.

David moved in with us and became a full-time nanny to Jody. Pavel did a lot of work from home, even though he was based in London, thankfully he was technical and had a fab set up.

Dad had been discharged from hospital. He had received the news about Jane almost the minute he came out of his coma. He had been told that's what he was needed for at the police station the night of the crash.

He had no idea what Ron had been up to but had since learnt everything from Veronica. He sat us down and had some difficult conversations with us. Difficult for him because he obviously idolised his big brother and even more difficult for Fiona.

He did say that whatever he'd done, his brother had really looked after him, and he would always love him for that. He explained that she must have had something on him and was bribing him because he had genuinely looked out for us all.

He was elated to see Jane but got the same response as I did. My heart sunk for him. He'd been through enough. We spoke about it afterwards, and we both decided she was deeply disturbed by her death being faked and all the other shit she'd gone through and that it was no wonder. We agreed to be gentle with her.

It had taken a few weeks of heavy adjustment for him, and I had mixed emotions about the whole thing.

He soon got back into the swing of things and said that he would have to go back to London as his business wouldn't run itself. He agreed that Pav would stay and do accounts from home but would be required to go down every few weeks to meet with stakeholders.

He made sure his brother was buried first. It had been a huge affair. Obviously, he was a very influential man. I felt sad and cried a genuine tear. I'd liked him and felt he had done so much for me but couldn't forgive him for being part of the Jane cover-up and everything else he had concocted with that woman. He would have gone to prison for an awfully long time if he had have lived.

Fiona asked for a transfer to Sheffield University. She said she had some close friends there and felt it would be better to be away for a while. We would always remain family; she was the first person I'd opened up to, and I loved her for that.

I had enrolled at Manchester University and was due to start this week. I wanted my degree in psychology. I actually wanted to be a psychologist, so it would be a long haul, but I was up for it. And best of all, I had the fees to cover it and live more than comfortably.

I felt both sick and excited about it. I had the childcare in place, now I just needed to face people, but it would be an excellent start to my healing journey, and I needed it more than ever now. I was determined to release my demons, and bit by bit, I would.

Jane had calmed somewhat, but she was still reclusive and stayed in her room a lot. There was an awkwardness when she did come out, even though everyone made an effort with her. She had various counsellors and was referred to a psychologist who was based at the hospital. She had been prescribed medication and was in contact with the crisis team in the event of any meltdown.

I sat and spoke to her often, but she was hard work. It was almost as if she was there but didn't want to interact because it was me. I couldn't believe that the reflection in the window was there in front of me. I'd been speaking to her for years in my head while looking into her face.

But she wasn't the reflection; she was real, and I found that I couldn't look in her face. Because it wasn't her, and in some odd way, I still missed her, I missed her in my reflections.

She reminded me of my mother so much that it was difficult to warm to her. She was insistent on blaming dad and me for leaving her with Susan. There was no getting through to her that we'd all felt her wrath. I'd even tried to explain about what happened with Jamie and how Susan had come to have such a badly scarred face. I hoped it would unite us somewhat, but it didn't. It was almost as if she switched off to anything I said and only came to life when she was explaining her sordid ordeal, which *was* horrendous.

I think I was disappointed because we could have helped each other through it. But it wasn't to be, and I secretly hoped that she would join dad one day in London as I wasn't sure that she could care for herself and she didn't want me.

But I had Jody, who had thrived and loved being around so many beautiful people. She seemed to have forgotten about her ordeal, although she was still cagey around Jane. But she was so funny and so cheeky, and she followed poor David around everywhere he went. He pretended to be put out by her constant attention, and it was amazing to see a nearly thirty-year-old man bond and have banter with a two-year-old. It really was special. She absolutely adored him.

She spent time with Ann and Andy, but I wasn't ready to let her stay overnight yet. They'd been here for dinner, and she'd gone there. It wasn't that I didn't trust them; it was more about her being away from me; the thought made me go into a panic. But I was working on it, and they were all patient, and for that, I was thankful.

Pavel loved her and gave her so much attention. Him and David really were the best uncles you could ask for. She called then Paf and D, and it made me so happy to see it all growing around us. She had settled really quickly; she loved people, that was for sure. I was proud of her, and I knew if anything happened to me, she would be safe forever.

I didn't trust Jane though, and that was playing on my mind constantly.

Chapter 40

The weeks passed, and I had been thinking about someone else quite a lot lately. Jamie Morano.

The boy who left me for dead; well, emotionally, not physically. I wondered where he was and what he was doing. He had been the only person that I'd ever let in, that I'd ever truly loved, and he had left me devastated, seeing him with my mother in that horrific video.

I had no idea about his situation; was he married, did he have kids? I didn't care. I needed to see him again. I needed closure so that I could move on.

I did a bit of digging and found a number that led me to him. I needed to settle it once and for all. The timing probably wasn't the best given what was going on, but it wasn't leaving my head.

I was getting ready to go and meet him, or at least, Charley was. I couldn't tell him my real name in case he ignored me. I headed to The New Moon restaurant, not far away from my mother's old house.

I was hoping he wouldn't recognise me; I'd changed a lot from the eighteen-year-old girl back then. I was now a twenty-six-year-old woman on a mission to show him who was best. I wanted him to regret losing me. I wanted him to want me.

I went to the restaurant alone; I was late on purpose. I didn't want to be hanging around. I told the front of house my name, and they led me to a table where he was already waiting.

He stood up and I could see his confusion, and

the cogs were going; I could hear them whirring around in his head. He finally recognised me.

He put his hand on his chin, shook his head. 'Julie?'

I smiled and nodded my head.

'Jamie Morano.'

'God, well, this is a shock,' he looked serious. 'Who is Charley then?' he asked, his hand still rubbing his chin.

He looked me up and down, and his face softened. I had no doubt he liked what he saw. He saw me with my hair almost blonde, my huge, luscious mouth and my piercing dark eyes. I was shapely and womanly. I only ever looked like this around a wanton male. Other than that, I was a drab mother with a heavy cloud over my head.

'I didn't think you'd meet me if you knew it was me,' I explained. 'After everything that happened, I didn't think you'd ever want to see me again.'

'I've thought about you for years, so I'm glad you're here now.' He meant it.

I flicked my hair and stuck my chest out as I flirted with him. I would have him. I had to have him.

We sat down.

We ate.

We drank.

We talked.

And all the while, he couldn't take his eyes off me. He couldn't concentrate on his food. I loved making him feel uneasy. The sexual tension was oozing through the restaurant. I even think the waiter felt it as he brought over our food. I loved the feeling it gave me.

I went to the toilet, applied more makeup, smiling at myself as I did so. I looked in the long mirror and watched myself as I lifted up my figure-hugging, red dress and peeled off my red lace knickers. I was half hoping someone would come in and catch me; the thrill was nearly too much.

I joined him back at the table and slowly passed him my red lace knickers.

'I want you so bad,' I said, bold as brass. I knew I had him.

He sat there with my knickers in his hand, staring at me. I didn't flinch, but the feeling between my legs was getting warmer. I nearly wet myself when he brought them up to his face and smelled them.

'I want you so bad Julie,' he leant across the table. 'I never stopped wanting you. You were and still are beautiful.'

He stood up, paid the bill, and we were off as soon as we got in the car park. The tension was too much, and he grabbed me and kissed me hard. I pushed his hand up my dress so he could feel what was waiting for him.

We got in his car and drove to his.

As soon as we got into the house, I ripped off his clothes, leaving mine on. He kissed me hard, and I could feel the stiffness of his cock. I moaned as I wanted him to want me so bad.

We were very quickly in a bedroom. I didn't even take note of any of it; I just saw a bed.

I pulled off my dress so he could see me in full view. He grabbed my breasts and started to suck them hard. I needed harder. I was desperate as he stroked his hands up and down my body. I writhed with pure pleasure as I remembered his clumsy young hands that were now so big and strong. I lay on the bed and opened my legs wide, stroking myself while he watched. He couldn't help but touch himself, moaning with pleasure as he did so.

'Put it in,' I demanded.

He lay on top of me, kissing me and licking my neck as he put it in. I felt such a strong surge of desire and lust as he thrust himself in and out gently. I wanted it hard, and I wanted it to hurt.

I turned and knelt on all fours and screamed, 'fuck me hard.' He didn't have to be told twice as he went full throttle. I felt him in my stomach but wanted to scream in ecstasy as he thrust in and out.

'Slap my arse,' I demanded. He slapped me hard; I wanted more, so I said, 'harder.' He could barely contain himself. I threw myself on my back and pushed myself up to his mouth with my legs wrapped around his neck and said, 'lick me'; he licked away.

I threw my head back and concentrated on his hot tongue as it darted everywhere, making my legs shake and my whole body go into a beautiful spasm. As it did, I came hard in his mouth, squirting lust everywhere. I got on my knees and gave him the best suck of his life, and he yelled loudly as I let him come all over my face.

And while he was lying there, I had my cig and looked out of the window reflecting on life.

No matter what it takes, you have to be true to yourself,

You must never let her go.
Never let them treat her so bad,
Thus, changing her whole beliefs and forcing
rejection of your self worth,
Never let them do that, ever.

Chapter 41

A bang on my bedroom door broke my reverie. I nearly jumped out of my skin. I'd been thinking about my night with Jamie again, but it was done now, and there was no going back. I'd wanted closure, and I'd got it, so I needed to leave it be.

David ran in with Jody in his arms. She was giggling as he jiggled her about throwing her in the air. I rolled my eyes. I could never get any peace with these two, nor did I ever want any from them.

'Tell you what, little lady, you're cheaper than going to the gym. I've lost over a stone me, running about after you. Not sure what I'm going to put on tonight, nowt fits me, I'm going to look like a bag of rags!' He was talking to himself rather than Jody.

Then he turned his attention to me.

'Right lady, I'm going out, remember? You need to prise this one from me while I get me glad rags on.'

He was going to The Royal Oak with Pav to see some of the old crowd. I could have gone if I had wanted to, but I refused, still reluctant to let Ann have Jody overnight. It made me feel sick to be apart from her. Although, next time, I was definitely going to sort it because I was starting to regret it already.

I grabbed Jody from him and swung her in the air; she giggled. 'Bath and bed for you, my little lady,' I grabbed her tightly, kissing her blond curls.

'Bat and bet,' she repeated. David and I laughed.

'She's been here before that one,' he said like a

proud father. The amount of love he had for her was adorable.

'Right, I'm going. But babe, just watch her tonight. Crazy Aileen, I mean.' He pointed towards the door as if Jane was stood there. 'I've caught her twice now with our Jody, nothing to shout about but enough to know, she needs an eye on her that one.'

I shuddered when he said that. I decided we'd stay in our room tonight. We had a telly, and Jody would sleep while I watched Friday night's channel four.

He gave us both big hugs and kisses and sashayed out of the room like he owned the place. I had to laugh; he never failed to make me smile.

I bathed Jody and enjoyed her splashing around that much that I jumped in with her, which made her laugh and get so excited. She splashed and kicked about in the water until most of it was on the floor, and the bath was nearly empty.

I loved drying her with our big fluffy towels and putting warm pyjamas on her little body. I got into my own pyjamas and carried her over to her little bed that was carved from wood with a canopy over the top of it, fit for a princess. I smiled as I tucked her into it.

'Doo doo,' she murmured, and I grabbed her dummy off the side and watched, stroking her hair as she soothed herself to sleep. I had never felt at one with anything, but this little girl made me feel connected with myself, if only for a moment; she made me feel life. I kissed her cheek as she slept, then went over to my side of the room.

As I went to put the telly on, there was a knock

on my door. It could only be Jane as there was no one else in the house. I didn't want to wake Jody, so I walked over to the door and answered it. She was standing there, looking slightly dishevelled.

'What's up?' I asked her.

'You need to explain to Jody that she can't come into my room.' She was pulling a face like a child, looking like a scared rabbit, but beneath it, I could see the real her.

'What has she done that warrants a bar from your room?' I asked.

'She moved some of my stuff.' She said it with such anger, I half expected her to say she'd smashed her prize possessions.

'I didn't know she had been in your room? When was this?' I questioned. I was losing patience now. This was ridiculous.

'She was in there with me. David couldn't be bothered with her, so I took her in with me for five minutes.'

She did the grin.

'She's two years old Jane, but I'll explain to her that she is never allowed to go in your room again.'

And I shut the door. I meant it. I didn't want her near Jody. She could play nicey-nicey all she wanted to; she was starting to give me the creeps.

She knocked lightly again.

As I opened the door, she barged her way into my room.

'What do you want Jane? We're trying to settle down for the evening.'

'Don't slam the door in my face again. Who do you think you are?' she said. And with that, she marched off.

I made my mind up to phone dad tomorrow and sort this out. She had to go, she could live with him, or I was going. She reminded me too much of my mother and the old days.

I put the telly on low and climbed into bed. It was Friday night, and channel four was really taking over, with its American sitcoms and late-night chat shows. And right now, I welcomed the escapism.

I watched Cheers for half an hour. The camaraderie of the Boston Bar made me feel nice, and I almost wished I was there. I snuggled down and laughed as Sam, the manager of the bar, chatted up *another* model, in doing so, making his co-host jealous. The banter was hilarious and made me smile.

After Cheers ended, I reached for my bottle of wine and poured myself a big glass, getting ready to watch a program called "The Word", which used a jazzy format for interviews, live music, features and even live games. Channel four didn't seem as strict as the other three channels, and the guests on "The Word" could do just about anything to be as controversial as they wanted. It was fun to watch, if not a bit daft.

The presenter's accent seemed very forced, yet I was drawn to him. He had a way about him. I couldn't remember his name, Terry something or other.

I was getting the feeling between my legs. The thought of the night with Jamie was making me feel excitable and giving me a very unwanted thrill. I was fighting it because there was no going back for more. I had to get him out of my head now. I was finding it hard to keep my eyes open, and the red wine wasn't helping.

I felt my eyes going but forced myself out of bed to check on Jody. I realised that she didn't have her bottle or "boc boc", as she called it and that she would soon be waking up for a sip of her milk.

It brought me back to life, and I left the bedroom to go and get the bottle.

I ran across the top of the landing, wishing I'd have put my dressing gown on. I was freezing. I got to the stairs and ran down them, shivering as my bare feet touched the cold stone. I went into the big kitchen, leaving the light off.

I opened the huge fridge door, and the light lit up the room. I grabbed her bottle from one of the cupboards and filled it up with fresh milk. I felt a bit peckish, but there wasn't really anything ready to eat other than a plate of leftover meat from dinner. I gobbled down a great big slice of it, put the milk away and ran back up the stairs. I was out of breath by the time I got to the top of them; they were big stairs.

When I got back to the bedroom, I noticed I hadn't shut the bedroom door, which confused me as I was sure I had. I looked up and down the landing and went back into my room.

I decided to have a cig before I did anything else and perched in my usual spot on the windowsill. I took a drag and stared at my reflection. That was me through the window, nobody else. I tried to give myself a smile. And actually, got one back.

Before I got back in bed, I grabbed Jody's bottle and went over to her side of the room. I put the bottle down next to her bed and leant over to where she lay. But she wasn't there. Her quilt was covering her pillow, and I thought it had been her little body. My heart sunk right down into my toes.

I took a deep breath and knew where she would be. I was feeling angry now, angry because I just wanted peace. It was my time for peace, and I'd have it if that weirdo hadn't turned up. I hated myself for saying it, but she was really starting to fuck me off.

I ran to my bedroom door and looked either way up and down the big landing. There was silence.

I went up the landing to where Jane's room was and was shocked to see her bedroom door open. I went in. It was dark apart from a few candles. I shuddered. How could she give me the creeps? She was my twin, for God's sake. But she did, and I know she was lurking in this house somewhere with Jody.

I took another deep breath and headed off back down the landing to see if she was in the huge bathroom. I nearly shouted for Jody but didn't want to alarm her if she was already feeling uncomfortable. The bathroom was empty.

I looked out of the big window from the landing and could see the lights of a car driving down the lane. I hoped it was David and Pavel, but knowing them, they'd be back at Irene's eating kebabs and drinking cans of lager. I would have given anything to be with them right now.

I headed back to the stairs. Jane was standing at the top of them holding Jody tightly in her arms. Jody was quiet; she knew she wasn't safe. She was so clever, she kept calm, more than I felt.

I felt the heat rising through my body. I tried to sound as normal as I could, even though my head was filled with a black smog that had been building up for weeks. I wanted to run over and knock her fucking head off.

'What are you doing?' I asked her.

She nearly jumped out of her skin.

'She just scratched my face, this horrible child.'

She put Jody down next to her and bent down to chastise her, she was wagging her finger in her face, and little Jody just stared up at her taking it.

I walked over towards them both. She started laughing. I didn't care; I couldn't let it knock me off my stride. I needed to get my little girl away from her and from the stairs.

I bent down to grab Jody, and as I did, Jane lashed out and tried to punch me in the head.

As she did, she lost her footing and did a full three-sixty turn. I could see on her face that she knew what would happen, and she screamed as she went flying down the stairs.

I grabbed hold of Jody and covered her ears and face so she couldn't hear the screams or see her aunt fall down the stairs. It all happened in slow motion. She fell with her arms flying in the air. I heard every part of her body thud on every stone step that there was.

I gasped as I heard the final thud. I didn't dare look down, but I did. She was dead; there was no doubt about it. I sobbed as I looked down. I could just about make out her face. I couldn't believe that she had gone the same way we were led to believe she went almost twenty-one years ago.

David and Pav were standing at the front door as white as ghosts.

'It's ok babe,' David said. 'We saw it all. She fell babe. It's not your fault.'

Epilogue

I never had quite got over losing her the first time, but the second time was vastly different.

So many nights, I wished I could have her back, wished I could have protected her. But when she came back to me, I hadn't really felt like I had her back at all. She was a stranger and not the little girl who was my twin sister Jane.

But I grieved for her death again.

I grieved what I thought we would have – the bond that twins have from the moment they are in the womb.

Once more, I was left staring at her in the window, trying to make sense of it all. I looked hard into her eyes; there was a coldness there, no tears, no frown; they looked still and lifeless.

I looked away from the refection and headed downstairs, trying to focus on other things. Like tonight.

It was Bernie and Az's engagement party, and I couldn't wait. I hadn't had a night out since my night with Jamie.

I wandered into the kitchen and poured myself a glass of wine. I knew David would be ages getting ready. God knows what took him so long.

The local paper was on one of the sides, and the headline caught my eye.

"Death of local man ruled suspicious."

I grabbed the paper and started to read with interest.

"Police are investigating the death of a local man, Jamie Morano, who was found dead in his home just a few weeks ago.

The cause of death has been determined as poisoning and is being treated as suspicious.

Morano was seen leaving a restaurant earlier that evening with a young woman in a red dress. His friends say that he had been going on a date with someone called "Charley" and it is thought this is who he left the restaurant with. It is not clear whether the couple parted ways or whether they went back to Morano's together.

Investigating officers are keen to identify and speak to this woman who is yet to come forward.

"We do not yet know whether this woman is linked to Morano's death, and we would like her to come forward to give her story. She may have been one of the last people to see Mr Morano alive, and it is vital that we speak to her."

Morano's family are devastated by his death. They describe him as a kind, loving lad who was extremely popular and had no enemies.

They are asking anyone with information about this mystery woman or his death to contact the police.'"

I felt momentarily guilty. I had only met his family a couple of times, but they had seemed like decent enough people.

Then I remembered the feeling of watching that video of Jamie with my mother, and the guilt subsided.

Jane and Jamie had been the last links to my past

traumas, and now they were both gone.

Jane's accident was tragic, but I would be lying if I said I wasn't a bit relieved to be rid of her.

And Jamie's death was a little less of a shock. I'd gone to get closure. And closure is what I had got.

Susan. Jamie. Jane. They were all gone.

Finally, I was free to move forward.

It doesn't matter who you are and where you come from
What matters is the journey you take
The soul that carries you is eternal
The reflection you see is only a mirrored form
Your inner self is the truth
Turn within and search until you find you
Your own true mind, your own true peace is waiting
Believe that your strength is all within
Outside factors banish, unless they feel good
The good in and the bad out
Most of all, remember that you are with YOU forever
Be kind to yourself, be gentle with her, she was once a beautiful child
And most of all, love yourself and love those that really love her.
Because if you knew who walked beside you, you would never be afraid.

David broke her reverie.

'Julie, Julie, oh you're there, I couldn't find you?

'Yeah I'm here, Julie replied... I couldn't find me either, but then I realised I was here all along...

Also by Lynette Heywood

Not So Innocent

Web of Hope